THE
LAWYERS

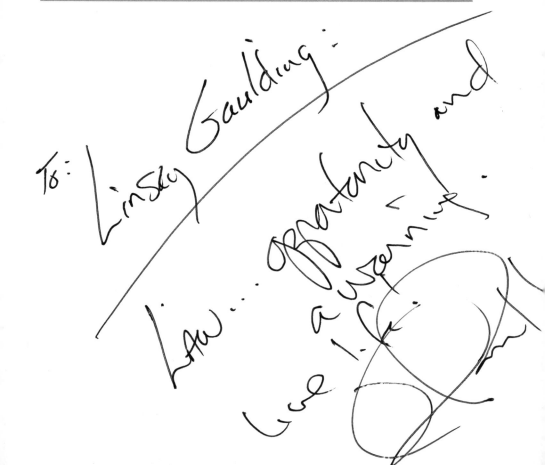

To: Linsey Gaulding:

Law.... opportunity and a warning:

Good luck.

THE LAWYERS:

Class of '69

a novel by
John M. Poswall

JULLUNDUR PRESS
a Golden Temple Publishing company

This book is a work of fiction. Names, characters, places and events are products of the author's imagination or are used fictitiously. Any resemblance to actual events, locations or persons, living or deceased, is purely coincidental. We assume no responsibility for errors, inaccuracies, omissions, or any inconsistency herein.

First printing 2003

ISBN 0-9729992-4-8

LCCN 2003103761

ATTENTION CORPORATIONS, UNIVERSITIES, COLLEGES, BOOK CLUBS, AND PROFESSIONAL ORGANIZATIONS: Quantity discounts are available on bulk purchases of this book for educational, gift purposes, or as premiums for increasing magazine subscriptions or renewals. Special books or book excerpts can also be created to fit specific needs. For information, please contact Jullundur Press, a Golden Temple Publishing company, 1001 "G" Street, Suite 301, Sacramento, CA 95814; toll-free 866-449-1600; email goldentemplepub @aol.com; website www.thelawyersclassof69.com.

Acknowledgment

While none are responsible for what I have attempted, and certainly not for my mistakes, I wish to thank many. When I began my research, the encouragement of Boalt's first woman dean, Herma Hill Kay, carried me forward. Joanne Maguire and Patricia McCabe, at the United States Supreme Court, provided valuable records, which led me to Nancy Meister of Whitman College. K. D. of the Sutter Resource Center Library provided clinical gynecological research, which was interpreted by Dr. Steven Polansky, OB/GYN, whose support and enthusiasm were unmatched. Only once did he defer to another, Dr. Malcolm Ettin, and then on a jugular issue.

Judge James Mize has always been my expert on divorce law; Ron Marks on flying and the Central Valley; and, Bill McCarthy on everything nautical or about San Francisco. Carmen Bernard Adame of Mexico lectured me on Mexican culture and language and Luis A. Céspedes added the nuances of the rich language. Diana Kennedy, while internationally known for Mexican food, is thanked for introducing me to the world of literary agents and marketing. In her place, her protege, Peg Tomlinson, reviewed the Mexican dishes—and the Indian menus stolen from the cookbooks of the effervescent Julie Sarne.

To my staff at PWK&C, especially Natalie, Jill, Sally, Julie, and Pat—and all the law clerks I have sent researching—your help is ever present and never undervalued.

And then there were the "readers" who plodded through early, heavy manuscripts and gave honestly, I hope, of their criticism: Peg Tomlinson, Judge James Ford, Sally Davis (LCSW), Catherine O'Brian, Wade Thompson, Betty Moulds, Natalie's mom, Ella Kelly, Jill Spitz, Rebel Curd,

Cindy Simonsen, Carolee Simpson, and Jennifer Doidge—and an editor known only as "Lead Dog."

But there is one person without whom this book would never have been completed: my young law partner, meticulous editor, and brilliantly talented individual, Aram Kouyoumdjian.

—John M. Poswall

Author's Note

This is a work of fiction, but it is set in a very real legal and historical context. Historical figures and prominent lawyers of the times interact with fictional characters. However, anything attributed to them, including their actions, thoughts, motives, or speech, is purely fictional and invented for the purposes of this novel.

Similarly, the law students depicted in the Class of 1969 at Boalt Hall are fictional, even though the issues they faced are real.

"What was it all for, anyway, if I could not make a real difference?"

—WILLIAM KUNSTLER,
My Life as a Radical Lawyer

Book I

Chapter 1

Rose

SHE HAD DECIDED to drive up Thursday evening from Salinas—alone. Of course, she would spend the night in San Francisco. That was a given.

It was 7:30 in the evening when she reached San Jose on 101. Instead of heading on to San Francisco, as she had done on so many weekends they had spent together, tonight she connected to the 880 and 80 into Berkeley. This time, and for the first time in 30 years, she drove to the campus of the University of California. It was an impulsive act. She thought she might just drive by the law school.

Driving up University Avenue, toward the Campanile in the distance, she recognized a few of the used furniture and antique shops where she had shopped to fill her apartment when she first moved into the south campus area. She was surprised by all of the Indian clothing stores and restaurants that had not been part of her Berkeley experience. As she drove closer to the University, she realized that the names of some of the roads had changed; others were now one way. She turned right on Shattuck and drove down, recognizing Dwight Way. She turned left and proceeded toward the Claremont Hotel. She pictured its tower caught in the news stories of the Oakland Hills fires a few years back. The eucalyptus trees had roared to a halt at its feet.

When she crossed Telegraph, she finally felt she was in Berkeley, the Berkeley of the '60s. She found some irony, however, noticing the Bank of America. In the '60s, students lined up to protest, if not to bomb. Now they lined up, orderly, waiting their turn at the ATM machine.

She remembered People's Park was somewhere near College Avenue but could not find it. Turning left on Piedmont, she noted that the fraternity houses seemed to be in full bloom. Finally, on the corner of Bancroft and Piedmont, ahead and to her left, was the law school. It looked different. On the one hand, a structure made bigger with additions. On the other, the familiar small, compact, original building on the side of a hill, somehow inconsistent with its national—indeed, international—reputation. A place that had so affected her life.

She parked and walked down the hill, past the school, to the west side through which she had entered the school daily, for her three years of law school.

"When I think thus of the law, I see a princess mightier than she that wrought at Bayeux."

Funny. She remembered the first time she had seen those words on the side of the building, along with the famous words of Justice Cardozo at the other end. They appeared so solemn to a 21-year-old girl from California's Central Valley, one of only 14 "girls" in the entering class that fall of 1966. Some princesses.

Even now, 33 years later, she stopped at the word "Bayeux." She wondered, if the words were so important, appearing on the white rectangular building like the writing on a sarcophagus, why on earth would anyone plant a tree in front to obscure them from public view? Perhaps it was enough to know they were there, inscribed on a building, the memory of which would be etched forever in the psyche of all who passed through.

The door was open, as she expected, for all those who would labor into the night in the law library stacks. She walked past the old lounge. The bulletin board still contained lists of job applications, recruiters' schedules, but there were new things: *the Berkeley Women's Law Journal, the African-American Law & Policy Report, Ecology Law Quarterly, La Raza Law Journal, the Domestic Violence Project, HIV Outreach.*

She looked down the hall toward the suite of rooms where she had spent so much time. They were never much to look at. State-issued metal desks, metal shelves, metal chairs with mahogany-colored cushioned seats, she remembered. But the *California Law Review* was in this basement, in those rooms below the classrooms. If one wanted to be recruited by the top firms in the nation—and only the top firms came to Boalt—or seek one of the prestigious clerkships at the U.S. Supreme Court, perhaps with Chief Justice Warren, a Boalt alumnus, Justices Brennan, Marshall, or Douglas, or the California Supreme Court and its Chief Justice Pinckley or Justice Parks—both of Boalt Hall—entree was through this basement. At the end of the first year, 27 out of 276 students would be selected as the editors and writers of the *California Law Review*, the official scholarly national publication of the law school. One would be the editor-in-chief. Rose Contreras had been that one.

She felt anger as she ascended the concrete stairs, turning her back on the corridor to the law review offices. She did not feel like the conquering hero—or heroine—returning to the field of her triumph.

"Hey, lady, they're wet," a voice came from the top of the stairs. She saw the African-American man with a bucket on wheels, squeezing dirty water out of a mop. "Can't you see the sign?"

She had not, of course. She remembered the front stairwell and turned instinctively. But that door, too, had been reserved for the exclusive use of law review members, and she had relinquished the key upon graduation, when she had reentered the real world.

"I am just walking around the school," she answered, remembering it was *her* school back then. At the end of January, after first semester, everyone knew where they were in the class. And *everyone*, including the 262 men, knew they were behind Rose Contreras.

She resumed her ascent, to the first floor of Boalt, to the three large lecture halls where, on the first day, the class had been divided. Two hundred and seventy-six students assigned randomly to three "sections." Ninety-two students with whom to compete throughout the year, throughout school, and in most cases, throughout life.

While "sections" only applied to the first year, the reality of the trauma of first year was that these were the people one would come to know best, form study groups with, and forever remember, as if, together, they had endured a hostage taking, and they had been the hostages.

The lecture halls were not any different from each other. At least they did not appear to be. Then, is there a difference, one bull ring to another? To the matador? To the bull? Does a gladiator notice the difference in arenas or just the size of the opponents?

Stark. Bright, extra white light, 25 feet up at the front of the room, reflected off the high walls, through white plastic dropped ceilings, obscuring the individual sources of light. Not light; illumination. As was supposed to occur on a daily basis here.

Acoustic tile, with its characteristic golf-spike holes, covering the walls down to the wainscoting of light wood. Walls that grew shorter as the stairs climbed from the podium, along 11 rows of semicircled countertop desks, behind which, anchored, stood plastic bucket seats, waiting. The symmetry of rows broken only, as in an arena, by aisles dividing the semi-circles into three pieces.

From the podium on the table, on a raised platform, the professor could look out and see the small number painted in front of each student's place and with the corresponding seating chart, arranged in alphabetical order, call on those who would sit behind numbers 1 through 206. Because the class totaled only 276, the 90 or so students in each section were allowed some freedom, within the confines of the room and the alphabet.

The room had not changed much. The low counters now accommodated wheelchairs. Probably the result of the ADA—Americans with Disabilities Act. What had not changed, however, was the feeling. After 33 years, it was as if she was entering the room for the first time. It had been…awe. And fear.

She had not believed it—that she had been accepted at Boalt Hall. She bought her books—used—and started reading, immediately. But when, that first morning, alphabetically, the voices started, her face flushed with embarrassment. She realized she was out of her league. The cadence started at the bottom right corner of the room from the professor and continued across the semicircle.

"Michael Amundson, B.S. economics, Stockholm; M.A. English, Yale."

"John Arnold, B.A. engineering, Stanford."

"Jim Axeldrod, B.A., M.A. political theory, Cornell."

By the time the person in front of her counted off, she was convinced she had made a serious mistake. What had she been thinking? Why was she in law school anyway? Certainly not because her father had been a lawyer. Her father—and her mother for that matter—were farm workers with only permanent residency papers. Neither had finished high school. Rose had been born in the United States and had the distinction of being the first—she had a younger brother—member of her family to be, by reason of birth, an American citizen. She was a long way from the fields, perhaps too far.

The count, now to her right, resumed in her awareness: "Jackson Bridge-port III, B.A. history, Harvard, postgraduate study, comparative legal systems, Oxford."

That drowned out the next few in her consciousness until she realized the person next to her, who had introduced himself upon sitting down simply as James, was finishing with "United States Military Academy, West Point."

She quietly spoke the words, half through her left hand on which she was resting her chin, looking down at her binder, as if writing with her right:

"Rose Contreras, B.A. English, Fresno State College."

Someone loudly cleared his throat to her right, down a row. Or did he laugh? Her face reddened. She waited, endlessly it seemed, for the spotlight to move upon the student to her left.

"University of Chicago…NYU…USC…Columbia…UCLA…" The names were echoing in her head as if it were a sound chamber.

There must have been some women's voices, but she did not remember hearing any or their announced pedigrees. She just wanted to survive in this environment that she had not even imagined existed. Nothing in her life had prepared her for this moment.

As she sat there on this evening she felt again those feelings of isolation as a woman; remembered the doors held open and the doors slammed shut; the people she had helped and those who had helped her.

Thirty-three years back to this classroom, this seat. She could still feel Jackson Bridgeport III looking at her with that disgusting, demeaning smile from his seat below and to the right. She was glad she had slammed him—publicly. But it did not console the anger, now pain, she felt about her treatment at—of all places—the United States Supreme Court.

She became aware of a sound she had not heard earlier. Mechanical. Shifting. She turned around to see the large clock embedded into the back wall, high up next to the ceiling. Just a square cutout in the acoustic tile with large Roman numerals and a metal minute hand seeming to pause to step forward, as a Grenadier Guard might in ceremonial march. It was 10:15 P.M. Rose had been sitting in her first year seat for over two hours. She shook her head. How did I do it? she thought.

"And why?" she said out loud to no one but herself. Rose stood up, walked down the stairs as she had that first time over 30 years ago, glanced at the professor's podium on the raised stage, and walked to her right and out of the double doors of her section room. The janitor held the door.

Rose was crying.

Chapter 2

The Reunion

"WE WERE THE last class of the '60s at Boalt Hall," the speaker was telling his fellow classmates. It was the 30th reunion of the class of 1969. Officially, it was the University of California, School of Law, at Berkeley. In the legal profession, however, to savor the appropriate respect, graduates would always answer, when asked where they went to law school, "Boalt Hall."

"In 1966, we came speaking of revolution; changing America; using the law to solve the problems of racism and inequality.

"Now we speak of mutual funds, living trusts, and look forward to retirement and grandchildren. We are legally defined as older Americans for nondiscriminatory treatment. For the first time in our lives the president of the United States is younger than us.

"It is small consolation that, at 56, we are eligible for the senior citizen discount at most breakfast chains. All of us, that is, except of course an obscenely wealthy classmate who made his fortune in class action litigation. No corporation in America will let him on its premises. Discretion forbids me from naming him—but lacking discretion and since he is not here, I will tell you his picture is on page 19 of the official reunion photos."

J. J. paused to let the chuckling subside. Then he asked, almost plaintively, "Did we really make a goddamn bit of difference? Did we change the law? Society? *Anything?*" He looked around. "Or were *we* changed?"

It was a thought that had crossed the minds of many in the class as each prepared for the evening. It surprised some now, and had been the source of a lifetime of doubt for others. If nothing else, the 30th reunion of the class of 1969 was a chance for comparisons. Perhaps that was why some did not attend. Or, perhaps, as the dean reflected over his Mt. Eden Merlot, absentees of the class of 1969 viewed the act of nonattendance as a final political statement; still protesting.

8

The Clarion Country Club, located in the Berkeley Hills just above Strawberry Canyon and a mile from the law school, had been selected by the reunion committee at the urging of Geoffrey Mason, head of the committee and a member of "the Club." That is what it was called by those who spoke knowingly of its traditions: the Club. It was unlikely that more than a few in the class had ever attended a function at the Club since membership was limited. In fact, the chairman of the reunion committee really was not a "member" at all. Rather, his firm held a membership, and he had imposed upon the founding partners of his firm, Baxter, Wainwright, Jones and Jefferson, to sponsor the event. It was hardly an imposition. All had themselves attended Boalt. Jones, Boalt class of 1941, and Jefferson, Boalt class of 1948, immediately agreed. Baxter, Boalt class of 1911, and Wainwright, Boalt class of 1923, did not object. They were dead.

But if the committee had given the nod to dignity in its choice of locations for the event, it had thrown caution to the wind in the selection of J. J. Rai as Master of Ceremonies. His name was Jawaharlal Jallianwalla Singh Rai, named by his Indian father after Jawaharlal Nehru, then a leader of the Indian independence movement, and Jallianwalla, the place in the Punjab known to every Indian schoolchild where in 1919 thousands of peaceful demonstrators were fired upon by British soldiers under the command of General Dyer. The massacre, Dyer proclaimed, was a "jolly good thing."

On that most memorable of days, the first day of class, Rai had insisted, in his best Punjabi accent—imitation, really, for he had never spoken any language but English—"but, but you may call me J. J." Everyone knew J. J. He made it a point of being noticed, in school and in the profession. He was a pretty good law student and an outstanding personal injury trial lawyer. His antics with juries were legendary and effective. He claimed that his success came as a result of his unpredictability. No judge, no opponent, and no jury knew what he would do next because, he explained, he did not know either.

"Hey, if Baxter, Wainwright, Jones and Jefferson is hosting this thing, how come I'm paying for my own drinks?" J. J. looked in the direction of Geoffrey Mason. "And does this club know I'm an Indian? Hell, if I knew they would actually let me in here, I would have worn my turban. Can't you see it? I pull up to Mason's club here, and a polite guy with white gloves helps me out of my new Jaguar convertible and says, 'May I park your car, raghead?' God, I love it here. Thanks, Mason."

Mason lifted his glass to J. J., laughing, knowing full well J. J. was capable of such a stunt.

"And did you see that invitation? 'Coats and ties required for Gentlemen.' Hey, Dean, what about the women? Naked?"

Rose accepted the slight rub on the back from her "guest." As the name tags proclaimed, those accompanying class members were either spouses or guests, and Rose was not exactly married.

Rose's reaction to the invitation was at first dismissive. She opened the large envelope assuming it was the semiannual appeal for money. Not that she gave; rather, she took an interest in classmates featured for their achievements or their financial contributions to Boalt, which often went hand in hand. She saw, instead, it was an invitation to the 30th reunion. She had never attended a Boalt reunion and had no expectation or thought of attending any in the future. Then she read the words: "Coats and ties required for Gentlemen."

It just hit a nerve. A deep, painful nerve. She tried to smile and shook her head. But the words took on a meaning far beyond the suggestion of a style of dress.

"I don't believe this," she said. It was then she resolved they would attend the reunion and would wear matching ties.

She looked back at her guest and tried hard to return the smile. As she did, she heard J. J. say, "Enjoy your dinner because the dean will be up here next asking for money." As J. J. passed her table, he smiled at Rose: "Just the warmup," he said. "Got to keep the Anglos off balance."

Her eyes followed him as he walked back to his table. His hair was still coal black, perhaps with a little salt at the temples. He had the swagger of someone comfortable with himself and the Armani collection that featured his trim body; a person who knew others pointed him out in a crowd and spoke of him. He stopped momentarily, put his arm around an attractive younger woman—another "guest"—and led her toward the bar. Rose smiled at the thought: J. J.'s single, again.

Rose's glance turned toward the doorway. At the entry to the dining room were Professor Ernesto Z. Reynoso and Justice Michael Cassidy. They were a study in contrasts. Michael Cassidy was soft-spoken, even shy, and nodded appreciatively as he was greeted. He wore a nicely tailored but conservative dark suit with a medium starched white shirt and a light blue tie. He had an attractive Asian woman on his arm. Professor Reynoso, with his large torso and imposing full beard, entered as if crashing a party in search of someone. His clothes appeared old and disheveled. He was alone.

Reynoso and Cassidy were certainly not together. But both were looking her way. Not at her but at her guest. Michael Cassidy smiled; Reynoso appeared pained.

The Honorable Michael Cassidy seemed to be enjoying himself, as he turned back to those greeting him. He liked being called "your honor." A graduate of Notre Dame, he had struggled at Boalt, staying in the middle of the class. Given the caliber of the class, this did not make him stupid, just…well, average. But average in one of the top law schools in the nation.

In the profession, he was given the respect always accorded the answer, "Boalt Hall." But at the Boalt reunion, it was the designation "the honorable" that gave Michael Cassidy heightened standing, he hoped—at least with faculty and those who appeared before him, first in the Alameda County Superior Court, then the First District Court of Appeal in San Francisco, and, most recently, at the California Supreme Court where he now sat as an Associate Justice.

But to those classmates who remembered—and law students always remember standings in the class—he was still average. Class standing was forever; at best, he might be considered an overachiever having attained a position on the California Supreme Court. More likely, he ended up where average students who know a governor end up: on the bench.

"I believe you know Justice Cassidy, Dean," came the introduction by fellow classmate Jackson Bridgeport III. Bridgeport's wife meekly looked on. She was not included in the introductions.

Professor Ernesto Reynoso was hardly subtle in moving away to avoid being included in the formalities. He had no use for Cassidy, and everyone knew it. "Of course, good to see you again, Justice Cassidy. I think the last time was at the American Bar Association panel on class action litigation, wasn't it?"

"Right. London. And congratulations on your appointment, Dean Steinberg. You were my favorite professor, first year."

"Thank you. It's a challenging job. I'm sure I'll be calling on you to help with alumni matters, Justice Cassidy."

The cordiality dance was interrupted by an intruder.

"I didn't know there was a problem with class action litigation requiring a California Supreme Court *Associate* Justice to go all the way to London to solve it." There was obvious sarcasm in the comment, especially mixed with the emphasis on "associate."

All eyes turned to the man approaching the group from the bar. He stood out—and not just for his lack of deference. He wore cowboy boots, his hair was pure white, and he had the tan of a man who worked outdoors. In one hand he held a drink glass filled with dark liquid. His other hand preciously held the hand of his daughter. She was 10. Neither wore a tie.

"Randy," he gestured, holding up her hand and pointing, "this here is Michael. He's a judge now. We went to school together. And this is the new dean, Dean Steinberg. When I was at Boalt, he was our Contracts teacher." He left Jackson Bridgeport standing without introduction.

No one made the obligatory social gesture of introducing this intruder to the others. Nor did he volunteer his name. On his shirt, under a western dress jacket, stitched above his pocket, was an emblem. On it was a kayak descending a rapid, and, under that, "Brian."

No one recalled this Brian in the class and, tonight, apparently no one much cared who he was.

*   *   *   *   *

The entering Boalt Hall class of 1969 consisted of 276 students of whom 14 were women, 3 were black, 1 was Hispanic, and none was Asian. Their undergraduate degrees spanned the most prestigious universities of the United States, including Harvard (9); Yale (11); University of Chicago (5); New York University (6); Michigan (15); Columbia (6); U.C. Berkeley (33); Stanford (7); USC (13); West Point (2); UCLA (26); and Radcliffe (1). Some in the class had graduate degrees from such esteemed institutions as Oxford, Princeton, Harvard, and MIT. This was what, then, was known as "diversity."

But it was Berkeley; it was the '60s. When the class arrived in the fall of 1966, Lyndon Johnson had 400,000 American soldiers in Vietnam, Huey Newton and the Black Panthers were on the streets of Oakland, Cesar Chavez was organizing in the fields of California, and Ronald Reagan was about to be elected governor. And Bobby Kennedy and Martin Luther King were still alive.

Chapter 3

Jackson

HE HAD NOT meant to laugh. Actually it was more of a rush of air through his nose, a slight smile with his mouth closed, and a roll of the eyes directed knowingly toward the professor. Jackson Bridgeport III, "undergrad Harvard, postgrad Oxford," may have earned his arrogance but he just could not hide it. Three generations of Bridgeports had gone to Harvard. The grandfather, a U.S. senator from Connecticut; the father, a cabinet member in the Eisenhower Administration; and "Jackson 3," as he was referred to privately by the staff at the family estate. He had no doubt the meek little voice that had answered "Fresno State" would likely quit, as girls often did, once they understood the competitive nature of the law. "She'll be gone by Christmas," he whispered out of the side of his mouth to the law student sitting next to him, whom he did not yet know. Not that he made any effort to know anyone. His academic credentials of Harvard and Oxford put him second to none; thus, he looked down on everyone. He was not exactly thrilled to be at a public institution for the first time in his life.

Bridgeport, Bridgeport, Hall and Pendergast was founded in 1895 and, by 1966, had 378 attorneys in offices located from its origins in Connecticut, to New York, Washington, D.C., Cleveland, Chicago, and Dallas. It boasted a lineup that included a former attorney general of the United States, two prior ABA presidents, three retired federal judges, the former solicitor general of the United States, and, like its founder Jackson Bridgeport I, a number of former U.S. senators. Not surprisingly, all were Republicans.

Jackson III had applied to Boalt Hall at his father's insistence, and, of course, with his academic record, was accepted. While it was never an issue since birth that Jackson would be a lawyer, a family tradition, the executive committee of the firm, chaired by his father, had it as an agenda item to discuss the law school he would attend. He was told its decision: Boalt Hall. The firm had plans to open West Coast offices, Los Angeles for sure and possibly San Francisco. This was the reason given for the selection of Boalt Hall at the University of California. Privately, even his father found him an arrogant bore and hoped throwing his son into public education in California might loosen him up.

"Father," the youngest Jackson had protested, "I understand the benefit of a California legal education if I am to play an important role in the West Coast expansion of the firm. It would seem to me logical, however, and consistent with my background, that I go to Stanford."

"You don't understand California," his father cut him off. "They're different out there. Tradition, privilege, manners, decorum mean nothing to them. Not even in business. You need exposure to this new breed that we will likely have to deal with in our work for our clients in California."

With dismay, all Jackson III could muster was, "But Berkeley!"

Chapter 4

Michael

JUSTICE MICHAEL CASSIDY had been a stranger neither to the Club nor to Boalt in the 30 years that had passed since graduation. He had briefly been a member of the Club, an embarrassing fact that he had acknowledged at his confirmation hearing after Governor Wilson nominated him as an Associate Justice of the California Supreme Court. He had quietly resigned his membership; too quietly, some argued. When others successfully convinced the membership committee to rescind the ban on woman members and to affirmatively seek minority members, Michael Cassidy sat quietly on the District Court of Appeal.

Neither his membership nor his quiet, timely resignation "because of the press of judicial business" escaped those who opposed his conservative views, however. The American Civil Liberties Union, the National Association for the Advancement of Colored People, La Raza, the California Trial Lawyers, and all major liberal groups in the state opposed his nomination. It was a losing fight, and they knew it. He had been declared "qualified," though not "well qualified" or "exceptionally well qualified," by the California State Bar. The governor had the votes necessary for approval, and no amount of opposition could change that fact.

The undisputed spokesperson for the opposition was a professor from Boalt Hall who, at a public hearing, called Cassidy a "14-carat bigot" and a "person who had squandered the best public legal education in America, at Boalt Hall, on a vendetta against the public interest and the poor."

"Why are they attacking me so personally when I'm going to be confirmed anyway?" Cassidy had wondered to the governor's judicial appointments secretary. "Do they think I'm going to forget this?"

"No, Judge. They *want* you to remember."

The governor's appointments secretary was right. Professor Ernesto Zapata Reynoso wanted him to remember. Every day Justice Cassidy took the bench, as Professor Reynoso knew he would, he wanted him to remember: "Zapata" is out there.

But if it had been a Boalt Hall professor who led the charge against him, he knew he owed his Supreme Court position to a fellow Boalt classmate in the class of '69: Jackson Bridgeport III. Without Bridgeport, not even the governor could have gotten him confirmed. Ironically, as much as Zapata wanted people to know of his opposition, Bridgeport offered his help only on condition that it not be disclosed.

Chapter 5

The Reunion

HE HAD HIS daughter Randy ask, figuring the chance of rejection was less. He had not really known Rose well in school and doubted she would recognize him anyway. But he wanted to sit at her table. Not for himself. He knew his time had passed. Rather, for his daughter, Randy. He wanted her to meet Rose.

"Can my dad and me sit here?" she asked Rose, pointing to the two empty chairs at the table for eight.

"Sure," said Rose, smiling at her, then looking back at Henry Steiner, who was in mid-sentence.

"And you remember there was that guy who had his name legally changed and was always being quoted in the papers. The *San Francisco Chronicle* would say, 'Today Steven F. Poland addressed the rally and said…' but the same story in the *Berkeley Barb* would start 'S. Fuck Poland addressed the people's rally and demanded…'"

Henry was still laughing as he raised his glass and began to sip the wine. It was then that he noticed the little girl who had slid into the seat next to him.

"Was his name really Fuck Poland?" she asked.

There was silence. Everyone at the table was looking alternately at Henry and the little girl. Henry cleared his throat and took another drink of wine while pondering an apology to the little girl and her father. Randy cracked a slight smile.

"If it was, that would be fucking funny." Henry lost it. Red wine all over the pressed white table cloth.

Her father came to his rescue. "I am sorry. My daughter thinks she wants to be a lawyer. I thought bringing her here to the reunion might dissuade her."

17

"And it's…?" asked Rose.

"Brian," he said. "And Randy."

Rose's guest asked what the others were too hesitant to ask: "I take it you're a lawyer then, Brian."

"No, no, I am definitely not a lawyer," he said with a slight glance downward toward Randy, but avoiding her eyes, in case she might say, "Tell them, Daddy."

"Well, me neither, so maybe we could talk about—"

"White-water rafting," he interrupted, as he saluted them with his drink.

Chapter 6

The Classroom

"MR. CASSIDY," THE professor announced, without looking up, as he deposited his books on the podium, "could you state the salient facts of *People v. Stevens?*"

"The defendant encountered a sleeping person in a public place and robbed him," replied Cassidy without hesitation. "A violation of Penal Code §212."

"Mr....uh"—looking at his seating chart—"Jacobs, are those the salient facts?" asked the professor.

It was still early in the first year, and the professor of Criminal Law knew few students by name. Some professors would know all the names by now. Others would not bother knowing any until grades came out. Then they knew who not to waste their time with.

"No. Not at all. The important point Mr. Cassidy has overlooked is that the so-called sleeping person was a police officer who purposely laid a wallet on his stomach in plain view to passers-by."

"So…" It was going as expected. The professor pounced. "Mr. Jacobs, was it significant for you the victim was a policeman or that he was really not asleep?"

"Both. It was a set-up. That's entrapment," opined Brian Jacobs, taking the side of the accused. His own experience with "law enforcement" remained in the form of his broken nose and deviated septum, which had left his otherwise handsome face off-centered.

Turning back, the professor asked, "Mr. Cassidy, do you agree?"

"No. Honest people don't steal. The officer only gave someone with a criminal intent the opportunity to steal. He did not endow him with criminal intent. Does society really have to wait for criminals to strike on their own terms, before taking action? I don't think so."

"Then why not go further, Mr. Cassidy? Why not seek out those with a criminal predisposition and arrest them before they act?"

"Perhaps they should be watched more closely," responded Michael Cassidy.

"And who are 'they'?" asked someone from the professor's left. It was Leon Goldman. He had walked in late, without apology, and dropped his backpack on the desktop. His appearance—long hair, goatee, wire-framed glasses, with jeans and an old sweater—contrasted with the Ivy League, clean-cut looks, jacket and tie, of Michael and many of the men in the class. He was, he suspected, exactly who Cassidy had in mind to be watched. This, Leon firmly believed, was the reality of the dissident in history: To be watched by an ever-increasingly paranoid power structure. He had acted in contravention of society's expectations his whole life, under his leftist parents' tutelage. It had been a good education. Now he was searching for his role as an outsider to what he saw as a morally bankrupt American society. A legal education, he thought, might make him more effective in radically altering that society for the better. It was a means to an end. Nothing more.

Chapter 7

Leon

SOME OF LEON Goldman's earliest memories were of his mother sitting at a folding table covered with books and papers as his father stood nearby, handing out political pamphlets on street corners in Seattle. There was always an issue to be protested, a government action to be opposed. When he was eight years old, his parents were on the streets warning that Truman would use the Bomb against Asians, in Korea. When he was 11, they were urging the people of Seattle to write their congressman because of their fear that Eisenhower would use the Bomb to aid the French in Vietnam: "Say no to colonialism." They were relieved with the fall of Dien Bien Phu, the defeat of the French, and the victory of "Uncle Ho."

The next year they were caravanning across the country with a group from the Washington American Civil Liberties Union, the ACLU, to protest on the steps of the nation's Capitol: "McCarthy is Un-American"… "Support the First Amendment."

As Leon grew up, he endured some embarrassment because of his parents' views. He could not be a Boy Scout because his parents opposed young boys being put in uniform. It was hard when they pulled him out of 5th grade because the school board insisted that he, with all the others, salute the flag and recite the Pledge of Allegiance.

"America is not one nation…and it certainly does not provide liberty and justice for all, and my son will not be compelled by any government to lie for it, swear allegiance to it, or take an oath invoking a god," his father shouted at the school board, whereupon Leon was formally expelled.

Kids threw rocks at his house. He and his family were shunned because they were outspoken in their views, which most of their neighbors believed were unpatriotic. Through it all, Leon retreated to books. Even at 14, when he entered high school, he had the traits of an intellectual—a rather dispassionate but insightful, logical analyst of facts, albeit with a heavy Marxist view of history—which was impressive but did not make him much fun. His social skills suffered, although it seemed of no consequence to him. It was hard to tell, later, if he ever doubted his judgments or second-guessed where they led him.

Leon's dad, Leonard Goldman, had come to Seattle as a young man and had gotten a job as a worker on the docks. Even before Pearl Harbor, the docks were busy loading ammunition onto ships appropriated to help Europe in the war effort. When the Japanese struck at Pearl Harbor, Leonard Goldman had no reservations about defending the country against them. After all, they had launched an unprovoked attack upon the United States, had they not? Nor did he have any doubt about the magnitude of the Nazi menace in Europe. He heard stories from relatives of what was going on in Germany with the Jews.

Leonard Goldman became a Communist by accident—actually, because of an accident. While he was working below deck, a load came loose and fell. He escaped the load only to be hit by the block and tackle at the end of the cable as it swung violently. It hit him in the right leg, instantly shattering the proximal end of the tibia and the knee. He was lifted out of the hole by the same crane equipment that had injured him, onto the deck, and carried to a waiting ambulance.

In 1942, good orthopedic surgeons were on duty either in Europe or in the Pacific, not in Seattle. Leonard's leg was casted, and he was sent to a convalescent facility overlooking the Boeing aircraft factory. In the months that followed, it became evident that the casting of a severely comminuted fracture did nothing to heal his leg. As a consequence, his body did the best it could. As it did, fusing the bone into a shortened and weakened leg, with no joint left at the knee, he sat in pain for months, watching aircraft roll out of the Boeing facility, watching the sun set on the ocean beyond, and watching Edith Weinstein, a volunteer nurse's assistant. Edith's regular job was in adult education, and it was through her that he began what would become a passion for reading.

It started with current news of the war and led to discussions with Edith about the origins of the current conflicts in Europe and in Asia. In addition to the *Seattle Times*, he began reading newspapers of the Longshoremen's Union and pamphlets written by its president, Harry Bridges, an avowed Communist. The pamphlets referred to various books, *Das Kapital*, *The Communist Manifesto*, and *State and Revolution* by Lenin, which he devoured as if reading a Bible, and then labored through *Imperialism: The Highest Stage of Capitalism*, also by Lenin.

He read of the capitalist exploitation of workers, the seizure of raw materials in Asia and Africa, of colonial wars as an extension of capitalism. He questioned whether nationalism was alien to socialism, which he understood to be a workers' paradise: "From each according to his ability; to each according to his needs."

Was it not nation states that caused wars in which the poor and the workers of one nation went off to fight the poor and the workers of another nation? What did workers in one part of the world have against other workers around the world? he wondered. Capitalist countries pursued war to protect markets, to suppress worker uprisings, or to thwart national liberation, like England in India; Belgium in the Congo; France in Indochina; and even England in America. And had not Britain and America, in one of Winston Churchill's earliest debacles, attempted to land troops in Archangel in 1917 to suppress the Russian Revolution? It was crazy. War made no sense. It had to be stopped. And the way to stop it was through the recognition of the common interests of the workers of the world.

Leonard limped out of the convalescent hospital in June of 1943. He would limp the rest of his life and would use a cane. Two weeks later, Edith and Leonard took a train to San Francisco to attend the annual convention of the Longshoremen's Union. Harry Bridges was the keynote speaker.

Harry Bridges, with his unusual cadence of speech, Australian with a twang, and full of revolutionary fervor, ignited Edith and Leonard's passions. They joined in the singing of "The Internationale," and Leonard signed up as an organizer for the Longshoremen's Union and, at the same time, the Communist Party of America. In the years that followed, Leon would hear of his father's travels to New York, Nova Scotia, New Orleans, Galveston, wherever ships would port. Leonard was a recognized figure, with his black hair, his muscular build, and his ever-present cane that he would wave above his head in speeches on the internationalism of the workers' struggle. He was a true "Wobbly" as the workers of the world were called. Cane and all.

On July 4, on the last day of the San Francisco convention, Leonard and Edith were married in a simple civil ceremony. They thought perhaps a rabbi should preside, but neither had family on the West Coast, and each professed, upon reflection, to be atheist, or at least to have very strong doubts. They picked July 4 to dedicate their life together to a new revolution in America. Harry Bridges gave the bride away.

On May 8, 1944, a son was born to Edith and Leonard Goldman. He was named Leon, after Leon Trotsky, a leader of the 1917 Russian Revolution.

Chapter 8

Michael

MICHAEL CASSIDY ATTENDED Notre Dame as an undergrad, at the urging of his father, attracted more by its football legacy than his Catholic upbringing. He tried out for a back-up quarterback position, but really was neither fast enough for its option running offense nor big enough for college ball. He hung on, at least with good seats to games while on the bench, and played sparingly on the special team for on-side kicks. He also joined the college's ROTC which, with his father's help, would later provide his ticket out of the draft.

Accepting admission at Boalt Hall was a coming home for Cassidy. He was raised in San Francisco, living in exclusive Pacific Heights overlooking the Marina District. He attended St. Ignatius, receiving the exclusive education for which the Jesuits were legendary. Better than Sacred Heart, run by the Christian Brothers, and with a better football team. Every year, at the Trophy Ball, the award was given to the school that excelled in sports and "S.I."—as those in San Francisco called it—won three out of the four of his high school years. He played at Kezar Stadium on Thanksgiving Day his senior year and threw for a touchdown against Sacred Heart but hardly won the game, as his father claimed. S.I. was up 21 to 6 with three minutes left when Michael was put in to hold the lead after the first string quarterback left the game with a fractured rib. But it was enough to get him his varsity ring and a date for the Trophy Ball.

His father, Terrence Cassidy, was a well-known attorney, practicing corporate and real estate law. He was also a leading Republican in a Democratic town.

But going to Cal-Berkeley was not like Notre Dame or even the exclusive San Francisco that Michael knew. Michael had little patience for the hippies, yippies, or latest version of beatnicks. He saw no value in drug use

25

and definitely did not adhere to a belief that a greater awareness or consciousness flowed from drugs any more than getting bombed at a fraternity
kegger made his frat brothers more erudite.

"Fine," he argued at Sather Gate to a gatherer of signatures for the
latest marijuana initiative, "let's tax you for growing it, sales tax for selling
it, and impose liability on you for anyone who gets injured by someone on
it, okay?"

"Man, like it's no one's business what I do with my body."

"It's mine," he said, "when you show up at the emergency room with
no insurance because you can't keep a job.

"What a wonderful society," he added. "Everyone bombed." With that,
Michael turned and left. He heard the shouted, understandably delayed,
response: "But if everyone got bombed, no one would get bombed!" It was
the ultimate recipe for world peace.

He shook his head and began the climb up the hill, up Bancroft Avenue, to the seclusion and sanctuary of rational thought, Boalt Hall, the
law school.

Chapter 9

Brian

ON APRIL 11, 1967, Governor Ronald Reagan went to bed at his regularly scheduled time at the home bought for him in the Sacramento suburbs by the "Friends of Ronald Reagan." Nancy Reagan stayed up until 2:00 A.M., furious.

"Can't you arrest them?" she had shouted at the state police. "They have no right to do this to Ronnie and me!"

But the demonstrators had every right. They had brought their protest to the home of the governor of California. At 10:00 A.M. the following morning, Aaron Mitchell was scheduled to die in the gas chamber at San Quentin. Of course, he had sought executive clemency from the governor. A hearing was held. The governor did not attend the hearing on clemency. Instead, he sent his legal affairs secretary, Edwin Meese III. The governor liked a mini-memo on an issue with a recommendation he could check "Yes" or "No." The governor had checked "Yes," and Aaron Mitchell would die the next morning. Nothing to lose sleep over.

Brian Jacobs drove to Sacramento in the late afternoon, right after class, with other members of the National Lawyers Guild. They arrived on the west steps of the Capitol, where signs had been prepared by organizers of the rally. For two hours, speakers addressed the rally. One, a young black assemblyman, an attorney from San Francisco, decried the disproportionate number of blacks on death row and in the general prison population, and charged: "The penal system of this country is used to further the genocide of young black men."

His name was Willie Brown, and he was, Brian was convinced, right.

By the time the speakers had finished, it was late in the evening. Approximately 200 protesters, including Brian and his group of law students, took up their signs and lit their candles. Slowly and quietly, they began the

35-block walk, in the early evening Sacramento air, on the sidewalks, up "J" Street to 45th Street to the private residence where the governor lived. Occasionally, the still air was punctuated with a car horn, or the yells of "Gas him!" from cars of fraternity members from Sacramento State College who passed by the procession on their way to Shakey's Pizza.

Of course, it did no good, and the fraternity boys had their way. Aaron Mitchell was gassed the next morning. No first-year Boalt student of the National Lawyers Guild missed Contracts class to stand outside San Quentin at 10:00 A.M. Not even Brian. He drove back from Sacramento early in the morning, read the assignment before getting a couple hours of sleep, and made his morning classes. He had every intention of excelling in law because he excelled in everything.

Brian was raised in Gloversville, New York. His parents owned a large house in town and an old summer cottage with a screened-in veranda on one of the lakes 30 minutes from town. They were not rich, in the Eastern sense, but, as the only pharmacist in town, his father had done pretty well. He invested his earnings in a nearby area north of town that he and a local lawyer developed into a family vacation spot, complete, they bragged, with the oldest operating carousel in North America. His mother, a graduate of Smith College, taught English literature at the junior college in Johnstown.

Without regard to his parents' position, and the fact that he lived in a rather small community, Brian was known for his own accomplishments and was recognized as a leader. Everyone expected great things of Brian—especially Brian. As valedictorian of his high school class, leader of the debate team, and student body president, with excellent grades, he had no trouble being accepted at New York University. The year was 1960 and his life was about to be given meaning. John F. Kennedy was elected president of the United States.

At first, it was simply the cadence of the language that he admired. Then the idealism expressed. The humor, the vitality. The realization of the power of language in the hands of this "new generation of Americans." Brian watched every minute of the 1960 Democratic Convention, televised from Los Angeles, as he sat glued to his family's 24-inch black-and-white television set, even through dinners on his TV tray. He had his own list of the states on a poster board and color-coded the delegate count.

Brian knew that if the nomination was to go to Kennedy, barring something like Eleanor Roosevelt pulling it out for old Adlai Stevenson, it would be on the first ballot, before those delegates legally committed were free to be stampeded or bought off by another candidate. Lyndon Johnson. He could not even stand to listen to Johnson. The Texas accent. "Crude" was the best way he could describe him, especially when held up against John F. Kennedy.

By Washington, it was Kennedy 710, 51 short of the nomination but with enough votes to guarantee it. Everyone in the hall knew it was over. So did Brian with his meticulous count of the delegates.

When Kennedy was nominated, Brian was so euphoric that he could even accept Johnson as vice president because Kennedy needed the South and, Brian expected, the South probably had as much use for a Northeasterner as he did for a Southern politician. After all, Eisenhower had sent in federal troops just so young black children could go to school. Selecting a Southerner was a price that had to be paid to elect Kennedy. As Adlai Stevenson himself had said at a campaign stop in Sacramento, California, "The stakes are too high because the alternative to a Democratic victory is—Richard Nixon."

At NYU, Brian joined the Young Democrats and debated members of the John Birch Society who were convinced that Dwight Eisenhower, Earl Warren, and most everyone else were Communist. He knew he wanted to "do something" with his life, heed the call to "public service." For Brian, that meant being a leader, which translated into politics.

The election of John F. Kennedy confirmed that belief. That is when he first started thinking of law school as the road to politics. He imagined himself a U.S. senator. Even president someday.

Chapter 10

The Classroom

IN 1863, TWO ships left Bombay for England, arriving at the Liverpool Quay a month apart. Both were named *Peerless*. Both carried Surat cotton meeting specifications appropriate for the use to which one—a merchant named Wichelhaus—intended to put the "middling fair merchant's Dhollorah" Indian cotton. But when one of the ships arrived at the Liverpool Quay early the next year, Wichelhaus refused to accept the 125 bails of Surat cotton at the agreed-upon price. Instead, he claimed, he had intended to purchase the same type and amount of cotton that had arrived upon the earlier *Peerless* ship which had left India a full month prior. Raffles, who had bought the cotton in India and contracted with Wichelhaus for its delivery, sued Wichelhaus for breach of contract, claiming that he had offered the goods to Wichelhaus, who had refused to accept them and pay for them as promised.

"Mr. Zierdan, do you agree, as the court found, that the defendant Wichelhaus breached his agreement to buy the cotton?" The professor of Contracts looked up from his seating chart toward the top row seats.

This is how it had been done from the inception of the law school at Berkeley and its dedication in 1911, following Ms. Elizabeth Josselyn Boalt's gift of two pieces of property in San Francisco to be sold to raise money for the construction of a building at the Berkeley campus to house the Department of Jurisprudence named in memory of her husband, John Henry Boalt. The case book method, as it was called, was not the creation of Boalt Hall. It was, however, a truly American creation that owed its origins to Harvard and its dean, Christopher Columbus Langdell who, in 1870, introduced the case method. Its adoption throughout the United States went hand in hand with the Socratic method, creating a system in which students were active participants in a learning process requiring rigorous examination of facts and law from real cases described in published opinions of the courts of England and the United States.

"Of course. The opinion of the court is silly. I mean, cotton is cotton. It was the same stuff, at the same price. The confusion over which ship doesn't really have anything to do with the contract. It was to buy cotton. What difference does it make how the cotton got to England?"

"So, Mr. Zierdan, it wouldn't make any difference then if the good ship *Peerless* your client had in mind when he agreed to supply cotton sank on the way to England? He would still be obligated to deliver even though his cotton was now sitting at the bottom of the ocean?" The professor raised an eyebrow.

"Well, no…but…"

"But, Mr. Zierdan?"

It was too late. The professor had turned and was selecting his next target.

"Ms. Contreras, perhaps you can help Mr. Zierdan with his client's sunken ship—and case. What's wrong with this contract?"

"No *consensus ad idem*…no contract," Rose uttered. It was the first time a professor had called upon her.

"Oh, my goodness, the lady speaks a foreign tongue!" the professor exclaimed in mock surprise.

"No *consensus ad idem*; 'no meeting of the minds,'" he announced triumphantly. "How can you have a contract without the basic element, a meeting of the minds, an agreement on what it is you are doing together?

"Mr. Goldman, you don't agree?" Actually, Leon had said nothing, had not even raised his hand. He had just shaken his head, not even that noticeably. But already in the sixth week of first-year Contracts, his intellect, and occasionally his ideology, had surfaced. These exercises were, after all, intellectual duels. Professor Steinberg, B.A., New York University, LL.B., Harvard, the author of the definitive work on Contracts, used in the best law schools in the nation, thrived on dueling with the best and the brightest. He had little patience for the rest. Soon the shake-out would occur: first exam grades. At the end of the first year, invitations to join the law review would go out. The lines would be clearly drawn, the pecking order established, forever. Some students would never be called upon again. Others would not dare raise their hand.

Leon took his glasses off, exposing the dark circles from a lifetime of intense reading.

31

"No. The analysis by the judges is the product of a legal system dedicated to upholding the order of business. Thus, their analysis focused solely on form. Nowhere do they ask: 'What is the harm? What difference does it make to anyone?' It is the law for its own sake; a set of rules, mantras, without regard to consequences."

Silence. A few darting looks around the class confirmed the "oh, shit" consensus. Without breaking his stare, and after sucking his teeth audibly, the professor asked: "Mr. Goldman, you would allow courts to go behind the words of a contract, which is clear and unambiguous on its face, and explore the secret, unexpressed thoughts of a party who seeks to get out of a contract?"

"Of course," came the immediate retort.

"Ah, but, Mr. Goldman, how can one possibly have a uniform system of enforceable contracts that business depends upon—"

"My point exactly," Goldman interrupted. "The law is a system designed to support the uniform practice of business. It has little or nothing to do with the unexpressed, but real, intentions of people. And, I might add, we are all here at Boalt as trainees in that legal system, as evidenced by the corporate curriculum."

More "oh, shit" looks: "Big shit."

"Ah, yes, Mr. Goldman. The perceived servitude of the law to corporate interests. 'Relevance,' I believe you call it, isn't that it, Mr. Goldman? You only want to learn of the law what is 'relevant' to your times. Well, let us continue and see where this gets us.

"Do you agree, Ms. Contreras, with Mr. Goldman?"

Rose had not expected the question. She was caught between Mr. Goldman and the professor, and was asked to choose sides.

"Well," she began, "I think you are both right."

"Oh, my goodness, again. The lady speaks Latin and is tactful, too. How can we both be right, please tell us, Ms. Contreras?"

"You seek order; a system that commerce can rely upon. Mr. Goldman seeks to vindicate the real intentions of the parties. In reality, even though expressed in the Latin mantra of the law, the justices in the *Peerless* case ultimately did attempt to reach the subjective intent of the parties, even though the contract on its face appeared unambiguous. When they found that the parties had a misunderstanding about the words used in the contract, they refused to enforce it. A strict objective rule, looking only to the words used, and not subjective intent, certainly would be more reliable in a uniform system of commerce. Such a rule would have reached the opposite result here and enforced the contract."

"Ms. Contreras," beamed the professor, "have you been reading ahead in your case book? Does the name Oliver Wendell Holmes have meaning to you?"

He turned back to Leon. "They would have loved you in England in 1864, Mr. Goldman. Subjective intent was determinative. But in the United States, this approach was criticized, especially by Oliver Wendell Holmes in his lectures on the Common Law and in his *Harvard Law Review* article in 1899 on 'The Theory of Legal Interpretation,' as making enforcement of contracts more difficult, less predictable. He advocated an external—or what others have called an objective—theory of contract interpretation. In essence, courts would look at the words and conduct of the parties and interpret an agreement, a contract, in accordance with the ordinary meaning a 'reasonable person' would attach to the terms. No reading of minds. An objective, dispassionate, 'business-like' approach.

"So you see, Mr. Goldman, the 19th-century merchant capitalist colonial empire of Great Britain was, like you, more sensitive to the real intent of real people than was America, the land of the free. The beauty of the Common Law. It changes with the times."

Seeming to reverse fields, the professor asked: "Mr. Bridgeport, would you agree that a strictly objective standard would be better for a well-run system of contracts? That is, one where the court looks at the 'reasonable' interpretation of the contract instead of trying to determine the parties' actual, subjective, secret, mental processes? Look at what they actually express rather than what they might have meant to say?"

Bridgeport had been following the exchange with some satisfaction that the long-haired radical socialist, Goldman, was getting thrashed publicly. He saw his opportunity to pile on.

"Certainly. If a contract doesn't mean what it says, then how can you have a system of commerce or even a definitive marijuana purchase?"

That drew some snickers and a brief sense of relief that the tension was subsiding. Instead, the professor shot back: "What if there had been a third *Peerless* ship then, Mr. Bridgeport? What would happen to your orderly system of commerce in cotton or marijuana?"

Confused, Bridgeport said, "I don't understand."

"Well, we have the situation in the 1864 case of *Raffles v. Wichelhaus* that the justices of Queen's Chancellery were presented with one party saying 'I meant the *Peerless* leaving India in October' and the other party saying 'I meant the *Peerless* leaving India in December.' What if there had been a third *Peerless*, and the words of the contract could objectively, reasonably, be interpreted to mean, and the court found, that a reasonable person would assume it meant the *next* ship named *Peerless* to leave India with cotton, and factually it turns out that neither of the two we have been describing was the 'next' ship to leave India?"

Sensing Bridgeport had not yet caught on, the professor continued. "In essence, the court objectively determines that the contract binds the parties to the third ship—one that neither party subjectively contemplated. What do you think of your objective theory now, Mr. Bridgeport?"

He had not seen it coming. But then, why should he have? Professor Steinberg was the master in Contracts, and the podium and his lecture hall were his weapons. "Perhaps, gentlemen," he stated, looking at Goldman and, alternately, at Bridgeport, "you would be wise to bring *analysis* to the study of law, and not ideology.

"Class dismissed."

That afternoon, Leon Goldman checked out from the law library Oliver Wendell Holmes' *The Common Law*. Leon had a passion for history. He was not as committed to a legal education. Giving Professor Steinberg his due, he was willing to entertain the possibility that perhaps there was more to Western history than the economic exploitation of capital and labor.

"The parents aren't going to like this," he thought to himself, as he headed down campus with Oliver Wendell Holmes under his arm. With law school, he did not have time to attend the speeches, programs, rallies, and concerts listed in the flyers handed out at Sather Gate or posted on the kiosk near the Student Union. But at least, walking through the Berkeley campus to his apartment south of Telegraph Avenue, he felt somewhat connected to what he had left behind, "down campus."

Chapter 11

Rose

JACKSON BRIDGEPORT III was raised in a home complete with a floor-to-ceiling library. Leon Goldman's parents provided him a home full of books, pamphlets, and lively Marxist discussions of history and economics. Rose Contreras grew up with *Reader's Digest*, an occasional *National Geographic*, and any other magazines her mother could obtain from the houses she cleaned. Rose's mother, who had not finished high school in south Texas when she met and married Rose's father, was determined that things would be different for her daughter. Because they moved with the seasons, from place to place, depending upon crops, they never had a subscription of their own. Not that they would have spent the money when they could get the used magazines free. In addition to working alongside her husband during harvest time, Rose's mother always managed to find new homes to clean, and new magazines to bring home to Rose, always asking first if the magazine was ready to be thrown out. Occasionally, she would bring home a *National Geographic* with the map still inside, and Rose would add it to her wall of maps.

Rose's father, too, knew the value of education even though he spoke very little English, despite being 20 years older than Rose's mother and having spent most of his working life in the United States. Having come from Mexico at about 22—he was not sure of his birth date—he had lived most of his life in farm labor camps with other Mexicans and learned only the English necessary to follow directions. When one picked, irrigated, thinned, hoed, ditched, sprayed, loaded, and drove, there was not a need for a lot of dialogue with the *patrón*.

After Rose's parents married, they moved to California and followed the work throughout the Central Valley. Occasionally, they would go up to Washington for the apples. Most of the other workers were single men, but they appreciated and were respectful of the *señora* among them. Rose's mom, with her English without an accent, was often asked to write letters and make phone calls in English, obtain money orders, or do other things difficult for the nonfluent workers. Usually, a more private area was reserved for the Contreras family in the farm labor camp shack, even if it was no more than a corner separated by a blanket hung on a line. And, of course, everyone loved baby Rose and brought her candy, and used clothes and toys given away or found discarded, including, once, a little bike with training wheels.

It was rare for Rose to spend more than three or four months in any school during the elementary years. This made it hard to make friends, to establish relationships, although occasionally she might see kids in a later grade who were with her for a few months in an earlier grade, as she passed through with the crops, depending on weather. If cotton was early that year in Kern County or the grapes late in Lodi, or her parents left early for the peach harvest in Yuba City or onto the artichokes, the strawberries, the prunes, or the walnuts, Rose's school would be dictated by the crop.

Rose's parents never asked her to do work; they preferred that she did not. But she learned to shake almonds with a mallet, to thin clusters of peaches, to irrigate fields, and to pick walnuts until her hands were stained black and her knees indented from dirt clods. By the time she was 15, she could drive a D-4 Cat, pull a spray rig through rows of trees with a field tractor, pick up bins of peaches, and load field trailers with a forklift on the back of a tractor. But for a child, growing up in the lush fields of California, this was simply fun, not work. Most of the time Rose would be seen by workers who would teasingly throw fruit at "Rosita," sitting on a folding chair, reading. She loved to read. Anything. In every town, she would find the public library and check out books.

One summer evening, Rose's mom answered the door of the small one-bedroom house the family rented in Salinas. It was in a poor neighborhood, with houses closely adjacent, packed into what would be called a slum in an urban area. Clearly no one but renters lived there. So it was unusual to see a young man, Anglo, with a sports coat and tie, carrying a briefcase, standing in the glow of a single light bulb that illuminated the steps to the door.

"Good evening. Do you have children?" he asked.

Mr. Contreras wondered if there was a problem.

"*¿Quién es?*" he asked.

"No sé," his wife answered. Turning back to the young man, she asked, "What do you want?"

He saw Rose sitting on the couch, reading, and began his pitch. "Do you care about your children's education?"

"¿Qué dice?" her father asked.

Mrs. Contreras interpreted for her husband. In Spanish, he told her, "Ask him in."

The *World Book Encyclopedia* was the only set of books the Contreras family ever owned. Yes, the parents cared deeply about their children's education and this one set of books, they were promised, had virtually all of the knowledge of all of the countries, everywhere—everything a young person needed to know to be successful in school. It even had plastic overlays showing different levels of the body from the external skin to the skeletal system.

The young man with the briefcase of opportunity had made a sale and a nice commission. He also caused the Contreras to think about what else they could do for their children's future. Rose was 13 and had just finished 8th grade, half in Salinas and half in a two-room school in Live Oak, California.

Her brother, Pablo, was four. The Contreras family needed to find a place it could stay year-round, for the sake of the children's education.

In the fall, Rose started high school in Gonzales, California. Her family moved to a small house on property owned by the DiGeorgio Corporation, adjacent to 1,400 acres of farmland also owned by the company. With the house came a year-round job and assurance that the children would remain in one place to attend school.

In high school, Rose made friends easily, although her circles and activities were limited. In her white gym blouse and shorts, with her shoulder-length hair pulled and tied back, she felt she looked much like the other kids. While not overly interested in sports, she enjoyed the camaraderie of her teammates. At 130 pounds, 5 foot 6 inches—2 inches taller than her dad—she was actually not a bad field hockey player and a good softball hitter in girls' intramural sports.

But she was not one of the "in" crowd of Valley residents who had spent all of their school years together. While accepted, and even well liked on the sports field, she was not asked to socialize or double-date with her teammates. Her parents were very reluctant to have her date at all, although they allowed her to attend school events under strict limitations.

But, in the Valley, Anglos, while friendly, did not date the daughters of Mexican farm workers.

It was also obvious to her classmates that Rose was smart. Her years of reading in the fields had given her a vocabulary beyond that of others her age, although occasionally her pronunciation would be of one who had only seen the word, never having heard it spoken. This, too, set her apart as different, if only because she was so bright.

Her teachers encouraged her to attend college, something she had not thought possible growing up in labor camps. At graduation, she was named "Most Likely to Succeed" by her classmates, received her CSF—California Scholarship Federation—pin and a Bank of America Scholarship of $50 for excellence in literature.

"You should consider becoming a lawyer," she had been told by a counselor at Gonzales High School. "You are so articulate; you are very bright. You could help people logically work through situations."

Her parents were proud of her. Her father bought a camera for the occasion. After the graduation ceremony, the family returned home where dozens of workers, neighbors, and friends came by. Even the superintendent of the DiGeorgio facility accepted the invitation and stopped in. There was music, chips and salsa, beer and pop.

Rose's father gestured to the superintendent to pose with Rose for a picture. He readily agreed. When everyone left that evening, Rose's dad came over to her, held both her hands, and kissed her softly on the forehead.

"Rosa, quiero que llegues a ser alguien importante." Rosa, I just want you to be somebody.

Rose went to Fresno State because she never thought of going anywhere else, except maybe a junior college. The acceptance of her student loan application, and her parents' help, made it possible for her to choose a state college. She lived in the dorms but had little time to socialize. She took the maximum number of units permitted to graduate in three years. Her father picked her up most weekends so she could spend time with her family. In the summers, she joined her mother in the fields as a way of helping pay her parents back for the educational costs they were providing.

As she entered her final year at Fresno State, she began to think what she would do with her education and her future. She had maintained a 4.0 grade point average throughout college and had come to the attention of a number of professors who had urged her to consider postgraduate training. She took the Law School Aptitude Test, mostly out of curiosity, and was startled to find that she scored in the 98th percentile. For the first time, she accepted that she might well be eligible not just for any graduate school, but a top school. She applied to Boalt Hall—in Berkeley. She knew there was no way she could pay for Stanford or any other private institution and did not want to be too far from her family. Despite her qualifications, she was again surprised when she was accepted.

Rose was not sure what she would do with a legal education but somehow liked the idea that perhaps she would be another Perry Mason. She knew that she did not ever want to be his secretary, Della Street.

She knew she had to "be somebody."

Every time she came home from Boalt to visit her parents, there were only two pictures in the living room. One, on the wall, was of Our Lady of Guadalupe. The other was on the mantle. It was the high school graduation picture of Rose with the superintendent of the DiGeorgio Corporation plant.

Chapter 12

Brian

THE CONVERSATION AT the reunion turned to Brian, initially more out of politeness than interest; a lull in the serving of salad.

"So. Are you really a white-water rafting guide?" asked one of the wives.

"Sure am. That and a cattle rancher. It's pretty restful."

"This must be a real contrast for you this evening, Brian," suggested her husband. It was Geoffrey Mason.

"No, not really. We have a lot of pretentious people coming out to Bozeman thinking they can raft a river."

The conversation at the rest of the table noticeably stilled, and all eyes turned at the gratuitous insult. That is, all eyes except those of Brian's daughter Randy, who, with her head down, was busy eating all of the sourdough bread, carefully separating the inners from the crust, salting the former, eating it, and piling the latter on her dad's bread plate.

"You see," he began, "I found there is really a tremendous similarity between litigation and white-water rafting." This seemed to spark some interest at the table. He still knew how to work an audience.

"There is a feeling when you are cross-examining the key opposing witness in front of the jury, especially a professional witness who makes his living testifying. You know only one of you is going to walk away the winner. You start out slowly. Tentative. Testing. You win a few. He gets in a few shots. There is the occasional eddy. But slowly you get your rhythm. Then it starts in earnest. You are moving a little faster, then swiftly with the current. The decisions become instinctive, instantaneous. Each of you is alone now.

"The jurors sit, watching. They are not participants. Opposing counsel sits, seeing it happen, but he can't stop it. The witness is starting to show signs of panic.

"There are no safe inlets. Nowhere to hide. There is no way out. You plunge over the edge. If it is done right, you survive. If it is done wrong, you probably drown.

"It's exhilarating. It is the moment everything in the case was built toward. You've lived it in your dreams a hundred times. It's better than an orgasm.

"Well, I get that same feeling every time I run a class 4 or 5 river. The difference is, I'm outdoors, and"—he paused a moment for effect—"no one needs to be destroyed."

The young Hispanic waiter put the chilled salad fork in its place in front of him.

"So, Brian," said Rose's guest leaning forward with real interest, "you were a lawyer?"

"Of course," he said, glancing at Rose. "Boalt Hall, class of '69."

Rose and the others at the table could not help but think how much older he looked than they. Life had obviously taken a toll.

As they were trying to place the face, Geoffrey Mason interrupted their thoughts.

"So why did you come to the reunion then if you feel we are all pretentious bastards?"

"I just wanted to see if you had changed at all, Mason."

Mason looked at him hard for a moment, then laughed. "Brian Jacobs! You're a real bomb thrower and, as I recall, there were plenty of those in the class."

"Mason, at least get it right. At People's Park, it was a gas canister they alleged, but couldn't prove, I threw."

Brian Jacobs was never a bomb thrower. If the truth be known, he might have to admit that he was a pacifist. In fact, he had notified his draft board, just as he entered Boalt Hall, that if the occasion arose, and they were to issue an induction order, he would refuse orders to serve in Vietnam in any capacity, even as a medic.

However, he declined to apply as a conscientious objector because he did not believe he met the legal interpretation and because he felt the government had no right to inquire into what his personal beliefs might be, even for military conscription.

The draft board had posed a hypothetical. The questions came from a 65-year-old woman who looked more like his grandmother than someone who sent young men off to war:

Clerk: "Well, suppose the Vietcong invaded the United States. Wouldn't you defend your country?"

Brian: "They haven't. We invaded them. I intend to serve my country, not wantonly kill innocent people for it."

His response did not go over well, but the occasion to refuse induction never arrived because Brian reached his 26th birthday at the end of his first year at Boalt, before his number ever came up at the draft board.

For the two years before he entered law school, Brian had a deferment from induction. He was serving the United States of America at something that made sense to him and was consistent with the strong sense of idealism he felt. He served in Africa, in the Peace Corps. And he was married.

Brian was strongly influenced by John F. Kennedy and the New Frontier. He graduated from high school in 1960. During his senior year, he put up lawn signs, went door to door to get out the vote, and watched as Kennedy captured the aspirations of millions of young people like him. Everything was possible. That's when he started thinking about law school as the road to a political career.

At New York University—NYU—he studied political science. In the summer of his second year, he joined a group of students who went South to help tutor children in rural Alabama. He had no intention of "agitating," or becoming involved in any demonstrations or "freedom rides." He just thought he could help. He quickly found that his presence alone, a white college student from New York tutoring young black children, was "agitating" and generally unwelcome by white Southerners.

At first, people in the small town seemed curious. After a few days, as people learned what he was doing, he was ignored. When he sat at the counter of the diner next to his motel, no one waited on him. He knew better than to make a scene. After a week, when he returned one evening from tutoring, there was a note under his door: "This room has been rented. Please leave."

He knew, of course, what was going on, but he did not push the issue. He bought a tent—to his surprise, the clerk sold it to him—to pitch near the small Baptist church used as the school. When he paid at the register, the store owner stood nearby and with a nod allowed the clerk to accept Brian's money.

"Camping?"

"Looks that way," said Brian cheerfully.

"Be careful. Huntin' season," smiled the owner, who then spit on the floor and turned his back to Brian.

It started slowly, in late morning, as Brian was teaching his class. He was writing on a chalkboard and almost missed the sound. As he turned, the 23 children were all looking up at the ceiling. He looked up and saw nothing but the exposed rafters supporting the corrugated metal sheets that made up the roof. He could see through the holes made in other times that the metal had been used before being put to service for the Lord on the Baptist church.

Finally, he heard it too. A few pebbles. Rolling and sliding down the slope of metal sheets and falling to the ground alongside the church. Then a few more. Then what sounded like hail on the roof. The children sat, frozen, their eyes telling what they instinctively knew and of which he had no idea.

"Kids," he thought, but he was apprehensive. The first thing he noticed, with relief, as he walked out of the church house was the police car across the street. The next thing he experienced was a fist in his face.

Boys play at boxing, and men imagine fighting and hitting someone, as in the movies. But the reality of being hit, full face, with a large fist of an adult male, the nose breaking, the intense pain across the orbital floor as bones splinter, the white blindness, and the total loss of balance and orientation, defies any expectation or ability to return fire. Then more punches. Then kicks as he lay against the church door. The sound of ribs breaking, just like the snapping of chicken bones. He heard the feet walk off the deck, away. Nothing was ever said. No threats; no epithets. They were not necessary.

Next, he felt himself being lifted to his feet. He had no idea how long after. He fell against the wall while being helped up. He could not see anything; the blood covered his eyes, his face. A voice announced: "Mr. Jacobs, you are under arrest for assault and battery, being drunk in public, and disturbing the peace."

He felt liquid being poured on him and panicked at the thought of being set on fire. Then the can hit him. With relief he recognized the smell of beer.

He was pulled roughly, placed in the back of the police car he had seen, and taken to jail. He had little recollection of the next two days, but was never taken to court, arraigned, or, for that matter, seen by anyone or allowed a phone call. Late in the evening of the second day, he was told that bail had been posted, and he was led out of the building to a waiting car.

"Brian," said a stranger, offering him assistance, "we are taking you to the airport in Birmingham. You are going home."

As he got into the backseat, he was aware of another person in the front.

"Hi, Brian. I'm Shelly. I'm a paralegal. We heard what happened to you and contacted your parents in New York. They sent the $500 bail and a plane ticket. You'll be home by morning."

A deputy leaned into the front window and smiled. "You smell, boy. Too much to drink?"

Brian flew home, in the same blood-stained clothes he had worn for two days, barely able to sit in the cramped airline seat. He had managed to clean his face and wash part of his body at the airport, but had been unable to remove his shirt without assistance. His parents met him at the airport in New York and drove him home to Gloversville.

A few days later, he found a card stuffed in his shirt pocket. He did not remember her putting it there. It read:

> Shelly Leibowitz
> Paralegal
> Kunstler and Kunstler
> Attorneys at Law
> New York

He called the law office, after ten days, when he could think straight. He was still dizzy from what had been termed post-concussion syndrome, and he had a permanent deviation of the septum despite the surgery to repair the fracture and dislocation of his nose and the fracture of the orbital floor. His ribs ached, and he slept sitting in a chair because of the pain.

He asked for Shelly Leibowitz. The receptionist put him through to another paralegal who came on the line: "This is Mark Greenberg. What can I do for you, Mr. Jacobs?"

"I have Ms. Leibowitz's card. She helped me out of jail in Alabama about two weeks ago. I need to talk to her about the trial."

"What trial is that?" asked Greenberg.

"Well, my parents posted bail for me, and I don't know what the procedure might be. That's why I called."

"There won't be any trial, Mr. Jacobs," answered the paralegal.

"I don't understand. My parents posted bail."

"Brian, this is a little game they play down there in Alabama. Everyone understands the rules. You go down there from up North, they beat you up, arrest you, throw you in jail, and set bail. You are bailed out and go home. You don't set foot back in Alabama. They don't come looking for you. End of problem for everyone."

Brian could not believe what he was hearing. He was beaten up in the presence of a law enforcement officer. Then he was arrested. Now his lawyer's staff was telling him to forget it.

"But I want to have a trial. This isn't right. I am guilty of nothing. The officer knows that…and so do the children I was teaching," he said, pleased at remembering that there were witnesses to the event.

"Brian, you are lucky. You have someplace to go. These people, and those children you mentioned, they live in Alabama. They have no choice; no place to go; no ticket out. We have limited resources, Brian, and we have to pick our fights. Sorry, but you ain't it, buddy, understand?"

"But what about my parents' $500?"

"Price of admission," responded Greenberg.

"I suppose you mean exit."

"No, Brian, I mean admission. Admission to a front seat to the reality of racism in the law. It's about power. And in Alabama, the people you met? They is the government."

Brian called a few weeks later and again asked for Shelly Leibowitz. The receptionist offered that she was out of town. He inquired and was told that she was with Mr. Kunstler in Albany, Georgia, "with Dr. King."

The remainder of that summer he rested at the family cabin on the lake. He believed more than ever that he wanted to do something with his life, something of value, something to help those oppressed, who, at that moment in America, seemed to him to be the Negro and racial minorities. He also knew that he did not want to be physically beaten again for the help he provided.

It was just before Christmas that year, while he was in the library studying for midterms at NYU, that he saw Shelly. As he walked into the reserved book room, with a copy of *The Making of the President 1960* to study for a political science class, he saw her sitting with her back to him. There was no missing her black hair in tight natural curls. She was wearing jeans, her left foot tucked under her body, her right hanging down with a sandal dangling off the end. He stood behind her, looking down, not knowing what to say. Finally, he leaned forward, next to her left ear, and said: "You are under arrest."

Brian and Shelly would, as most of that generation, remember exactly where they were and what they were doing at 12:30 P.M. central standard time on November 22, 1963. They were in bed, making love, at her apartment on East 67th overlooking Central Park with the sounds of the Everly Brothers drifting softly from the radio in the living room area:

> *Dream, dream, dream,*
> *that I love you,*
> *in the night...*

He heard it first, and jumped.
"What? What did I do?" she asked.
"Listen," he said.

> We interrupt this program for an announcement just received. The president has been shot. President Kennedy has been shot. There is no word at this time how serious the injury may be. We will be going to the network news in Dallas momentarily. We repeat. President Kennedy has been shot, in Dallas, Texas.

They jumped out of bed and ran, naked, to her small television set. The sight of Walter Cronkite in the middle of the day confirmed the news was ominous. They never left their television set until Cronkite removed his glasses and, wiping away a tear, announced: *"President John F. Kennedy died today in Dallas, Texas. The victim of an assassin's bullet."*

They held each other, naked, sobbing. All Brian could say was: "Those fuckers down there got him."

*   *   *   *   *

If Brian and Shelly needed an excuse to marry, the Peace Corps gave it to them. They had given a lot of thought to what they wanted to do with their lives. Shelly wanted to teach the lower elementary grades. As she said,

46

"get them before it's all over—before racism comes, before bigotry, while their flower is still opening to the world."

Brian still believed he could best help those in need through a political career and decided the road to politics was through law school. But he had hitched a ride on the dream of John F. Kennedy, and Kennedy was dead. He needed more time to think, to regroup. The Peace Corps, in which the spirit of Kennedy lived, appealed to both of them. After Alabama, he took seriously the surprising juxtaposition by Indian Prime Minister Jawaharlal Nehru of what the Peace Corps had to offer; "privileged young Americans could learn a lot from poor villagers."

They applied but quickly found that while their exceptional liberal arts records qualified them, the Corps could not guarantee that they would be assigned to even the same continent, let alone the same project, unless they were married.

The wedding was held in Gloversville, at Brian's parents' summer home on the lake. The Leibowitz family insisted that their rabbi perform the ceremony.

Gloversville could handle the Jews, but it was hardly prepared for the two Volkswagen minibuses full of long-haired, bearded, ragtag black and white young people that descended upon it. In black suits and Birkenstocks, with the girls sporting flowers in their hair, over their clean muumuus, in an obvious attempt to look "dressed up," they were as much a sight as a circus. In the back of the bus was their leader, a man of 45, hair combed from left to right over his head to cover thinning and baldness, in a suit and tie, with his glasses attached around his neck on a narrow cord but resting on the top of his head.

"Bill," Shelly screamed, when she saw him, despite the fact that she was on her father's arm about to walk between the chairs to the boat dock to be married. "Dave, Wendy, Bonnie, guys!" They were, of course, attorney William Kunstler and his "paralegals" with whom Shelly had worked in the South.

The party went late into the night, with most of the paralegals and a few fully dressed guests jumping or being thrown into the lake. In between, the newlyweds and their young friends talked of going to Africa, seeing the world, leaving and looking back on America. Others argued for the need to stay and confront society, as Dr. King was doing. Kunstler was glad to hear that Brian was thinking of law school, but made it clear that a life in public office was a waste of a good legal education.

"Brian, you've been to Alabama. They busted your head for teaching black children to read. If you were in Alabama, would you run for public office? Alabama is America in a white sheet. The people in power are going to stay in power, Brian. You have to decide: Are you going to be on the inside, or on the outside?"

One of the paralegals handed Kunstler a hand-rolled cigarette that seemed particularly sweet in smell. "Change is going to come in the streets, Brian," Kunstler continued, "not by the benevolence of good politicians in power. They have to be pushed, kicking and screaming, out of the way."

Finally, in a phrase that Brian would remember throughout his career, Kunstler put it in the jargon of the street: "Brian, baby, you is either a 'pushor' or a 'pushee.' Make up your mind."

Kunstler looked seriously at Brian for a moment, raised his glass, and said, "Mazel tov, Brian," and downed his champagne. Throwing the glass into the lake, Kunstler got up and returned to his dancing paralegals.

Chapter 13

The Classroom

"TAKE A MOMENT to read the problem," said the Torts professor, as he handed a batch of papers to each aisle for passing out. "Keep in mind, the elements of a negligence cause of action: a legal duty, a failure to act reasonably, proximate cause, and injury."

PROBLEM:
1. Adam, age 15, who is unlicensed, drives his parents' car down Telegraph Avenue.
2. Adam hits a pedestrian who is legally in a crosswalk and who, in turn, is thrown into the intersection, where Bruno, swerving to avoid the pedestrian, crashes into a power pole, which falls, injuring Charles sitting in a bookstore reading the collected works of Camus, and killing David, a quadriplegic living in Oakland, whose life-giving respirator fails without electricity because of the downed power pole. Meanwhile, the pedestrian is taken by ambulance to Kaiser Hospital in Oakland but unfortunately is caught in a shootout between the police and undesirable elements, and ultimately dies 10 years later as a result of complications from wounds inflicted by police fire.

THE ISSUE:
   Was Adam negligent; to whom does he owe damages?

"Let's start with negligence. Any problem there, Mr. Marquette?"

"No, Adam was driving without a license, which makes him negligent."

"So," asked the professor, "if he killed and injured all these people, but had a license, Mr. Marquette, you would feel better?"

"Well, driving without a license was a proximate cause of injury, since he didn't have a license, and therefore, if he had refrained from acting unreasonably, he would not have been driving with his inexperience and lack of training," responded Mr. Marquette.

With thinly veiled sarcasm, the professor looked around the class, as he raised his voice. "Does anyone else see any facts, any evidence in the problem, as posed, to suggest Adam was either inexperienced or lacked training?

"Mr. Bridgeport?"

"Well, his age, 15, suggests that, plus the fact that he had no license."

"Suggests! Suggests!" screamed the professor. "Do you plan on being a lawyer or a fortune teller? Are you reading Tarot cards? Most pedestrians are run down by *older licensed* drivers! There is nothing in the problem that tells you anything about the facts of the accident except where it occurred and where the pedestrian was hit. Don't assume facts not in evidence."

He calmed himself. "Now, is there anyone who can point to any negligent act of Adam?"

The professor waited. After the outburst, the first-year students were hesitant to venture forth.

"So I assume you are all content to permit children to drive cars on Telegraph Avenue and wreak havoc, destruction, injury and death, without consequences?"

"We could kill the little son-of-a-bitch," came a reply.

"Good, Mr. Rai. Thank you. Mr. Rai at least has a suggestion, grounded in the Common Law—vengeance! But where is the negligence, Mr. Rai?"

"The problem indicated that the pedestrian was legally in the crosswalk, which means he had the right of way, and Adam must have violated that right of way, and that would be a breach of the duty of a motorist which proximately caused the accident."

"But what of the fact that Adam was only 15?" asked the professor. "Shouldn't he be held to a lesser standard than an adult?"

"Generally, yes, but not while engaging in an adult activity. There is only one set of rules of the road."

"Thank you, Mr. Rai, for saving Berkeley from marauding children. Not that there are not enough marauders already."

With some semblance of relief that an answer had finally been received, the professor continued.

"Now that we have established that this little bastard was in fact negligent under the law, let's turn to the question of to whom Adam is liable and specifically to the issue of proximate cause. Mr. Cassidy. Could you explain how Justice Cardozo's opinion in *Palsgraf v. Long Island Railroad Company* bears upon this problem?"

Michael Cassidy hesitated. Professor Van Dyke loved Torts and expected everyone else to do so as well. As far as *Palsgraf*, Van Dyke had written articles devoted solely to this one leading case on legal causation and had taught, written upon, and spoken about it so widely that he could, and would, yearly recite from memory the facts verbatim from Justice Cardozo's famous 1928 opinion. That time was about to come, but Cassidy had momentarily derailed the Long Island Railroad.

"I am sorry. I haven't read it," Cassidy confessed to a hushed classroom.

"Haven't read it! Haven't read it! You're a law student in Torts and you haven't read *Palsgraf*? It was assigned for today! When were you planning on reading it? Do you think you can go through Torts without reading *Palsgraf*?"

"I'm sorry. I was up all night..."

Professor Van Dyke cut him off. "You are supposed to be up all night, for God's sake. You're a law student."

Cassidy added, hoping it would help: "My wife had a baby. A baby boy." It did not help.

"Your wife had a baby; you didn't have a baby. I didn't expect your wife to read *Palsgraf*. I expected you to read *Palsgraf*."

Thinking for a brief moment, in the pause, the professor looked back at Cassidy. "Was this a planned pregnancy?"

Cassidy lied: "Yes."

"Well, then, you could have planned to read *Palsgraf*."

With this, the class began laughing. Over the noise came the professor's voice dispatching Mr. Cassidy: "So tonight, you read *Palsgraf* out loud, to your wife. And to your child. Maybe he will be a better law student than his father."

Professor Van Dyke closed the book in front of him and did what he had done for 36 years, since coming to Boalt Hall from his clerkship with the Chief Justice of the Court of Appeals of New York, the legendary jurist Justice Cardozo, the author of the *Palsgraf* opinion. He began to recite to the class the facts of the opinion as he had read the final draft in the chambers of his judge and as it now appeared in every major law school case-book in America.

The story of the plaintiff Ms. Palsgraf's fateful day at the Long Island Railroad Station:

> Plaintiff was standing on a platform of defendant's railroad af-ter buying a ticket to go to Rockaway Beach. A train stopped at the station, bound for another place. Two men ran forward to catch it. One of the men reached the platform of the car without mishap, though the train was already moving. The other man, carrying a package, jumped aboard the car, but seemed instead as if about to fall. A guard on the car, who had held the door open, reached forward to help him in, and another guard on the platform pushed him from behind. In this act, the package was dislodged, and fell upon the rails. It was a package of small size, about fifteen inches long, and was covered by a newspaper. In fact it contained fireworks, but there was nothing in its appearance to give notice of its contents. The fireworks when they fell exploded. The shock of the explosion threw down some scales at the other end of the platform, many feet away. The scales struck the plaintiff, causing injuries for which she sues.

"Mr. Ford, how would Justice Cardozo have addressed our problem?"

"Cardozo would have focused on negligence and asked to whom does Adam owe a duty. Only those who a court or jury found could reasonably be expected to be put at risk by Adam's behavior could recover," answered Ford. Happy with his answer, he added, "Mrs. Palsgraf wasn't a foreseeable victim."

"So," asked the professor, "does the dead pedestrian's family have a case? After all, he would not have been in the ambulance but for his inju-ries caused by Adam."

"I don't think so," replied Ford. "It is not reasonably foreseeable that he would be shot on the way to the hospital. That is a rather remote possi-bility to conceive of for one who only violated the right of way of a pedestrian."

"But what if," asked the professor, changing the facts, "the evidence showed that he would have died anyway from his injuries, even without being shot. Would that change your view of Adam's liability to the heirs, Mr. Ford?"

"But he didn't."

"Oh. So Adam gets a free pass for imposing fatal injuries because the Oakland police performed the *coup de grâce* on a dying pedestrian?" Dismissing Ford, Professor Van Dyke turned to another student.

"Mr. Jacobs, are you ready to exonerate Adam for the pedestrian's death?"

"No," replied Brian, "but obviously, I would also hold the police responsible…"

Interrupting, the professor asked, "And not the undesirable elements that caused the police to shoot?"

"I didn't say that. Cardozo talks of holding persons accountable for the dangers they create and that are reasonably foreseeable. The issue is not negligence but proximate cause."

"Except," responded Mr. Johanson when the professor nodded toward his raised hand, "the pedestrian didn't even die for 10 years. How can that be considered proximate to the accident?"

"Ah, yes, proximate cause."

Every year a student could be relied upon to spring the trap created by Francis Bacon, Lord Chancellor of England, when he penned the words:

"*In jure non remota causa sed prexima spectatur.*"

Professor Van Dyke looked around the class and repeated slowly: "*In jure non remota causa sed prexima spectatur.*"

Translating, he added: "In law the near cause is looked to, not the remote one."

Professor Van Dyke continued, "With these two words, 'proximate cause,' Francis Bacon has confused the law of torts for 200 years. Proximate implies close in distance or time. But if one has a duty in law and violates that duty, and a person is foreseeably injured, what difference does it make if the person is 1 foot or 100 miles away, or is injured today or dies an agonizing death as a direct result 10 years later?"

"Mr. Bridgeport, how would you resolve the problem?" Bridgeport was being given a rare second chance.

"I agree with the dissenting opinion in *Palsgraf*. If a person violates the duty imposed by law, I see no reason why he should not be responsible for *all* consequences that flow, foreseeable or not. Perhaps that way more people would obey the law. Unlike Mr. Jacobs, I would hold the criminal undesirables, not the police, liable for their conduct that caused the police to exchange gunfire contributing to the pedestrian's death."

"Ms. Contreras, you have a different view?" asked the professor.

Rose began hesitantly. "Cardozo approaches the problem as one of negligence, defining to whom a duty is owed. The dissent approaches the same facts from the perspective of causation. Both are focusing on to whom the defendants will be liable. Each concludes, really, that the issue is one of public policy: Just how far do we want to extend responsibility for actions?

"The problem is that if we approach the matter as one of causation, like the English case of the ship *Polemis* that burned at Casablanca, Morocco, simply as a result of a plank being dropped into its hold, and somehow, strangely, and unexpectedly, causing an explosion of the benzine cargo, then virtually every consequence can be found to have a seed of causation in the defendant's conduct, as in our problem. Clearly, none of the injuries would have occurred 'but for' Adam's conduct. On the other hand, if we asked to whom defendant owes a duty, after an accident, how do we decide some will recover, and others won't?

"Is the test foreseeability? If so, isn't it true that, in retrospect, to borrow a phrase, 'on a clear day, a judge or jury can foresee forever'?"

No one raised a hand. No one spoke. Finally, the professor smiled warmly at Rose, then looked around the lecture hall.

"There, ladies and gentlemen, you have in a nutshell the problem with the law of negligence and what judges have been struggling with for hundreds of years. The words simply mask a public policy decision: Should this plaintiff recover from this defendant on these facts? It is your job as attorneys to see the right facts are persuasively presented to justify the result.

"Thank you," he added, as he picked up his books, signaling the end of the lecture.

As the class straggled out, Professor Van Dyke raised his left hand and pointed his index finger at Rose. "Ms. Contreras. Please stop by my office this afternoon." It was not offered as a question. Rose nodded.

At 4:00 P.M., immediately after her classes for the day had ended, Rose climbed the stairs behind the entry to the library to the fourth floor. As she ascended the stairs and turned into the hallway, she found a narrow corridor with closed, windowless, wooden doors, each with the name of a professor stenciled in black. She knocked at the door marked Professor Van Dyke.

The door opened, and she saw behind the man at the door a small cubicle cluttered with books, articles, and papers. A manual typewriter sat on a small moveable metal stand next to a secretarial desk, the only place an inhabitant could sit and work.

"Miss Contreras. Come in."

He cleared the single remaining chair in the room of a stack of library books with 3x5 cards stuck in them, placing them on the floor next to the chair.

Over his desk, on the wall, was his law degree. Harvard 1926. Under it was an honorary doctorate from the University of Melbourne and a proclamation announcing his designation as holder of the William Prosser Chair in Torts, at Boalt Hall, dated 1962 and, to the right of it, his designation as the Reporter of the American Restatement of Torts.

As Rose sat, she saw his most valued item in the room. It was to the right of the door that she had entered, to be seen by anyone exiting, if only Professor Van Dyke daily. It was an old photograph from the Court of Appeals in New York, dated 1928, showing Chief Justice Cardozo and his law clerks. There stood, unsmiling, in starched white collar, coat, and tie, a young Maurice Van Dyke. The caption read: "Mr. Van Dyke, thank you for your two years of service as my clerk. Fondly, Cardozo."

"Ms. Contreras, I am finishing up an article to be published next fall in the *Columbia Law Review*. The entire edition will be devoted to the opinions and writings of Justice Cardozo. I would like your assistance in cite-checking the cases and authorities I use. Of course, I expect you to read each case cited. Here is the first section. I would prefer you do one section at a time. Return it to me with your comment sheet. We will do one section a week so you can plan your time accordingly. Any questions?"

"No."

"Fine. Good day, Ms. Contreras."

She walked out. Stunned.

Chapter 14

Michael

MICHAEL CASSIDY'S BABY, born just before the recitation of Ms. Palsgraf's injury on the Long Island Railroad, was named Robert F. Cassidy. His friends would know him as "Robbie." When he would later go to Boalt Hall himself, his law review article would be signed with his full name: Robert Fong-Cassidy. He would insist upon the hyphenation.

Michael met Mai Fong, the mother of their child, at the Buena Vista Café during spring break in his senior year at Notre Dame. He and two couples had stopped for an after-dinner drink, having had crab with warm melted butter, and San Francisco bread, at Alioto's on the Waterfront. Very touristy, but he had been away and felt like hitting the Wharf and even riding the cable car up and over to Union Square where he had left his car earlier in the evening. An Irish coffee was called for before hanging off of a cable car, especially on a cold San Francisco evening. That meant the Buena Vista Café.

"We've got to get Michael laid," suggested someone in the group.

"Sorry, Michael, but I don't do Catholics," laughed one of the young women.

They had known each other since high school and enjoyed teasing their rather reserved friend who, they were convinced, was the only remaining virgin among them.

"All right, Michael, I'll do it," announced one of the men, "but I am going to keep my eyes closed."

Through the laughter, Michael heard, "What can I bring you guys?"

They were sitting next to the window at wooden tables that resembled library desks. He looked up and saw Mai, the cocktail waitress, who had been standing at his side through the bantering.

"Five Irish coffees," said one of the girls.

She returned in a few minutes, placing coffee in tall glasses before each of the couples and placing the fifth in front of Michael. "And one virgin Irish coffee for the boy." She smiled slightly, walked away, and disappeared among the crowd at the bar.

When Michael left the Buena Vista that evening, he stood for a while across the street waiting for the Powell and Hyde Street cable car. He watched the cocktail waitress, in her black skirt and white blouse uniform, through the blue and red surreal neon lights of the Buena Vista casting their glow in the evening fog on the people seated on the other side of the windows.

Michael came back alone to the Buena Vista every night that week. Each night he asked for "the usual," and each night she placed it in front of him, announcing, "One virgin Irish coffee for the boy."

On Tuesday, he told her his name. On Wednesday, he asked if she would like to go for a drink.

"No, I don't drink," she replied with the same slight smile.

On Thursday, she actually waved as he walked in and brought his drink without waiting for his order. "So, what brings you to the Waterfront, sailor? Looking for action?" she asked as he took his first sip of Irish coffee.

He nearly gagged. He did not know if he was being propositioned or ridiculed. After four days, he knew only her name, as did everyone else who could read the name plate above her small left breast. He realized she had done nothing different in those days, serving other customers, taking their orders, smiling, walking as if oblivious to her surroundings, amongst the noise of people drinking and laughing, and the smell of burnt coffee beans and cigarette smoke. At that moment, he felt foolish.

All he could think to say was, "I'm sorry."

"Oh, you mean about the tips all week. I figured you were just inexperienced. I mean in bars, too. So aren't you going to ask me out for Friday?"

Again, he was surprised. "Well, yes, I mean I am not just trying to pick you up. Like at a bar or something."

"This is a bar." She looked around the room as if verifying her statement.

He smiled. "What I mean to say is, will you have dinner with me Friday evening?"

"No."

"Excuse me?"

"You said, 'Will you have dinner with me Friday evening?' and then I said, 'No.' Michael, you've got to keep up with the conversation. You remember Adlai Stevenson at the United Nations during the Cuban Missile Crisis: 'Mr. Zoren, don't wait for the translation. Yes or No.'"

Then she held up her hand. "Hold that thought, Michael. Review the transcript while I'm gone. I have an order up."

She rushed off to the bar and picked up a tray full of drinks which she delivered to a group of apparent tourists, all with cameras strung around their necks or over their shoulders.

She returned with a second Irish coffee for him.

"Notice how the service gets better in anticipation of better tipping. Can you believe those Caucasian tourists," she motioned to the table, "all carrying cameras? Now, where were we?"

"You said, 'Aren't you going to ask me out for Friday?' and I said, 'Will you have dinner with me Friday evening?' And you said, 'No.'"

"Good," Mai exclaimed. "You did review the transcript. That means you are paying attention. So where does that leave us?"

"I have no idea," Michael said, shaking his head.

"Let's review," she replied. "We met on Monday. You came back Tuesday. You asked me to go out for a drink on Wednesday. Today is Thursday, and you asked me out for Friday. What, are we going steady or something?"

Michael added, "And I leave Sunday morning to go back to Notre Dame."

They looked into each other's eyes as if in a dare to see who would break off the stare. It was as intimate a moment as he had ever experienced. It lingered. He smiled slightly and offered the last alternative: "Saturday?"

"Bingo!" she shouted, a little too loud for his comfort.

"Oh, I'm sorry. I forgot. You're Catholic and Bingo is a sacrament. Well, as Confucius say, you've got your ticket and you can pick up your laundry Saturday, at 6:00 P.M., here. And leave a better tip, will you, Mikey?"

He drove home to his parents' house with its spectacular view of the city at night. He knew he would not be bringing her here. His father was still up, working in his study.

"Michael, when do you have to go back to school?"

"Sunday morning."

"We have a table at the Mayor's Tribute Dinner on Saturday. It's formal, so you might want to check and see if your tux is here."

Michael had forgotten. More probably, never knew what his father had planned for him.

"Gee, Dad. I have a date."

"Well, bring her along. If you expect a career in business and politics in this town, you've got to be seen at these functions. Good Catholic girl?"

"You know, we just met and only had a brief conversation, which barely touched on religion, so I haven't pinned that down yet."

"What's happening with law school? Have you heard from Boalt?" his father asked as Michael reached the doorway.

"Not yet," Michael answered, "but I have been accepted at Hastings so I have got that as a back-up."

As he walked out of the room, he heard his father shouting, "My son isn't going to no goddamn 'back-up' law school! I will have someone call the dean at Boalt."

Michael knew better than to protest. His father would do what his father would do. That was how business was done, his father had told him since childhood. He would "call someone."

Michael could not sleep. At first, it was the anger he felt toward his father. Would it always be like this? Wherever he went, whatever he achieved, would it be because his father "called someone"? His anger gave way to exhaustion. He found himself smiling, thinking of that first evening, when she had delivered the Irish coffee: "And one virgin Irish coffee for the boy."

She had the flat facial features of an Asian and could make her face expressionless, and droop her eyes, like a lizard. But after deadpanning one of her smart-ass comments, she could acknowledge with satisfaction, with her eyes, the shock she had caused. Then they would open wide, crease back on the sides in an acorn shape, to reveal dark brown pupils. She wore no makeup that he could detect but had the faint smell of body powder. She was, for Michael Cassidy, compelling.

It was also evident that she was very bright, as well as funny. Outrageous, spontaneous, and totally unpredictable.

On Saturday, he was at the Buena Vista early. She arrived late. By 6:15 P.M., he doubted that she was coming and felt rather conspicuous, neatly dressed in a suit, sitting alone, with two empty drinks and a small white box to keep him company, at a table for two by the window.

Then he saw her get out of an older car, wave to the driver, and stroll to the sidewalk. Her black hair came down to her waist, and, as she threw it back, she saw him in the window.

She stopped at the sidewalk, opened her purse, and placed it on the ground in front of her. Then she froze. As the first group of tourists approached her, she started moving her arms up slowly, one at a time, as if walking. Then her trunk turned and bowed partially to the approaching strangers. Her head moved, as if on a track, slowly, until it halted, mechanically, and a frown appeared on her face. Her right hand moved down and pointed to the bag.

The group stopped, as did a young couple walking in the opposite direction. "A mime," said one of the young people and put 50 cents in the open purse.

The frown turned to a smile, an eye winked, and the left hand rose and gave a wave at the wrist. Then the face turned back on the tourists and frowned, with the right hand still pointing at the purse. "You're supposed to give her money, Harry," one of the women said. The men in the group reached for their wallets and dropped some change in the purse.

"Thanks," Mai said, bent over, picked up the purse, and walked into the bar.

On entering the Buena Vista, she received applause from the customers who had apparently also watched the evening's main event. The staff just smiled. "That's Mai," commented Michael's server.

"Sorry I'm late. Had to wait for my brother to get off work to give me a ride."

Then she looked up at him and paused before exclaiming, "Jesus Christ! Whoops. Did it again. Holy cow! Is that okay? No Hindus in your family? What are you all dressed up for? Me? Are you out trying to get laid again?"

She noticed the box. "What's that?"

He pushed it across the table and she opened it. In the box was a single white orchid, the stem wrapped with wire, and a pin in it. "It's for your hair."

"Good," she said, looking down at her jeans and sweater, "since there is no place to attach it on this low-cut, strapless evening gown."

She excused herself, taking the orchid corsage. In a few minutes, she returned from the bathroom with the flower in place, pinned on the left side of her hair. She leaned over, kissed his cheek, and said, "Let's get out of here. I work here."

He had found a parking space along the road so they did not have to walk into one of the parking garages. He helped her into his father's Lincoln Continental, walked around to the driver's side, and got in himself. She said, "Let's just drive."

"Where?"

"Sunset on the Golden Gate. Hurry." Then she added, as they drove, "The irony of a clear night is that it takes a certain amount of clouds to make a good sunset." But the sun had set before they reached the Presidio, leaving little but twilight with early stars appearing. They crossed over the Golden Gate and headed north on Highway 101.

"I actually learned in Sea Scouts to navigate by the stars," Michael said, motioning to the sky and leaning forward to look through the top of the windshield.

"I'm impressed. So navigate us to a burger and fries."

"You don't believe me?"

"If you can find a burger and fries, looking at the stars, I'll believe you, Mikey," she said, frowning at him.

He turned back to the windshield, scanned the sky, found a star and pointed: "There, burger and fries. Five miles north, three miles east."

They continued driving without another word. In five miles he left Highway 101, headed east-southeast for three miles, until she saw the water and the A&W drive-in dead ahead. He pulled in and stopped. "Your order," he asked, with satisfaction. She acknowledged his navigational skills with a nod of the head and a look at the sky.

"Hamburger, hold the onion, in case you try to kiss me," she answered.

"Anything else?"

"That was your order," she clarified. "I want everything on mine, fries, and a root beer float."

He drove out of the drive-in with their order in bags, turning left down the road bordering the Bay.

"Where are we going?" asked Mai.

"You'll see," he smiled, obviously pleased with himself.

Down the road, he turned into a parking lot and stopped in front of a low building.

"Can't we get a parking lot with a view?" she asked. "Not that I'm complaining. I mean we are close to the dumpster."

"Get out," he laughed.

"What? The evening is over already? Can't I even eat my burger?"

"We're not eating in the car."

She followed him toward the building, but he went around instead of through the door marked "Members Only."

The insignia on the door read "Founded 1869." The San Francisco Yacht Club prided itself on being the oldest yacht club on the Pacific coast.

Older certainly than the St. Francis Yacht Club, which some suggested was for the *nouveau riche*, the pretentious. The truth was somewhere in between.

First, the "San Francisco" Yacht Club was not in San Francisco at all, but on Belvedere Island. Second, the St. Francis, which was in San Francisco, was really a faction that took its yachts and departed for San Francisco in 1926 over a dispute about relocating the San Francisco Yacht Club.

As for pretentious…well, yachting was for those who could afford it. As the saying goes, a yacht is a hole in the water into which one pours money. Ironically, now, many of the members of the St. Francis were also members of the San Francisco Yacht Club because the St. Francis did not have enough slips to accommodate all of its members. Even more ironically, many members of the San Francisco Yacht Club did not even have yachts. But they could claim membership, hang around the clubhouse bar, show up for the famous Saturday and Sunday breakfasts (wearing, of course, nonskid, nonmarking deck shoes), and enjoy the salt air, seagulls, and the view of one of the most beautiful bays in the world.

Mai was enjoying the intrigue of trespassing upon affluence until an older couple came through the locked gate, held it open, and greeted them.

"Good evening, Michael. I see your dad's got the boat at dock."

"You have a boat here?" Mai asked.

"Well, my family does. But it's not a sailboat so we use the guest dock to bring it here occasionally for special events."

"What's the special event?"

"You," he answered. "I brought it in from Richmond this afternoon. Better view of the city."

At the dock was a 65-foot Hatteras with gleaming lacquered teakwood railings, planked decks, chrome cleats, and lights glowing from an inner salon warmed by rich woods, Oriental rugs, and upholstered sofas. Mai was unusually quiet as she boarded the boat and entered the salon. Michael took her below, showing her the staterooms, the galley, the heads—one complete with a tiled bathtub—and returned to the salon. She sat at the bar as he served up the hamburgers and fries from their bags.

"And I believe the root beer float is for the lady," he said with the disdain of a French waiter, as he put the root beer in front of her.

He opened the under-counter reefer and pulled out a bottle of Roederer champagne. "Do you mind?" he asked. "I just wanted to look at you with a champagne glass in my hand."

"None for me?" she said sticking out her lip.

"I thought you didn't drink."

"I don't. On Wednesdays. This is Saturday. I make exceptions for Saturdays, fine champagne, and first dates."

She leaned over, reached under the bar, and pulled up a flute. "Hit me," she gestured. As he poured, she looked behind him to the back bar. Centered there was a life preserver with the word "AVARICE" stenciled around the top half of the circle.

"What is that?" she asked.

Michael looked. "Didn't you see that coming aboard? That's the name of the boat."

He clinked his glass with hers.

"My father named it. Someone suggested the word and he looked up the definition: 'an extreme desire to amass wealth.' The next day he had it painted on the ship's transom."

She looked at him over the top of her flute, listening to the bubbles and said, in all seriousness, "That is really sad, Mikey. Really sad."

They spent the night. Mostly on the floor of the foredeck, huddled in a blanket, making up names for constellations, including those created by the passage of airplanes on their way in and out of San Francisco Airport. Or those created by the lights of homes on Belvedere Island or on the hills above Tiburon. Most of his constellations were real, but with the names changed. Hers were all totally imaginary.

It was between constellations and champagne that he looked at her laughing in the reflected light. She saw his look.

"Mai…"

"Mikey, you have been calling me 'My' for a week. It's pronounced 'May-I.' You really need to learn more about Asian pronunciation."

"I'm sorry."

"That's okay. Now try it properly," she said.

"May I."

She moved her head sideways and up, looking at his mouth, and said, "I wish you would, Mikey. I really wish you would."

He kissed her softly, holding her body against his, exhilarated and afraid. He moved his lips to her eyelids as she snuggled into him, and then to her forehead.

He lay there holding her, taking in the smell of her hair, the feel of her slender body, wondering what to do next. What was expected of him?

He waited for any signal, any movement. And waited. After a while, he surmised, correctly, that she was asleep. With some disappointment, and significant relief, he held her and closed his eyes.

He awoke abruptly before dawn to the horn of a tug guiding a cargo ship through the Bay. He was uncovered and cold. Mai was asleep beside him, with the blanket wrapped tightly around her. He went below, checked the time, poured two glasses of orange juice, and returned forward on deck.

"Mayday, Mayday," he whispered in her ear. "Two people stranded who don't want to be rescued. Help. Help."

She started speaking without opening her eyes. "All this. A luxury ship. Fine champagne. And you can't even get laid. Avarice, Mikey, avarice. I don't know what we are going to do with you."

She did as he asked. Drove—more like, raced—him to the airport and, after dropping him off, took the car to his parents' home, parked it outside, and put the keys in the mail slot, next to the door. She walked down the steps, away from the large, elegant Pacific Heights mansion.

But then she stopped at the sidewalk, turned, and walked quickly back to the door. She knocked firmly the cast iron door knocker shaped like a lion's head. She heard someone shuffling on the other side of the door. Michael's father, in slippers and monogrammed robe, answered the door holding a newspaper.

"Good Sunday morning, sir," Mai began. "Have you given thought to your eternal soul? Have you reflected on a life of giving, rather than receiving, a life of sharing the bounty of the Lord, instead of one of *avarice?*"

Michael's father just looked at her. Without saying a word, he pushed the door, letting it click shut.

She turned and looked at the view from the porch. "I have seen the face of avarice. Now I must do the ritual cleansing. Home, Mai, for a shower and a bagel."

The following week she sent Michael a small package. He opened it to find a set of chopsticks with a note: "I am worried about your eating habits, Mikey."

She never told him about meeting his father. Nor did his father mention the strange missionary who had preached on his doorstep the Sunday Michael had "a friend" drop off his dad's car keys.

*   *   *   *   *

There is something about long-distance relationships and letters. Perhaps it's dreams and fantasies uninterrupted by the tedium of life. Imagination without consequences. Lovemaking without anyone going to the bathroom.

In the months that followed, Michael expressed feelings to Mai that he had never admitted to anyone, including himself. He told her of his admiration for her, her intelligence, wit, and freedom from convention. He wanted to learn from her. He wanted to be better, for her. He wanted to love her. He wanted her to love him.

Mai's letters always entertained. In time, they also told of her aversion to the preoccupation with money. Her father was a realtor—almost exclusively to the Chinese community in San Francisco. He had spent his entire adult life, and much of his family's time, seeking wealth—without success. Not that he had not provided for his family; he had. But a decent living was not enough. There was the drive to be rich. To be able to go to the Chinese Center and donate large sums of money and be recognized, perhaps with a plaque on the wall. To be thought of as a leader in the Chinese community. Someone politicians, at City Hall, would come to for "the Chinese vote." Instead, her father was more likely to be at City Hall defending health and safety violations at apartment houses or duplexes he purchased without sufficient capital to renovate.

The four children, Mai being the oldest, spent most weekends during the high school years and college summers painting apartments, scraping wallpaper, and cleaning out the residue of former tenants. In the process, she saw her mother become old by 40 and her father suffer two heart attacks. There was more to life, she concluded, and she was going to find it even if she had to invent it herself.

When she looked at Michael, she saw someone who needed reinventing. A sweet guy worth the effort.

It was June when he returned to San Francisco after graduation. He had been accepted for the fall semester at Boalt Hall, and they were looking forward to being together, she in her senior year at San Francisco State, and he at Boalt. His parents had attended graduation ceremonies at Notre Dame and gone on to New York. He returned home alone, to Mai waiting at the airport. That night, for the first and what would be the only time in her life, Mai spent the night with Michael in his parents' home.

They both knew what would happen when they came together. Neither of them anticipated that it would be within hours of landing at San

Francisco International Airport. If she had to guess, Mai thought it would be at the boat. He was still trying to think of what friend he might impose upon for the loan of an apartment for the evening when they arrived at his parents' home to drop off his luggage. Behind the door at which she had once preached the joy of giving was a literal gallery of takings from the art of Europe, the rug-making of the Middle East, and the antiquities of Japan. On the teal green plastered upper walls of his father's mahogany wainscoted library, illuminated by recessed lighting at the ceiling and capped with an octagonal coffered ceiling, were individually lit oil paintings by Dutch masters, their dark tones made richer by a large Persian rug covering all but a few feet on each side of the room. In a large bay window sat a large unusual desk.

"The desk actually came off of a Spanish galleon captured by the pirate Francis Drake. The Spanish called him a pirate. Of course, the British called him Sir Francis Drake. I guess it's a matter of whose ox is being gored."

"Was that an attempt at Spanish humor, Mikey?" Mai interrupted. "Ox being gored."

As they passed the dining area, Michael pointed to the large glass-encased vestment occupying the entire wall, floor to ceiling, at the head of a black lacquered teak table: "That's a 17th-century Samurai warrior ceremonial costume. In the lacquered box at the base of the glass case is an actual Samurai sword from the same period."

"And you put it in a box why? You don't want people cutting their meat with it?" asked Mai inquisitively.

He ignored her comment.

"Let me show you my room." They ascended the large curved marbled staircase, with ornate pewtered hand railing, to the second floor. At the top of the stairs were large double doors.

"What's in this room?" asked Mai.

"That's my parents' room. My room is down here."

"Well, let's see this room," said Mai as she opened the doors.

What she entered was less of a room and more of a suite appearing to hang in air over the city of San Francisco. One wall consisted completely of windows, floor to ceiling. The drapes were drawn, showing the full panorama of the San Francisco Bay, with the Golden Gate to the left, Alcatraz directly ahead, and, below, the lights of the city coming on at dusk. For a moment, even Mai was speechless. Finally she uttered: "Oh, my God!"

"It's a pretty spectacular sight, I have to admit. Better than my room," said Michael.

"Do you think they watched?" asked Mai.

Confused, Michael asked: "Who? Watched what?"

"Your parents. Do you think they watched us the evening we were on the boat? This looks like it's on a direct line of sight to the boat. If we could see San Francisco, couldn't they see us?"

Michael realized she was talking about the last evening they spent in San Francisco, when they were on his parents' boat.

"From here they could see Belvedere but not into the cove. So we were safe. As I recall that evening, there was nothing to watch anyway. Nothing happened."

Mai turned from the panorama of the window and walked toward Michael. "And I have been meaning to talk to you about that exact point."

Very serious in her expression, she stopped, her body very close to his, with her head tilted up, continuing her gaze. Finally she asked: "Just what exactly do you intend to do about that, Mikey?"

He put his arms around her and leaned down and kissed her. As she stood on her toes in her sandals, he could feel her body and realized that other than the sandals and the loose pull-over dress, Mai was wearing nothing. They fell onto his parents' bed and kissed more deeply. She laughed and managed to lighten his apprehension with, "Oh navigate me, my captain."

She began undoing his shirt. "No point going to your room, Mikey, if the view is so much better here."

Her expressed self-assurance hid little real experience. The difference was that what he approached with guilt and trepidation, she welcomed with delight and anticipation.

Mai became pregnant on their first night together. Contrary to the answer Michael would give to Professor Van Dyke, the pregnancy was not planned, neither by Michael nor Mai. His parents would never be convinced that "the Chinese girl" had not "gotten herself pregnant" to force Michael into marriage. That was not why he married her. The timing, yes; but the reason, no.

His father was furious: "You don't have to marry her, damn it! She can have an abortion."

Michael was stunned by the suggestion. He had not even considered it as an alternative: "We're Catholic! That would be murder."

"Yes, we're Catholic. This Chinese girl isn't. She is probably Buddhist or something. They don't believe like we do. It's her choice."

"Dad. It is my child, too."

"You don't understand," his father pleaded, "it's the rest of your life that is at stake here."

Michael thought about his life. He thought about life with Mai. "You're right, Dad. It is what is at stake here. My life. I am going to marry Mai."

They were married the third week of school, in September, at Holy Spirit Chapel of the Newman Center, in Berkeley, just two blocks from their apartment on Dwight Way. Under the circumstances, the Cassidys felt it was best not to have the wedding in their parish in San Francisco. Michael's father made a few calls, and matters were worked out. Required lessons in Catholicism for Mai were waived, but Monsignor Kelly insisted she sign an agreement to raise the child in the Church.

The Fong family was not happy that Mai had married a Caucasian. Her father took some consolation in the fact that she was marrying into a wealthy family. At the small reception following the wedding, in the Newman Center, Mai's father offered Michael's father a business card, suggesting the possibility of a real estate investment. Mr. Cassidy took the card, thanked Mr. Fong, and threw the card in the trash at the first opportunity.

As they sat in the front pew watching, the Cassidys were convinced that Michael was throwing his life away with this marriage. Even before the Berkeley priest began the mass, in English instead of Latin, someone with a guitar started singing words from Ecclesiastes 3.1:

> For everything there is a season,
> and a time for every matter under heaven:
> A time to be born....

Robert Fong Cassidy was born five months later. In the lesson of Mrs. Palsgraf's case, two people owing a duty to each other as a result of a foreseeable, yet unborn, third person, undertook to faithfully carry out that duty on behalf of the three of them.

Chapter 15

Leon

GROWING UP THE son of the neighborhood Communist isolated Leon Goldman from many of the other children but made him keenly aware, at a young age, of class differences in America and the world.

In some ways, his father had his own foreign policy, and, through the Longshoremen's Union, could enforce it. Ships from South Africa were refused unloading by the ILWU in protest against apartheid. Ships heading to countries with oppressed workers—read: "No Unions Allowed"—were refused loading. The docks of America, he saw, belonged to the ILWU, which stood solidly behind its leader, Harry Bridges.

Unless his father was away organizing, the dinner table was the place set aside for discussions of world events. There, Leon heard, as early as he could remember, of the Negroes, of slavery, of union busting, monopolies, Standard Oil, J. P. Morgan, the railroad barons, and the oligarchy of wealth that ran America.

"The coming uprising of the Negro in America is this country's curse for slavery. And don't think things have changed. The exploiting class has just learned a lesson: Keep cheap labor overseas. The new policy is colonialism and slavery combined," his father argued, "the best of each without the burdens of slavery gone awry, on our own soil, or the cost of owning colonies and dealing with movements of self-determination."

The history Leon learned was the history of the struggling classes, of John L. Lewis of the United Mine Workers, Walter Reuther of the Congress of Industrial Workers, Samuel Gompers of the AFL-CIO, of Sacco and Venzetti, and, of course, the struggle of the international workers of the world. Because so much of free speech law involved the suppression of unions, Communists, and other dissidents, Leon learned early that free

69

speech and democracy were illusions, not rights freely given to workers or oppressed classes, but rather tools of the rich and powerful.

In 1954, if he had been asked in class, Leon would have surely been the only one to have heard the name Dien Bien Phu or the "glorious victory" of Ho Chi Minh over the French colonialists. But then, in fourth grade, most of his classmates were concentrating on learning the capitals of the states.

When Leon's father was arrested in 1957 and his pamphlets seized, it was cause for celebration, not despair, at the Goldman household. With the help of the ACLU, Leon's father challenged the seizure and his arrest as violating his constitutional rights to distribute Communist views and pamphlets on public property. The property he had chosen for distribution was the U.S. Federal Courthouse itself, in Seattle.

Years later, when Leon began his studies at Boalt Hall and entered the huge reading room of Garrett McEnerey Memorial Law Library for the first time, he sought out the Federal Law Reporters, turned to 264 F.2d 256 (9th Cir. 1959), and sat and read with pride the Ninth Circuit's decision in *Goldman v. United States of America*:

> Plaintiff Leonard Goldman, an avowed Communist, and an organizer for the ILWU, argues that his rights to speech and assembly under the U.S. Constitution were abridged by seizure of his publications and, further, that his arrest, even though on government property and at a courthouse of the United States, similarly was violative of his First Amendment rights. He finally asks that the anti-sedition statutes under which he was arrested be declared unconstitutional. The Court, sitting en banc, concurs. The case is remanded for trial on plaintiff's claim of damages against the United States of America.

Leonard Goldman told his attorneys to dismiss the claim for damages. His interest was solely the vindication of his rights—all citizens' rights—to political speech. He refused to take a dime or put a price on the right to free speech. And just to make sure no one forgot (and perhaps to rub the government's nose in it), Leonard Goldman was at the same federal courthouse where he had been arrested, the day after the appeals court opinion was made public, handing out his pamphlets and protesting the control of both political parties, Republican and Democratic, by big business. In case anyone had trouble hearing the booming voice he regularly used to address workers at open-air meetings on the docks, Leonard brought a bullhorn. The federal District Court judge, on the sixth floor, who had sentenced him, only to be reversed, could hear his protest clearly.

Though he was only 13 when his father was arrested, Leon saw first-hand the workings of the legal system, and particularly the advocacy for the constitutional rights of outsiders, like his father, by the American Civil Liberties Union. His parents had become active in the ACLU since many of the issues they believed in were espoused by the ACLU. Leon was impressed by the scholarship of the lawyers, which appealed to him, especially as it represented a historical approach to the law. The briefs in his father's case, which he used for a term paper in high school civics on Peter Zanger, traced the sedition laws of England, the Founding Fathers' awareness and concerns about sedition restrictions on the press, and the origins of the First Amendment prohibitions themselves. His father may have been self-taught, but he read "Congress shall make no law" abridging speech to mean *no law*. And, as Leon would read in law school, so did Justice Hugo Black of the U.S. Supreme Court. Dad read the Constitution as well as the learned justice—even if both were in the minority on its interpretation of free speech.

In 1960, Leon and his father had a sharp disagreement that lasted 1,000 days. Leon thought perhaps John F. Kennedy could make a difference in America. His father assured him that Kennedy represented simply the "next generation of wealth," not a "new generation of Americans."

"He is Joe Kennedy's kid. Do you think Joe Kennedy is going to let his son do anything that is going to hurt the rich?"

Leon tried to argue: "I don't think even a father can tell his son what to do if the son is president of the United States."

"And how do you think he gets there?" his father asked, his voice rising. "Joe Kennedy buys it for him!

"We are not talking a father's pride. We are talking Joe Kennedy, a Nazi sympathizer, a friend of Joe McCarthy, buying the presidency. Don't tell me he'll let his kid run the country."

"Senator Kennedy has been reaching out, talking about the Negro and the poor," protested Leon. "Voting rights protection."

"Sure, pacify them; offer them crumbs. Does anyone think, for a moment, why should any citizen have to ask for what is rightfully his all along? Who are those uneducated Negroes going to vote for? The ones who gave them the vote! It's the same game that has kept them down since slavery. At least with slavery, they knew they were slaves."

On the evening of November 22, 1963, Leonard Goldman called his son at his dorm room at U.C. Berkeley. Leon was a sophomore, a history major.

"I know you felt strongly about him," his father said, referring to the assassinated president. "Maybe you were right. He was trying. But Leon, don't you see? They just couldn't let him succeed."

Leon was not sure his father was right, but he knew he was not wrong. He just did not know which "they" in the class struggle called America had gotten to John F. Kennedy first.

When he got to Boalt Hall, Leon never told his father that one of his professors was an assistant to the Warren Commission on the Assassination of President John F. Kennedy. It would have just confirmed for his father the link between the assassination, corporate America, and the training of more lawyers to do its bidding.

But his father was pleased with Leon's undergraduate education at Berkeley between 1962 and 1966. He saw the Free Speech Movement as the beginning of the revolution, the rising up of the students against the privilege of their parents and the system of education that indoctrinated them.

For his part, Leon saw the Free Speech Movement as nothing more than the opening up of the rest of society to the rigorous examination of ideas that had been a part of his everyday life since childhood. He welcomed it on the one hand, but also understood that it spelled the end of innocence, the beginning of responsibility for a world his generation was inheriting. If slavery begat the present disorder, if colonialism was unfolding into wars of national liberation and, if developments in medicine made sex free, then the world was about to be turned upside down, and only centrifugal force would hold the travelers to the planet.

Leon was there, in Sproul Plaza, when the crowd pushed forward, surrounded the campus police car, and Mario Savio stood on the car to address the crowd. Leon sat down in the Plaza with thousands of other students, preventing the police from moving the car when Savio was arrested and placed in the backseat. But he left, rather than face arrest, because—he reasoned—he was a person who reasoned. He used logic and persuasion, not physical force or obstruction. Not that he did not understand and admire the teachings of Gandhi and the tactics of nonviolence. He not only understood them and wholeheartedly approved of them, but believed that they represented the only real hope in a society where any violent insurrection could be crushed. Politically, he believed in the proletariat but also believed in the vanguard of the proletariat, the intelligencia, who would lead and direct, and he saw himself, without arrogance, in this latter group. Years later, when he looked back on the pictures of Sproul Plaza, he could not help noticing that many of the "radicals" sitting there that day were wearing ties.

In the other areas of the revolution—"free love" and hallucinogens— he was neither a leader nor a follower. He thought sex was a private matter, not a sport, and as far as drugs were concerned, he had too many allergies to smoke or inject anything. The constant inhaling Leon did at Berkeley was from his nasal spray to control his asthma.

Leon's attraction to the law arose in part from his readings in history, his exposure to the ACLU and civil liberties, and, of course, his parents' Communism, and their constant refrain for a need to champion the rights of the economically oppressed. He understood, perhaps better than others entering Boalt in 1966, that the law was the manner of ordering society and that economic control by one segment, and oppression of another, was rendered through laws. It was by understanding the workings of the law that one could begin to reorder society, to free the oppressed, and bring everyone a fair share of the wealth.

As he read history, and particularly Soviet history, he wondered why his father had named him Leon, for Leon Trotsky. After all, Trotsky had fallen from grace long before Leon Goldman's birth and had been murdered in 1940 in Mexico, presumably on Stalin's orders. Knowing his father had come to Communism in the early '40s, when the Comintern, the international Communist movement, was in its heyday, he found it hard to understand why he would then be named for a disgraced Communist.

"It was Trotsky who saved the Revolution, not Lenin, not Stalin. He was everywhere, defending against the White armies that sought to crush the Revolution, with, I might add, the help of America and England. He saved Petrograd, stopped the assault on Moscow, and preserved the Revolution."

His father calmed down a bit and added, "And I did it for your grandparents."

"My grandparents? They weren't named Leon or Trotsky."

"Nor was Trotsky," his father said. "If you want to help the oppressed, you should remember your heritage of oppression."

Leon still did not understand. Finally, his father provided an explanation. "Leon," he said with both hands on his son's shoulders, "the Revolution was saved by a Jew. Trotsky's name was Bronstein. We all need to remember who we are and where we came from, if we are going to change history."

Chapter 16

Jackson

JACKSON BRIDGEPORT III was not a Rhodes scholar, as his father had been, but thought a year at Oxford would round out his resume before he started down the path of legal study and the family business of law. Since he did not need a resume for anything other than ego, it was, in reality, a year off between Harvard and law school.

He planned on taking a few classes and seeing Europe, with special emphasis on skiing in the Alps and searching for the perfect vodka martini most everywhere else.

In the first month at Oxford, he, along with his class of graduate students, was invited to tea at the home of Sir Nigel Graves, a former cabinet secretary and noted professor of international law. Sir Nigel taught the graduate class in European Comparative Governments. After many weeks, Jackson was still struggling to understand Sir Nigel, whose English sounded strained by a mouth full of marbles.

The tea, to Jackson's disappointment, actually involved the serving of tea, along with the eating of small crumpets and biscuits that were nicely arranged on a table with embroidered white doilies. The home was small by American standards, but it had survived longer than the American republic and had housed professors of Oxford for over 300 years. The large fireplace in the living room still bore the soot and stain of having been used for cooking. Yet it was a house that echoed the discussions, down through the ages, of the British Empire, the East India Tea Company, the splendors of the Raj, Kitchener, East of Suez, and the events that had been controlled from this small island country. The walls contained books bearing names such as Disraeli, Gladstone, Marlborough, and Churchill. Bridgeport was convinced that both the house and the Empire had seen better days. He would have preferred a cocktail.

There were 12 students in the class, and Sir Nigel greeted each as they approached him, at his place by the tall fireplace. It became apparent that he was maintaining this location to blow puffs of smoke from his pipe up the chimney. As he turned from his position at the fireplace, he motioned with the pipe, shrugged his shoulders, and said, by way of explanation: "The Mrs."

Even in his own home, there were apparently laws that applied to the renowned Sir Nigel, expositor of international rules of conduct for nations.

Sir Nigel began his annual welcoming speech to the class as a server went about the group refilling teacups. She was young, petite, no more than 90 pounds (or whatever stones that equaled). Her brown hair was cut very close, like that of a little boy, but her eyes were large and green. Her blue eye shadow and a light pale swath of color across her upper cheek, but without lipstick, caused the focus of attention to be drawn even more to her eyes.

"Tea?" she offered.

"Thank you, and do you have any more cookies?" Bridgeport asked, wanting to prolong the eye contact without being obvious.

"You mean biscuits?"

"Well, I am not sure. They were over there on that table."

"Well, they are not there now, are they?" she said in the manner of the English, ending an answer with a question.

"No, that's why I asked."

"I will see if we have another tin," she replied and walked toward the kitchen.

She came back as Sir Nigel was finishing up with a flourish with one hand, as he tugged on his lapel with the other, and a quote from "the poet of the Lake country." At least that is what Bridgeport thought the words were, still doing his best to understand Sir Nigel's pronunciation of the English language.

"Have you served at one of these before?" Jackson asked, attempting to make conversation.

"Yes," she said, holding out a plate of biscuits, each sitting individually in a white paper holder.

"Do you understand a word he is saying?" he whispered, nodding his head in the direction of Sir Nigel.

She looked around conspiratorially, turned back, and whispered: "Yes. Every word my father spoke."

Jackson had met Sarah Graves, daughter of Sir Nigel.

Jackson Bridgeport's tall and lanky frame towered over Sarah, especially in his wing tips. While his penchant for suspenders and bow tie certainly set him apart from the English students, his strong New England accent, which would sound distinctive at Boalt Hall, marked him as just another Yank at Oxford. His arrogance and pontification might understandably be mistaken for confidence and erudite discourse by an impressionable 17-year-old English girl.

For all her father's academic credentials, Sarah had little interest in school. She had, however, an abiding love for art. It was about a month later that he saw her again. She was sitting on the commons, next to a path, painting. It was one of those rare days, since he had arrived, when the rain let up to a slight drizzle, with the sun breaking through the clouds. He would not have seen her, had he not been approaching from the front and been able to look into the tent-like structure she had erected over herself and her easel with a waterproof tarp.

"What are you doing?" he asked.

"Oh, hello, Mr. Bridgeport. I'm painting the conker trees."

"The what trees?"

"The conker trees. Don't you have conkers in America?"

"I don't think so. What are conkers?"

"Well, they are the fruit of that tree. If you look high up into the tree, you can see the prickly ball-like objects. In the spring, they will split and open up, showing a deep shiny tan, well, nut, I suppose, that the children call conkers. If nature has its way, a conker will fall to the ground and sit. Slowly, it will break open, and a white yellowish tube will come out and find the ground and grow. Someday, I suppose, if left alone, it would be a tree. Of course, if you want a good conker, it's best to knock them off the trees before they fall themselves. That way you have a better chance of getting a King Conker and defeating all the other children on the street at Conkers."

"I have no idea what you're talking about," smiled Jackson, "but I admire your creativity in finding a way to watercolor in the rain. May I see your painting?"

She hesitated for a moment and offered the explanation that it was not finished. Finally, she turned the large easel at an angle so that he could lean under the canvas and see it from one side.

"I call it *The Avenues*," she said. "That's what we call this part of the commons."

The watercolor was in muted pastels, showing a wide, wet avenue on each side of which was a row of trees extending up to a slight hill and disappearing down the other side. Park benches, in the rain, empty of people. A solitary person walked, her back to the viewer, carrying an umbrella and holding the hand of a child wearing Wellingtons. The child appeared to be carrying what looked like a butterfly or fish net. The colors, the shading, the differences of light, the reflections on the wet surfaces, and the bark on the tree showed a serious and accomplished artist. What stood out, however, more than the beauty of the art, was the fact that the painting was no more than four inches by seven inches on an easel that would easily accommodate a board six times that size.

In the weeks that followed, they met and talked, often over fish and chips. She, and for that matter, Sir Nigel himself, had really traveled very little outside of England. After all, England was England. People came to Oxford to study. There were more treasures of Egypt in the British Museum than there were in Egypt. The advantage of empire was that one could loot the riches of other countries and bring them back to one's own country, even if it consisted of a small island just off the coast of Europe. There was also the fact that as distinguished as Sir Nigel was, he had been the equivalent of a civil servant and college professor throughout his life, which did not lend itself to wasteful spending. Not that he did not adore his daughter, but he was of the belief that a girl was more in need of a husband than world travel and education.

Sarah, for her part, was quite shy, enjoyed her art, but would not consider asking her father for money to travel to faraway places to view art that could be easily seen in books at the Oxford library. She had, on occasion, traveled to London and viewed the exhibits at the British Museum, the George IV Museum, and the Victoria and Albert Museum. What she saw, primarily, was the art of the past. If there was art she wanted to see, it was modern art.

Jackson was not unfamiliar with art. He had certainly taken the requisite college courses. In addition, he had actually taken an interest, primarily from the point of view of his family's investments, in modern art. While at

Harvard, he had spent a lot of his spare time in New York and was familiar with the pop artists and the incredible amount of interest—not to mention money—that certain people like Andy Warhol were generating. The Museum of Modern Art was featuring many of the new "modern" artists, and the "in set" of New York used the occasions of artists' openings as great opportunities for parties.

At Christmas, Jackson asked Sarah if she would like to go to New York to spend the holidays with his family. He suggested it would be a great opportunity to visit the Museum of Modern Art, perhaps even "the Factory" of Andy Warhol and other "beat" locations in Greenwich Village frequented by the new generation of artists. Noticing her hesitation, he emphasized that it would all be "very proper" and that his parents would formally extend an invitation to her, through her father.

With Sarah's consent, Jackson's mother called Sir Nigel directly and invited his daughter to join "the family" at the apartment they maintained in New York for the holidays. It was understood, although certainly not expressed, that Sarah would have her own room under the supervision of the family, with everything on the "up and up." Sir Nigel thanked Mrs. Bridgeport for the invitation and accepted on behalf of his daughter, knowing full well that he did not have the ability to give his daughter the experience being offered by the Bridgeport family.

Jackson and Sarah traveled together, on Trans World Airlines, to the old Idlewild Airport in New York that had been renamed JFK Airport after the slain president. He had told his mother about Sarah, the petite English girl with the delightful speech and proper manners. It was actually his mother who had suggested the visit.

They arrived on Christmas Eve morning at the Fifth Avenue apartment, in time to accompany the family to caroling at Rockefeller Center, and returned to a Christmas Eve open house hosted by Jackson's parents. Sarah was overwhelmed by the hundreds of guests, including the mayor of New York, and stood most of the evening, quiet, next to Jackson.

On Christmas morning, Jackson took Sarah for a ride through Central Park by carriage. A light snow had fallen, but the day was brisk and the horses unimpaired on the dry pathways. Sarah felt like she was in a coronation, and she was the queen. That evening, to her surprise, there were presents under the tree for her. Jackson's mother had selected a beautiful cocktail dress at Bloomingdale's, a size 2 petite that fit her loosely. Jackson handed her a present. She opened the attached card: "To Sarah—A Very

Special Girl." She unwrapped the present and opened the small box, with both trepidation and confusion. In it was a very thin gold link chain with a single hanging diamond. If she had known about these things, she would have estimated its weight at 2 carats. She looked at Jackson, dumbfounded. "I thought it would look nice with the dress my mother bought you for New Year's Eve," he said, matter-of-factly.

The week that followed was a blur of activity. Jackson took her to the Museum of Modern Art in New York. They also visited the Guggenheim, and upon her insistence, as promised, they went to Greenwich Village.

On New Year's Eve, on the balcony of his parents' apartment, with Sarah wearing the dress that his mother had purchased and the diamond he had given her, and with the sound of music filling the apartment as the guests danced in the new year, Jackson Bridgeport kissed Sarah for the first time. All she could think was that she had come a long way to Fifth Avenue in New York, in these fineries, for a young English girl. Just like Cinderella.

By the time Sarah returned to England, she had been dubbed "Mouse" by Jackson's family, a term that would stick and, in time, be used disparagingly by them. But that Christmas, they found her, well, "delightful…so English." Jackson's father was pleased that this pretty and proper young lady was the daughter of Sir Nigel Graves, of whom he had never heard, but he was impressed by the title and Sir Nigel's position both in the English government and at Oxford.

When Jackson told his parents, at the end of his first term at Oxford, that he was thinking of marrying Sarah, they welcomed the news. In fact, they insisted that she have, on loan of course, the heirloom wedding ring worn by Jackson's great-grandmother. It was huge on her small, narrow hand and had the general effect on anyone who saw it of causing the jaw muscles to relax and the mouth to drop open. Jackson's parents were also relieved, since Jackson had shown little disposition to intimate relationships or displays of affection. Sarah, they were convinced, would make a good wife and mother to her professional husband and be an asset to his career.

As a wedding present, channeled through the law firm, the Bridgeports provided a leased home near Grizzly Park in the Berkeley Hills for the married couple to use during Jackson's three years at Boalt. The preferred view from a home in the Bay Area was, of course, of water and bridges. They were not disappointed. To the right was San Pablo Bay. To the left, the Bay Bridge. Below them were other houses tucked away among the trees down to the Berkeley campus, with its Campanile rising as if a beacon to ships, and beyond the mud flats decorated with junk sculptures. In the distance directly ahead was the Golden Gate Bridge—the gem of San Francisco Bay—connecting two peninsulas and framing the sunset.

As a housewarming present, Jackson gave Sarah a painter's easel, complete with paints, brushes, and everything she would need, even a smock covered with paint splashes. She set it up immediately in a little alcove of the sun room. On the morning that he started Boalt, she began painting the Golden Gate, or at least the north tower protruding through a blanket of fog hanging over the Bay.

Her paintings were small, just like her; the colors muted so as not to offend, just like her; the process of painting tentative, just like her. But her excitement was evident and the views spectacular, from the foggy mornings to the sunsets caught between clouds and the water on the horizon leading to the Pacific.

Bridgeport threw himself into the study of law, working harder than he had ever done in his academic career. He found his name of no consequence in the classroom. Outside class, the talk was of assigned cases, not vodka martinis. On exams, a number on the standard blue test book, not a prestigious name, was all that identified him among his classmates. Already, in the first semester, it was clear that Jackson Bridgeport III was likely to place well behind many of the "radicals" in the class, which caused him to further resent them personally, as well as their politics and expressed values. While he could not compete with them successfully in law school, he could privately disparage their lifestyles and the causes to which they intended to dedicate their legal education.

"These people are dreamers," he would pontificate to Sarah. "They see criminals as victims of society. They see corporate America as the enemy. They have no idea of the real world. Wait until they have to work and pay taxes to support all of their welfare and poverty programs."

It never occurred to Sarah to remind him that he had never worked or paid taxes, or experienced hardship. She seemed content to paint.

At the beginning of the second year, a garden party was held at the home of the dean to welcome back the class of 1969. By then, the invitations for the law review had been made known, and the lines had been drawn through the class as to where each student stood in relation to another. Bridgeport was in the top 20 percent of the class, but not in the exclusive ten percent invited to join the prestigious *California Law Review*, whose alumni would display a framed law review certificate in a prominent position on their law office walls—which visiting lawyers would acknowledge even 30 years later.

As was her habit, Sarah, when not at Jackson's side, stood off, alone. That was what she was doing when she first met Rose Contreras.

"Are you a law student?" asked Rose.

"Oh God, no."

"So what are you, then?"

"I am Jackson Bridgeport's wife."

"You're English, right?"

"Yes."

"Well, over here 'who are you' and 'what are you' are not the same question," said Rose. She touched Sarah's hand and smiled. "I bet you are a lot more than just Jackson Bridgeport's wife."

Sarah laughed. "You're right. I am an artist, a painter."

"Great. I wish I could paint. It must be wonderful to have a talent like that. I would love to see your work sometime, if you would let me."

Rose paused. "I'm sorry. I don't even know your name, only who you are married to."

"I'm Sarah. Well, they call me Mouse, mostly."

"And I am Rose."

Sarah and Rose were still talking of Sarah's painting and the differences between art in England and America when they were interrupted by the dean tapping a spoon on his wine glass. "I would like to congratulate all of you for actually returning after what I suspect was the most terrifying and disruptive year of your lives: your first year of law school."

The collective laugh of the students, and some serious gulps of wine by the spouses, revealed that the dean was on target. Rose excused herself when she saw Jackson Bridgeport returning with a glass of wine for his wife.

As Sarah and Jackson drove home after the event, Sarah recalled that she had not given Rose her phone number so they could get together to view art.

"Jackson, do you know a woman named Rose who was there tonight?" she asked.

"Of course."

"Is her husband in your class?"

"No. She is. That was Rose Contreras. She is number one in the class."

Sarah was shocked. Rose seemed so nice. Nothing like she would have expected of a law student, especially the top person in the class at Boalt. She had not even talked about law.

When Sarah began her painting the next morning, after Jackson had left for class, she thought about Rose again. It was then she realized that her husband regularly told her what he did each day, his arguments in class, his schedule of study, but had never, in the first year at Boalt, asked to see her art, as Rose had in their first meeting.

She would remember Rose and their meeting, 13 years later.

Chapter 17

The Classroom

"MR. BRIDGEPORT, CAN you explain what is wrong with the attempted testamentary disposition discussed in problem number three?"

Wills and Trusts. A required course. In fact, everything in the first year, and the second for that matter, was obligatory. That is the way it had been for the professor, and his professors, and that is the way it had been at Boalt, and at every other major law school, "from time immemorial." Every state in the union that tested law students, and they all did, tested new admittees to the Bar on Contracts, Torts, Civil Procedure, Criminal Law, Corporations, Wills and Trusts—"the great body of the law"—no matter that most graduates would never practice in these areas, let alone the rest of the curriculum of Tax or Antitrust, or ever encounter an International Conflict of Law question in their lifetimes.

Their "relevance," however, for law schools was that a professor had dedicated his life to the subject, written extensively upon it, sparred with other professors at other leading law schools on the nuances of it, and had been proclaimed the authority on it, whatever "it" was.

But with "it" came an endowed chair, probably named for someone else who was also an expert on "it," along with grants for all of the books that the library could hold on "it," especially if they were written in Old English or Latin. When suitably situated in one's chair, one would become the head of a section of the American Bar Association on "it" and, ultimately, the Commentator on "it" for the Restatement of the Law, or a Reporter of the American Law Institute, or obtain some other similar title. At this level, professors spoke to each other in published articles in law reviews; traveled and spoke internationally to conferences on subjects that only other professors or federal judges cared about; or spent a year at some foreign university, generally unable to speak the language and occasionally wheeled out to the eager students who had no idea what the hell "it" was, but sat in reverent awe of the "distinguished visitor." These professors were, however, the keepers of the flame—the group in the inner sanctum of the legal society entrusted to pass on the tablets upon which was chiseled the law. This is how it had always been. But the altar of the law, was, ultimately, the classroom.

"In conveying Blackacre to *A*, for life, then to *B* for 25 years, then back to the heirs of *A*, the conveyance violates the Rule in Shelley's Case," answered Jackson Bridgeport III.

Even the language of the law was unintelligible to outsiders. It had to be learned. This way only "lawyers" could know the law and make a profession out of interpreting it for lay people, much like priests learning Latin. In class, all land was "Blackacre." People were *A* or *B*, or the heirs of *A* or *B*, or some other letter. Someone then living was not living, he was a "life in being." All strived, it seemed, not just to own "an" interest in land, but the ultimate that English law could bestow, a "fee simple"—unrestricted ownership, lock, stock, and barrel.

"Mr. Johnson, do you agree?"

"I am not sure. It seems that the intervening 25-year conveyance to *B* will prevent the merger of the remainder to *A*'s heirs and preclude the applicability of the Rule in Shelley's Case. What I am having difficulty with is whether the estate to *B* of 25 years, after *A*'s life estate, violates the Rule Against Perpetuities since it is more than 21 years before *A*'s heirs will obtain the land from the death of *A*."

"Well now," gleamed the professor, "let's start with Mr. Johnson's claim that the Rule Against Perpetuities is violated. Mr. Patrick."

Patrick with total assurance: "The Rule Against Perpetuities prevents the vesting of interest, unless the interest must vest, if at all, within 21 years after lives in being at the creation of the interest."

"Well done, Mr. Patrick, you have correctly memorized the Rule Against Perpetuities."

Laughter from the class. "And why do you think it might apply here?" asked the professor.

"Because the conveyance is to *A* who is alive, but only goes to *B* after *A* dies, and *A* can't very well conceive heirs 21 years after he is dead," Patrick opined with satisfaction.

The professor looked at him quizzically. "Really?" He turned to the class: "In 1581, English law was willing to conclusively believe, for purposes of testing the legality of conveyances, in the fertile octogenarian—the idea that an 80-year-old could conceive or deliver a baby. After all, the Bible speaks of Sarah bearing Isaac at 91 years of age. But you are right, Mr. Patrick, the law never contemplated children being born years after the death of the progenitor or as some of you ladies might call him, the 'sperm donor.'" This drew some hoots.

"You laugh," said the professor, "but no less an authority than Professor Leach of Harvard Law School, writing in the *ABA Journal*, has raised the issue of frozen astronaut sperm held by the government, which, if used after a fateful space accident, could violate this 12th-century feudal rule. This is not just history, ladies and gentlemen. It is the generation of frozen sperm and space travel to which you are witness."

Having moved from the Bible to frozen astronaut sperm to make his point, the professor returned to the law. "But what about the Rule in Shelley's Case? Will this drafting pass muster or is the testator's intent going to be frustrated?"

Cassidy raised his hand.

"Mr. Cassidy."

"Even when a will gives immediately to *A* and later to *A*'s heirs, separated by another estate like the 25-year term to *B* here, the rule still applies. It doesn't make any difference whether the remainder is mediately or immediately to take effect on *A*'s death as long as it is a remainder in *A*'s heirs that is attempted. The result is a merger of the interests in *A* of a fee title."

The professor looked toward the upper level of seats. "So what happened to *B*'s right to 25 years of uninterrupted tenancy?" he asked, pointing to Mr. Rai.

J. J. looked up and quickly concluded: "He's shit out of luck."

Above the roar of the class came the shout of the professor: "No! No, never, Mr. Rai. The beauty of the law! He has a great case. Against the lawyer who drafted the will!

"You may wonder," the professor continued, laying his glasses on the desk, "what is the 'relevance' of the medieval history of property rights. Why did the law decide these rules were necessary? Who benefitted? What was being accomplished?

"In a feudal system, all land was owned by the King. The way to reward and curry favor was to give the use of land to others. These grants were not of ownership, but tenancy, meaning a period of time that may be measured by years or the life of someone, usually the person to whom the

King was giving it. In exchange for tenancy, as with a landlord, something of value, some continuing obligation, flowed. In turn, tenants might create subtenancies. This system was evidenced as early as 1086 in the Domesday Book cataloguing the holdings of William the Conqueror. It reflected, in essence, the political and military character of feudal tenure. While the King owned the land and his tenants were dependent upon him for his favor, you can see that the King in turn was dependent on his tenants. If tenants failed to pay rent, didn't raise armies, or found ways to avoid the incidents of the King's ownership by transferring the land to their heirs, or to others, the King's authority would be eroded." He paused.

"The Rule in Shelley's Case, for example, which actually was enunciated as early as 1324 in Abel's Case, was likely a way to avoid the feudal consequences of a person's death and the transfer of property to his heirs. Originally, since the King owned the land, when a tenant to whom the land had been given died, the King was under no obligation to give the land to the tenant's heirs. Usually, he would—but only after extracting what was called relief, something of value, a payment. In effect, the King would have 'sold' the land twice: Once to the father; the second time to the son."

He added, looking around, "And, for the young ladies in the class, I guarantee it was a very chauvinistic, male-dominated legal system."

"Was?" came a response from a soft voice in the back of the classroom.

"Ah, yes," the professor responded without breaking stride, "and as to certain other rights, I must regretfully report that while the King or Lord did have the right to select a female subject's husband in England, unlike some parts of feudal Europe, he did not have the *droit de seigneur*, the custom of *prima nox*, which loosely translates into 'first knock' on the assumed virgin bride.

"But let us return to relevance," the professor protested in the face of loud moans of male displeasure with this wrinkle in the English feudal system. "Some clever 12th-century lawyer figured out that the modern day equivalent of inheritance taxes could be evaded by the wording of the original conveyance. Hence, the law's response: The Rule in Shelley's Case.

"While the rule may have been established for one purpose, over time it came to serve different social purposes. Specifically, freeing land one generation earlier from restrictions on alienation. Do you see, if *A* limits his gift to *B* by saying 'for life' and adds 'to *B*'s heirs thereafter,' the land is tied up during *B*'s life. But if *B* owns the land outright, which is what the

Rule in Shelley's Case effectuates, then he can divide it up, sell it, freely alienate it, and move to Florida, thereby allowing society to use the property free of a long dead donor's control from the grave. And, Mr. Rai, the kids are, in your words, 'shit out of luck.'

"Look at the Rule Against Perpetuities. Same thing. It limits the period of time when a person can tie up title to land into the future.

"Mr. Roland, you have a question?"

"Yes, if one owns land, why isn't he free to do with it as he pleases?"

"Good question. How would you answer that, Mr. Goldman?"

Goldman had been following the exchange with interest. "I suppose it's a question of whose freedom. Every restriction by a present owner on how his property is to be used in the future by another owner is a restriction on the second owner's freedom to do what he wants with the property."

"Very good," nodded the professor, "except the Rule Against Perpetuities only deals with the transfer of property, or title to property, not the use to which property is put. But, Mr. Roland, would you in your quest for a landowner's freedom to 'do with it as he pleases' permit A to grant to B 'but only so long as he shall use the land as a wildlife habitat?'"

"That sounds like a reasonable restriction," responded Roland.

"So," smiled the professor, "you now permit restrictions on freedom if you agree with them?"

"Well, he doesn't have to buy or accept the land if he isn't willing to accept the restriction on the deed."

"Oh, some kind of arm's length transaction concept, is that what you mean?"

"I suppose so," shrugged Roland.

"To test Mr. Roland, let's change it a little. A grants Blackacre to B and his heirs but only so long as the land shall be used solely as a wildlife habitat where white people may contemplate nature. Violations of the condition shall result in a reversion of the land to the grantor or his heirs. How do you feel about freedom now, Mr. Roland?"

Having been led down the proverbial garden path, Mr. Roland had no response.

"Let's add something to the example. This grant was made in 1776 by one of the signers of the Declaration of Independence. See a problem, anyone?

"Mr. Jeffries."

"The problem is the condition under which a reversion occurs has sat in the deed for 190 years. A violation today would result in a forfeiture of the land by the present holder to the heirs of *A*." Mr. Jeffries smiled at Mr. Roland.

The professor looked around the room with satisfaction. "Now," he gleamed, "do you understand how feudal concerns are your concerns as lawyers?"

Chapter 18

Michael

MICHAEL CASSIDY'S FATHER reluctantly came around to his marriage once Michael was in the full swing of his first year at Boalt Hall and had agreed to clerk at his father's firm for the summer. His mother, on the other hand, was wooed over by the sight of her grandson, Robbie. Mai, they did not know how to take; she was just a phenomenon to them. She was everything but sedate and proper. She was, in a word, a prankster. She loved life and every minute of it. She laughed almost constantly and seemed to take everything lightly. She was, they had to agree, a terrific mother, although her habit of breast-feeding in public made them uncomfortable. Well aware of the disruption she caused in their lives, Mai was not about to reign in or alter her lifestyle for anyone's uptight parents. She was, however, considerate of her in-laws' interest in their grandson, encouraged it, and left the child with them two nights a week while she resumed classes at San Francisco State College. Michael was, of course, in the law library at Boalt Hall most nights, studying.

Saturdays were reserved for Michael, Mai, and Robbie alone, unless Michael had to study for an exam. Mai saw to that. She planned day outings for them, a day at Stinson Beach, the Planetarium, a picnic in Golden Gate Park. Occasionally, they would even venture down campus to Telegraph Avenue, more as spectators than participants. Mai was curious and open to new ideas; Michael was uncomfortable and irritated by what he saw. Unlike Mai, he found it hard to walk barefoot in a public park; it just did not feel "proper." Nor would he, could he, wear a "costume" to a party. Mai, on the other hand, could be said to be in costume most of the time. On Monday mornings, Michael put on his coat and tie, secure in the uniform of a law student.

Mai finished her units in summer school for her bachelor's degree and decided to pursue a master's in the fall of Michael's second year at Boalt. The summer had been busy with the baby, her summer school, and Michael's summer clerkship at his father's firm. It was with some relief that she greeted his decision not to pursue a future career at his father's firm.

"I just feel I want to do something more with my life," he told her.

"We all want more, Michael. Your dad wants more money. My dad wants more respect. Me, I want more sex. So what do you want more of?"

It was clear he had been thinking about the subject for some time. "Don't you ever have the feeling that things are getting out of control, that society is deteriorating? That we have a responsibility to set it straight, before it is too late? It is as if we are on a collision course in this country, with the crossroads just ahead and no one putting on the brakes. Don't you see it?"

"I think we all do, Michael. It's as if there is a revolution coming. That is the same thing a lot of the people in the streets are saying. But I almost feel that there are people in power, pushing, who want that to happen. That this isn't an accidental collision of trains at a crossing."

He looked at her, not knowing how she had totally missed the point. "That makes no sense. It is those outside who want in, pushing. Militants, Negro groups like the Black Panthers and Black Muslims, and even those civil rights groups. And the student groups, who seem to embrace every charismatic anti-U.S. revolutionary in the world. All of them seem to be pushing a class warfare agenda. The government, as I see it, is just trying to maintain order."

"You mean keep them in their place?" She did not like his lecturing tone.

Now he displayed frustration and anger: "Not even you can believe Negroes burning down their own neighborhoods, like Watts and Hunters Point, qualify as urban renewal projects."

"Their own neighborhoods?" Her voice rose. "I doubt seriously they owned any of those neighborhoods. Rich, white people, like your father, and corporations way outside of the line of fire own those neighborhoods."

"I doubt that would stop your father from leasing the property to Chinese people." Michael regretted the words as they left his mouth.

What had started as insight into his feelings was now a full-blown race riot: "My people weren't your slaves, Michael. They were only coolie laborers. You need to understand a little about how white people in America got all their power if you're going to ever understand why others may think it is not legitimately wielded over them."

With that, she got up, grabbed her books, and headed for the door. "Congratulations, Michael, on deciding society needs your help. I'm going to school. I suppose you, on the other hand, are off to join the National Guard."

The door slammed and woke the baby. Michael was left to discuss his future plans with Robert Fong Cassidy. Robert F. was in no more of a mood to hear of his future than was Mai. He just wanted his diaper changed.

During that first summer, Michael and Mai had kept their Berkeley apartment while he worked at his father's law firm in San Francisco. Good apartments, up campus from the "Berzerkleys," were hard to find. His father showed him off: "This is my son. At the firm for the summer. Going to Boalt. Just finished his first year." They each grew tired of the jokes about Berkeley. Pointing to Michael's Ivy League, Brooks Brothers looks, his dad explained: "Boalt is not Berkeley."

Michael got a sense of the life of a business attorney and bond lawyer. Bond law seemed to be primarily about finding a way to pay for things for which local officials would not dare vote directly. Or, in the case of many of his father's clients, ways to market land for development that could not compete in the market without a government subsidy.

At Sam's in the financial district—"order the sand dabs"—or Tadich's—"order the Caesar"—Michael would lunch with his father's business friends and political associates. It was hard to tell where the line between business and politics separated the two. Like a tip on a horse race, the reality of knowing in advance about an upcoming political decision could mean money to those properly situated. Or just a sympathetic ear, well placed. His father had explained a basic rule of business and politics: "You listen to those who think like you, because they are the ones who support you. You help your friends." By the end of the summer, Michael knew he did not want to be seen as his father's son for the rest of his career.

It was, however, through his father's contacts that he met a person who would give direction to his life and inspire him toward a life of public service. One evening after work, during the summer of 1967, he joined his parents for dinner at Ernie's Restaurant in San Francisco. When he arrived, he found his parents seated with another couple.

"Michael, Michael," his father greeted him loudly from across the room. As he approached, his father announced: "This is my son, well, our son,

Michael. He's at Boalt. Just finished first year. Michael," he continued, "we actually have a member of the faculty here tonight. Well, he is a part-time member of the faculty. He's doing more important work these days as Governor Reagan's legal affairs secretary."

Across the table, the man rose, almost bashful, a broad smile on a cherub round face, close-cropped blond hair, and a soft voice: "Hi, Michael. Nice to meet you. I'm Ed Meese."

Chapter 19

Michael

"I STILL THINK public service is what I want to do. I am not sure if that means elective office or—"

She cut him off. "I hate to tell you this. You live in San Francisco and you are a Republican."

"As I was saying—or serving in some capacity in government. My legal training is really all I can bring to the table. But I truly believe the law is the answer."

Mai looked at him and said, "How can the law be the answer? It's the problem."

"Ever hear of Yick Wo or Woo Lee?" Michael asked.

She was taken aback by the question and had no idea where the conversation was going.

"No."

Actually Michael had not either until one week before when he had read of them in Constitutional Law. But he now threw out the names like an authority on the plight of these two Chinese gentlemen.

"They each had a laundry in San Francisco."

"Am I supposed to know every Chinese guy with a laundry in town?" she asked.

"Well, there were 240 Chinese guys running laundries in San Francisco at the time."

"So?"

"So, 150 of them were arrested."

"Well, I guess I must have missed that. Maybe I was changing diapers." Then she asked, "Arrested for what?"

"Running a laundry in a wooden building."

"What's wrong with a wooden building?"

"So, no white guys were arrested for doing the same thing."

"What's new? Where did you read this interesting piece of news? In Herb Caen's column in the *Chronicle*?" she asked.

"It happened in the 1880s."

"No wonder," she interrupted, "I was busy that century."

He continued, delivering a tutorial: "San Francisco authorities passed an ordinance banning laundries in wooden buildings based upon the dangers of fire. But in reality, there was resentment against the Chinese, and the ordinance was enforced to arrest only Chinese laundrymen so as to give a monopoly to the businesses of large institutions financed by Caucasian capital."

Again, she interrupted: "Some things never change."

He continued: "In 1886, the United States Supreme Court held all persons, even noncitizens, like these Chinese laundrymen, were entitled to be treated equally, free of any discrimination because of race, color, or nationality, under the Fourteenth Amendment of the United States Constitution."

He paused to let it sink in and made his point: "I believe in that too, Mai. I want to see it come about as much as anyone protesting in the streets. But I have to do it my way, which is not to grow long hair and smoke dope, okay?"

"Okay," she answered, "but I think a little weed, now and then, might loosen you up, Mikey." She smiled at him. "So what do you want to do?"

"I have decided to take a summer internship in state government, with the legal affairs secretary to the governor."

The word governor caught her attention. "Which governor?" she asked.

"*The* governor."

"The governor of California?"

"Yes, the governor of California," he answered.

"Reagan?" she shouted.

"It's not really for Reagan. It's with Ed Meese, the legal affairs secretary, dealing with legal issues."

Again. "Reagan!"

"Meese is actually on the faculty at Boalt Hall as a lecturer. It's a legal internship which will put me in the middle of everything that goes on in Sacramento," he explained.

"Sacramento!" She seized on the word. He was relieved she was off Reagan.

"You want to move to Sacramento? In the summer? Do you know how hot it is up there? Sacramento *and* Reagan!" She was back to Reagan.

"What's the good news?"

"My parents don't live in Sacramento."

Finally, she said "okay" in vain submission, with her arms hanging down, her body bent over. "But I am going to tell my friends we are leaving for the summer to work on Robert Kennedy's campaign. I can't tell anyone I know that we're going to Sacramento to work for Reagan."

He tried one more time. "It's the law; not Reagan."

"Michael, you know what you said about the law freeing all those Chinese laundrymen?"

"Yes."

"Well, Mikey, it was the law that put them in jail in the first place. Remember that when you are advising those right wing nuts in Sacramento."

"I am not going to be advising anyone, and they're not nuts."

"Oh, yeah," about to trump, "then why did they install extra thick glass on the governor's window when Reagan took office?" She answered her own question quickly: "To protect him and the other right wing nuts from the squirrels in Capitol Park!"

With that, she squeezed her nose and mouth together, held up her hands like squirrel paws, and attacked him, biting and scratching, grunting "nut, nut, nut." He fell back on the couch, laughing, unable to push her off.

Finally, she stopped, sitting astride him.

"Michael, you mean well. But I think the world is a little more complicated than nice rules of law applied to every situation. There is a human side to each case and no rule can take into consideration every situation. If you don't look at the human, Mikey, you're just imposing arbitrary rules. And nobody likes arbitrary rules."

She reflected for a moment. "Maybe that is why we are in different fields. You are in the law because you look to rules; I am in social work because I look to individuals."

Then she turned very serious, still astride of him, and asked with a frown: "Isn't that the essence of totalitarianism? Right or left? Isn't that what Eric Hoffer says? The individual versus the state?"

Michael, with equal seriousness, began to answer: "Well, I think…"

"Shut up," she said playfully. "I am getting turned on by this totalitarianism talk. Sitting on you. Unzip and push them down, now!"

*　　*　　*　　*　　*

Sacramento turned out to be an exciting time for Michael. While he rarely saw the governor, he worked in the east wing of offices entered through the large wooden doors on the first floor, over which prominently was displayed the sign "Governor's Office." The Legal Affairs Office took him past the governor's suite, where cabinet meetings were held, and where the inner office—the one with the extra thick glass—was located. Ed Meese's office was next door in the east side of the suite that made up the governor's offices.

When Michael entered the large wooden doors to the governor's office, off the main corridor of the Capitol building, visitors would look at him, wondering who he was. Inside, the attractive, redheaded, nicely dressed receptionist would buzz him into the private corridor, with an acknowledgment and smile, ensuring that those waiting would believe he had access to power. He was surprised to find that he had unlimited access, in fact, through Meese, to all levels of the executive and legislative branches of government. He visited prisons, sat in on parole hearings, and watched deliberations of the Adult Authority on the fate of famous prisoners. Since he was from the "Governor's Office," private deliberations of prison officials were not abridged in his presence: "He could do the time standing on his head. That religious conversion is crap. They are all Catholics this month because they like the new chaplain. If he was a rabbi, they would all be Jews. Wearing those funny little yarmulkes. Deny the parole. Let the son-of-a-bitch rot." The file was stamped "5 Year Review."

Sometimes he felt invisible. Even riding with Meese and other high officials, nothing was held back because of his presence: "We need to build the ultimate prison for these people. No televisions. No yards. Nothing. An 'uncle' prison."

Later he asked what the cabinet secretary had meant by an "uncle" prison. Meese smiled and told him, "That's a prison where the worst of the worst stay until they say 'uncle.'"

For two weeks, Michael was assigned to the Criminal Justice Committee, writing bill analyses, watching lobbyists testify before the committee. Another week he followed the representative of the District Attorneys Association from legislative offices to committee rooms, and participated in breakfast strategy meetings. The line-up became clear: The ACLU representing the criminal element versus law and order. Them versus us. By a quirk of history, the lobbyist for the District Attorneys Association was always a Deputy District Attorney from Alameda County. Meese had come out of the Oakland D.A.'s office. Others, who had or would move on to higher positions, came through the Oakland office. It was, he saw, a stepping stone to governmental positions.

Once a week, over donuts, Michael would do the morning summary of the latest California Supreme Court and Appellate Court opinions, called advance sheets, at a breakfast meeting with Meese and other lawyers who joined them from the governor's office or the District Attorneys Association.

"You mean the governor and all those guys are dependent on you to tell them what the law is?" Mai asked. "A second-year law student? I heard he wasn't very smart."

"I don't tell the governor anything. He is not there—"

"Well, that explains why he is even dumber than they say," she interrupted.

"I meet with Meese and the lawyers. They are too busy to read every opinion that comes out. I just summarize for them. It's standard law clerk work."

"And I hear Reagan can't read anyway," she added.

When Michael finally did meet Ronald Reagan, he was, as most who met him personally were, overwhelmed. The governor was leaving for a conference and walked out of his office, with a few aides in front of him, when he saw Michael standing next to Meese.

"Governor, I want you to meet Michael Cassidy, our summer intern from Boalt Hall," Meese said.

Reagan greeted him warmly, shaking hands and telling him how much he appreciated his helping out, and added, "You've got a fine teacher in Ed here. We rely on him for all our legal advice." The governor started to leave but turned and asked, with a big smile, "You're not one of those revolutionaries from Berkeley, are you?"

All Michael could say, without thinking, was, "No, governor. I am at the law school."

Michael tried to describe the moment to Mai later...still starstruck. "He is bigger than life. Very athletic. Very tan. His hair is really wavy and he just occupies the room. He is so charismatic without even saying anything. It is as if he was up on that big screen. He is just bigger than life. I can't explain it."

"And he hates students," Mai added.

"That's not true. He just thinks there should be less agitation and disruption, and more education."

It sounded like a line out of one of Reagan's speeches.

"Chink or Mex?"

She had enough of the same political disagreement and was moving on.

"Food?" he asked.

"In a manner of speaking. Let's walk through McKinley Park. Robbie will show you his new favorite duck. We'll let him chase it for a while, get tired, then we'll have Mex, and we can come back here, he'll fall asleep, and you can have me. Chink and Mex."

"An offer I can't refuse."

"You better believe it." She smiled, picked up the baby, and handed him to Michael.

Chapter 20

Rose

J. ANTHONY HAWK knew talent when he saw it, and Rose Contreras was the best law student he had ever judged. Hawk, a legend himself at Boalt, a former clerk to Chief Justice Earl Warren of the U.S. Supreme Court, and the youngest president of the San Francisco Bar Association, regularly judged Moot Court at Boalt. The second-year students teamed up and argued a "case," for which they prepared briefs. The judges, often real appellate court justices and distinguished alumni, grilled the students mercilessly. Most students crumbled; a few survived. Rose did not just survive, she backed the judges up on their heels.

Hawk shot off a letter to Rose the next day.

Ms. Contreras:

Based upon your performance in Moot Court, which I had the pleasure to judge, I resolved to send you this letter. Since then I have also learned that in addition to your oral advocacy skills and obvious intelligence, you are the Editor-in-Chief of the *California Law Review* for the coming year and presently stand first in your class. This offer would have been made had I only witnessed your Moot Court advocacy.

I wish to extend to you, on behalf of our firm, an offer of employment upon graduation. Should you seek a judicial clerkship, as I would expect, the offer will remain open throughout your clerkship. In essence, you have a job here any time you wish.

Should you like to interview other firms, before making a final decision, we would be glad to assist you in that effort. In the meantime, check us out.

I would enjoy meeting with you at your convenience.
Sincerely,

J. Anthony Hawk

The stationery looked real. The envelope bore a canceled stamp. If it was a joke, Rose thought, it was an elaborate one. There was still a year and a half before graduation, recruiters would not even be at the school until the fall, and here she sat looking at an unsolicited, unconditional offer of employment from a partner at one of the most prestigious up-and-coming law firms in San Francisco.

She had not even spoken to Hawk, not really; she had just argued, rather firmly, with him over a point of law in Moot Court.

As the significance of the letter sank in, Rose started to smile, then laugh, then scream out loud, wildly waving the letter. It was then she realized that she had no one with whom to share her excitement. Her classmates, at least the men, were her competitors. The women…well, she really had not had time to spend getting to know the few women in the class. There were really so few that it was not even statistically likely in the complex that made up the law school, with four or five bathrooms to choose from, and sixteen hours in the school day, that she would even encounter them. There was no separate women's lounge or facility for the sparse contingent. As for her assigned Moot Court partner, he would likely resent that she had been singled out for the offer, even if he would not say so. Her law review colleagues recognized her ability; they did not have to like it.

She decided there was only one person to tell.

"*¿Bueno, una assocciación seria y de respecto?*" Her father asked if it was a respected firm.

"*¿Cuanto pagan?*"

She explained these things were negotiated but that she believed starting salaries in San Francisco upon graduation would probably be around $15,000 a year.

"*M'hijita. ¡Quince mil!*" Fifteen thousand dollars! He was ecstatic. He kept repeating, "*¡Quince mil! ¡Quince mil!*"

Rose's mother got on the phone, and Rose repeated what had happened to her. When she finished, her mother asked, "Can you come home this weekend?"

Rose could not. She had to study. As she hung up the phone, she could still hear her father in the background, repeating to someone—perhaps no one—"*¡Quince mil!*"

Returning to school in the evening, Rose was unable to concentrate on her law review research. "The Rights of California Creditors to a Deficiency Judgment Against the Debtor After Exhausting the Security" was not holding her attention. She left the article on the library table and went to the reference librarian.

"Do you have the Martindale Hubbell *California Directory of Law Firms*?" she asked.

She took the large encyclopedia to a table and turned to San Francisco and the listing for Janrette, Hawk, Ross and Stephens.

Michael Janrette. Dartmouth College (B.A., 1953); Harvard Law School (LL.B., 1956); Clerk, Justice Hugo Black, U.S. Supreme Court.

J. Anthony Hawk. Yale University (B.A., 1955); Boalt Hall School of Law, University of California at Berkeley (LL.B., 1958); Clerk, Chief Justice Earl Warren, U.S. Supreme Court.

Malcolm Ross. University of Chicago (B.A., 1955); Boalt Hall School of Law, University of California at Berkeley (LL.B., 1958); Clerk, Judge Charles Browning, U.S. Court of Appeals, Ninth Circuit.

Jeremy Stephens. West Point (B.A., 1953); Boalt Hall School of Law, University of California at Berkeley (LL.B., 1960); Major, U.S. Army.

Areas of Practice: Business and civil litigation, bond law, admiralty and political law.

Representative Clients: California Democratic Party, Port of San Francisco, San Francisco Housing Project, South Bay Municipal Utility District, Fresno Irrigation District, Kern County Woolgrowers Association, Shernotzky Vodka Imports, Greater Bay Ferry Boats.

There were four partners and only four associates listed. Yet a check of the microfiche of the *San Francisco Chronicle* showed the firm mentioned often. A piece in the *Bay Area Legal Journal*, announcing the firm's formation just four years before, described it as the "hottest firm in the city" and as "a boutique firm with an impressive array of clients in large measure because of its liberal Democratic ties." The article went on to compare the firm favorably with the largest San Francisco law firms, describing it as a "nimble giant slayer," rather than a plodding giant.

Rose was excited about what she read. She had not, until now, given much thought to what she planned to do after law school. At first, everything had been about getting accepted. Then, about survival. Then, success. Now…what?

"What do you want to do with your life, Rose?" she asked herself, surprised it had taken this long for the question to arise.

She decided that she would call Mr. Hawk for an appointment. But first, she would tell Professor Van Dyke about the offer.

Rose had finished the research for Professor Van Dyke during the first summer of law school, and the article had been published, as anticipated, as the centerpiece in the Symposium Edition of the *Columbia Law Review* devoted to Justice Cardozo. From time to time, she had seen Professor Van Dyke in the library, where he seemed to live at all hours. He would always greet her with the formality of a professor of law: "Good evening, Ms. Contreras" or "Good morning, Ms. Contreras."

When she had completed her final research assignment, he had taken her notes, set them down without reviewing them, and said simply: "Thank you, Ms. Contreras."

After the article appeared, she received a package in the mail. It was a copy of the *Columbia Law Review*, with Professor Van Dyke's article in it, and a note attached on the inside, dated, and on his stationery: "I hope you learn to appreciate Justice Cardozo as much as I have." It was signed, "Van Dyke."

Rose took her offer of employment to Professor Van Dyke's office. She knocked, as always, on the closed door. As was his habit each time, he never said, "Come in." In fact, his door was always locked. He opened the door: "Yes?"

"Professor, I have received an offer of employment, and I would appreciate your advice."

"From whom?" he asked.

"Anthony Hawk, on behalf of Janrette, Hawk, Ross and Stephens of San Francisco," she replied.

"Mr. Hawk was one of my best students. But Ms. Contreras, there are always jobs. Legal education is not about jobs. You should apply for a clerkship first, at the Supreme Court, as did Mr. Hawk. I will write you a letter of recommendation."

All this while Rose stood in the hallway and Professor Van Dyke stood holding his door handle, just as he had answered the door. She hesitated, not knowing what to say next.

"Good day, Ms. Contreras," he said, catching her by surprise and politely closing the door.

It took a couple of weeks before she could get away to meet with J. Anthony Hawk. She explained that with second-year finals pending it would be hard to come over to San Francisco until summer break. He understood.

"Just call when you have a little time. No hurry," he told her.

Her mother urged her to come home for the summer, but Rose explained that her law review editorship required her to spend most of the time at Boalt organizing and selecting articles for assignment, editing, and publication. While she had article editors, student editors assigned to law review candidates' papers, and managing editors to deal with style, Rose insisted on reading everything herself. But she worried that she needed to make some money to supplement her scholarships and loans, and take the burden off her parents for the amounts they were contributing. She felt very guilty taking from them while at the same time not getting home to help with the summer harvest, or even picking walnuts on weekends in the fall. She knew if she did not accept her parents' help, her father, especially, would be hurt.

On her first visit to the law firm, it was Hawk who brought up the subject of summer employment. "We would normally offer you a full-time summer clerkship here, but I suspect your law review work is going to take up most of your summer. I know it did for me."

Rose was relieved that he did not expect her to work the summer. "I didn't realize how lectures were a break from reading. I am looking forward to third-year classes just to get a little rest."

"Well, just for diversion," he suggested, "we could send over, by messenger, our weekly filings of lawsuits, briefs, and the like, and you could join us for our Monday morning conferences. We would pay you $200 a week to participate. You wouldn't have to do any work. You would get an idea of what we do, what goes on in the real world, and we would get the benefit of your company. How does that sound?"

"Great. But what would you get out of it?" she asked.

"Oh, I have the feeling that you will get in your two cents' worth during our conferences."

He was right. She started with a few questions, but even the questions raised eyebrows. She was smart, as they all were, but her approach was different, even for the best and the brightest that made up the "hottest firm in the city." The real reason for the abbreviated summer job, however, was that J. Anthony Hawk knew Rose Contreras could be a star, and he wanted that star at Janrette, Hawk, Ross and Stephens. He also knew she had a lot to learn about the law and the experience would either harden her or break her. He was betting on Rose, not the legal system.

"Van Dyke is right," he told her one morning, on the phone. They had gotten to know each other well over the summer and had abandoned the formality of the law, at least in private conversations. "Rose, you do need to apply for a clerkship. As number one in the class and editor of the *California Law Review*, you are obviously a candidate for the United States Supreme Court. You know, each of the last three editors has received a clerkship. Like Van Dyke said, you can always get a job. You can only be a clerk at the Supreme Court once in your life, and it will follow you for the rest of your legal career. Only a select few go through those doors, Rose."

"And Van Dyke said he would write a letter," she added.

"Of course he will." He added, almost matter-of-factly, "You will understand better when you teach."

Rose was confused by the comment. Teaching had never been mentioned and had never even crossed her mind. "I have no thought of teaching," she said.

"Rose, when you teach, and you will, you will come to realize that it is in the law school where the legal system can be changed. Those young faces, eager minds, not yet cynical; not yet making too much money to choose anything else."

"Tony, you sound like one of the cynics."

"Well, maybe that's why I teach. But do you understand why Van Dyke selected you to research for him? Do you know?"

Rose really had not given it much thought other than to assume, from her class performance, that she was capable of helping. "I guess he was too busy to do it himself."

"And you think he needed a first-year law student to help him write the definitive work on the legendary Justice Cardozo, the person he clerked for, and about whom Van Dyke is the world's foremost authority?"

"Well, when you put it that way, no. Why? Why did he ask me to help him?"

"Because he saw something in you, Rose. Because he believed in you like Cardozo believed in him when he selected Van Dyke, a young law student, to be his clerk."

Hawk let his words sink in before continuing. "Rose, it is about legacies. Van Dyke knows that Cardozo's decision to pick him changed his life forever. It gave him entree, it gave him status. It anointed him to carry on the work, to affect the evolution of the law. When that mantle is given, it is given only to someone who can be trusted to carry it."

"Where is the legacy?" asked Rose.

"Whose picture is at the door of Professor Van Dyke's office? Someone long dead who is remembered every day by his disciples, and is mentioned in every recitation of the now-famous Van Dyke's background. When you present your credentials to the United States Supreme Court, or anywhere else that you go in the law, there will be included a letter of introduction from the famous Professor Van Dyke for whom, your resume will show, you clerked while in law school."

"You make it sound so sinister, like a secret society," said Rose.

"No, Rose. If it were secret, it would defeat the purpose. Can you imagine Jesus and the secret disciples? Would never have gotten the church off the ground. And, if Jesus had picked the wrong disciples, they would never have spread the word."

There was silence but a smile as Hawk's analogy sunk in. Then he spoke again. "You've read Oliver Wendell Holmes' quote on the building at Boalt, haven't you?"

"Not really. The trees block half of it."

"Well," Hawk added, "Holmes speaks of 'dim figures of the ever-lengthening past.' As the bearer of the Van Dyke letter, you are now connected through Van Dyke to Justice Cardozo. You will leave your mark on the law, Rose, and help others, who will in turn build upon your work and continue the connection. That's how it works. Legacies."

Rose thought for a long time. "It sounds like a lot of responsibility," she finally said.

"It is, Rose. More than you can know." Hawk did not say so, but he was worried for Rose.

Chapter 21

Michael

"YOU'RE NOT GOING to believe this, Mikey. Your governor has declared fuckin' martial law!"

Mai threw her books through the doorway as she entered the apartment. She had just left for school and returned abruptly.

"There are soldiers with bayonets on every corner. I can't get through!"

"What are you talking about?"

"Soldiers. Not cops. Soldiers! With rifles, bayonets, camouflage uniforms, like the fuckin' 92nd Airborne all over Berkeley. They've invaded. He has finally done it, Mikey. He has imposed martial law. A police state!"

Michael Cassidy was getting a head start on outlining for final exams, while at home with the baby. He had followed the protests on television and in the papers but had not ventured down campus. Apparently the university wanted to build a high-rise parking garage—"God knows you can't find any parking anywhere"—but chose a block that street people had dubbed "People's Park." The matter had been escalating, he knew. Some law students had even offered the law school as a forum to "mediate" the dispute. He was not clear what there was to mediate. The university owned the property and needed parking for students and staff. The squatters, who tilled gardens, slept on the land, or watched their dogs fornicate, had no legal standing.

"Come, see for yourself," said Mai as she picked up the baby and headed for the door. By the time he had put on his shoes and grabbed a coat, Michael had to run to catch up to her halfway down Dwight Way. She proceeded on to College Avenue. Already crowds were gathering. At each corner stood an Army jeep, its antenna waving, with a driver, an armed soldier in the passenger seat holding a rifle, and a communications specialist talking softly into a handheld microphone. Along the road, at about

10-yard intervals were armed soldiers at parade rest with bayonets mounted on their rifles.

"This is crazy, Mikey!"

The crowd grew. Students began, without prompting, to sing "We Shall Overcome."

It seemed strange to Michael to see white students singing a black civil rights song, but then "Stop the Draft" and other slogans used at the Oakland Induction Center hardly seemed appropriate to shout at National Guard troops "protecting" a vegetable garden.

A line of four jeeps pulled up. An officer in the first one stood, brought a megaphone to his mouth, and announced: "This is an illegal assembly. If you do not disperse, you will be arrested."

Suddenly, the students, first a few, then en masse, started running. Someone was shouting "To the park, to the park." As they ran, looking down College Avenue, Michael could see others joining from each intersecting road into a stream of people, making their way to People's Park. Too many for the individual soldiers to impede.

Mai started to run.

"Where are you going?"

"To the park."

"Mai, don't get involved." But she was off. And with the baby. He followed her. "Mai. Mai! The baby!"

The students might as well have published their intentions because it was clear that law enforcement had prepared for their actions. They had anticipated that the students would rush the park if they had not, in fact, encouraged them to do so. Once they congregated there, probably a thousand students, the National Guard troops closed off all the intersections. The Alameda County Sheriff's Office brought up large vans, obviously in wait, out of sight, to deal with the expected student response. It was as if the presence of the Guard was designed to provoke the exact response it did.

For days, Governor Reagan had been treating the disturbance in Berkeley as if it had been taking place in Vietnam and the students were the Vietcong. He had called it "part and parcel of the revolution." He had warned ominously—it now appeared—that "if it takes a bloodbath, let's get it over with. No more appeasement." He was determined to be no Neville Chamberlain. Of course, the students were convinced he was Hitler in the scenario. Now they saw his Wehrmacht on the streets of Berkeley.

The students sat down. Everything went silent.

The students seemed well-pleased with their action. It was nonviolent. There were so many of them, it would take the officers all day to carry each away. It was a sit-in.

It began as a faint drone, hardly noticeable. As it drew closer, a few heads turned to the sky. Over the trees, and over the dormitories surrounding the park area, they looked with some puzzlement. Two helicopters came into sight. A few students pointed. Others cheered and waved, until they noticed Sheriff's deputies putting on gas masks. By then, the helicopters were overhead, emitting a fine spray from pipes mounted above the landing frames. Eyes began to burn as the smell and feel of pepper gas engulfed the park. At the edge of the crowd, Michael saw Sheriff's deputies rolling tear gas canisters among the seated students.

Large vans appeared from side streets, moving forward, slowly, their rear doors open. Officers with batons followed. Michael watched as deputies grabbed protesters by the hair, hit them, or threw them toward the vans. A gauntlet of officers pushed students forward until they reached the van. Some were helped in. Others were beaten around the legs as an incentive to get in. In one van, full of protesters, a deputy threw a tear gas canister. Michael grabbed Mai, who was sitting among the students in the park, and lifted her to her feet. "Come on. Come on. Let's get out of here."

She resisted. She was shouting and crying with burning eyes. "This is America! Fascists! Fascists!"

He saw Brian Jacobs leaving and dragged Mai in the same direction. Two deputies approached them, grabbed Brian, threw him to the ground, and handcuffed him. Michael shouted, "Hey, he didn't do anything! He's a law student." A deputy grabbed at him. Mai interceded, holding up their child: "Baby gasser, baby gasser. Look what you've done." The deputies quickly moved on, not wanting to be delayed in handling a medical emergency with a baby. There were heads to bash.

Michael took the baby from Mai knowing she would follow. The smell of gas followed them all the way up to their apartment at the top of Dwight Way. It was in their clothes, in their hair, and on their skin. Two blocks beyond the police barricades they stopped at a water faucet alongside a house. With the help of a passerby who gave them a shirt, they washed out the baby's eyes and cleaned the pepper gas off his exposed skin.

Mai did not speak of what had occurred the rest of the day or evening. She did not go to school. She just sat rocking the baby. When she and

Michael were in bed together that night, the lights off, he knew she was lying in the dark, staring at the ceiling. Finally, she said, "How can you be part of them?" and turned and went to sleep.

Michael lay awake throughout the night. What he saw that day had shaken him also. There was no place for the military on the streets of America. Of course, if law enforcement could not handle a situation, like in Watts, order did have to be restored. But the students were not violent. Yet they had to be evicted. The means seemed excessive. But law violators could not be allowed to select the means. Perhaps a show of force was all that was intended. After all, he had met the governor and knew the governor's staff, Ed Meese and the others, as well as members of the Alameda County District Attorney's staff. They were well-meaning people who believed in the law as much, if not more, than a group of street people who had attempted to occupy property that did not belong to them. What was law if not rules to be obeyed and enforced?

It was three days before Brian Jacobs returned to school, his arm in a sling. He, along with hundreds of other protesters, had been arrested and taken to Santa Rita, the "farm," instead of the downtown Alameda County jail for normal booking. Law students, under the guidance of activist volunteer attorneys with the National Lawyers Guild and the ACLU, fought their way through the hurdles set up to delay interviews, bail, and release, ultimately filing a federal *habeas corpus* writ and a separate civil rights action for damages on behalf of those detained.

Yielding to the students of the law school, Boalt Hall's administration acquiesced to delay finals by one week for anyone who felt the need for extra time because of the down-campus disruption. It would not, however, agree to cancel finals. The law students accepted the compromise, especially those who saw finals as their last chance to advance their class standing and improve their opportunities for employment.

Nor did any law student, after three years of hard work, boycott graduation. A few wore gas masks. Some wore "Free Brian" buttons for Brian Jacobs, who was still facing prosecution. Most wore toilet paper armbands in protest of the "bombing" and "siege" of Berkeley by the authorities. Michael was not among them.

In the spring, before the events at People's Park, Michael met with Ed Meese at the governor's office. They went to lunch together, joined by the District Attorney of Alameda County, Lowell Jensen. Michael was flattered when Meese called and said, "Michael, I know you're interested in public service, and I have some ideas I would like to share with you."

Michael went to Sacramento, excited about the prospect of working for Meese but not eager about the possible move to the capital. More correctly, he was not eager to argue with Mai about working for Governor Reagan.

Meese introduced him to Lowell Jensen: "Michael was our star intern last summer, Lowell. He's at Boalt. We think he would do well helping implement the governor's law and order program. What I was thinking—and Michael, you can tell me if you are interested—was that Michael get some real-life trial experience as a prosecutor in your office, Lowell, and perhaps in a year or so come on loan to the governor's staff as my deputy."

"Well, Michael," began the D.A., "as you may know, a lot of top people in state government, including Ed, have come through the Alameda County D.A.'s Office. It would be a real opportunity for you. Ed won't say this, but, Michael, Ronald Reagan is going beyond Sacramento, and it wouldn't hurt if you were with him when that happened."

Michael decided immediately that he would accept the offer. He just did not know if he could get it past Mai. He had asked if he could "discuss" the offer with his wife.

"Of course. Just let me know by April 15th," said the D.A. "Crime doesn't stop in Oakland, and I've got to have enough prosecutors to keep up."

Michael called his father and told him of Meese's offer. His father was pleased. "Reagan is going to be president of the United States," he said. Hearing his son's excitement, he did not mention that he had discussed his son's future with Meese some weeks before.

As he drove home from Sacramento, Michael decided to tell Mai just about the job offer at the District Attorney's Office. No point in discussing moving to Sacramento in a year or a year and a half. After all, it was possible—he knew, unlikely—that Ronald Reagan would not be reelected in 1970. When and if the time came, he would discuss it with Mai.

The night of People's Park, he knew he had been right not to tell Mai about Meese's plan for him to join Governor Reagan's administration. It would be hard enough being a deputy D.A. for Alameda County. He just hoped his first assignments would not include prosecuting Brian Jacobs or any of his other classmates who had been at People's Park that day.

Chapter 22

Leon

BRIAN JACOBS HAD made it clear to his draft board that he would not go if called. Michael Cassidy enjoyed, by the inadvertence of fatherhood and the benefit of marriage, a statutory preferential status that mitigated against being called. If called, his father had assured him, without prompting, that he could "call somebody" and get a place in the National Guard Reserves for his son, to avoid service in Southeast Asia. Not that Michael opposed the war or military service. He would just prefer avoiding the confrontation with Mai.

Jackson Bridgeport III had no excuse, except the inconvenience and the "waste of a Harvard education" in serving in the military. To guarantee no disruption to his carefully planned legal career, an examination at the famed Helverstein Clinic in New York was arranged through his father's law firm. After a thorough examination by a world-renowned cardiologist, a "murmur" was detected, which, within the meaning of the selective service physical regulations, could qualify as a "cardiac abnormality." It was, according to the cardiologist, consistent with a heretofore unrecognized cardiac anomaly reported in an unpublished article describing a disease said to be responsible for undetectable "arrhythmias" in the heart, which, as medical literature well attested, were anomalies the presence of which could cause death from undetermined causes. The weight of the attached curriculum vitae, listing the teaching positions and published articles of the doctor, more than made up for the thinness of the diagnosis. The perplexed general practice medical advisor to the draft board dared not quibble with an internationally recognized cardiologist. Accordingly, Jackson Bridgeport III received a 4-F permanent medical deferment from military conscription. The cardiologist continued receiving research grants from the Bridgeport Family Foundation.

Leon Goldman was so close to being legally blind that he required the equivalent of Coke bottle bottoms to read. He could hardly see the eye chart, let alone the letters, and that was on a good day when his allergies were not acting up.

While Leon had no chance of ever being drafted, due to his medical condition, he felt strongly, as did his parents, about the immorality of the United States' role in Vietnam. He saw it as a continuation of French colonialism and as damaging to American society. Free of the draft himself, he counseled others about avoidance. He studied the Selective Service Act, learned the regulations and their interpretations, and networked with lawyers, theologians, and doctors to make available every opportunity for deferment. But he would not counsel people to lie, even to an immoral government, about their beliefs or medical condition. Instead, he believed, the moral answer to immorality was nonviolent resistance and noncooperation. For those who could not risk or accept prison for their beliefs, he suggested flight to Canada. He was not opposed to encouraging illegal acts; he was opposed to endorsing immoral acts in the face of immorality.

As a consequence of Leon's involvement, the railroad to Canada, for many, ran through Seattle and his parents' home. The Goldmans were very proud of their son, and, for the first time, saw some value in his being a lawyer.

When not counseling "draft dodgers," Leon Goldman worked his summers during law school at the Alameda County Legal Aid Society. In the poorest neighborhood of Oakland where he worked, he understood the connection of landlord-tenant law to the Common Law origins he had studied at Boalt. The tenants in Oakland lived not unlike those in feudal times, struggling to earn enough to pay for the privilege of living in dilapidated buildings, dependent upon the whim of the landlord for the roof over their heads. Tenancy, he reflected, had not changed that much in some parts of America from feudal England. At least, he learned, the rules were the same.

It was with some dismay that his parents learned that he had won an Am Jur Award in property law. The award, consisting of a certificate and the book on the particular area of law, was awarded each year by the publishers of *American Jurisprudence* to the person receiving the highest grade in a particular subject. Leon tried to explain to his parents that to reorder society, one needed to fully understand its underpinnings.

"Dad, if you are going to blow up a bridge, wouldn't you want to know which were the supporting members?" he asked.

His dad was not buying it. "Don't be a smarty. You are being trained to be one of them. Learn about workers' rights, not property rights. Workers don't have property. The monopolies and owners have the property."

When Leon excelled in Creditors' Remedies, which he studied in his third year at Boalt with the legendary Professor Steven Reisenfelt, his father was convinced that Leon was on his way to a life as a collection attorney.

"Workers are debtors, not creditors. When are you going to learn something useful to workers? You are going to lose touch with those of us on the outside. You can't change from the comfort of an insider, Leon. They will change you first."

But Leon had no intention of losing touch. He intended to live where he practiced and help those who had no one—the victims of poverty and discrimination in a society too ready to discard those who could not compete. Their problems were food, shelter, employment, and medical care, not corporate law, SEC 10b security violations, antitrust, and the subjects occupying law journals. He could see that those he intended to help would never be able to pay him. Nor could he expect regular law firms to support this type of work. He certainly did not have the resources himself to support a firm dedicated to helping the poor.

The answer, ironically, was provided by the government in the form of Legal Aid through Lyndon Johnson's Great Society programs. Marxism was right: "Democracy has within it the seeds of its own destruction." He would be paid as a government attorney to take on society, and often government, on behalf of those society shunned.

In the third year at Boalt, while his classmates were interviewing with prestigious law firms throughout the nation, Leon Goldman accepted a position with the Alameda County Legal Aid Society to head its new section on housing. Throughout the summer, studying for the Bar exam, and in the fall, beginning work, Leon did not even have to move from his one-bedroom apartment off Ashby Avenue in Oakland.

His father was not happy with Leon's choice. "You are a government lawyer!"

"I am working for the people, against landlords, and, when necessary, against the government," Leon protested.

"Yeah," his father retorted, "who sends you your pay?"

Before Leon could answer, his father answered for him: "The government. And who is the leader of the government? Nixon."

Leon's first day on the job, as head of housing law, was equally discouraging. He met Angela Africa—she had rejected her "slave name" of Brown, replacing it with "Africa"—the head of the Oakland Fair Housing Commission. The Commission was located in the same building as the Legal Aid Society. Angela was tall and athletic, attired in a long, flowing African print gown. She was wearing her hair pulled back tightly in a bun, through which she had put six-inch arrow-shaped wooden sticks. On her feet were gold sandals. Multiple bracelets covered her forearms. Her fingernails, brightly painted, were long and pointed like bear claws. Her appearance, demeanor, and loud voice would not allow her to be dismissed. She commanded, demanded, attention.

As Leon entered the building, Angela stood looking at him, with one arm bent, her hand resting on her hip. She looked him purposely up and down, her eyes bulging, her half-glasses low on her nose, and finally announced: "So you is the little white boy who gonna kick ass and help da po folks." She paused for effect, looking him up and down again, and uttered: "She-e-et!"

Chapter 23

Jackson

BERKELEY WAS A disaster, as far as Jackson Bridgeport was concerned. He took his football very seriously. Correction. He took beating Stanford very seriously. If he could not go to Stanford, at least he expected Cal's football team to beat Stanford as some kind of vindication. His parents came to visit the school in his first year on "Big Game" weekend. They stayed at the Claremont Hotel with a beautiful, if somewhat sterilized, view of Berkeley. They visited the law school and accompanied Jackson to the "Big Game," studiously avoiding Sproul Plaza or Telegraph Avenue.

In their Cal colors—gold stars for the women, blue and gold ties for the men—and a Cal Bear blanket across their knees, the Bridgeports could have been cast in a Cal version of "Knute Rockne of Notre Dame."

Cal lost 13 to 7.

Jackson's parents never came out again, until graduation.

The second year, Jackson finally made it to Stanford and received some satisfaction. Cal beat Stanford, at Palo Alto, 26 to 3, scoring 21 points in the fourth quarter. The concept of "piling on" appealed to Jackson. He would use the 1967 game as an example in his practice, instructing associates, "When they are down, kick 'em."

Jackson Bridgeport's euphoria was short-lived. In his third year at Berkeley, Stanford kicked Cal's ass 20 to 0. Jackson left at halftime with the score 17 to 0. It was perhaps a lesson, one that Jackson Bridgeport would undoubtedly learn the hard way: "What goes around, comes around."

It was "suggested" after his second year that Jackson might spend the summer at the new Los Angeles office of Bridgeport, Bridgeport, Hall and Pendergast. Not as much to work as to become familiar with the environment and the personnel. There were already 40 lawyers at the new Los Angeles office, and it was understood that he would be put in charge of a section at the first opportunity. Jackson thought it should be "litigation," given his perception of his strength in oral advocacy. To those who later observed him in action, both in and out of court, it could better be characterized as oral disdain and unrelenting abuse. But in Los Angeles, it would pass as a "style" of "civil litigation" sought by those who wished to crush their opponents.

After a few weeks in the Los Angeles office in the summer of 1968, Jackson and Sarah flew to the family's summer home in Bridgeport. A few days later, Sarah flew on to Oxford to spend six weeks with her father. In the quiet of the English countryside, she resumed painting subjects other than bridges of the Bay. In one more year, they would move to Los Angeles and, Jackson promised, she could pursue her art professionally. They could move as soon as school was out, since his plans were already established and he had a job with the family firm. In fact, she was assured, the firm would have a real estate company searching for a home in a desirable area of Los Angeles in the spring and she could "expect to participate in its selection." She thought that an odd choice of words—"participate in its selection"—but knew she had little say in how their lives were run, seemingly through the law firm of Bridgeport, Bridgeport, Hall and Pendergast.

At graduation, Jackson's father was furious that the ceremonies were permitted to be spoiled by graduating law students wearing toilet paper as armbands. Nor could he believe the dean would hand a diploma to someone in a gas mask. "These people have no business practicing law," he fumed to Jackson. "Maybe you should have gone to Stanford."

It was, of course, too late for Jackson Bridgeport III. He could take no satisfaction in the fact that Stanford beat Cal in the fall of 1969, after graduation, 29 to 28, with Dave Penhall passing for 321 yards.

Chapter 24

Brian

THERE WAS NEVER any doubt that Brian would pass the Bar exam in August of 1969. His admission to the Bar, however, was delayed for six months.

Brian celebrated with his friends from class, his study partners (at least those who were still in the Bay Area), when the results were announced that fall. But, unlike them, he received a letter advising him that there were questions of "moral turpitude" that raised issues concerning his "fitness to practice law."

As he read the letter, he trembled.

"Can they really do this?" Shelly asked.

> The Committee of Bar Examiners is evaluating your application for admission. Certain information has been submitted which raises questions concerning your moral fitness to practice law. The information is listed below. You have 30 days to respond. Thereafter, the Committee shall determine if the matter requires further action in which case an Accusation shall be filed before the Office of Administrative Law Judges for a full evidentiary hearing.
>
> You are entitled to be represented by counsel at all stages of the proceedings.

He turned to the attachments, a cover sheet stapled to official-looking court documents and reports. The cover sheet chronicled, in rap sheet format, the following:

> 1. Arrest, May 21, 1969. Berkeley, California. PC 241 (Assault); PC 409 (Failure to Disperse).
> Disposition: Dismissed. Interest of Justice.

2. Arrest, July 7, 1962. Troy Ferry, Alabama. Alabama Code 1473
(Assault and Battery); Troy Ferry Town Ordinance 1273 (Drunk in
Public); 923 (Disturbing the Peace).
Disposition: Bail $500, forfeited. Failure to Appear. Bench Warrant
Issued.

The first attached police report, of the Alameda County Sheriff's Department, pertained to the incident at People's Park and alleged that Brian had thrown a tear gas canister at police at the park and had refused to obey a lawful order to disperse.

The second report he had never seen before. It was the "official" crime report from Troy Ferry, Alabama, of his beating and arrest.

> Subject seen by arresting officer loitering near a church where young black female children were attending school. As the arresting officer approached, subject was observed to be unsteady on his feet, with bloodshot eyes, his breath smelling of alcohol. Arresting officer formed the opinion that the subject was drunk in public and may pose a risk to the young children. Subject was offered a ride to town at which time the subject became abusive with profanity in the presence of said children. Without warning, the subject attacked a group of young men who had stopped to render assistance. At this point, the subject had to be restrained and was placed under arrest.

The court docket evidenced bail, his failure to appear, and the resulting bench warrant for his arrest.

It was Shelly who called William Kunstler. "Bill, we need your help," she said, explaining the substance of the letter from the committee. Kunstler listened.

"Shelly, the last thing you need is me. I have just finished the Berrigan trial where I am accused of conspiring with the Jesuits and the Communists to obstruct the draft. I have also been held in contempt by that fuckin' Nazi judge, Herr Hoffman, for defending my clients too vigorously in this Chicago 7 trial. I don't think the California Bar would look too favorably on me at this moment standing up for Brian. I suspect they don't think I'm 'fit' either to practice law."

The feeling of despair echoed through the phone lines. Kunstler finally relented. "Let me make some calls."

That afternoon Brian received a phone call. "Mr. Jacobs, the dean would like to see you tomorrow at 9:00 A.M."

Brian knew it was more bad news. He worried that maybe the Bar was just carrying out orders from Reagan and now the university was falling into line. Maybe the law school was going to take away his diploma for not disclosing his Alabama arrest when he applied. He tried half the night to recall every form, document, or application he had submitted to Boalt for admission. Had any of them asked whether he had been arrested?

He arrived early at the dean's office and waited outside. At exactly 9:00 A.M., he entered the glass doors to the reception area and told the receptionist, "I have an appointment with Dean Jennings. Brian Jacobs."

The receptionist was pleasant, even friendly.

"Yes, Brian. The dean will be just a moment."

As she said this, the door opened and the dean stepped out. "Brian. Come in." He seemed to Brian to be genuinely pleased to see him. Perhaps he was not part of the fascist conspiracy after all.

As Brian walked in, he was surprised to see Gerry Marks, a graduate of Harvard and now a lecturer in Constitutional Law, by way of a clerkship with the U.S. Supreme Court, sitting on the couch in front of the dean's rolltop desk.

"Brian, I think you know Gerry. He is going to be putting this thing together for us."

Brian was puzzled. "What thing?"

"Your response to the Bar," answered the dean. The dean smiled and, for the first time in 24 hours, Brian breathed out. Then he realized how exhausted he really was.

"In 1937," the dean began, "I went to Yale as an undergrad. In addition to doing very well in class, I made the swim team."

Brian looked up. He had no idea what the dean was talking about. He watched the dean go to the wall next to the door where he stood for a moment. Then the dean reached out and took down a picture. Holding it in his hand, looking at it and smiling, he brought it over to Brian. It showed six young men wearing swimsuits, in a line, arms around each other's shoulders, with "Yale" written on a large towel laid in front of them.

"We graduated in 1941."

Brian looked at the black-and-white picture of the young men. It could have been taken from any college yearbook.

"All of them went off to war after graduation, except me." The dean began to point as he spoke. "Mike here died at Guadalcanal. Jerry at Normandy. The rest all came home. On the left, that's Supreme Court Justice Malcolm Stanley; Charlie, next to him, is CEO at Boeing. That's me on the other end with my arm around Bill. Bill Kunstler."

Brian looked closely at the picture. William Kunstler. The radical lawyer. In a swimsuit on the Yale swim team with a future justice of the U.S. Supreme Court. And the dean of Boalt Hall.

"Brian," the dean looked at him solemnly, "we are going to bring you home."

And they did. When he reviewed the submissions prepared on his behalf, Brian was surprised by a letter, a letter that would grace his office walls for 23 years until May 8, 1993, when he finally turned his back on the practice of law and walked out of his law office forever.

Committee of Bar Examiners
California State Bar
100 Market Street
San Francisco, CA
Re: *Application of Brian Jacobs*
Dear Sirs:

In the early 1960s, many young men and women went to Alabama to help the struggle for human rights. They were abused, beaten, and some were killed. Still they came, despite the risk to life and future. Why? some asked. My husband answered them:

I am in Birmingham because injustice is here.

There comes a time when the cup of endurance runs over and men are no longer willing to be plunged into the abyss of despair.

I guess it is easy for those who have never felt the stinging darts of segregation to say, "Wait." When your first name becomes "nigger" and your middle name becomes "boy"…and your last name becomes "John"…then you will understand why we find it difficult to wait.

One day the South will know that when these disinherited children of God sat down at lunch counters, they were in reality standing up for what is best in the American dream…

...[I]n some not too distant tomorrow the radiant stars of love and brotherhood will shine over our great nation with all their scintillating beauty

Brian was one of those young men. I know my husband would join me—if he were here—in urging his admission to the practice of law.

The letter was signed Coretta Scott King.

As much as Coretta Scott King's letter had inspired him, the letter of the dean enraged him. It detailed the dean's Establishment credentials, his participation on the president's National Advisory Commission on Civil Disorders, and his role in establishing standards for legal education through the ABA Committee for Law School Accreditation. It then, in Brian's view, dismissed his actions in Alabama, and at People's Park—all the important stands he had taken in his young life—as "spontaneous, impetuous conduct, born of youthful idealism that I can confidently assure the Bar will restrain itself in the pursuit of professional responsibility and decorum."

If Brian had learned anything from Alabama, from his Peace Corps service in Africa, from Berkeley, and now the State Bar, it was that the law was simply the wielding of power. He had also decided that the answer was not restricting that power, but changing the hands that wielded the law. As long as the wrong people were making the rules and imposing them upon the unrepresented in society, he would be there to stand in the way. No longer with his face. He now knew the rules. Boalt had given him that, and he had mastered them.

In disclosing the secrets of generations—the rules, the analyses, the thought patterns—society had left itself bare, in the same way sharing military secrets presupposes a common purpose. If there had been a common purpose, a shared idealism in 1960, it had been shaken in 1962 in Alabama, shattered on November 22, 1963, in Dallas, and it had died on April 4, 1968, in Memphis, Tennessee, on the second floor balcony of the Lorraine Motel. It was buried as Brian watched the results of the California primary as Robert Kennedy lay dying on the kitchen floor of the Beverly Wilshire Hotel in Los Angeles, the night of June 4, 1968.

As long as America was a racist, oppressive society, Brian would oppose it. And not by rules of civility, professionalism, or decorum designed to keep every cog in its proper place and the machinery of the law grinding on. He would not even use the terms "lawyer" or "attorney." His card read simply:

Brian Jacobs
Advocate

He knew now, in the words of William Kunstler, he would be one of the pushors, not a pushee.

Chapter 25

Rose

IN THE FALL of the third year, recruiters descended upon Boalt from New York, Washington, Dallas, Chicago, Los Angeles, San Francisco, and every major city that headquartered a national law firm or a firm that strove for national recognition. Since Boalt was one of the leading law schools in the nation, its top students could expect to be the subject of fierce competition for their attention. Those on the law review especially, if they wished, could spend a good part of the fall on all-expense-paid trips visiting law firms throughout the country. For the 1969 class, salaries had shot up from the year before as a result of New York firms offering "obscene" amounts of money that were promptly matched throughout the country. The market for Boalt graduates, just like those of Harvard, Yale, and Stanford, was a national market.

Law firms were confronted, however, with a dilemma. Many of the brightest students were questioning a legal career beckoning them with only money to offer. What contribution, they asked, did the prospective employer make to society? What type of pro bono work did it do? Clearly, the innovative firms, and most especially those that could afford it by reason of their hefty fees from corporate clients, offered "summers in Selma." In these programs, young lawyers who had dutifully put in their 2,200 billable hours per year for three years could spend part of a summer doing civil rights work in the South.

Rose had decided to forego big firm recruiters and submit applications for judicial clerkships, as recommended by Professor Van Dyke and Anthony Hawk. She submitted her application to the U.S. Supreme Court and, as a backup, also submitted an application to the California Supreme Court. As promised, Professor Van Dyke had written her a letter which, as required, went directly to the courts.

While it was expected by everyone, Rose was still excited when the letter arrived bearing the designation, in stylized print, of the Supreme Court of the United States. She would be interviewed, it proclaimed, by Justice Talmadge Reynolds in his chambers on November 12, 1968, at 4:15 P.M. She was to report to security at the entrance by 3:50 P.M. for her appointment and would be shown to the justice's chambers.

Preparing to go to Washington and, for that matter, for her first flight on an airplane, she marveled at what had happened to her. She was still, after all, a girl from Fresno. Now, on the wings of a letter from an internationally known professor and her own hard work at Boalt, she had been summoned to Washington to meet with a justice of the highest court in the land. Professor Van Dyke believed in her. Anthony Hawk believed in her. Her ability to compete with 275 others from the finest schools throughout the country, and to come out on top, had finally convinced Rose to believe in herself. It was not just the pride of her parents; it was now a fact.

Nevertheless, her confidence, and sense of anticipation, could not conceal her excitement in traveling to Washington, D.C., the nation's capital. Coming in from San Francisco on the evening of the 11th, on Pan Am, she peered out of the window to see national monuments, the White House, the Washington Monument, and other sites that she had only seen on the news or in books. Even staying in a hotel in a major city, one recommended by Anthony Hawk, was a new and exciting experience. This, she thought, must be how lawyers live as they travel throughout the country, meeting important clients and arguing important issues of law.

On the morning of the 12th, she went to the Supreme Court early to stand in the public line with the hope of getting a seat in the courtroom for oral arguments scheduled for that day. But first, she stood at the foot of the steps leading to the court doors, looking up the long flight, imagining the many people who had climbed these steps to argue landmark cases, like Thurgood Marshall, who had argued *Brown v. Board of Education* to integrate schools and now sat as the first black justice of the court. She climbed slowly, deliberately, thinking that she, someday, would return to ascend these steps again to address the Court, not as a law student in private, but as an attorney in public, arguing a case that would impact the nation. She reached the top and turned, standing between the columns, surveying the view. This, she thought, must be what it was like when Sir Hillary climbed Everest. And here she was, after years of climbing, at the top of a legal mountain, about to enter chambers seen by few.

The elegance of the white marble, like a palace, added to the solemnity. As she walked in, she almost expected John Marshall, the first Chief Justice, or other historic justices, to walk down the hall.

Entering the courtroom itself, she was met with heavy velvet red curtains that formed a wall blocking the view of the inner courtroom. Stepping through the curtains, she was surprised to see how close the justices sat to the gallery. The raised structure, behind which sat nine black leather highback chairs, appeared right in front of her. She was overwhelmed by the historical significance of what she was seeing, until, that is, the guide beckoned her to move forward to the seats for those who intended to sit through the entire session, behind the single "bar" of the court that separated those who had been admitted to practice before the court, but ahead of the "5-minute" section for tourists.

As she sat, her heart jumped at the thumping of the gavel by the marshal declaring, in a loud voice:

> The Honorable, the Chief Justice and Associate Justices of the Supreme Court of the United States. Oyez, Oyez, Oyez. All persons having business before the Honorable, the Supreme Court of the United States, are admonished to draw near and give their attention, for the Court is now sitting. God save the United States and this honorable court.

Everyone stood abruptly, as if equally taken off guard by the thumping of the gavel. From behind a curtain, the justices of the Supreme Court, as if choreographed, came and took their seats in the large high-back chairs, with the Chief Justice at the center. Immediately, as the last justice took his seat, the Chief Justice called the first case:

"*Tinker versus Des Moines*...Mr. Johnston."

The Chief Justice looked up. A tall man rose from the counsel table and strolled to the podium between the two tables reserved for attorneys appearing on a matter before the Court.

"Mr. Chief Justice, and may it please the Court," he began, as did all arguments, in keeping with the ancient formalities of the Court.

Mary Beth Tinker, 13 years old and in the 8th grade, was about to make history, if only because she had been suspended from school. She had worn a black armband in class to protest the Vietnam War. It seemed an innocuous enough act but it, as much as the war itself, had clearly

126

evoked strong emotions. Now, in the solemnity of a Supreme Court hearing, these same emotions, or at least the proper role of "children in the nation's future," would be debated.

Counsel for Mary Beth was explaining how Mary Beth had quietly worn her armband, without disruption, to the class. For this, she had been sent home. He had gotten about three minutes into his 30-minute allocation of time when he was interrupted. Just like Moot Court, Rose thought. Here it comes. Her adrenaline was rushing, as she witnessed the events, as if she herself were about to do battle.

Justice White: What if the student had gotten up from the classes she went to and delivered the message orally that her armband was intended to convey and insisted on doing it all through the hour?

Johnston: In that case, your honor, we would not be here, even if she insisted on doing it only for a second, because she would clearly be—although she would be expressing her views, she would be doing something else.

Justice White: Why did they wear the armband to class, to express that message?

Johnston: To express the message, yes.

Justice White: To everybody in the class?

Johnston: To everyone in the class, yes, your honor.

Justice White: Everybody while they were listening to some other subject matter was supposed to be looking at the armband and taking in that message?

Johnston: Well, to the extent that they would see it. But I don't believe there was any—I don't believe that the...

Justice White: Well, they were intended to see it, weren't they?

Johnston: They were intended to see it in a way that would not be distracting...

Justice White: And to understand it.

Johnston: And to understand it.

Justice White: And to absorb that message...

Johnston: And to absorb the message...

Justice White: While they're studying arithmetic or mathematics, they're supposed to be taking in this message about Vietnam?

Johnston: Well, except that, your honor, I believe that the method that the students chose in this particular instance was specifically designed in such a way that it would not cause that kind of disruption.

Justice White: Again, why did they wear the armband?

Johnston: They wore the armband to...

Justice White: ...convey a message.

Johnston: ...convey the message; that's right.

Justice White: They anticipated students would see it and understand it and think about it?

Johnston: That's correct.

Justice White: And when they did it in class, they intended the students to do it *in* class?

Johnston: I think it's a fair assumption that the method of expression...

Justice White: They intended the students to think about it outside of class but not in class?

Johnston: I think they intended, I think they chose a message, chose a method of expression, your honor, which would not be distracting...

Justice White: ...physically; it wouldn't make a noise, it wouldn't cause a commotion, but don't you think it would cause some people to direct their attention to the armband and the Vietnam War and think about that, rather than what they were thinking about, supposed to be thinking about in the classroom?

Johnston: I think perhaps, your honor, it might for a few moments have done that, and I think it perhaps might have distracted some students, just as many other things do in the classroom which are allowed, from time to time.

Rose cringed. "Don't admit 'distraction,'" she was arguing silently. "Call it…say…it might cause someone to…mentally note a matter of national importance rather than something as frivolous and distracting as a boy's haircut or a girl's stocking, which are distractions we tolerate daily."

Rose saw the white light go on at the podium, telling Mary Beth's lawyer he had five minutes left. She nodded approval when he informed the Court he would "reserve" his remaining time for reply. But if Mary Beth's lawyer conceded too much, the school district's attorney went too far. An older gentleman—about 70, Rose guessed—he clearly believed personally that "students should be seen and not heard." He sought to compare 13-year-old Mary Beth to hundreds of unruly black students who had descended upon a jail to protest the arrest of civil rights sit-in demonstrators in Florida. When confronted by Thurgood Marshall, the Court's first and only black justice, he tried to link Mary Beth's black armband to the riots at the Chicago Democratic Convention that summer, the radical Students for a Democratic Society and its leader Tom Hayden, Dr. Spock, the March on Washington, and draft card burning. It was too much, although Mary Beth would be pleased to know, Rose suspected, that her black armband, silently worn, had caused such havoc. The attorney for the school district justified suspending Mary Beth and her armband because, after all, a former student of one of the high schools in the district had been killed in Vietnam. Some of his friends were still in school. If they had seen Mary Beth and her armband, apparently, they may have acted in a way that would have been difficult to control. Hence, went the argument, suspend Mary Beth and her armband.

There was a hush in the room when Justice Marshall asked, "Do we have a city in this country that hasn't had someone killed in Vietnam?"

The importance of the question was obvious. If there could not be demonstrations against U.S. policy because they might distress someone who knew another who had been killed in Vietnam, then there could be no demonstrations throughout the country because there were more and more people being killed in Vietnam every day.

Ironic, Rose thought. Mary Beth was protesting to mourn the deaths on both sides and to seek an end to the killing—so that no more students would be drafted and sent to die. But it was this very message that students were not to convey to other students.

Mary Beth with her armband had supported Robert Kennedy's proposal for a truce. Now, Robert Kennedy was dead. Richard Nixon had been elected president just two weeks before the argument, and even he professed to have a plan to end the war. But Mary Beth could not have one. Not in school.

Sitting in the courtroom of the U.S. Supreme Court, Rose wondered why Mary Beth, her brother, and five others were the only students wearing armbands among the 18,000 pupils of the Des Moines School District. Was not that the best measure of the failure of a school system, that so few spoke up?

* * * * *

"Miss Contreras."

Not a greeting. Not a question. A statement. "Sit down."

Justice Talmadge Reynolds continued making notes in the margins of the galley proof, striking sentences, changing words, occasionally writing "No!" Finally, he looked up at her. "Another justice's draft opinion," he added by way of explanation.

He continued reading and making notations.

"So, Miss Contreras, you wish to be my law clerk for the next two years. What do you know about me?"

"Harvard Law School, class of 1932; clerked for Justice Cardozo, New York Court of Appeals, 1932–1933; clerked for Justice Frankfurter, United States Supreme Court, 1933–1935; taught law at Harvard for five years. For two years, you were assigned to the secretary of Navy dealing with Lend-Lease in the Roosevelt administration. After that, you served in the United States Navy, 1941–1945. You were a prosecutor at the Nuremberg War Crimes Tribunal. Then assistant attorney general in the Truman administration. You practiced law in New York and resumed teaching at NYU Law School until you were appointed assistant attorney general in the civil rights division of the Justice Department in the Kennedy administration and, of course, appointed by President Kennedy to the United States Supreme Court in 1962."

"Very good, Miss Contreras. That is what appears on my official biography. But what do you *know* about me?"

"Well, you are recognized as a leading authority—*the* leading authority on the Court—on the Commerce Clause. Your 1961 article on its use to expand civil rights in public accommodations, businesses, and activities that affect commerce—arguably everything—formed a legal basis for the

Kennedy-Johnson legislation in the area and led the way to the federalization of civil rights."

He interrupted. "It didn't form *a* legal basis, Miss Contreras, it formed *the* legal basis."

Rose acknowledged the not-too-subtle distinction. "Well, certainly many scholars have argued that your thinking formed *the* legal basis for the civil rights legislation."

He interrupted again. "Yes, I have made that argument myself," he said without a hint of modesty.

Yet, he seemed uncomfortable, Rose observed. Certainly, a Supreme Court justice had no reason that she could imagine to be uncomfortable in his own chambers with a third-year law student. But this was as new an experience for him as it was for her, she was to find out.

"Anything else?" He looked at her, waiting.

"I have heard that you are tyrannical with your staff, abusive with your law clerks, and generally a very difficult person to work for."

Rose maintained eye contact upon finishing. She was not, at that moment, sorry she had said it. She wondered why she had done so. Whatever the reason—maybe because it was well known and she felt he was daring her to be truthful—it was out there, hanging.

A slight smile of satisfaction lifted one corner of his mouth. "Miss Contreras, you're here because Professor Van Dyke wrote me. You know he and I are in an exclusive club of persons who were privileged to clerk for Justice Cardozo."

"Yes," answered Rose with relief, "I worked on Professor Van Dyke's article on Cardozo my first year in law school. I certainly feel privileged to have worked with Professor Van Dyke."

"Well, Van Dyke said you were brilliant. He wrote a marvelous, glowing letter. I just had to meet you. He only writes one letter a year, you know."

"Yes, I have heard. I am deeply honored that Professor Van Dyke chose me for that letter." She sat back in her chair, more relaxed.

"Well, I must say Professor Van Dyke never said you were pretty, too, Miss Contreras. I must say I am surprised."

"Surprised?"

"Yes, well, a woman in the law…smart *and* attractive."

Rose was well aware that there were not that many women in the law. She was taken aback, though. "Attractive." She had never really thought of herself that way. Or that her looks would be a subject during an interview with a justice of the U.S. Supreme Court. As she sat pondering, not knowing how to respond, Justice Reynolds continued.

"Well, I mean, a very attractive woman such as yourself, I would have expected would probably be married by now. Do you have plans to get married and have a family?"

"No. I have plans to have a clerkship and then get a job."

"Well, clerkships are something finite. There are only so many. We certainly want to award them not only to the brightest and best of students throughout the country, but also those who are going to contribute to the profession. Do you intend to practice law and stay in the profession?"

"Of course. I have worked extremely hard to get to where I am. Why would I throw it all away?"

"Well, that's my point. If a very pretty young lady like yourself is simply going to get married in the next few years, and have babies, and give up her career to follow her husband, then the prize of a Supreme Court clerkship could well be wasted on her. Do you see my point?"

"No. Your male law clerks get married, don't they?"

"Yes, of course, but that's different. Why, last night I told my wife that you were coming in today, and I can tell you Mrs. Reynolds was a little jealous, and I can imagine what she would say if I hired a pretty, young, single girl as my clerk."

For once, Rose was speechless. She was in the chamber of a justice of the U.S. Supreme Court; in the temple of the Constitution. "Justice under law." She surmised that she was being told she could not have a job, the most prestigious job for a graduating law student, because the *wife* of a justice might not feel comfortable that her husband was in the stacks, so to speak, with a "pretty young thing."

She had studied the law; she had studied Justice Reynolds. She had read his articles, every last damn one of them. Where in there was the answer to "my wife might not understand"?

"I wish to be honest with you, Miss Contreras," began Justice Reynolds as if honesty was always a virtue and one that had raised its head for the first time in the interview.

Rose interrupted: "Oh, I appreciate that, Justice Reynolds. Perhaps I should talk to your wife."

"Excuse me?"

"Your wife." Rose was now sitting upright on the edge of her seat. "It seems she is the one with the problem. Perhaps I could dress really badly, hair unkempt, no makeup, and interview with her? I would act really smart so she wouldn't suspect anything was really going on between us."

Justice Reynolds recognized sarcasm. "Miss Contreras," he said with a mixture of anger and a hint of embarrassment, "this interview is over."

"Oh? I thought it was over before these high heels walked in, Justice Reynolds."

With that, Rose stood up, paused, turned, and walked to the door, maintaining all the dignity and poise she could muster. She opened the large door with the antique handle and walked through, leaving it wide open. She resolved not to cry, at least until she reached the street. It was in the pause that Justice Reynolds knew he had been bettered.

On February 24, 1969, three months later, the U.S. Supreme Court decided *Tinker v. Des Moines Independent Community School District*. Justice Abe Fortas delivered the opinion of the Court. Little Mary Beth Tinker won her right to protest with a black armband in school. The Court upheld that the First Amendment did not stop at the schoolhouse door. To hold otherwise, said the Court, would be to "teach youth to discount important principles of our government as mere platitudes."

Justice Reynolds voted in favor of Mary Beth. Rose could only conclude that Mary Beth must have been really, really ugly to get Justice Reynolds' vote. She herself, Rose concluded, would have to settle for "mere platitudes" from the U.S. Supreme Court.

While flying back to California, Rose did not know how she would explain her behavior. The Dean, Professor Van Dyke, other professors, students, her parents, and Anthony Hawk, all knew she was interviewing at the Supreme Court. Boalt had placed a clerk at the U.S. Supreme Court from each of the graduating classes since she had been in law school. Would she be seen as letting down the school? The faculty? Professor Van Dyke? Would all of the justices be told of her conduct? Would the faculty, many of whom had themselves been clerks at the U.S. Supreme Court, be called? Be warned? Be told, in no uncertain terms, that Boalt would not be welcome at the Supreme Court in the foreseeable future? No more "troublemakers" from Berkeley?

Rose did not know with whom she could share her humiliation and anger. Professor Van Dyke was supportive, but his office door represented the distance of generations and gender between them. And it was his letter that had sent her to the Court. She felt she had let him down. She had no "girls" in the class as best friends or confidants. Being number one in an overwhelmingly male class did not lend itself to intimate conversations about failure. Anthony Hawk was probably closer to her than anyone else in the law, but he was her potential future employer. She was not going to discuss her "bizarre" behavior with him and jeopardize her job prospects.

By the time she reached San Francisco, Rose had resigned herself to the embarrassment and potential damage to her career.

It never came. Instead, on February 27th, three days after the *Tinker* decision, Rose received a letter from the chambers of Justice Reynolds. It read simply:

Dear Miss Contreras:

I want to thank you for applying for a clerkship for the 1969-70 term. Your qualifications are, of course, exemplary, as are those of the select handful of law school graduates each year considered for clerkships at the United States Supreme Court.

The decision is always difficult. I regret that I am unable to offer you a position. You should take pride in the fact that you were nominated, and supported, by your faculty.

I am sure you will bring credit to the practice of law.

Sincerely,

Justice Talmadge Reynolds

Justice Reynolds apparently, for whatever reason, never discussed Rose and their "interview" with anyone.

While waiting for the repercussions from her meeting at the U.S. Supreme Court, Rose followed up on the dean's suggestion that she interview at the California Supreme Court. It was, after all, the leading state supreme court in the nation, unabashedly liberal, and at the forefront of tort and civil rights law. Not only was it followed by supreme courts of other states, it was often cited with approval by the U.S. Supreme Court, which often followed its lead, albeit years later.

Having heard nothing from the U.S. Supreme Court yet, Rose was able to say, with a straight face, that "yes," she was a "candidate" at the U.S. Supreme Court, but was "seriously considering passing up whatever offer might come from the Court" if she were first offered a clerkship "with the Chief Justice or one of the leading justices of the California Supreme Court."

What she meant, of course, was, "Please offer me a clerkship so I can tell Justice Reynolds to shove it."

The Chief Justice of the California Supreme Court greeted Rose enthusiastically. Instead of being led to chambers by a secretary, to a seated justice, Rose was surprised when Justice Pinkley's door opened, and he personally came into the waiting area, his sleeves rolled up. "Rose, isn't it? Come in. Come in. Good to see you." While shaking hands with Rose, he told his secretary, "Terri, come in a minute, will you. Rose and I are going down to join Justice Parks for lunch."

He turned and reentered his chambers with his secretary and Rose following. Things looked promising. She was apparently going to be taken to lunch by two justices of the California Supreme Court. Where do justices eat? The Financial District? The Garden Room of the Palace Hotel, under the dome where she had taken her parents? She really did not know. But this was San Francisco, and she assumed it would be exclusive. Justices of the Supreme Court do not go to Denny's, she thought.

"Terri, find out when Justice Parks is ready for us. Rose, let's chat."

He led her to a seating area in his room, instead of sitting behind his desk. "Justice Parks and I are both Boalt graduates. Of course, that was a long time ago. A very long time ago," he added, laughing.

"Privately, we do have a preference for our alma mater when it comes to selecting law clerks. After all, it is the best law school in California…with Stanford runner-up." He laughed again. "I guess you probably don't follow the Big Game, Cal versus Stanford?"

Rose was ready. "I heard we didn't do too well this year," she replied, wanting to sound like she gave a shit what a group of Neanderthals on testosterone overload, and athletic scholarships, did in the name of intercollegiate rivalry.

"Not too well! Not too well! That's an understatement," laughed the Chief Justice. "I'd say 20 to 0—with 17 to 0 at halftime—qualifies as piss poor." He added, apologetically, "Please excuse my language, Miss Contreras." He looked at her with embarrassment.

"The only reason it wasn't worse is because I think Stanford's first string went home at halftime, and they put their song leaders in. And even they scored points and held our boys to nothing." He was enjoying himself, even if Rose could not understand what this had to do with a clerkship at the Court.

The phone rang, and the Chief Justice excused himself to Rose and picked up the phone. "Good. Tell him we'll be right down." Hanging up the phone, he stood and announced: "Justice Parks is ready for us. He is the senior justice, even though I am the chief, so we go to him," he said, laughing again.

They walked into the richly carpeted hall and down the corridor to a tall wooden door with the name of Justice Parks engraved on a brass name-plate. Rose knew Justice Parks had been on the Court for 16 years, after serving on the First District Court of Appeal. He was regarded as an intellectual on the Court, a prolific opinion writer, and a scholar of the law of torts. His opinions had led the way nationally in the development of product liability, consumer rights, and civil liberties. Once, when asked why his opinions were so long, he responded that he did not have time to write shorter opinions.

Rose followed the Chief Justice into Justice Parks' chambers, where Chief Justice Pinkley knocked on the inner door and waited.

"Come in," came the reply and they entered, with the Chief Justice holding the door for Rose.

Sitting in front of her, at a huge desk, made bigger by his diminutive size, was a bespectacled, thin man peeling an apple with a penknife. In front of him was a cloth napkin laid out on the desk, with law books and papers moved to either side to clear a space. He was carefully peeling the apple, going completely around with each cut, dropping the peel on the napkin. "Justice Parks, this is Rose Contreras, the applicant from Boalt Hall," Justice Pinkley said.

Both Rose and the Chief Justice remained standing in front of the desk. Justice Parks had finished peeling the first green apple and was starting on a second.

"Would you like a piece of apple, Miss Contreras?" he asked, looking at her briefly.

Having blown it on the Cal-Stanford question, she decided to accept. "Yes. Thank you, your honor."

"Peel, body, or core?"

She surmised that he was not offering her an apple, rather a dismembered part. She chose peel, thinking it might be the easiest to handle while being interviewed.

"We don't have much time here for long lunches like practicing lawyers do. I always eat at my desk, then take a walk around the corridors for exercise. Would you like some water too?" he asked, handing her two circumferences of apple peel on his penknife.

"No, thank you."

Rose took the pieces and nibbled on them. She watched Justice Parks stand a skinned apple on end and cut it vertically, first one side, then the next, until he had cut four sides, leaving a core entombed in a rectangle.

"Professor Van Dyke wrote that you are the best graduating student of your class. In fact, he said you are among the best he has ever seen. You should be honored to be singled out by him. He only writes one letter a year, you know."

"Yes. I have been told that, Justice Parks. I am deeply honored to be the one this year," she recited now as if by rote.

Justice Parks began cutting the wedges of apple into thirds. "Do you know what would be expected of you as a law clerk to this Court, Miss Contreras?"

"Of course. A great deal of research, writing, long hours, many of the things I am doing now in writing my own law review article and reviewing other articles for publication as the editor of the *California Law Review*."

"How well do you handle deadlines, Miss Contreras?" Justice Parks asked.

"Very well. Isn't that really what law is about? Everything has a deadline."

"Yes, well, here, Miss Contreras, it sometimes may feel like a drop-dead line," he replied, looking directly at her for the first time through his wire-rimmed glasses. "Please, sit down." She and the Chief Justice, who had also remained standing, both sat in chairs directly in front of Justice Parks' desk.

Rose really was not sure where the conversation was going or what Justice Parks' point was. The Chief Justice remained quiet. Rose decided to do the same. She waited.

Justice Parks had finished cutting the wedges and now cut each piece of peel into thirds. Rose realized her *faux pas*. She had bitten off pieces from the whole of each circumference of peel. Then again, she did not have a penknife.

"We had a young lady three years ago. She didn't work out. Nervous breakdown. So, you see, we're concerned."

Rose looked over at the Chief Justice. He shifted in his chair uncomfortably and looked away from her. Rose looked back to Justice Parks who had stabbed a piece of apple with his penknife and was putting it into his mouth.

Here we go again, Rose thought. But she was determined not to get upset, not to confront. Make the most convincing argument, a legal argument, she told herself.

She waited to make sure her voice would not betray her.

"Justice Parks, I am the editor of the *California Law Review*. I know you also were the editor of the law review when you were at Boalt. So you know the time involved and the pressure of constant deadlines. I am number one in my class—have been for three years—and I can guarantee you I will maintain that position and will graduate number one at Boalt. My class includes 262 men. Boalt is one of the top three law schools in the country, as it was when you and the Chief Justice were there, so you know how tough the competition is. Unlike any other member of this year's law review, I also competed in Moot Court and received national honors, although I have to admit I did not win. Again, I know you have been kind enough to give of your time at Boalt in judging Moot Court, so you know about the time, work, and attention involved in presenting before eminent jurists and achieving national standing. I clerked for Professor Van Dyke and assisted him in his publication last year in the *Columbia Law Review*. I am sure you know that Professor Van Dyke insists on the highest standards of work and research. My own law review article, on deficiency judgments in California, is in galley proofs and will be published in the May edition of the law review. So, Justice Parks, I think I have demonstrated I am more than capable of competing with anyone, man or woman, in the study or practice of law and the stresses that it imposes."

She paused and thought perhaps that a little humor—"for the boys"—might break the tension. So she added, "Besides, I hear the other girl was from Stanford, so what did you expect? I'm from Cal, and I would like to be here clerking when we kick their butts in the Big Game in the fall."

"Atta girl," shouted the Chief Justice, raising his right arm in a power salute.

Justice Parks had now begun on the core of the apple, surprisingly taking the whole thing in hand and crunching it as he pushed it slowly into his mouth with his index finger.

He finished chewing and swallowed.

"Well, Miss Contreras, Boalt is not necessarily reflective of real life," Justice Parks finally said. The interview was over.

"You know, he's right, Rose," Anthony Hawk told her.

After receiving her second "thank you…you should be proud" letter, but no clerkship, Rose had finally told Hawk what had occurred during her interviews.

At first he had sat quietly, just listening. When she recited the events with Justice Reynolds at the U.S. Supreme Court, he turned his chair and faced out of his window, first because he was horrified, and then because he envisioned Rose confronting Reynolds. He had to laugh. He turned back: "You said that to a justice of the Supreme Court of the United States?"

"Yes," she said, partly laughing also, but trying to keep her voice steady so as not to cry.

"You've got balls!" he responded.

They laughed together, Rose wiping her eyes. "No. That seems to be what's missing on my resume, 'cojones.' Maybe I could change my name. 'Rose Con Cojones.' Would that get past Mrs. Reynolds or would she want to see for herself?"

With frustration, she asked, "If they had no intention of hiring me, why waste everyone's time?"

"Van Dyke," Hawk answered. "Everyone knows he writes one letter a year. A Van Dyke letter is a guaranteed interview. He is held in such respect. He opened the door. He can't guarantee they'll change the rules for you, though."

"What rules?"

"Men only."

He held the index finger and thumb of each hand in the air, as if framing a sign. He said the words again in the same manner as he would read a sign that said "white" or "colored."

"Look around you, Rose. There are no women on the United States Supreme Court; none on the California Supreme Court. A handful of women in your class, most of whom, if history is any measure, will not be practicing law full-time in five years, and certainly not in the lucrative, high-profile areas of law. Justices pick law clerks who become professors who become justices who pick law clerks who become professors who pick law clerks who become justices. It's the legacy I told you about. It's a legacy of men, Rose. Law is a patrilineal society."

He paused for effect.

"Don't you see there is a lot riding on your failure?"

"I think you mean to say success. A lot riding on my success," Rose corrected him.

"No, Rose. Your failure. There are 262 men in your class who believe it's a fluke you beat them. The best thing that could happen, for the society of male lawyers, is if you went to the Court as a law clerk and failed. Then the justices could say, 'We had a girl here once. Didn't work out. Nervous breakdown.' How many more years could someone like Justice Parks use your failure to keep women out? Failure, Rose. The majority of your colleagues in the law want you to fail, so they can collectively say, 'See? Women don't belong in the law.'"

"Maybe I don't," said Rose.

"Any woman who can tell a United States Supreme Court justice to go fuck himself belongs in the law!"

His language and anger surprised her. Now he was shouting. "Did you think it was going to be easy?"

"I never thought about it. I mean, I excelled at everything. I thought I had earned it."

"Rose, Justice Parks said it. Boalt is not the real world. Van Dyke knew what he was doing. He picked you. The first woman to receive his letter. You are part of his legacy. Legacies are made over lifetimes. You haven't even begun to earn it!"

They sat quietly, neither of them saying anything for a long time. She looked out of his office window to the city below. He looked at her in the reflection of the window, wondering how it would all turn out.

"Well," she finally said, "is that job offer still open here?"

"So," he said smiling, "on the rebound, I'm looking pretty good to you right now, huh?"

"Yeah," she smiled back. "For a male."

That fall, after taking the Bar exam, Rose went to work for Janrette, Hawk, Ross and Stephens. Her father was proud of her. He asked for business cards to hand out to everyone he knew in Gonzales. She tried to explain that they were unlikely to use the services of her business litigation and bond firm. He did not care. He wanted everyone to know his daughter was "*una abogada muy importante en San Francisco.*"

That same fall, new law clerks to the justices of the U.S. Supreme Court went to work. Their names were Kenneth, Gustave, Richard, William, Robert, James, Charles, George, Douglas, Harry, Michael, Jerry,

Thomas, Charles, William, Robert, Thomas, Gary, David, Leonard, Silas, William, and Edward.

The U.S. Supreme Court was established under the Constitution of 1779. It was 165 years later that the first woman, Lucille Lomen, clerked for a justice of the Court. The year was 1944. Some have suggested there were not enough men, since many were off to war, to fill all of the clerkship slots, which also accounted for the increase in female law students. It is doubtful that the unavailability of men accounted for the filling of a single clerkship by a woman during the four years of World War II. But there was one, just one. Lucille Lomen was picked by Justice William O. Douglas on the recommendation of the dean of her University of Washington Law School and the faculty of Whitman College, where Justice Douglas himself was the most distinguished alumnus. Justice Douglas was a maverick. In the same year, 1944, he penned the only dissent to the Japanese exclusion cases, holding that the United States had no authority, even in time of war, to detain Americans of Japanese ancestry in camps without evidence of disloyalty. Perhaps Lucille worked on the opinion and was at his side, as his only law clerk, when the United States dropped the atomic bomb on Hiroshima. She did, by all accounts, an outstanding job for a justice viewed as working his clerks the longest hours, assisting on the opinions of the most prolific member of the Court.

On June 21, 1996, in Seattle, Washington, at age 76, Lucille Lomen died. A tea was held in her memory at Horizon's House, a senior retirement home where she lived. Her obituary carried the notation "law clerk, Justice William O. Douglas, U.S. Supreme Court." The prize of a clerkship at the U.S. Supreme Court followed her throughout her life, and in death into her obituary.

During the 22 years after Lucille served at the U.S. Supreme Court, no other woman was chosen as a law clerk. In the fall of 1966, as the class of '69 began study at Boalt Hall, Margaret J. Corcoran of Harvard clerked for Justice Hugo Black. In 1968, Martha A. Alschaler of the University of Chicago clerked for Justice Abe Fortas, becoming only the third woman in history to clerk at the U.S. Supreme Court in its 189-year history. She now teaches at Harvard Law School.

In 1969 there were no women selected as law clerks to the U.S. Supreme Court—not even Rose Contreras, number one in her class at Boalt Hall.

Book II

> "WHEN I THINK THUS OF THE LAW, I SEE A PRINCESS MIGHTIER THAN SHE THAT WROUGHT AT BAYEUX ETERNALLY WEAVING INTO HER WEB DIM FIGURES OF THE EVER-LENGTHENING PAST—FIGURES TOO DIM TO BE NOTICED BY THE IDLE, TOO SYMBOLIC TO BE INTERPRETED EXCEPT BY HER PUPILS, BUT TO THE DISCERNING EYE DISCLOSING EVERY PAINFUL STEP AND EVERY WORLD-SHAKING CONTEST BY WHICH MANKIND HAS WORKED AND FOUGHT ITS WAY FROM SAVAGE ISOLATION TO ORGANIC SOCIAL LIFE."
>
> —JUSTICE OLIVER WENDELL HOLMES
> *Engraving over the southwest entry to Boalt Hall School of Law, U.C. Berkeley*

Chapter 26

Michael

HE BLAMED GEORGE McGovern for her leaving him.

It had taken Mai four years of part-time classes to get enough units to qualify for her master's degree. Along the way, she had become active at San Francisco State in politics, which, between 1967 and 1972 meant anti-war activities, intensifying as the presidential election approached. It began with teach-ins about the war, listening to campus speakers. She felt especially vulnerable as she learned more, because she was, after all, Asian. This war seemed to contain elements of racism, similar to the atomic bombing of Japan, not Germany; the "relocation" of Asians, not Italians, during World War II. Those who were sent to fight the Asians, for the white American society, were disproportionately black and poor.

But if she felt she would find virtue in recent Asian history, she was wrong. Preceding the Americans, and the French before them, China had persistently attempted to conquer Vietnam. Japan had its own history of conquest and brutality. Vietnam itself was no stranger to invading foreign soils.

Nor did Mai find comfort and support in the Chinese-American community, or with her own parents. Parroting Nixon, her parents believed that "Communism must be stopped" and negotiations would be seen as weakness. Mao and Nixon, it seemed, were interchangeable: "All power comes out of the end of a gun," or, in the American case, a B-52 bomber at 40,000 feet.

Mai refused to stop organizing draft protesters and resisters at the Oakland Induction Center, but she agreed, out of deference to Michael's job as a Deputy District Attorney for Alameda County, to avoid being arrested along with the demonstrators who regularly chained themselves to train tracks or threw blood on induction records. She, along with other female students, handed out pamphlets to inductees, urging them to refuse to step forward when called. Their slogan was, "Women Say 'Yes' to Men Who Say 'No'."

On June 18, 1971, George McGovern announced his candidacy for the presidency of the United States. The next morning Mai read the story of McGovern's announcement and focused on a McGovern quote in the *San Francisco Chronicle*:

> Thoughtful Americans understand that the highest patriotism is not a blind acceptance of official policy, but a love of one's country deep enough to call her to a higher standard.

She tore the quote out of the paper, taped it on a small piece of cardboard from a cereal box top, and attached it to the refrigerator door. From that day, every day, to November 5, 1972, she worked tirelessly for the election of George McGovern as president of the United States.

When McGovern won the California Primary, on June 6, she believed it could happen. When he was nominated at the Democratic Convention in Miami, she believed the end of the war was in sight and a new day for America was possible. When Nixon trounced McGovern and won a second term as president, taking 48 of the 50 states, Mai blamed Michael. She also never voted again. When Michael left for Sacramento to work on Governor Reagan's staff, George McGovern stayed in Oakland with Mai, on the refrigerator.

Chapter 27

Brian

IT WAS 1974 and he was where he loved to be—in the face of America. In front of a bank of microphones, with the television cameras rolling.

> We have today filed a multimillion-dollar civil rights lawsuit against the Chicago Police Department for the wrongful death of Emanuel Jackson, and for the violation of the constitutional rights of the Black Panther Party.

Brian Jacobs was flanked by a group of young black men, standing at the equivalent of parade rest, their black berets slightly tipped to one side, their matching black leather coats picking up the camera lights of the mid-morning press conference. Timed to make the noon and five o'clock news, and commuter traffic radio.

The parents of the deceased, the usual plaintiffs in a wrongful death case, were not present. The father was a crack addict, serving time at the moment; the mother had expressed no interest in Emanuel but consented to the use of her name if it meant she might recover some money out of the suit.

> As you know, charges against all those arrested in the police attack upon the Black Panther headquarters were dismissed because of the violation of their constitutional rights by the police. So we have come here, to the U.S. District Court for the Northern District of Illinois, to bring the police and the city of Chicago to justice under the Constitution.

Brian gestured toward the federal court, the backdrop he had selected for the announcement. Then he worked up to what he knew would be the "lead-in," the quoted line capturing its content. He was handing the media what they wanted. He paused so the sound clip would be clean:

This was a legal lynching. That's why we have filed suit under the Ku Klux Klan laws against the Chicago Police Department.

Five seconds. Perfect.

Shelly paused also, so as not to step on Brian's lines, then stepped forward with a handout to the press. It provided all of the details of the attack on the Panther headquarters, the seizure of literature, and the shootout that had left Emanuel Jackson dead, three other Panthers injured, and four police officers wounded. In the ensuing criminal prosecution, the search and the seizure of pamphlets had been held to be violative of the First and Fourth Amendments to the U.S. Constitution. The shooting by the Panthers was held to be in self-defense, in response to an illegal entry and threat of imminent harm to them by the police. Having won the freedom of the Panthers, Brian was on the offensive. Not only would Chicago have to lick its wounds, it would have to pay the Panthers, and Brian Jacobs.

Brian knew his civil rights case would never go to trial. After he won the constitutional ruling on the conduct of the police, it was all over. The city would have negotiated and settled without a suit. But then, Brian would never have had his press conference.

He had been trained well. The news teasers did not disappoint him. "Today, in a multimillion-dollar lawsuit filed in federal court, an attorney compared the Chicago Police Department to the Ku Klux Klan. Film at 11."

"Public interest litigation is, first, public," he told a conference of budding young lawyers eager to hear the latest star on the national Movement stage, a month later in San Francisco.

If you want to be a lawyer, confine yourself to the courtroom. If you want to be a Movement lawyer, take your case to the streets. Your job is to change a society, not move a judge. Sometimes, you even have to lose in order to win and show the absurdity of the law. It is not about winning cases and, as you can tell from these clothes I am wearing, it definitely is not about making money.

That always drew a laugh. His clothes looked threadbare. But then that always seemed to help his opponents underestimate his abilities. It was also the look that best fit at liberal fundraisers. A little quirky. A little intellectual. Generally leftist. One who believes in The Cause.

"Mr. Jacobs, how can it not be about money when you file multimillion-dollar lawsuits?" asked one of the young lawyers, apparently hopeful that a career committed to The Cause could yet be profitable.

Brian smiled. "Do you really think we would make the 11 o'clock news if we sued for $10,000? This society and its media measure news in dollars. The more dollars, the bigger the story."

"But when you settle…"

Brian cut him off. "The filing of a lawsuit is the news. Speech is most effective at its 'propitious moment.' For the media, the propitious moment is the filing of the lawsuit. That's when it's news. That's when it's fresh. Most of the time, all you are ever going to see or hear about is the filing of the lawsuit. No one is going to care five years from now, after a trial, and an appeal, that another nigger was shot in Chicago. That's history—not current events."

The audience of exclusively young white lawyers was shocked by his use of the term for Negroes. He rarely used it. But when he did, it was for shock effect and only in the presence of white liberals, or white judges and white district attorneys, and, in the latter instances, when he was quoting a police officer using the term about his clients. Then, he relished it, spit it back to the witness, judge, or prosecutor, repeating it until everyone in authority was clearly uncomfortable.

When he helped attorney Charles Garry, in law school and shortly after, on the Huey Newton case, he had spent a lot of time with the Black Panthers. A white boy riding around East Oakland with the Panthers, he came to enjoy their company, talk their talk, drink "Panther Piss"—take cheap warm red wine, add lemon concentrate, shake, and pass the bottle—and fear white policemen patrolling like a colonial power. In the home of David Hilliard, the Panthers' Chief of Staff, he had sipped straight whiskey on the rocks—his first time ever—and laughed at jokes about "the white boy" choking on the whiskey, and politely smiled as they conversed with each other, starting each sentence with "nigger, you…" He understood "white boy" had its limits. He did not call no Panther "nigger."

I am accused of just seeking publicity. Of being hysterical for the camera. I called the murder of the Black Panthers in Chicago a "legal lynching." That made the headlines and my brethren in the law called it "inflammatory speech." They want "reasoned discourse." Reasoned discourse doesn't make the 11 o'clock news. But to those who want reason, I say, the term "legal lynching" is, in fact, the genesis of the Fourteenth Amendment to the U.S. Constitution and to the civil rights laws, including the Ku Klux Klan Act, passed after the Civil War.

In the period between 1866 and 1875, Congress understood, like no Congress since has, that it wasn't enough to end slavery; freedom required affirmative action to end the incidents of slavery. Congress passed the Ku Klux Klan Act making it illegal—a federal crime—for persons "to conspire together, or go in disguise upon the public highway or upon the premises of another for the purpose...of depriving any person or class of persons of the equal protection of the laws or equal privileges or immunities under the law." State law enforcement officers who failed to protect persons subjected to abuse were themselves liable for damages. These statutes had in mind the lynching and mob violence then targeting not only freed blacks, but their white supporters in the South. Black slaves were freed by the Thirteenth Amendment, but a lynched black man benefitted little by his freedom. So the federal Congress, in a *revolutionary* act, nationalized—*nationalized*—the rights of every citizen with these protective laws. Unfortunately, in the years that followed, the U.S. Supreme Court struck down the true intent of these laws and restricted the Fourteenth Amendment to apply not as a pronouncement of every citizen's rights, but as a restriction on state action. This allowed for over 100 years of "state rights" and continued segregation and repression of the "freed" slaves and their progeny that Congress had sought to end by these laws.

The anti-slavery origins of the Fourteenth Amendment are well documented—for those of you who would like to read further—in the scholarly work of the legendary Professor Tenbroc of the University of California, Berkeley.

So when I say "legal lynching" and invoke the Ku Klux Klan Act of 1871, I do so with an awareness of a history lost upon my fellow members of the establishment Bar and to warn any uniformed gov-

ernment official, or accomplice, "going about in disguise upon the
public highway" or elsewhere, that if you deprive any citizen of his
rights on account of race, then these laws were meant for you. When
a black man is shot in his home by the police on account of his skin
color, it is an incident of slavery, a legacy we have inherited and one
I wish to thrust in the face of America. Hence, the Ku Klux Klan Act.
It is no accident on my part and, in my opinion, no stretch of history
or jurisprudence, that I invoke laws designed to combat the incidents of slavery.

He paused and looked around the room, making eye contact. "So let's
be honest. Or, if you prefer, let's call a spade a spade."

Brian and Shelly had spent almost four years, by the time of the Emanuel
Jackson suit, on the road. It had started with "just helping" Charles Garry
in Oakland. Then came the Chicago Seven trial that brought Garry and
radical attorney William Kunstler together to "defend" leaders of the anti-
war protests at the 1968 Democratic Convention in Chicago. Garry and
Kunstler did not "defend"; they attacked. In short order, they took control
of the courtroom and public opinion, and put the government and judicial system on trial. Brian spent as much time writing press releases as legal
briefs, both of which he did with passion and convincing arguments.

Following the Chicago trial, he was occupied with police attacks on
the Black Panthers in Los Angeles, and again in Chicago. In between, he
and Shelly went to New York with a group of radical lawyers to try to
mediate the Attica prison riots. Again, William Kunstler was there. Brian
was with him the morning of September 13, 1971, when negotiations
failed and the State of New York authorized a full-scale attack in which
guards systematically killed, tortured, and brutalized the rioting black prisoners.

Brian and Shelly stayed on in New York, living in a spare room at
Kunstler's house, while Shelly wrote press releases and Brian worked on
coordinating the numerous cases and volunteer attorneys throughout the
country who looked to Kunstler for help in radical causes. Often, he would
be the lead attorney at trials in the far-flung network of radical causes, but
in Black Panther trials he was lead attorney only if Charles Garry was unavailable.

Finally, in the fall of 1973, Brian and Shelly started back to California,
only to be side-tracked at Pine Ridge, South Dakota. Kunstler had asked

them to just "stop in." They stopped, then stayed, on the Indian reservation, living out of their car and a lean-to tent till the spring. They did not feel particularly safe or comforted by the fact that they were surrounded by federal marshals, FBI and Bureau of Indian Affairs agents, police, state troopers, and National Guard troops. The stand-off would become known as the Second Siege at Wounded Knee.

After four years on the road, staying at the homes of volunteer attorneys, progressive members of the community, or just a motel when they wanted to be alone, Shelly and Brian finally returned to California. They had no assets other than the car and Brian's national reputation as an effective advocate for just about every group generally disliked by the public. This gave him a phone directory of names in every major city in the United States of people who wanted his services (usually free) and were willing to put him up for a few nights.

For Brian, it was exactly where he believed he needed to be. At the head of the charge; in front of the troops; visible. Not a tactician behind the lines; not a lawyer sitting in an office; not a revolutionary limited geographically if the fight was elsewhere.

Shelly wanted a child. She wanted a home. After four years of handing out his press releases, she wanted some recognition too. But mostly, she wanted a child.

"Los Angeles," she told him.

"Why L.A.?"

"Well…" She had thought it through. "If you are going to actually practice law, that means California, unless you want to start studying all over again for a Bar exam, followed by a fight over your 'fitness' to practice law."

He had taken the California Bar after graduating from Boalt Hall, as had almost everyone else in the class. Since each state has its own unique exam based upon its own laws, it made sense for a California law school graduate to take the exam on the state law most familiar to him. In going before courts in other states, for an individual case, from time to time he had been admitted *pro hac vice*—for the case—generally associated with a member of that state's bar. This is how he had appeared in dozens of other state courts. In the federal court system, he had "been admitted to practice" before each court on the nomination of a practicing, previously admitted member of that court. The archaic procedure was *pro forma* and essentially an excuse for each court to charge $25 "admission" to exert the dominion over an attorney's body as only a federal judge could.

But opening an office and hanging out a shingle required being a member of the Bar of the state in which he was to practice.

"Okay. California. But why L.A.?" he asked.

"Because there is no other city in California big enough for your ego."

"You mean my national reputation?"

"And it's the top media market in California and the sixth largest in the country," she continued, "so that should take care of both your national reputation and your ego."

"Fine, smart ass. The first press conference I'll call when we get there will be to announce, 'Mrs. Shelly Jacobs, wife of nationally prominent attorney Brian Jacobs, was knocked up somewhere between Pine Ridge, South Dakota, and Los Angeles.'"

"If you are planning on 'knocking me up,' you are going to have to do it between something other than two cities. Besides, with my IUD it is not likely. I mean, Brian, you are good, but in the fight between sperm and copper, copper wins most every time. But no harm in practicing for the time when we can actually afford a child."

A look of surprise. "I didn't know you had an IUD."

"Brian, what did you think I used for protection?"

"I don't know. I never really thought about it. I just figured we did something. The pill, I guess. We never talked about it."

"Right. It was my responsibility."

"Well, you're the one who would get pregnant."

"That's why I got it. You think I trust some guy to have condoms?"

"Some guy? What guy?"

"I mean in college when I had it inserted."

"What guy? Or are we talking a whole bunch here?"

"Brian, it was before I met you. Although I don't recall you ever having condoms either."

"Well, I didn't think you were that kind of girl."

"What kind? The type who would sleep with you?" Now she was getting indignant. "Why are you interrogating me, anyway? You must have had girlfriends before you met me."

"Yeah, but none who were going to be the mother of my child."

"Brian, I wasn't a virgin. I don't understand." She looked at him. He looked away.

"Oh, my God, Brian. You were! How could I not have known?"

Defensive and embarrassed, Brian responded, "Well, I thought I handled myself pretty well our first time. I guess I just thought it was *our* first time, not just mine."

She broke out laughing. She could not help herself, she grabbed him and pulled him to her, petting his head.

"Oh, Brian, I will be so much more gentle with you now that I know."

"You had better. This is my first pregnancy, too!"

Chapter 28

Leon

HE SAW HER, sitting in the crowded waiting room: her clothes, 20 years out of style, neatly ironed; her purse on her lap; her gray hair curled; her makeup too obvious. She looked to be in her early 70s. She carried herself with the same dignity, he suspected, as when the clothes were new and her neighborhood was white. She was the first to arrive and sign in on the sheet that now bore the name of four other people.

Leon Goldman, "Supervising Attorney" of the Alameda County Legal Aid office on San Pablo Avenue, started the daily sign-up system for clients. After a year of having tried to run the center like a private law office, he had given up. "Poor people," he had argued to his board, "don't function by appointment."

Leon did not bother going into his office before meeting his first client. There was no reason to believe it was any different than the way he had left it the evening before: the same metal table, the metal file cabinet, the two wooden chairs under the ceiling with missing tiles in the windowless room. When he had a scheduled appointment system, he would walk out of his office and down the narrow corridor that led to the waiting area, and more often than not, find, in the crowded room, no "Mrs. Jackson" or "Mr. Hall." Now, he was almost always guaranteed a "Next" who would be waiting for his legal assistance.

He looked at the sheet: "Mrs. Pawloski?"

He turned and, as expected, the elderly white woman rose.

"How do you do? I am Leon Goldman, Supervising Attorney. Why don't you come back to my office with me." His hair was still shoulder-length, his goatee in place, and, unlike his classmates in private practice, he did not wear a jacket or tie. His clients did not mind; they had no alternative.

He was the only attorney at the San Pablo Avenue office, which made him the Supervising Attorney. Most of the clients were seen by law students designated as "Housing Specialists" or "Welfare Specialists," depending on the nature of the problem described in the phone intake sheet. If the caller actually showed up at the office, the intake sheet went with the client to the room.

While Leon supervised all of the work, he made it a point to spend two mornings a week doing "drop-ins," to keep "in touch," he told himself. But after just a year, he was beginning to see the futility, as his father had argued, of bandaging the individual casualties of the capitalist system.

"Are you changing anything? You fight for a tenant here, a patient there. But the system grinds on. You are just a medic helping the casualties back onto their feet to keep the system running."

"Mrs. Pawloski," Leon began after reading the letter from the Alameda County Welfare Department, "the reason they have cut off your medical benefits is because your assets exceed the state guidelines."

"But I need to see the doctor every month for my lupus and for my prescriptions. I've got only a small pension from my husband's work for the railroad. I mean, I don't believe in people getting something for nothing, but we have worked hard all our lives. I don't have the money to pay for the doctor or the prescriptions."

"The problem isn't your income, Mrs. Pawloski, it's your assets."

"I don't even own a house. I just live with my daughter and give what I can toward the food."

"How old is your daughter, Mrs. Pawloski?"

"Forty."

"Is she in good health?"

"Yes, why?"

He knew what he was about to say would upset her. "Well, the regulation that is causing the problem deals with burial plots. You have a half interest in a burial plot listed on this worksheet from the Welfare Department."

It did upset her. Perhaps it was the memory of her husband.

"Mr. Pawloski got that from the Knights of Columbus. He is buried there. When I die, we will lie together at St. Philomenes Cemetery. It's already paid for!"

"Since it's already paid for, the welfare regulations say it's an asset, and they put a value of $1,200 on it, which puts your assets over the maximum allowable."

Mrs. Pawloski began to cry. "But I can't sell it. I want to lie beside my husband when I die. Who else would want to buy that plot? What am I supposed to do, drop dead on the street and be hauled to the dump? It's not right to punish people for taking measures to see that they are suitably buried."

She was embarrassed over her own outburst and tears. He was uncomfortable with both but agreed with her sentiments about wealth and poverty in America.

"Let me suggest something to you, Mrs. Pawloski," he said. "Go home. Talk to your daughter. What's her name?"

"Helen."

"Tell Helen you are selling her your burial plot for $600."

Mrs. Pawloski looked alarmed. "But I can't do that."

"Then," he continued, "you tell her that when you die, you want her to bury you in that plot. Okay?"

Mrs. Pawloski was not sure how she could sell her plot and be buried in it.

"And you also tell her that if she dies first, you are not going to bury her there."

"But how do I get it back?" Mrs. Pawloski asked.

"Tell her to write a handwritten will, leaving the plot to you."

Mrs. Pawloski looked concerned. "Will it work?"

"Yes. It's all legal," Leon assured her.

"But what do I do with the $600 my daughter pays me? I have to report it."

"Yes, but you tell your eligibility worker that you paid it back to your daughter for back rent, which you will do, so your daughter is out nothing."

Mrs. Pawloski shook her head. "Can I tell you something, Mr. Goldman? I have been a Republican all my life. But this just isn't right what they are doing to us old people. It just isn't right."

"No, it isn't, Mrs. Pawloski. But it's the law, and we're just using it back at them. If you have any problems getting your eligibility back, just call me."

She got up and exited the door that he held open for her. She did not say "thank you." Not that she was not grateful. More likely, she had had enough of the law for one day.

*　　*　　*　　*　　*

"You mean 'black people,' don't you, Mr. Gold Man? Black people can't be trusted to keep a a-point-munt!"

The tone, accusatory, surprised Leon. He was simply reporting to his board on changes, after one year, that he had instituted to better serve the community. The open list sign-up sheet was just one. Another change was the use of "clinics" to address problems common to a large number of clients. A "clinic" for landlord-tenant problems; a "clinic" for welfare rights issues; even a "clinic"—really a cooperative—to assist with child care.

The accusation came from Angela Africa, executive director of the Oakland Fair Housing Commission, who was attending the meeting of the board of the Alameda County Legal Aid Society to make a presentation later on the agenda. She was not a member of the board, most of whom were white attorneys. Her own agenda item dealt with discrimination in housing and a request for collaboration between the Legal Aid Society and the Alameda County Fair Housing Commission. "Request" was not something Angela Africa did. She demanded, confronted, accused, shocked, embarrassed, and shamed. It was a style of leadership that gave her credibility in the black community and was most effective with liberals who carried heavily the guilt of racism in America. In the Bay Area, she was on fertile ground. Her anger was genuine, but it was not personal hostility. Rather, it was a mixture of historical analysis and political calculation.

"And black people got to go to some 'clinic' like they got some loathsome diseases or somethin'. Do da white people over in San Fran Cisco, do they got to go to a clinic or do they get a 'a-point-munt' to see they's 'a-turn-ney' in private, Mr. Gold Man?"

No one had ever addressed him this way or suggested that he treated Negroes any differently than any other person. But Angela Africa was rolling now.

"And what's this child care shit? I thought this here was Legal Aid, not baby aid. You 'spect we go'n bring our babies down here so they can be raised by some white folk? What's that 'bout? We need legal rep-prez-sen-tasion, not baby raz-in."

"Miss Africa," the board chairman interrupted, "the board is receiving a report, an internal report, on operations. It's really out of order for you, a non–board member, to be—"

"Oh, so now I iz out of order 'cus I question treatin' black folk like second-class citizens?"

"Could I answer Ms. Africa since I am the one who instituted these procedures?" Leon asked the board chairman. He stood to address her. As he did, she lifted her head back so as to be, again, looking down her nose through her glasses at him.

"Ms. Africa, poor people, all poor people, not just black people, have a problem with appointments because they often don't have cars; they have to rely on friends or neighbors or public transportation for a ride. Often they don't have child care or someone to help if a child is sick or can't go to school. They have less control over their work schedules, if they work. Many don't have a phone to call and reschedule, if a problem arises."

"So," she interrupted, "you set up a waitin' list where theys have to come in and just wait. Like theys has nothing else to do all day 'cept to wait on some white lawyer to tell them their rights?"

"Look, Ms. Africa, I'm sorry I'm white but..."

"You should be! Why do you think all these black people come to see you? Because they like you? They can't afford any better than a Legal Aid lawyer and it's the white society that holds them down but gives them you. Now ain't that a co-in-sa-dance."

Then she added, as if an afterthought, "And why's you arranging babysittin' here?"

"We are not babysitting here. We are just trying to network and free up mothers so they can support themselves with work and—"

"Work! Work! Why should they have to work? Don't you think they should be home raz-in' their babies? Like white women? Are you married, Mr. Gold Man?"

"No, but—"

"And I bet you don't ride no public trans-po-tation. And I bet you haven't had no apartment manager tell you 'we got no vacancies for your kind,' have you, Mr. Gold Man?"

"No, but—"

"Well, Mr. Gold Man, we's go'n take you out of those offices and take you to the streets. I'm going to see to it, personally. You is go'n get an ed-you-kay-shon, Mr. Gold Man, door to door, all over Oakland. Then we's count how many times they slam the doe in my black face and how many times they invite your white heinie in to rent. Deal?"

With that, Angela Africa had, before her agenda item came up, convinced the board that it had no choice but to support her housing discrimination investigation. Leon was in the uncomfortable position of having a "client" telling the "Supervising Attorney" how to practice law. Her way.

Leon caught up with her in the parking lot after the meeting.

"Miss Africa."

She was walking with two young women to a waiting car, music blaring, a black male behind the wheel and two others sitting in the back sharing a paper bag. She ignored him.

"Miss Africa."

The two girls turned to look. The men in the car looked past Angela and at him. Angela Africa paid him no attention.

"You gonna share that shit?" she asked one of the men in the backseat as she reached in for the bag. She took a swig of the sweet Southern Comfort. The two girls got in the car, still eyeing Leon.

"Let's go party. I'll follow you." With that the car roared off. Angela turned to Leon. "What the fuck is your problem?"

"Miss Africa, I don't know what the problem is, but the only two times you have even deigned to direct anything at me it has been abuse. Have I offended you?"

"Yeah, you 'o-fend-ded' me. For 300 years you have been 'o-fendin'' me."

She walked to her car, got in, and started it. She took off but abruptly stopped, put the car in reverse, and came back to where he was standing in the parking lot.

"And don't you ever approach me without an invitation when I am talking with my people. You want to talk to me, make a 'a-point-munt.' I got no sign-up sheets for white people to sit around waitin' for my ass."

With that, she drove off. She felt she had done a good night's work. She knew Leon, a Boalt Hall graduate, could be making two or three times the starting salary of a Legal Aid attorney. After their confrontation, where she had challenged his commitment, she knew he would bend over back-wards to prove himself. She had herself a top flight lawyer.

*   *   *   *   *

He waited a week. Fumed for a week. Thought about her for a week. Then he called to make an 'a-point-munt' with Angela Africa. She kept him waiting. He could hear her on the phone, shouting, laughing…"tell him to kiss my black ass…the governor's a motherfucker…you bring those ebony babies in here, you hear girl, or I am goin' to come and steal 'um."

When he was finally led into her office, she looked over her glasses, frowned and asked, sarcastically, "What you want?"

"Miss Africa…"

"And what's that Miss, shit? Save that for the white girls."

"What do you want me to call you?"

"Nothin'. I don't want you to call me. You got something to say, just say it."

"Look," he demanded in exasperation, "you came to my board de-manding our help. I didn't come to you. If we are going to work together—"

She interrupted: "Who says we iz going to 'work together'?"

"Well, your proposal to jointly study discrimination practices in Oak-land."

"Study? Study. I don't need no study. I know these white people is dis-crim-in-a-tin!"

"What do you want Legal Aid to do?" he asked.

"I am Director of the Fair Housing Commission. They gave me no lawyers. We get a complaint, we s'pose to 'mediate' it. I am sick of mediatin' with racists. I want to sue the motherfuckers. And I want you to do it for me 'cause you iz the lawyer."

"Can I ask you something?"

"What now?"

"You have a master's degree in journalism from Columbia, right?"

"So?" She was impressed that he had taken the time to do some re-search about her.

"So, why do you talk like that?"

She looked at him. "Let me ask you something, Mr. Goldman. Why do you talk like that?"

"Like what?" Leon asked.

161

"Like a white person."

She paused to let her remark sink in. When she resumed, it was in softer tones: "Leon, you have an undergraduate degree in history from Berkeley. You went to Boalt Hall. In a few years, you will go back to your white society, having done your bit for conscience. I will still be here in Oakland. I will still be here, with my people. I will still be black."

He was embarrassed, again.

"So, Leon, excuse me if I forget to talk white."

It was partly true. He had the choice to leave. To reenter white society. But Angela had also made a choice to work in the poor black areas of Oakland. She was not, for all her rhetoric, from the ghetto. She was raised in a middle class home and attended predominantly white schools. Her father, a teacher, was also the track coach of her high school. He had gone to college on a track scholarship and coached Olympian long jumper Ralph Boston, the first man to jump over 26 feet in competition. In high school, Angela herself had been a track star, in the 100 and 200, and in the 400-meter relay. The white kids said it was "natural ability." She had a revelation: "Yeah; we are better."

It was this revelation that made her search out a black identity. She enrolled at Spellman College, in Atlanta, not to run track but to understand "her people." She discovered W. E. B. DuBois, born in 1868, the first black man to receive a doctorate from Harvard, a founder of the NAACP, and a prolific writer on the international implications of the struggle for racial justice. Rather than seek compromise, Dr. DuBois argued that since the world was disproportionately nonwhite, the future world would be, in all probability, what people of color made it. Knowing and believing in this future inevitability, DuBois was a black person confronting white society in uncompromising language. Ironically, DuBois believed that the struggle for equality would not be achieved through black dominance of capitalism, but—like Leon's father—an end to capitalism.

In Atlanta, Angela met Wesley Brown, a student at nearby Morehouse College. His parents were affluent and well-established in Atlanta's black society. Unfortunately, she found, after a year of marriage, this meant he could indulge in whatever recreational drugs he wanted. She had no patience with anyone wasting his life—or her time. Her divorce and bachelor's degree—the latter with honors—were conferred in the same month.

She went on to Columbia University, by which she was aggressively recruited, for a master's in journalism. It was while at Columbia, doing research on Dr. DuBois, that she first traveled to Africa. In Ghana, at the site of DuBois' entombment, in sight of Castle Osu and old Christianborg, from which millions of African slaves set sail across the Atlantic, Angela Brown became Angela Africa.

After Columbia, she landed a job at the *Oakland Tribune*. A black woman journalist at the *Oakland Tribune* was an anomaly. She turned it into an asset. With her loud clothes, crafted black populist dialect, and "Angela Africa" byline, she soon had entree to the political and civic scene of Oakland.

But if her speech was affected, her politics and commitment were unequivocal. Like W. E. B. DuBois, she, too, saw history—particularly American history—in terms of exploitation. Not just economic exploitation, but human—black—exploitation. It was not just theory to her. As a black woman, she took it personally.

Like Leon, Angela had choices. Most of the time, when dealing with whites, she chose to be black.

Chapter 29

Brian

THEY CALLED THE firm Jacobs and Associates, but it was just him, a receptionist-typist, and Shelly as a part-time paralegal. To supplement his income, he taught nights in a clinical program at UCLA Law School and was able to get much of the firm's legal research done by the enthusiastic law students. They, too, wanted to be involved in causes and use the law to fight injustice. They, too, had no business sense. If a destitute black family called for Brian's help, especially in a death penalty case, he would leave a paying drunk-driving client and fly halfway across the country, if necessary, and live in a motel for weeks at a time. Shelly would be left to find a source of financial assistance, perhaps through the NAACP Legal Defense Fund, the Death Penalty Project, the ACLU, or others who would help defray some of the costs. Brian's national reputation did have one benefit. Los Angeles, was, at least, a fertile fundraising ground for legal defense of radical causes. One month it might be the "Atlanta 5," next it would be the "San Quentin 7 " or whatever cause was "in." Even Brian and Shelly had to laugh at white guys with Afros, Nehru jackets, or peace symbols, assisting impeccably fashioned females out of Porsches.

Between causes, Brian would pick up court appointments in less political criminal cases. He believed the criminal justice system was, by definition, political. Since most of these appointed cases were drug busts or, as Brian called them, "Fourth Amendment violations," Brian's earlier work on behalf of the Black Panthers served him well.

The First Amendment, Brian found, also had a special value in Hollywood that went beyond political speech. When the District Attorney of Los Angeles County decided to run for office on a platform of shutting down "smut" in L.A., he ran smack into Brian and his federal lawsuit striking down prior restraints on First Amendment speech and seeking damages

164

from the county for illegal seizure of constitutionally protected material. The laws of pornography were so hopelessly confused that there was little chance that a public lawyer, especially a deputy district attorney who left the office early for softball practice three days a week, could expect to write an ordinance or seek an injunction that could not be successfully challenged by a good civil rights advocate. Brian Jacobs was one of the best. If a Supreme Court justice was forced, in frustration, to say of pornography that he could not define it, but he knew it when he saw it, Brian's job was to challenge the seizures of obscene material to ensure that no judge ever saw it. When confronted, on one occasion, with the question, "Does your client's film have any redeeming social value?" he answered, "Sure, judge. It keeps the perverts off the streets of Los Angeles for an hour-and-a-half."

Brian's "constitutional law" scholarship did not go unnoticed. In Los Angeles, free speech, free expression, and bodily freedom represented the pursuits and pleasures of not just perverts and pimps, but those in the movies and associated with the film industry. Paying clients.

Brian, true to form, practiced with flair. In one widely reported case of a client who had "allegedly" brought three tons of marijuana into Los Angeles Harbor on a stolen yacht, Brian successfully argued that the police had illegally seized the evidence. The D.A. dropped the charges and dismissed the case. None of this made the news. What made the news was the lawsuit Brian filed thereafter against the City of Los Angeles for the return of the illegally seized evidence—the 60-foot yacht—that his client had stolen "fair and square."

It only took one person in the circle of Hollywood celebrities to be successfully represented by Brian before he became the lawyer of choice whenever a celebrity or the child of a celebrity was arrested on drug charges. On the first couple of cases, his picture appeared in the *Los Angeles Times* with the celebrity at the first court appearance (or rather, the press conference following the court appearance). In time, he was called so early that he was often pictured with the celebrity as they rode together from the scene of the arrest to the police station.

L.A. being the town that it is, Brian would be permitted to delay departure of the police vehicle with his client until he concluded his press conference wherein he invariably professed the innocence of his client and referred to the police conduct as "shameful" or as "an attack upon the privacy guaranteed by the Constitution." In deference to his growing reputation, and probably in the hopes of an autograph from his client, the police would often politely inquire, "Will you be riding with us, Mr. Jacobs?"

With equal courtesy, he would answer, "Yes, thank you, officer."

So would begin another chapter in celebrity law and the protection of the fundamental rights inscribed in the Constitution of the United States for which Brian had received the finest legal education California could offer.

With a growing case load and the recognition that Brian had no concept of, or interest in, running a business, Shelly urged him to hire another lawyer. Jacobs and Associates hired a young lawyer, Paul Zarik, and, at the same time, a full-time paralegal. Paul had been a staff attorney with the ACLU of Southern California for two years, having spent his first year at the prestigious O'Melveny and Myers firm, after graduating from UCLA Law School with honors.

Paul was a native of Los Angeles, a very aggressive attorney, but with practical experience in private practice and a sense of how an office should be run. After the first "office meeting," Paul took over management. The paralegal was assigned the task of coordinating all of the law students who seemed to wander around the office at all times, often just hanging out and doing their homework. A real clinical program was established where assignments were handed out, deadlines set, and a designated third-year student given responsibility for the overall handling of a file, under the supervision of Brian or Paul.

Shelly was relieved to finally get out of the office, having assigned her duties to the new paralegal. She had been taking classes for her teaching credential and was starting practice teaching. She had also taken a few classes toward her M.A. degree in child psychology. She had decided to teach in the primary grades. She explained to Brian her feelings: "I am giving up on the grown-ups. You fight those battles. I am going to get the kids when they are little, six or seven, before they learn to hate. While there is still a chance for them. You have your great cases; the kids will be my legacy."

Now, when Brian heard a call from afar, and was gone, the office kept functioning under Paul. Shelly and the staff would always know where he was and what he was doing, most often by checking the evening news or by his frantic calls for research assigned to the law students. He was still where he wanted to be but at least making a living, too.

Chapter 30

Brian

"WHAT DO YOU mean, Governor Reagan won't be there? It's a clemency hearing for Christ's sake!"

Brian was trying to restrain himself. He had less than 30 days. His client was scheduled to die on October 15, 1974.

"Mr. Meese is the governor's legal affairs secretary and handles clemency matters. He will be handling the hearing, Mr. Jacobs," the secretary replied curtly.

"That's ridiculous. A man's life is at stake and the governor isn't going to be present at the clemency hearing?"

Who was he talking to? he thought. A secretary to the legal affairs secretary. Jesus!

"May I speak to the governor, please?"

"No."

"Is Mr. Meese in?"

"No."

"Is there anyone running the state?"

"Of course. The lieutenant governor, Mr. Reinecke."

"Is he in?"

"He is not involved in clemency."

"Apparently," Brian said with some cynicism, "the governor isn't either. Who is?"

"Mr. Meese."

Full circle. "Does Mr. Meese have an assistant?"

"Yes."

"May I speak to him?"

"Just a moment."

167

After a long delay, enough to read through a third of Brian's client's rap sheet before he shot the two white firemen with a high-powered rifle with a scope during the Watts riots of 1965, a voice came on the phone from the governor's office in Sacramento.

"Good morning, Brian. What can I do for you?"

"First, you can explain why the governor, who, under Article VII, Section I, of the California Constitution, is solely invested with the power of clemency, is not even going to be present for Stonewall Jackson's death penalty clemency hearing."

"Well, Brian, of all people I would expect you to be familiar with the governor's policy in these matters. I am sure you have read the article on clemency in the *California Law Review*. I think the cite is 55 Cal.L.Rev. 412 (1968). The governor made it very clear that he exercises the ultimate authority but relies upon his legal affairs secretary to gather the information and make a recommendation."

"And he can order people to their death without ever meeting them. Is that what you are telling me?" asked Brian.

"Now, Brian, I am not telling you anything. So don't quote me to that effect in one of your press releases."

"Could you, for the record," asked Brian, "tell me why the governor refuses to attend the clemency hearing?"

"Yes. The governor feels that since he is not an attorney, it is best to have his legal affairs secretary, Mr. Meese, handle this portion of information gathering in the clemency process."

"Does the governor understand that the 12 people who put Mr. Jackson on death row, the jury, were not attorneys either?"

"Yes, Brian. The governor understands that a unanimous jury of citizens convicted your client and unanimously decided that he deserves the death penalty. He also trusts that Mr. Meese will marshal and assess all facts and legal arguments for the governor's final decision."

"But he refuses to even meet the person he will condemn to die?"

"Brian, Governor Reagan did not condemn your client to die. A jury did. If anyone is responsible for his plight, it is your client, not the governor."

"If that is how he feels, why doesn't he just go over to San Quentin and throw the switch himself?"

"Brian, come on. The governor does not attend executions. He does not get personally involved. It is not political. He does his constitutional duty. Others do theirs. I know you will do yours."

Brian realized this speaker acted familiar and had called him by his first name throughout the conversation.

"Have we met?" Brian asked.

"I am sorry, Brian, I assumed you had asked for me when you called. This is Michael Cassidy. We were at Boalt together."

"Cassidy?" Brian searched his memory, turning card files in his mind. "Cassidy. The guy who didn't read the *Palsgraf* case because his wife had a baby!"

"Right, my son."

"What's his name?" asked Brian. He had tried confrontation and had gotten nowhere. Now he switched to friendly persuasion.

"Robert. Robert F. Cassidy."

"Robert F.? I thought you were a Republican."

"Not after Kennedy."

Michael did not volunteer that it was Robert Fong Cassidy.

"Remember Mike Marcus and Paul Harris in our class?" asked Brian.

"Of course. Law review."

"Well, since you mentioned the *California Law Review*, I am going to send you copies of their articles from the review. Michael's showed the discriminatory application of the death penalty to blacks. Paul's article is more sociological. Perhaps it would give the governor a little understanding of why blacks are disproportionately on death row. Michael, you went to Boalt. You understand how the law can be used for repression or it can be used for reconciliation. I am not asking the governor to let anyone go free, just to prevent one more murder of a black man in this society. It is really true, Michael, in America at this point in history, 'you're either part of the problem or part of the solution.'"

Michael Cassidy felt very uncomfortable. It was not just the feeling that the best and the brightest in his class were lining up against his views. He had weathered that at Berkeley for three years. No, it was "you're either part of the problem or part of the solution." Mai had said those exact words to him two years before, when she refused to join him in Sacramento and suggested a separation.

For two years, he had driven Highway 80, early Saturday mornings, to Oakland to pick up his son Robbie and return to his small apartment in downtown Sacramento, a few blocks from Capitol Park, which was his son's favorite playground. Even though Mai was not there, he heard her voice whenever they passed Governor Reagan's bulletproof thick glass windows: "That's to keep the squirrels away from the nuts."

Cassidy's life among the "nuts" was not made easier with the story that appeared in the *Los Angeles Times*, and was picked up by the *Sacramento Bee*, the next day. Then, it was not Brian Jacobs' job to make life easier for those who would execute his client.

The article read:

> According to Brian Jacobs, attorney for black militant Stonewall Jackson who is awaiting execution on death row unless granted clemency by Governor Reagan, "The governor refuses to do his constitutional duty and attend a clemency hearing for Stonewall Jackson. His office tells me the governor doesn't feel competent to hold the hearing. Frankly, if he doesn't feel competent to be governor, he should resign and not run around the country talking about becoming president of the United States."

It continued:

> "They also told me that Governor Reagan didn't want to get personally involved and wouldn't be handling the execution himself. The governor's staff made it clear that the governor feels that this execution is not his problem and Mr. Jackson, a black man, has it coming."
>
> Jacobs identified Michael Cassidy as the official who voiced Governor Reagan's position. Cassidy, a former Deputy District Attorney of Alameda County, is assistant to Edwin Meese, the governor's legal affairs secretary. Calls to Mr. Meese were not returned.

As Governor Reagan got off the plane in Dubuque, Iowa, and reached the doors of the airport lounge, he was confronted by ABC's Sam Donaldson who asked him, "Governor, is it true that you don't feel competent to handle a clemency hearing of a black man facing the death penalty in California?"

Another reporter asked if it was true that the only people executed in California, under Reagan, were black.

The governor was furious. He called Meese from the next campaign stop where he was helping others get elected in the November 1974 elections, building chits, all over the United States.

"Goddamn it, Ed. This has nothing to do with the color of his skin. That man deliberately shot and killed, with a high-powered rifle, two firemen doing their job, protecting life and property. With his scope, he could see their faces. Hell, if race is involved, it is a black man systematically executing law enforcement officers because they were white. He is not a black militant hero. He is a cold-blooded killer and a lawbreaker. Damn it, he *does* have it coming. And I am going to give it to him. This crap about playing politics; if I was playing politics, *I* would pull the damn switch myself. The people are fed up with rioting and lawbreaking. If I pulled the switch myself, I would probably be elected president tomorrow. This is about survival of our society, not politics."

Ed Meese delivered the message with more measured tones and with understanding: "Michael, you can't trust the press, and you certainly cannot trust a lawyer like Brian Jacobs. Our job is to enforce the law, not play to the crowds."

Michael offered to issue a press release with a true account of the conversation and the governor's position. Meese knew, however, how to deal with Brian Jacobs. He did nothing. Without a confrontation, the story died. So did Stonewall Jackson.

Chapter 31

Rose

"YOUR FATHER IS on the phone."

In the three years that Rose had worked in San Francisco, her father had never called her at work. In fact, he had never called her on the phone, anywhere. It was her mother who always called. Inevitably, her father would come on the line and ask how work was going, what cases she was handling, what major clients she had met.

"Are you sure?" she asked, as she stood and walked toward the secretary who was standing at the console with the phone in her hand.

"Yes, he said he was your father. Very heavy accent. A bit hard to understand."

Rose excused herself from the conference room and took the call in her office.

"Papá?"

He spoke immediately, in Spanish, *"¡Arrestaron a Pablo en la escuela!"* They have arrested Pablo at school!

Rose was stunned. Pablo, her brother, younger by nine years, had been arrested. He was a senior at Gonzales High School, a bright student who had never been in any trouble with the law. He was a student leader, active in student council. She thought he might be interested in law school, also.

"¿Por qué?" she asked.

Her father explained, *"Porque traia cachucha."* According to her father, Pablo had been arrested for wearing a hat. *"Regresa a casa immediatamente."* You must come home immediately.

She hesitated. She was in an important meeting—*"muy importante"*— with representatives of the city and the Sheraton Hotel on building a convention center on the Waterfront. But the importance of her meeting and the power of her clients meant nothing to her father, for once.

"Tienes que ayudar a tu hermano," he stated firmly. You must help your brother. She knew it was the end of the conversation. He had hung up. She sat at her desk and thought. Three years of multimillion-dollar bond issues, contracts, and business litigation had given her no clue as to how to deal with a high school arrest for wearing a hat. She realized it made no sense. She decided to call the school directly.

"Rose, what a pleasant surprise," came the principal's voice. "We hear you have done real well." Strange, she thought, after almost 10 years, and despite the fact that she was a professional, earning probably twice what her old principal was making, she still felt like the student.

"Mr. Parducci, my father called me and said Paul had been arrested on campus."

"No. No. Rose, Paul was not arrested. But he has been suspended, again, pending a hearing."

"Again?"

"Yes. Didn't you know? He has been making quite a point of defying school authorities. Even circulates a newspaper at school without permission."

"My father said it was because he wore a hat."

"Well, that too. He thinks he is some kind of revolutionary. He and his gang."

"Gang? What are you talking about?"

"My God, Rose. I can't believe you don't know. He has been very vocal. Calls his newspaper *La Raza* and members of his gang wear brown berets. They are affiliated with some outside group called MAYA, Mexican-American Youth something. Really has gotten people in the community quite upset. They seem to be advocating some kind of Mexican revolution here in the Valley."

"I didn't know," confessed Rose, "but why don't I talk to him. I am sure it is a big misunderstanding. He is going to graduate in June, and I can't imagine he wants to disrupt that or his college admission. Can I tell him he can come back to school on Monday if he apologizes?"

"Wish I could do that, Rose," answered the principal, "but now that the school board members are personally involved, it is out of my hands. If you had been his lawyer, I am sure it would never have gotten this far."

"Lawyer? Why does he need a lawyer? I thought this was just a problem of school rules."

"Well, Rose, that's what I thought, too. But he went and got himself a lawyer. And not just any lawyer. He got a California Rural Legal Assistance lawyer. Guy calls himself 'Zapata.' I think that's who is really behind all this. They are using Paul, just like they are using the farm workers. Cesar Chavez. CRLA. It's all the same. Now they've come into the schools, and they are using your brother and the other Mexican kids for their own purposes. You know Paul. He's a good student, just like you were, but he went off on this revolution thing, and now look where it's got him."

"Why is the school board involved?" Rose asked.

"This guy Zapata. He delivered a letter to every school board member, with a copy to the *Fresno Bee*. It's on the front page. An ultimatum. Reinstate Paul by Monday, with his beret, and let him circulate his paper, or else."

"Or else what?" she asked.

"Or, he says, he is going to federal court and suing each of the board members, and me, personally, for violation of Paul's constitutional rights. Can you believe it? Your brother is going to sue me!"

She did not admit it to the principal, but she could not believe it either. As she held the phone, she heard the voice of Justice Byron White, asking at the U.S. Supreme Court hearing in *Tinker v. Des Moines Independent Community School District*:

> But don't you think it would cause some people to direct their attention to the armband in the Vietnam War and think about that, rather than what they were supposed to be thinking about in the classroom?

"Rose, Rose. I said, your brother is going to sue me!" The principal's voice brought her back.

She hesitated. "I'll speak to him," she promised the principal as she hung up, although she had no idea what she would say to Pablo. This was not the brother she knew; these were not the actions of the type of student she had been.

Rose went back into her meeting. Her boss, J. Anthony Hawk, glanced at her. "Everything okay?"

"Yes," she replied. He continued his presentation—which she had prepared—explaining the legal requirements for a special convention center bond district that would commit the taxpayers of San Francisco to finance what private lenders were unwilling to do. For almost three years, Rose had learned the intricacies of bond law—the financing of convention centers, off-street parking structures, sports facilities, schools, and housing developments. Her firm's name on a proposed bond issue guaranteed its approval by a public entity and, more importantly, a bond rating attractive to Wall Street investors. She had appeared in front of county boards of supervisors, city councils, irrigation districts, and even school boards. Never once had she ever threatened their members with a lawsuit. She was there to facilitate, to help—never to disrupt or to challenge. While her firm was also known as a top litigation firm, its primary aim was the avoidance of litigation, not the solicitation of litigation. What was this guy Zapata thinking? What did he possibly hope to achieve by threatening? An ultimatum? My God, that will never lead to a resolution, she thought. What could possibly be worth endangering her brother's future? There must be a way out for everyone.

At noon, she told Anthony Hawk that she had an emergency at home and excused herself. "I will be in tomorrow morning," she added, although she was always in on Saturday mornings, as were all the associate attorneys, and the comment was unnecessary.

An attendant brought her car down from the building parking structure. "Leaving early?"

"Yes, got to run out of town."

"Well, have a nice weekend, Miss Contreras," he added as he closed the car door for her.

"Thanks, Jimmy."

As she headed across Market Street to catch the 101 South toward San Jose, she realized she had not been home for almost four months. At Christmas, she had only stayed three days because the San Jose Convention Center bond was being submitted to the voters again, and the firm's opinion letter had to be delivered by December 31. In fact, she drove the final draft to San Jose on Christmas Eve, and then went on to her parents' home in Gonzales. She arranged to pick up any last minute changes on December 27 and take them back to San Francisco for incorporation into the final document. When she was home for Christmas, no one had mentioned that Pablo was having any problems at school. They had only talked about how well she was doing as a lawyer.

Rose reached Gonzales late in the afternoon. Her father was sitting on the porch, alone, holding a newspaper in his lap, waiting. Her mother was in the kitchen. As Rose got out of her car, her father walked inside the house, the screen door slamming behind him, sat at the kitchen table, and spread the paper out before him, facing the empty chair. Rose walked in, kissed her mother, and sat in the empty chair across from her father. She knew her father could not read everything said about his son in the newspaper, but the mere fact that Pablo was in the paper, under the circumstances as he understood them, was distressing to him. He did not want any trouble and, already, his boss had told him that Pablo was involved with *malos hombres* and *comunistas*.

"Where is Pablo?" Rose asked, as she looked at a picture of her brother in a brown beret, looking back at her, menacingly, from the newspaper.

"With the lawyer," her mother said. Her father pushed a business card across the desk. "*Abogado.*"

The card, a rather cheap stock, Rose thought, read: "Ernesto Z. Reynoso, Abogado, California Rural Legal Assistance, 746 3rd Street, Gonzales, CA. Phone: (209) 645-4694."

She took the card and got up from the table. "I will go talk to them," she assured her parents. For the first time since she had arrived, her father's face showed something other than fear. "*Bueno, bueno, bueno,*" he said firmly.

Gonzales did not have many streets, but Rose had never noticed the CRLA office before. She found it at what she remembered to be an old dental office, a low duplex with a 6-foot by 4-foot cement landing at the front doors, at the end of a worn path across unkempt grass. A sign on one door said "California Rural Legal Assistance." On the other door a sign read: "Use other door."

The gravel driveway was completely occupied by a large 1965 Chevrolet pickup, with a homemade camper bearing a "Boycott Grapes" bumper sticker on the back door.

Rose parked on the street, walked up the path, and entered the office. While there were only a few cars on the street, the office was packed with people in a small reception area. All chairs were taken, mostly by mothers holding children. Men who looked like farm workers were standing along the walls. A receptionist was speaking on the phone, in Spanish.

Rose walked to the receptionist's desk and waited. To her left, she noticed a narrow hallway with offices on each side, just like a dentist's office. In fact, next to each door was a box to hold a file, apparently left over from the former tenant's days. They were actually in use with clipboards or files in each. At the end of the hall, she could see law books on shelves and what appeared to be a library table. In the library, on the wall facing her, was a picture of Che Guevara.

The receptionist hung up the phone and looked at Rose, who handed her a business card.

"I'm Rose Contreras. I would like to see Mr. Reynoso."

The receptionist looked at the card and started to hand it back to Rose.

"No," waved her hand. "I want you to give it to Mr. Reynoso. I am Pablo Contreras' sister. Please tell Mr. Reynoso I am here."

"*Pablo no esta,*" replied the receptionist.

"No, I didn't ask for Pablo. I want to see Mr. Reynoso. Give him my card." Rose pointed to the card in the receptionist's hand. The receptionist handed the card back.

"Look, is Mr. Reynoso here or not?" Rose demanded. Suddenly, she realized that they had been carrying on a conversation in two languages but that the receptionist only spoke one. Rose was speaking English but hearing Spanish.

From the end of the hall, she heard a voice thunder: "Zapata is in. Please come on back, Miss Contreras."

The receptionist smiled. Rose headed down the hall and into the library. At the end of the table, sitting at a manual typewriter and surrounded by books, was a very large, fully bearded man with dark hair, small wire-rimmed glasses, and a moustache that looked as if it had greasy hands recently run through it. His upper body appeared strong, not unlike that of a body builder.

Rose handed him her card.

"I am Rose Contreras, Pablo's sister. I understand you have threatened to file a lawsuit on his behalf. He is underage, and his parents do not consent. You have no authority to represent him."

The man spoke surprisingly softly. "Oh, but I do, Rosa. He is a 'person' under the Fourteenth Amendment so he has constitutional rights not dependent upon his parents—or his sister. Also, as a matter of state law, he is over 14 and able to appoint his own guardian, so, if necessary, Carmen will be appointed his guardian."

"Who is Carmen?" Rose regretted asking.

"Carmen is the paralegal you met when you came in."

"The receptionist. She doesn't even speak English."

"We call her a paralegal. More correctly an '*ayudante legal*.' But you missed the point. Do you know your history, Rosa? You live in California. Yes, that's pronounced 'Cally For-Nia,'" he said slowly, using the Spanish pronunciation.

"Under the Treaty of Guadalupe Hidalgo, when Mexico was forced to cede almost one-third of what became the United States of America, all official documents henceforth were required to be in English *and* in Spanish. Appointing Carmen as guardian *ad litem* compels the court to recognize this fact, Rosa, just to be able to communicate with her. Have you ever seen a federal judge brought down to the level of a poor Mexican, Rosa? It's wonderful."

"Look," said Rose, "I didn't come here to debate history. We don't want Pablo's future ruined by your cause. He is to graduate in June, and so far all you have accomplished is getting him expelled and causing my father a lot of anguish at home and at work. We want him back in school, not in a lawsuit."

"Your father had problems at work? Is the *patron* upset at the stirrings of the peons?"

Rose was annoyed.

"You can use all the political rhetoric you want, but it's not your butt on the line. You're just using Pablo for your cause. So what if you lose? You've got your government job. You've got your education. Do you think anyone really takes you seriously? Zapata? Leading a revolution? Come on! From your state and federally financed public employment with California Rural Legal Assistance? Why don't you take to the hills like Che Guevara here." She pointed to the poster on the wall. "Leave kids like Pablo alone. You're not a revolutionary. You're a fucking state worker with too much time on his hands."

He did not raise his voice. He almost seemed sympathetic.

"And what are you, Rosa? You're a Mexican trying to pass as something she's not. How do you feel when you see fear in the eyes of your parents because their son stands up and asks to be recognized for what he is? How do you feel when their livelihood is in the hands of someone who would fire them to repress their son?"

He broke eye contact with her at that point and dropped his eyes to the books in front of him. "You're a lawyer, right? Ever hear of *Tinker v. Des Moines Independent Community School District*?"

"I was there at the Supreme Court of the United States when the case was argued. I am very well acquainted with the case."

"Well, Rosa, do you think it doesn't apply to Mexicans? Is it, let the little white girl wear her armband in Iowa to protest the war in Vietnam, but don't let those dumb Mexicans wear berets to recognize their ethnic identity, in 'Cally For-Nia?" Again, he used the Spanish pronunciation.

"Next, they might start wanting longer handles on their hoes and something other than slums to live in while they do backbreaking work that no one else—except winos standing on street corners—can be rounded up to do."

He paused to let the significance of his legal analogy sink in.

"Your brother has done what no other Mexican in this community has ever done. He has stood up to the powers of this community, the big landowners, who run the school district. He has confronted them publicly on the front page of the *Fresno Bee*, and given them an ultimatum."

Rose saw her chance to jump in.

"Right. One that they will never accept."

"Exactly. We made sure that they couldn't accept it. If we had done it quietly—your way, I bet—with an apology and a promise to be a good Mexican, the county counsel would have told his board of education not to push it. Told them of the United States Supreme Court decision in *Tinker*. Also, by the way, there is another case, right on point from Sacramento: *Poxon v. San Juan Unified School District*." He threw a copy of a typed court opinion in front of her. She recognized it as an advance slip opinion—one so recent, it had not made it to the bound published reports yet. He was current on his research.

"From this very federal district. It says a principal cannot even require a student to submit his paper for prior censorship by the school. But you're right. When we threaten them, personally, in the newspaper, the lines are drawn. They can't back down. Not to a bunch of Mexicans."

"How does that help us?" Rose asked.

Reynoso noticed that Rose had said "us" for the first time in the conversation.

"Because we are going to take their action against your brother, toward Mexicans who seek only recognition of their ethnic identity, and shove it up their asses with the help of the Constitution and a federal judge." He said it in the same way he might have said "checkmate."

"Rosa, when your brother walks across that stage on graduation night, and he will, he will do it as a man—not as a shuffling Mexican."

Rose looked down at the books on the table in front of him.

"What are you doing now?" she asked.

"Preparing the lawsuit. The board is meeting at 9:00 A.M. on Monday to take up this matter. We will actually file, in Fresno, at approximately 9:05. The meeting will already be underway and the agenda set. There will be no going back. Then, at the end of the meeting, during the public comment period, I will go to the podium and personally serve them in open session."

"Isn't it enough that you file a lawsuit without rubbing their noses in it?" asked Rose.

"Part of the tactics. You're right. They will see it as rubbing their noses in it. It will inflame them. The press will be there. The board members are likely to say really stupid things when they are served in this manner. Talk of 'outside agitators,' 'Communists,' 'ungrateful Mexicans.' All of it will make the confrontation that much bigger, the evidence that much stronger that this is racially based, and the victory that much sweeter."

As he spoke, she noticed that for all his size and apparent strength, the full beard and messy hair that made his head appear huge, he had a soft face, an almost reassuring way of speaking, playful brown eyes, and smooth brown hands.

"Why do you call me 'Rosa'?"

He smiled. "Because you're not Irish, Rosa, you're Mexican."

She stood for a very long time, staring at the books. Then she sat and read through the *Poxon* decision that he had laid in front of her. He was right, she realized. They could not lose. How was she going to explain this to her father?

"I will help you on one condition," she found herself saying. She did not really know why she said it. Something told her she had no choice.

"I don't need your help," he answered.

"I will be on the pleadings, as guardian for my brother," she continued. "I can't be listed as co-counsel. My firm is bond counsel for Fresno County and most of the irrigation districts in the Valley."

She looked up at Reynoso and, without waiting for an answer, asked, "Where do we start?"

"Dinner," Reynoso answered.

Rose smiled and threw up her hands.

"I suppose that has to be Mexican, too?"

"Actually, I know this really good Chinese place."

"Great…Then back here to Mary Beth and Terri."

"Who?" he asked.

"Mary Beth and Terri. Didn't you notice the two landmark cases we are relying on? Both involve girls. Mary Beth Tinker and Terri Poxon. When Paul walks across that stage as a man, to use your words, it will be because of two girls."

Reynoso smiled. "You have a lot to learn about Mexican men. I suggest you not make that point again. We do have our '*machismo*,' you know."

"Zapata, huh? Well, I am going to call you Ernie."

Again, he smiled and held her eyes in his. "Then it's Ernie and Rosa."

He stood to his full height and leaned forward for balance. On both legs he wore full metal braces, held together with well-worn leather straps. He reached back to Canadian crutches that Rose had not noticed leaning against the bookshelf and attached them to his arms. He met her look of surprise.

"I don't think I would do very well taking to the mountains, as you suggested, if the revolution comes, but I could certainly be counted upon to write the Declaration of Independence."

She followed him down the hallway as he shuffled from side to side on his crutches. Everyone waiting nodded to him, it seemed to Rose, with not just friendship but reverence, as he passed. She followed him to his truck. He went around to the driver side and motioned to her.

"Get in," he said as he pulled himself into the driver seat. The vehicle was specially equipped with hand levers. He threw the crutches into the back area covered by the homemade camper.

When they arrived at the restaurant, the Rice Bowl—it was a converted bowling alley—Rose remembered her father. She had been gone all afternoon, and it was nearly 7:00 P.M. He would be waiting, worrying.

"I have got to call my parents," she said with slight panic in her voice.

"What are you going to tell them?" Reynoso asked.

She thought for a moment. She could not lie to her father, but she could not tell him what she was about to do. Not on the phone, anyway.

"I am going to tell him everything will be all right. Pablo will be back in school and graduating." She looked at Reynoso. "Right, Ernie?"

"Guaranteed, Rosa," he answered, holding up his palm as if to be sworn. "Honest Injun," he added.

181

"Are you even Mexican?" she asked, realizing she knew nothing about the person leaning against the counter of a Chinese dive on the outskirts of Gonzales, in whose hands she had apparently entrusted her brother's future and her own relationship with her family.

"I am Zapata!" he exclaimed loudly, loud enough to cause the owner to come running, as Reynoso turned and was escorted, shuffling, to his table. She watched him drag the metal-encased legs with obvious upper-body effort as he moved from side to side in a controlled fall forward. She could see why he had the appearance, sitting down, of a very large and strong man. The effort of years of lifting, swinging, and pulling his lower body along had built a hulk of shoulders, chest, and arms on a small waist and thin legs.

When she returned, she found him laughing with the owner, whom he introduced as Mr. Choy. She received a bow, and Reynoso explained that she was an attorney "from San Francisco."

Mr. Choy was impressed. He bowed to her repeatedly while smiling and gesturing for her to sit down. As she did, Reynoso began pointing and ordering, obviously for both of them, but in Chinese. A young woman server placed two glasses on the table.

"I think you'll like this. It is rice wine. Not up to California standards, I admit, but then everything can't be American, can it?"

He sipped his wine. Rose did the same. It was bitter.

"Yes," he began without prompting, "I'm Mexican, as you are, Rosa. My parents were both born in Mexico. I was actually born in Cambridge, Massachusetts. My father was on the faculty at Harvard for a one-year visiting fellowship from the University of Mexico in Mexico City. He was in the political science department of the University. He also had a law degree. Of course, in many countries, future revolutionaries all had law degrees. Castro, Gandhi, Lenin. Forty years ago, Mexico was in the throes of revolution. My father was an intellectual, a reformist, active in the movement that brought Lazaro Cardenas to the presidency. With government jobs and his teaching, my dad's assignments took us all over the world. When I was seven, we lived in China for a year as part of a delegation studying agrarian reforms. I started high school, or the equivalent, in England. When I was 15, we spent a year in India, at the University of Hyderabad. Fascinating year, 1947, when India achieved its independence."

He stopped to take another drink of his wine.

"So, all this world travel is the reason you are the so-called revolutionary Zapata?" Rose asked with raised eyebrows.

"No. I am Zapata because my father had a sense of history. The world travel gave me an appreciation of cultures. But more than that."

"There is more?" she asked. Her tone was mocking, but she smiled at him.

"Yes. I happen to be not only a connoisseur of fine food but a world-class cook of Indian cuisine," he exclaimed with pride. "I have traveled the world, enjoyed many cultures, but I have never forgotten I am Mexican, Rosa."

She sensed, uncomfortably, that the conversation had turned back to her.

"And you think I have?"

"That thought occurred to me when you drove in here in your new car and your business suit from your big-time San Francisco law firm."

He reached for a bowl of steamed rice with small pieces of pork, held it close to his mouth, and deftly began feeding himself with chopsticks.

"Oh, I get it. Mexicans have to remain poor to be Mexicans. Is that your point?"

"No," he answered, wiping his mouth hidden in his moustache and beard. "Mexicans should help other Mexicans so that we can lift up the community together. That's my point."

"That's crap." Rose was now feeling very defensive and, at the same time, conspicuous in her clothes that contrasted with his worn blue-collar appearance. "Every generation of immigrants has strived to 'make it,' get into the mainstream, the melting pot. Not to remain apart, but to become Americans. We are no different."

"Peppers don't melt. They heat up the pot, Rosa."

"What the hell does that mean?" She threw up her arms.

"It means there is history and antiquity in cultures. I don't want to melt. Cheese melts. I want the richness of our culture, Rosa, but I want it with economic and social justice for our people."

"Immigrants always start at the bottom."

"Yes, Rosa, but they don't usually stay at the bottom. Let me ask you this. If right now, in 1972, the fields of California were filled with Canadians, not Mexicans, do you think Canadians would be subjected to the same living conditions in labor camps, herded into vehicles like cattle, their children denied even basic sanitation, workers regularly exposed to chemical sprays without protective covering? America needs to be confronted with its own racism."

"If you want to be a Mexican so bad, then why don't you live in Mexico? You can lift up the whole country." Rose gestured, lifting her hands from the tabletop toward the ceiling.

Reynoso smiled. "Because then you wouldn't have had the opportunity to enjoy me, too."

It was 8:00 P.M. when the check arrived. He quickly reached for it. "*Machismo*, remember?"

"I am learning." She smiled.

As they drove back to the office, Reynoso outlined the legal strategy.

"We will file in federal court, Eastern District. They use a rotation system. Our paralegal will just wait by the clerk's desk and watch the court filings. As soon as the clerk stamps JSW on a new case file, the paralegal will jump in line and file our case next."

"What is JSW?" Rose asked.

"Not what, who. John Sherman Watson. Worst judge in the district. Appointed by Nixon. Fascist. He is the one we have to avoid. Since the clerk is on rotation, we will get Judge Stanley Pollock. Solid on the First Amendment.

"Once we file the complaint, our attorney will walk it in to Judge Pollock and ask him to sign the Alternative Writ with a TRO. The Alternative Writ will command the District to reinstate your brother in school, allow him to wear his beret and to distribute his *La Raza* newspaper, or to show cause why it has not done so. We will get a return of 14 days so we will be back in court fast."

Rose was listening, but the procedures were not ones that she had used in her business practice. "Are you telling me that the school can still keep him out for 14 more days before we even have a hearing?"

"No. That's the beauty of the TRO with the Alternative Writ. We want to prevent them from keeping Pablo out of school, hence the temporary restraining order."

"But they have already suspended him so they can hardly be prevented from suspending him," Rose added.

"Rose. You are about to get a lesson in mandatory and prohibitory injunctions." He said it in a way that was explanatory and not condescending. This was not her area of law.

"There are lots of problems with mandatory injunctions—federal courts telling state authorities they must do something. The law prefers prohibitory orders, telling someone *not* to do something. You are right. The District has already kicked Pablo out, and we want him back in."

"So what's the answer?" Rose asked. "An injunction doesn't seem to work."

"Well, it does, Rosa, because Judge Pollock is going to issue a prohibitory injunction *prohibiting* them from *continuing* to keep Pablo out of school. What that means, in plain language, is that if they cannot *continue* to keep him out of school, he is in."

"Sounds like an end run," Rose frowned with uncertainty.

"I prefer to think of it as the majesty of the law," said Reynoso, gesturing with his hand and bowing to his steering wheel as if he were in the presence of royalty.

"What if the judge doesn't issue the TRO?" Rose asked.

"He will. Our constitutional authorities are overwhelming. Besides, even a federal judge knows graduation is around the corner, and the school board only has to put up with Pablo for a few more weeks."

As they drove down 3rd Street toward the office, he asked her, "Can you type?"

"Not very well," she admitted. "We have secretaries for that."

"Well, you are looking at the secretary for this weekend," he said as he pulled into the driveway and turned off the motor. "You can start with the substantive constitutional law from the cases I have pulled. I will start typing the pleadings and doing the procedural and jurisdictional authorities. With luck, we will be finished by Sunday evening."

On Monday morning, at five minutes to 9:00, Rose was sitting in the front row, next to Ernesto Z. Reynoso, at the special board meeting of the Gonzales Unified School District. Promptly at 9:00 A.M., the members of the board entered from a side room, followed by the county counsel. They had obviously been in an executive session, meeting with their attorney. The chairman stood and waited for each member to reach his assigned seat and then, from behind his seat, in the center of the dais, announced, as was his custom at each meeting: "Please stand for the Pledge of Allegiance."

The audience stood. Except Ernesto Z. Reynoso. Rose hesitated, took her cue from Reynoso, and sat back from her half-risen position.

The chairman put his right hand over his heart. As he did, he looked over the audience. He saw Reynoso and Rose.

"Please stand for the Pledge of Allegiance," he repeated.

The chairman continued to watch Reynoso and Rose. Rose was staring back but watching Reynoso in her peripheral vision for a sign. Reynoso had his hands over his eyes, his head down, as if deep in thought.

"Mr. Reynoso," said the chairman. No response.

"Mr. Reynoso," said the chairman louder. "Will you be joining us in the Pledge of Allegiance to the flag of the United States of America?"

Reynoso looked up. He looked around. Then he systematically looked at each board member from left to right and, returning to the chairman with his gaze, said: "No, I will not. Not until this board recognizes by its actions that this is to be 'one nation…with liberty and justice for all.'"

It was both an act of defiance and a refusal to submit to a meaningless preamble, a loyalty oath to a system of government that did not measure up to the words of its Pledge of Allegiance. The chairman, with anger approaching fury, led the crowd in the pledge without Reynoso and Rose. It seemed to Rose that he came down heavy on "under God" and lightened up on "justice for all."

With the pledge out of the way, the chairman promptly called for a vote on the agenda item and, without discussion, the board voted five to zero to support its principal's suspension of Paul Contreras for violation of the District's policy against circulating unauthorized written material and disrupting school decorum by wearing a beret as a political protest.

Rose's old principal still could not believe it as he read the lawsuit served upon him at the school board meeting: "In the United States District Court for the Eastern District of California—Pablo Contreras, a minor, by and through his Guardian ad Litem, Rose Contreras, versus Gonzales Unified School District," each of the named board members individually, the superintendent, and the principal personally, accusing each of violating the constitutional rights of speech, press, and assembly of "said Pablo Contreras, an American citizen and a person of Mexican ancestry."

Nor would her father have believed it. So Rose did not tell him. Instead, after the board meeting, she returned to the CRLA office with Reynoso and confirmed, by phone, that Judge Pollock had issued the temporary restraining order prohibiting the District "from continuing" to preclude Pablo from attending school, wearing his beret, or distributing his newspaper. Then she went home and told her father that a federal judge had told the District that Pablo was right, and it was wrong, and that it must let Pablo graduate. She explained, repeatedly, that she had no choice;

that the District would not let him back to graduate so she had to go to court. She did not bother to explain that the District had no choice because Reynoso saw to it that there was no choice. Her father saw nothing to celebrate, no victory to claim. He was relieved that his son was back in school. He hoped he still had his job.

As she backed out of the driveway of her parents' home, to resume her life, her brother Pablo came running. He stopped on the lawn, in front of the house, with his brown beret, and raised his right arm and held his hand in a fist salute to her. Rose smiled, raised her own arm and made a fist in response, put the car into drive, and headed down the road back to San Francisco. She was not sure what had happened in the last 72 hours in Gonzales, but it felt good.

It was noon, Wednesday, before she saw the phone message. By then she was immersed in a problem with the City of Sacramento's off-street parking bond issuance and was three days behind on the San Jose project. The message was one word: "Zapata."

Chapter 32

Brian

"WHAT DO YOU mean, your IUD popped out?"

Brian was calling from Fort Benning, Georgia, where he had been in trial for almost three months defending a young black Army sergeant charged, under the Code of Military Justice, with desertion in the face of the enemy.

Sergeant Jerome Wilson had laid down his M-16 and walked away from a hamlet in the Mekong Delta when ordered to advance and destroy a village. Refusing a direct order to proceed, he instead had walked to headquarters, asked to see the Officer of the Day, and said, "I will not kill any more Vietnamese."

Wilson was arrested on the spot and charged with desertion, a capital offense. He was shipped back to Fort Benning, in shackles, placed in the stockade, and brought before a military court. He refused the proffered government JAG lawyer to defend him. Instead he asked that Brian Jacobs be contacted to represent him. Before being drafted, Sergeant Wilson, who had made an excellent soldier up to the point he refused to kill more Vietnamese, had been a member of the Black Panther Party.

When the call came through, Brian immediately agreed to represent Wilson. At the first hearing, Brian defied military protocol by pleading his client "Not guilty by reason of Nuremberg." Brian would not "defend" Jerome. He would put the U.S. Government on trial for its conduct in Vietnam and its use of black Americans to fight the colonial war.

"These things happen, Brian," Shelly said. "They are replacing it with a new type, anyway."

She did not tell him she had been experiencing pelvic pain for months leading up to the spontaneous expulsion of the IUD. Or that she had seen her gynecologist who had diagnosed PID—pelvic inflammatory disease.

188

The doctor assured her it was a rather common diagnosis and prescribed an antibiotic. When the IUD was expelled, she reported it to her doctor, and they both were satisfied that the shifting of the IUD was probably the cause of the pelvic discomfort. The antibiotic was discontinued. The doctor recommended reinsertion but with a new IUD called a Dalkon Shield. She had given some thought to discarding birth control and talking to Brian about a baby but decided now was not the time. Not with the trial. The new IUD was inserted.

"Well, at least you can't blame me. I have been gone so much I haven't had the opportunity to try to knock it loose." He laughed. Shelly did not.

"How much longer on this trial, Brian?" she asked.

"Didn't you see the news? I subpoenaed General Westmoreland, Henry Kissinger, and Robert McNamara. I've got them on the run. They can't let the American people know what the real policy has been. The civil rights organizations are picketing every day here in front of the base. We have even asked that a delegation from the nonaligned countries be permitted to attend the trial to document human rights abuses and that Jerome be declared a prisoner of conscience in violation of the Nuremberg rulings."

"Brian, do you know what is going on at the firm?" she asked.

"I know, Shelly. The Administration is pulling out all of the stops to get me."

"Brian, they are auditing everything. They say that all of the money the firm received last year from drug defendants was drug money seizable by the government. They are saying we have to forfeit all of it to the federal government. Brian, they attached my wages at the preschool for the taxes and penalties they say we owe!"

"I'm sorry, Shelly. But I can't let them get away with it. I just can't give in."

"Brian, they are the goddamn government of the United States, for Christ's sake! We can't beat them if they decide to take us out. Don't you understand that?"

"Shelly, I can't quit. I'm going to win this case." He sounded almost ebullient.

"Brian, the thing about the law is, it's a game. You can only win if they let you win."

He was silent for a long while. Finally, he answered, "You're right, Shelly. But they understand that the day they don't let us win, in the legal system, is the day we come at them with guns in the streets."

He paused again. "I'll be home when I beat them."

The Dalkon Shield did not perform well. Within weeks, Shelly was noticing the pain again, which seemed to radiate toward the hips, more on one side than the other. Her gynecologist again entered the diagnosis "PID" in her chart but noted under history the reinsertion of the new IUD as the probable cause of the pain.

"You're probably having contractions and cramping associated with the placement of the IUD," he told her. "Let's wait a few weeks and see. It usually goes away."

Three days later, Shelly was taken by ambulance to the Cedars-Sinai Hospital emergency room. It started with a fever. She thought she was just getting the flu. By the time she called for help, she was experiencing extreme pelvic pain, cramping, and bleeding. Brian got the call late at night—"too late to call off witnesses for the next trial day"—and arrived two days later, after Shelly had been admitted and a specialist, Dr. Martin Gershenson, had been called in to take over her care.

"Did you win your case?" Shelly asked.

He knew the question was more in the nature of "I could be dead." She turned her head away and looked toward the window as the doctor came in. She was not looking forward to this conversation—for more reasons than one.

"Mr. Jacobs, I am Dr. Gershenson. Heard you flew in from Alabama, was it?"

"Fort Benning, Georgia."

"Oh, right. Fort Benning. I was in the Army. Trained there in the 82nd Airborne. Pretty hot in August, as I recall. Well, your wife here—we were pretty lucky. But we've got a ways to go."

"Excuse me, doctor," Brian interrupted, "I've been up for 24 hours. Could you go over this for me? I am really in the dark here."

"Well, first, at the time your wife was brought into the emergency room, she was in shock from the consequences of the septic abortion which, untreated, could have killed her."

Brian reacted with shock. "What are you talking about—an abortion?"

"No. No. Don't misunderstand. Your wife didn't undergo a medical procedure for abortion. Her body, spontaneously, aborted an embryo of seven to nine weeks' gestation. This may well have occurred because of the presence of the Dalkon Shield IUD."

"I didn't know she was pregnant." Brian looked at Shelly. She continued looking out the window.

"Nor did she or her doctors, otherwise the Dalkon Shield, or any other IUD for that matter, would not have been inserted in a pregnant woman."

"But she had an IUD in place so she couldn't possibly have been pregnant."

"Well, strange as it may seem, we are not all that clear how or why IUDs work in humans. Some researchers think a foreign body in the uterus interferes with reproduction somehow, biochemically, or by causing an inflammatory foreign body reaction that releases various bodily chemicals and creates changes in the cervical mucus. Most likely there is also an effect on sperm. Whatever it is, we know they are generally effective, but pregnancies do happen. Not many, but a few. What is pretty clear, however, is that the IUD is not designed to abort fertilized eggs. It either does or doesn't do its work by preventing conception. If you're pregnant, it's probably too late for an IUD."

The conversation was going nowhere, as far as Brian was concerned. "Then why are we talking about whether an IUD was recently put in?"

"As I said, your wife had a septic abortion. A report from the Centers for Disease Control, just out the end of June this year, documents problems of the Dalkon Shield IUD. Incidents of complicated pregnancies, septic abortions, PID—all higher with this particular IUD in place."

"What's PID?" asked Brian.

"Pelvic inflammatory disease. That's what your wife was diagnosed with over the last six months."

Brian did not add that he had been unaware his wife had been diagnosed with anything over the last six months, but he continued what was fast becoming a cross-examination of the doctor.

"But you said she didn't have the Dalkon Shield until three weeks ago."

"Right. And she didn't have PID."

Again, Brian looked at Shelly, then back at the doctor. Shelly did not look at him.

The doctor continued, "In medical school, we derisively describe a diagnosis of PID as a 'pathetically inadequate diagnosis.' If the pelvic area of a woman hurts, call it PID. Means nothing. You have to ask why does it hurt. Here, she had expelled an IUD. That history probably stopped her doctors from looking further and confirmed, in their minds, that the cause of her earlier pain was a problem related to the IUD.

"When she was hospitalized, with a septic abortion, they once again would think PID—inflammation of the pelvis—quite possibly due to STD, sexually transmitted disease, or as a consequence of an IUD in place. Now, we have this report that just came out from the Centers for Disease Control saying this very IUD causes PID and septic abortion by reason of its unusual multi-filamentous structure, allowing a pathway for bacteria through the endocervix. It acts like a wick. Bacteria are absorbed. The Dalkon Shield has a crab-shaped upper end that causes microscopic lacerations through which the bacteria enter the bloodstream. What they have created is a design for disaster."

The doctor paused. Brian thought it was for effect, as he would with a jury.

"But you were right, Mr. Jacobs," Dr. Gershenson resumed, "causes don't run backwards. I believe the Dalkon Shield surely caused the loss of your child, but the pain your wife has been suffering for the last six months had nothing to do with any IUD. And it was not PID—whatever that includes. Mrs. Jacobs has ovarian cancer which, in an advanced stage, will cause the pelvic pain and referred pain to the hip, especially on the affected side."

Again, Brian looked quickly at Shelly. She still did not move, continuing to look out the window. He looked back at Dr. Gershenson. Dr. Gershenson, stenciled on his white long coat. Dr. Gershenson, on his opposite lapel. A hard plastic name tag. Dr. Gershenson, Cedars-Sinai Hospital, Dr. Morton Gershenson, Chief, Gynecological and Surgical Oncology.

"We didn't know it was cancer until last night. On pelvic exam, a mass was felt on the left side and the chief resident called me in. Frankly, with her history of sepsis, I thought it was probably an abscess. When we went in—"

Brian interrupted: "My wife underwent surgery last night?"

"Yes. As I was saying, I just expected to evacuate and excise an abscess but...well...the mass wasn't an abscess. It was clearly ovarian cancer. We couldn't know that without surgery."

Brian's brain had stopped at the word "cancer." The oncologist knew the reaction. "But everything points to cancer limited to the ovaries. I think your wife will be fine with the hysterectomy. She will have to take Premarin for the rest of her life and—"

"What's that?" asked Brian.

"Premarin? A conjugated estrogen—an estrogen replacement because of the removal of the ovaries. Actually, it's an interesting substance. It's collected from pregnant mares' urine..."

Brian was not interested in pregnant mares' urine. "And?"

"And what?" asked the doctor.

"You were saying, she would be on Premarin the rest of her life and...something."

"And, of course, with the total hysterectomy, she will not be able to conceive another child in the future," the doctor completed his thought.

After the doctor left, Brian stood in the middle of the room looking at where the doctor had been. He let it all sink in. Slowly he turned, as Shelly knew he would eventually, and looked at her. He thought of the day they met in Alabama, their time in Africa, the years on the road, sleeping in their car on an Indian Reservation, working together to build a law practice.

"Our baby?" He said it slowly. He repeated himself. "Our baby." It was not a question this time.

He walked out, knocking over a metal tray when he realized he could not slam the hospital room door. He drove out of the parking lot, his car tires screeching. It was a while before he realized that he was pulling into his office parking lot. He slammed the car door, catching his briefcase as he did. Why did he need it? He threw it back into the car. He started walking, looking for a bar. He was going to get drunk.

Shelly lay still in her bed, her head turned, as it was when he left, to the window. She watched the evening come, the darkness set in and, eventually, the breaking light of morning. She never moved. She never closed her eyes.

Shelly was groggy. The nurse was there to remind her she was in a surgical recovery room. Brian awoke, groggy, his head pounding. There was no one there to tell him where he was. He had spent the night in his car.

Chapter 33

Brian

"I CAME HOME, and I was a stranger in my own house."

Brian was sitting in his partner's office. Zarick was just letting him talk. He knew Brian needed to be able to tell someone.

"This last case. I was in trial for three months and probably in Georgia the better part of three months before that on motions and interviewing witnesses. Shelly's life just went on without me. Even now, with this cancer, I feel like I'm in the way. Something to be picked up along with the towels. She won't let me help with anything; won't even let me go to the doctor's office with her. Says it's her problem."

"Is she going to be all right?" asked Zarick, instead of directly asking, "Is Shelly going to die?" Cancer seemed, after all, a death sentence more than a diagnosis.

"I don't know," Brian answered, looking more frustrated than confused. "She won't tell me. It's like I am being punished for not being there. I mean it is not as if Shelly didn't know what it means to be a lawyer. We met when she worked for Kunstler. She was on the road with him traveling all over the country. It comes with the territory, with this kind of work. There are sacrifices involved."

"Maybe she feels she is the one sacrificing, Brian," Zarick said softly, tapping the arm of his chair with a finger, observing its rhythm.

"Jesus Christ, Paul, I am the one living in motels, busting my ass 20 hours a day, out there fighting those bastards."

"And you are the one getting all the glory."

"Glory? Glory? You think this is about glory? I've got a young black man facing, at best, 20 years in a federal military prison and possibly death for desertion. You call that glory? Some mornings I am so fuckin' scared I throw up before cross-examining witnesses. The only thing that keeps me going is knowing that we are fighting to expose what's really happening in Vietnam in hopes of—"

Zarick interrupted. "And does this young black soldier, whose life is at stake, know that you are fighting not for his life but to expose the government's policy in Vietnam?"

"What are you talking about?" Brian shouted. But he knew the answer and turned away.

"Did you tell him he's being martyred for a cause? Martyrs die so others may live. Does he understand that, Brian? Did you explain that to him, as his attorney?" Zarick asked.

"He knew what he was doing when he put that gun down. He wasn't seeking an easy way out. He didn't wander down to his draft board and file for conscientious objector status. He laid down his goddamn gun on the battlefield, Paul. So don't turn into some condescending fucking member of the Bar who assumes his client is stupid and you can plea bargain his conscience away for his own good."

"Brian, I am your partner, remember? I think I can understand how Shelly feels. You have been gone for months, leaving me here to cover your ass, and you attack me when you get back. Well, fuck you, Brian. Someone has to see that the rent is paid, the electricity works, clients still believe we are in business. Brian, what you have developed is a national reputation as the champion of free cases. I don't question your integrity, but there is such a thing as self-preservation. You have taken on more than the rest of us can chew."

"Isn't the fundraising covering the litigation costs?" asked Brian.

"Barely. But covering costs isn't the same as making money. It's covering costs. Costs of your motel. Costs of legal transcripts. Costs of witness travel. Nothing for attorneys' fees. Zero to the bottom line, Brian."

"What about the firm's income?" Brian asked. "My name still brings in cases."

"Some. But clients in big cases want you to personally work on their cases, Brian. They have to at least see you at court appearances to know you exist beyond the 5 o'clock news. When they see you on the national news while you're in Georgia, they know that you are not working on their case here. If you are going to build a practice in L.A., you need to be in L.A. I might add, and it's none of my business, I suspect if you are going to have a relationship with Shelly, you need to be in L.A., also."

"You're right…"

"…and…"

"...it's none of your business."

"Well, Brian, this is."

Paul threw some papers across the desk. One was on the stationery of the Internal Revenue Service announcing a "jeopardy assessment" for the tax year 1975, based on the assertion that a certain action filed in the U.S. District Court for the Central District of California made it appear that collection of federal income taxes might be in jeopardy and, accordingly, under applicable IRS Code sections, which were cited, an immediate assessment was being made. The assessment was for $1.5 million against all assets of Brian and Shelly Jacobs, the law firm of Jacobs and Associates, and all partners therein.

Accompanying the letter, on the familiar long pleading paper of the federal court, was a copy of an action entitled "United States of America vs. Brian and Shelly Jacobs, Paul Zarick, Jacobs and Associates, and the funds of Julio Juarez, Jose Martin Olivieria, Jami Torres, Michael Adame, Jose Baca..." He counted the names of 36 others, all of whom had been clients of the firm.

Brian read through the entire 32-page document. It alleged that all of the identified clients had been engaged in drug trafficking and had retained the services of his firm, paying all fees and costs with money derived from drug trafficking. It asked that all such money be forfeited to the government. It further alleged that all accommodations, meals, and travel expenses, together with all funds raised to defend the pro bono clients represented by the firm, constituted income at their reasonable value to Brian and the firm, and had not, in the previous five years, been so declared by Brian and Shelly on their personal returns or by the firm since its inception. Taxes on all, together with penalties and interest, were accordingly, immediately, due.

There was not any question in Brian's mind: The government was striking back. For the first time in his life, he entertained the thought that perhaps he could not win.

The court-martial trial was over. Brian's client had been found guilty and sentenced to 20 years. There was never really any chance of the death penalty. No one in 1975 wanted a martyr to the memory of those who opposed the Vietnam War. Gerald Ford had pardoned Richard Nixon. It was time to move on. A good JAG lawyer might have avoided the trial with a plea and a lighter sentence. But then again, a good JAG lawyer would not have questioned America's policy in Vietnam, South America, the Third World, or the developing quagmire in Angola, as did Brian.

Brian was home, in L.A., but in a house in which he did not feel welcome and in a law partnership that was collapsing around him.

"Your way, we go down in flames. Let's try my way," Zarick told him. Holding up the government lawsuit, Zarick said, "You've got to give them credit. They are very smart. They sued us civilly to get the drug money. They didn't bring criminal charges for conspiracy, because they knew they couldn't win. What they will do is prove we represented criminals, not that we are criminals. Then they will show that the source of the criminals' money was criminal activity. They tar us, by association, and take the money we legitimately earned, without having to prove we did anything wrong."

He flipped to the last two pages of the complaint, the section dealing with the receipt of goods or services instead of fees. "This tax angle. They treat us as if it is just another collection matter. The 'reasonable value' of 'in-kind' payments. Like we work for food.

"Brian, we've got to be equally smart. What we've got to show is that they are really attacking every lawyer in America and anyone who does pro bono work for charity. If you eat a meal at a homeless shelter while helping out, you owe Uncle Sam. That's the logical extension of their argument."

Brian was not particularly interested in the legal argument. "This is retaliation for taking on government policy. It is an attempt to crush radical lawyers. To stop The Movement."

Zarick jumped in before Brian got on a roll. With rising frustration, he shouted, "Brian, so what? Who cares?"

"I care, for one. All those people who are being oppressed care. Progressive people throughout the country. Blacks. American Indians. Prisoners. Those who don't have the ability to stand alone against the government. They care."

"Right, Brian. A bunch of losers. We need people who can stand up against the government and win. That's the difference between you and me. I want to win; I don't want to die fighting."

Zarick was calm now. He picked up the lawsuit again and, holding it in his hand, said, "Don't you see, Brian? They have fucked up. They have taken on not just you, and all those losers outside of the system, but every practicing lawyer, even conservative ones, who don't want to lose their fees to the government because of the source of their clients' money. No lawyer wants to ask a client, 'Where did you get the money?'"

Zarick looked at his watch. "I have asked Rebecca Stanley to meet with us. She's a staff attorney with the Southern California ACLU. She was also a law clerk to Judge Lionel Johnson in the Central District. The ACLU has agreed to represent us, to challenge the government's actions. She agrees with me. We need mainstream support. I have already called the Southern California Criminal Defense Attorneys Association and it will join on the brief. So will their national organization. The big one is the ABA. We have an inside to them. You are not going to believe this. At Yale, Bill Kunstler roomed with the incoming ABA president. The son-of-a-bitch knows everybody. The ABA will file an *amicus curiae* brief, but only if the National Lawyers Guild doesn't. They want to defend the principle. But they don't want to do it in the company of crazies."

Zarick held up his hands as if to fend off blows. "Sorry. Not my description."

"Then on the in-kind issue, Rebecca says the ACLU can get a lot of churches to join our position. She asked if it was okay to say you were Jewish but not practicing." Brian looked up. "Just kidding, alright?" Zarick was smiling.

Brian was not especially comfortable. "You're wrapping us up in the ABA and the Catholic Church? What kind of a statement are we making here?"

"None, Brian. We are trying to save our ass. But look, this is L.A. You want to make a statement? Make a movie. Buy an ad. But our court strategy has got to be one that can win, and in a hurry. Or we lose everything. I have been before this judge that's assigned to our case. He will go to bat for the ABA and the church. He could care a flying fuck about some criminal lawyer, and that's how they see us, Brian, these federal judges, not as lawyers representing criminals, but as 'criminal lawyers.'"

The strategy worked. In the face of the entourage of prestigious organizations and individuals who joined the ACLU on the brief supporting Brian and the firm—including the dean of Boalt Hall and 15 other deans recruited by him—the government withdrew its action.

The legal victory brought a great deal of favorable publicity. Brian was asked to address the Los Angeles County Bar Association's Annual Meeting and, later in the year, to be the commencement speaker at UCLA Law School. In honor of the ACLU, he entitled his speech "Eternal Vigilance"— the motto of the ACLU. But he also had in mind the vigilance of a lawyer to be ever mindful of the danger of straying too far from the idealism of the law student.

With the victory against the government, with the help of traditional legal and charitable organizations, came a level of acceptance that Brian had never sought or expected. He was the lawyer who defended the paramount right of attorneys! While it was couched in the language of the Sixth Amendment's "right to counsel," it was really the "right to be paid," a right all members of the profession held inviolable. Now that he was one of them—at least in their eyes, if not his—he found that he received more referrals of cases from firms which previously would not have given him the time of day, let alone a referral. Of course, the referred cases were those that business firms felt were below their standards to accept. Among the referrals was one Willy Swanigan, the husband of a housecleaner at the residence of Jackson Bridgeport III.

"Mr. Jacobs, I can't afford no trial. Mrs. Bridgeport ask her husband on account my wife is the housekeeper. I never been in no trouble. I just want where I can keep my license 'cause I can't work if I lost my class one driver's license. Maybe you could just get a deal. Mr. Bridgeport and you went to school together, I hear."

He handed Brian a business card. "What happened to your face?" Brian asked the small black man in front of him, as he looked at the business card of Jackson Bridgeport III, Bridgeport, Bridgeport, Hall and Pendergast.

"They beat me. Said I wasn't doin' the 'so-brighty' test right. One kept hittin' my knee bone here, so I would lift up my one leg. The other one said I breathed on him smelling real bad, so he hit me in the face with the stick."

Brain was looking at Willy Swanigan and seeing Alabama.

"Yeah, Willy, I will help you with a deal. You come here tomorrow at 8:30 in the morning, and we will drive over together. Before you leave, I want my partner to meet you. He has a Polaroid camera, and we will need to take some pictures."

He took Willy Swanigan down the hall and walked into the library where Zarick was seated across the table from two UCLA law school students.

"Paul, I would like you to meet Willy Swanigan. Mr. Swanigan is a new client. He can't afford to pay us, but I am hoping the City of Los Angeles will pay our fees. Do you have the camera?"

The biggest mistake that the City of Los Angeles made in the case of *People v. Willy Swanigan* was not dismissing it. Instead, it charged Swanigan with felony battery on a police officer and with resisting arrest. The District Attorney offered, after the preliminary hearing, to dismiss the case, but only if Swanigan signed an agreement releasing the officers and the City from liability. No one, Brian was convinced, would believe that one 135-pound, 5-foot 6-inch black man would take on two police officers, with a combined weight of over 460 pounds, with guns and nightsticks, on a highway at night, after being pulled out of his car at gunpoint. Nor did the four fractures of the patella appear consistent with falling on the shoulder of a road, as the police alleged. The broken nose and loss of vision in one eye were admittedly from a nightstick, but the stick was used, allegedly, in an attempt to push Swanigan away as he attacked the two officers.

Brian was so convinced of and so outraged by the police misconduct that he did not bother telling Swanigan of the District Attorney's offer to dismiss. He was afraid Swanigan might take it.

Brian was well aware that if Swanigan pled guilty to any criminal charge, there could be no civil lawsuit against the Los Angeles Police Department for violation of Swanigan's civil rights, excessive force, battery, and malicious prosecution.

"Don't worry. They beat you because you are a black man, Willy. They are going to apologize to you and they are going to pay you. I am going to see to it."

"But couldn't we just work out a deal?"

"They will deal with us at the right time, Willy," Brian assured him.

"But I can't afford to…"

"Don't worry," interjected Brian, "you don't have to pay us."

"I just want my license. Can't you get my license?"

"Nobody is going to take away your license, Willy. We will see to that, too."

Brian could see that Willy Swanigan was not convinced.

"Do you play cards, Willy?"

"Cards?"

"Yeah. Like poker."

"Some. Not much."

"Well, Willy, if we were playing poker, and I saw all your cards, and I knew my cards would beat your cards, don't you think I would be pretty crazy not to bet you?"

"Maybe. I don't know."

"And if I could win myself a lot of money—a lot of money—and I knew I had the winning cards, because I had already seen your cards, don't you think that would be pretty hard to pass up?"

"I guess."

"Well, Willy. You've got to trust me on this. You've got the winning cards. And I am going to win you a lot of money by the time this is all over."

Chapter 34

Leon

IT STARTED AS she had promised. She dragged his "skinny white heinie" around Oakland. A white (and white-sounding) secretary would call and inquire about a rental vacancy. But it was Angela Africa who would show up, nicely attired in a business suit and enunciating precisely in her best Columbia University diction, and seek to rent the apartment. If she was turned away, for any reason or pretext, Leon would call and immediately visit the same rental. If it was suddenly available to him, even with his long hair, he would return with Angela Africa and confront the manager or owner. This, not for litigation, since he could hardly be a witness and a lawyer in the same case; no, this was Angela's way of giving him a street ed-you-kay-shon.

With his education, Leon pursued, over the next three years, scores of individual cases of housing discrimination against landlords in Alameda County. He successfully sought penalties under the Unruh Civil Rights Act, changing society one bigot at a time, he reasoned.

"You're losing the war," his father argued. "There are more of them than there is of you. They just keep coming. They will wear you down."

Leon had to justify what he was doing, at least to himself, but he knew his father was right. So was Angela. Feeding a conscience was not the same as changing society. For Angela, there was some satisfaction in "suing the motherfuckers," especially since she had the white boy on loan from white society to do it.

Angela was also right that he would leave. They always did. But she was wrong to believe he would leave Oakland or his work in discrimination law.

After five years at Legal Aid and upon being asked to become the Director of the Alameda County Legal Aid Society, Leon decided to enter private practice. It was because he wanted to do more, to be more effective, that he left. The Legal Aid method was to provide legal services to individual clients. It had become obvious that if discrimination was to be fought, it had to be on a broader scale. Collective cases. Multiple defendants. Class actions. The government did not mind providing free attorneys to the poor; it just did not want them to be too effective. It was time for Leon to leave.

Fortunately, one of Leon's housing discrimination clients was a shop steward for the Iron Workers of America, Local 647, working on naval vessel and aircraft carrier construction. The union was interested in a legal referral service, and the steward recommended Leon. The idea caught on, and Leon started his practice, three blocks from the Alameda County Courthouse, around the corner from Lake Merritt, with four local unions signed up to receive services at reduced rates. The referral system paid the rent. It also meant Leon was writing wills, handling divorce cases, defending drunk drivers, and counseling union members on anything they wanted to talk about in their free half-hour consultation.

Leon held an open house upon entering private practice in the spring of 1975. His father was proud of his son representing working men and unions. Leon's hair still reached his unbuttoned shirt collar, but he now wore a dark rumpled suit, with a tie, loosely knotted.

Leon invited Angela to the open house. Predictably, she asked, "Why? You need a token Negro?" Surprisingly, she came. Not surprisingly, she was late. He knew her well enough to know she ran on B.P.T.: "Black People Time." But then she stayed, when the others left.

She sat in his office chair, kicked off her shoes, and put her feet on his desk. She reached for her drink.

"Well, now that you gonna be a rich white boy, I 'spose you think you can have all the brown sugar you want?"

"Damn it, Angela. There you go again with that talk. I know you do it just to embarrass me."

"Leon, now tell me, you like me to talk black, don't you? You find it exciting. Wild. Primitive—that's it, that's the word I'm looking for. Primitive. It arouses you. Am I right?"

"Angela. You are obviously a beautiful woman—"

"Wow," she interrupted, as usual, "beautiful woman. No, that's what you tell those skinny white girls. Not me. I am an African queen. Exotic."

"Okay. Exotic."

"That's better."

"Exotic with a mouth on you—"

"Now you is talkin' about my big lips?"

"No, your smart-ass mouth."

"Oh, so you like a black woman to just present her big butt and keep her mouth shut?"

"Why is it always about race with you? Black and white; white and black?" Leon was smiling, but he meant it.

Angela dropped her feet to the floor, stood up to her full 6 feet in her heels, smiled back as she walked toward him. She stopped, pressing her breasts against him, running one hand through his hair and pulling his head to her. Over his shoulder she sipped her drink and then leaned close to his ear, letting the moisture of her mouth, mixed with her drink, moisten his ear as she spoke: "Because the white master always wanted the African women. Black pussy is black magic. Trying to escape capture under the weight of that white body. Wild. Makes a man feel like a man. Is that what you want, Leon?"

Leon felt himself getting hard. She felt it, too. He put his arms around her, grabbed her hair, and pulled her face back.

She was smiling. "Just checking," she said. "See, 300 years and it still works."

With that she pushed him away softly but firmly, downed her drink, and walked to the door.

"Nice party, Leon. Call me."

Chapter 35

Brian

THERE WAS NEVER a chance that they would lose their home to the IRS because Brian and Shelly did not own a home. Brian had never cared that much about where he lived. But he knew he did not want to live in this place anymore. When he walked into the bedroom—their bedroom—he sensed the presence of another who had been there. Another man.

It was months before they talked about the baby. It was hard not to call it the baby, even though it was, as the doctor had said, an embryo at only seven to nine weeks of gestation. It was easier to focus on the surgery to remove the cancerous ovary and on the recuperation and recovery.

For the six weeks after surgery, Shelly's mother flew out to stay and tend to her daughter. When Brian came home each night, Shelly's mother had dinner waiting. For the first few weeks, Shelly avoided him by occupying a separate bedroom and eating in bed. On the persistent urging of her mother, some might say nagging, Shelly eventually joined them at the dinner table. Evenings had all the semblance of a family: "How was your day?" "What did you do?" "How are you feeling?" Like a family. Never discussing the real issues, those things just beneath the surface.

When her mother finally left, Shelly avoided him again by leaving early, coming home late. Or working on a lesson plan or whatever justified sitting alone, quiet, in another room.

A few months after Shelly's surgery—a Saturday morning—Brian was sitting at the kitchen table reading the newspaper. Shelly was sitting at the counter, looking into her coffee cup.

"He wasn't a lawyer."

Brian heard her. He knew instantly who "he" was. He continued to hold the newspaper separating his face from view. He stopped reading, as if secretly listening to a conversation from behind a wall.

BRIAN

He waited. Waited for an explanation. Who was he? Why? How could she do it? He was ready if she tried to blame him. His work. He had to fight them, didn't he? Someone had to do it. She knew when she married him. They shared their commitments, didn't they?

He waited.

When he lowered the paper, she had left the room.

Chapter 36

Jackson

JACKSON BRIDGEPORT III was right: Litigation was his forte. He had the personality to represent those who wanted their own way, at any cost. And his law firm was happy to see the charges reflected by this attitude. If he had a weakness, it was that the same disdain and arrogance that intimidated opponents and witnesses could not be hidden from judges and juries. His effectiveness depended upon the abuse of a superior economic position, the collapse of an opponent, not the persuasiveness of his flawed personality. His personality made him an effective "litigator;" it made him a lousy trial lawyer.

While Bridgeport, Bridgeport, Hall and Pendergast practiced "gentlemen's law" in Connecticut, Los Angeles was another matter. This was the West and, out here, "litigators" were people hired to kick the shit out of anyone getting in the way of a real estate development, zoning change, or business deal. "Litigators" were hired to threaten. To sit at the table as a warning. "Litigators" did not litigate the merits; they prevented anything ever getting to the merits.

"Don't just stomp 'um; hang 'um along the highway so no one else will ever do that again…like Spartacus."

In five years of practice, when most young lawyers were still hoping to handle their first business litigation case, Jackson Bridgeport III had already acquired a reputation in the legal community of which he was justly proud: He was an asshole. A very big asshole.

As Brian Jacobs felt public interest litigation needed to be public, broadly disseminated, to be effective, Jackson Bridgeport III felt exactly the same way about a good thrashing. Capital punishment, to be a deterrent, Jackson reasoned, needed to be brought to the attention of those who might harbor the thought of killing. Similarly, if one wished to discourage opponents, examples—public examples—needed to be made. That is why he invited a *Los Angeles Times* reporter to the videotaped deposition of Martin "the Supermarket Lawyer" Sypnicki, in the fall of 1975.

Did you fall in a supermarket or shopping center? Call the Law Office of Martin A. Sypnicki. "The Supermarket Lawyer."

In front of every major mall in the greater Los Angeles basin, the bus benches had his message. Radio spots, in English and Spanish, belted out the same message. His ad in the Yellow Pages added: "Falsely accused of shoplifting?" It also showed a picture of an older woman lying next to a supermarket produce bin with grapes and water on the floor.

Martin Sypnicki—actually, one of his "paralegals"—had filed a complaint for Carmen Rodriguez alleging an injury at the Los Angeles Valley Mall where Mrs. Rodriguez, 34 years old and pregnant, had fallen on coat hangers left in the changing area of a clothing store. The suit alleged negligence on the part of store personnel for not keeping the walkway area clear of hangers obviously deposited by customers trying on clothing. It further alleged that the shopping center itself was well aware of the danger created upon its leased premises and was, therefore, also responsible.

There was nothing out of the ordinary when Sypnicki's secretary told him there was an attorney on the phone calling on the Rodriguez case. He was prepared to suggest a quick settlement "to avoid the cost of litigation."

"Sypnicki. This is Jackson Bridgeport III of Bridgeport, Bridgeport, Hall and Pendergast. I am calling you on your Rodriguez case."

"Yes, Jack," he answered, trying to be friendly. No point fighting. "Will you be defending? I'll be glad to give you an extension to answer so we can discuss Mrs. Rodriguez's injuries."

"I don't defend two-bit cases, Sypnicki. That's what our insurance lawyers do. No. I called you to give you a chance to dismiss the case."

Sypnicki did not know what to say. "What—"

Bridgeport interrupted. "Sypnicki, you've got a nice little racket going. I am sure all the stores roll over, give you a few dollars like a slot machine paying out. You've done well for yourself, Sypnicki. Night law school graduate. First one to get those bus stop ads out. Your radio spots. Well, my clients asked me to do something about you. I told them that I would handle it. So here's the deal, Sypnicki. You dismiss your case. You pay $500 to cover the costs of my time calling you, and you agree not to handle any suits against my clients anymore. I will send you the list of my clients' real estate holdings in the area. It is rather extensive."

"You think I am going to dismiss my client's case for nothing? Why should I?" interrupted Sypnicki.

As Sypnicki's voice rose, Bridgeport's lowered, and he calmly explained: "Because it is no longer worth your while, Sypnicki. I will personally run you into the ground if you don't."

"Are you threatening me?"

Bridgeport's response now suggested boredom: "Of course. Do we have a deal?"

First contact from the defense was normally not this aggressive. Sypnicki thought the young lawyer was probably posturing. He decided to start the negotiations low. "I will take $7,500 for Rodriguez. Discuss that with your client, will you, Jack? She is really hurt," he added, seeking a sympathetic response.

Instead, as Sypnicki remembered later in the telling of the story to a reporter from the *Los Angeles Daily Journal*, Bridgeport's voice coldly told him: "You didn't hear me. I don't care if she is hurt. There will be no offer. Once I hang up, I will not call you again. I am going to make an example of you, Sypnicki, or the next guy. Your choice. Which is it?"

Bridgeport waited a few moments. When Sypnicki could not think of a response fast enough, Bridgeport hung up.

Bridgeport did not immediately file an answer in the coat hanger case. Instead, three days after their conversation, Sypnicki was served with a lawsuit filed in the U.S. District Court for the Central District of California in Los Angeles, alleging that the Law Office of Martin A. Sypnicki and its principals, attorneys, secretaries, investigators—even the receptionist— were engaged in a pattern of wire fraud, mail fraud, and extortion, and were acting as a criminal enterprise within the meaning of the federal Racketeer Influenced and Corrupt Organizations Act, commonly known as RICO, in filing inflated, fraudulent and/or false claims for damages against businesses in Los Angeles. The lawsuit listed almost 200 lawsuits or claims filed over the previous five years against 57 different listed businesses and shopping centers. Bridgeport's complaint was obviously the product of extensive research and investigation into Mr. Sypnicki's practice predating the phone call ultimatum.

Clearly, Bridgeport did not expect Sypnicki to agree to his "offer" of settlement. He did not want a settlement; he wanted Sypnicki. He wanted

to show, to warn the world publicly, just how great and feared a litigator—
how big an asshole—Jackson Bridgeport III could be.

Bridgeport had meticulously gathered together dozens of Sypnicki's
prior clients who were unhappy with the settlement of their cases. Those
who were mildly discontented became even more disgruntled under the
careful suggestion of Bridgeport's investigators. The investigators did not
say it directly, but they implied that Sypnicki was being investigated for
"improprieties" that could result in the State Bar compelling restitution of
a bigger portion of the insurance settlement to them than they had received from their attorney, Sypnicki. But first, the witnesses needed to
confirm that Sypnicki had sought them out as clients, sent them to the
chiropractic offices he was working with, run up so-called treatment bills,
and split the settlement three ways, between himself, the chiropractor, and
the client.

Most of the alleged shoplifters had been contacted by an investigator
from Sypnicki's office at the time of their first appearance in court. It was
suggested to them that Sypnicki could not only get the charges dismissed,
but could obtain a settlement "if they hurt you when they accused you of
stealing" or "forcefully arrested you," or both. Most contacted this way
remembered that they were punched, shoved, or perhaps "hurt my back
when they pushed me down," or had other complaints. The three-way
split still applied. But the client's third went to pay the criminal defense
fees. The client got nothing. Sypnicki got two-thirds; the chiropractor,
one-third.

By the time of Sypnicki's deposition, Bridgeport had obtained over
500 files, by court order, from Sypnicki's office, involving claims going
back 10 years against every major shopping center in Los Angeles. He also
obtained Sypnicki's financial records on each case, which led to obtaining
the financial records of 40 chiropractors paid out of client settlements.
Bridgeport (or rather, his young associates) took extensive depositions from
everyone—including Sypnicki's last five receptionists—who had worked
for Sypnicki's office for the past 10 years. Sypnicki's malpractice carrier
used up the limits of his malpractice policy in defending him and withdrew from the case. Sypnicki was left to defend himself, although he had
the good sense to borrow what he could to retain a criminal defense attorney for the possible criminal implications and to respond to the complaint
lodged with the State Bar disciplinary committee by every former client
who testified. Actually, Bridgeport's office assistants prepared each com-

plaint for submission to the Bar and even paid the postage for mailing. The witnesses just signed on the line provided. After 23 days of videotaped deposition, Sypnicki, "on advice of counsel," refused to answer any further questions. By then, the Law Office of Martin A. Sypnicki was closed, its five lawyers, 18 "paralegals," and clerical staff scattered.

Then there was Mrs. Rodriguez. According to her medical records—before Sypnicki sent her to chiropractors—she had sustained trauma to her lower lumbar spine when she had fallen on her buttocks. The symptoms suggested a bulging and possibly herniated disc at the L5-S1 level. Because of her pregnancy, the doctor advised that she wait for X-rays and other diagnostic tests, and return after delivery of the child. However, he noted, vaginal delivery would be complicated by and/or might aggravate the disc injury, and even compromise her spine, with the pressure involved. Fusion surgery, he opined, would be likely within a year.

More important, for Bridgeport's purposes, was the entry under Social History. Mrs. Rodriguez was separated from her husband, a dissolution petition was pending, and child custody was in issue. "Past Medical History" documented "substance abuse x 3 years" prior to pregnancy. Bridgeport saw his opening.

"Get all the court records on the divorce. Rap sheet. DMV. Have the investigator talk to the husband. Find out how bad he wants custody."

Mrs. Rodriguez had no way of knowing what would happen to her at her deposition. Sypnicki had sent her a paper telling her he was no longer her attorney; she had to find someone else. She did not read the legal newspapers and had no idea what was happening to Sypnicki.

Mrs. Rodriguez could hardly sit down after the accident, with the baby pressing on her pelvis, and the pain from her back radiating across her buttocks and down her left leg. It had been hard dressing her six-year-old and walking the child out to the bus stop. One morning, as she came back into the house and sat down, she saw the good-looking white-haired man on television: "If you have been hurt in an accident..." She needed a new lawyer, since Sypnicki had abandoned her. She called the number on the screen. She was assigned an attorney—not the white-haired actor in the television ad. That is how Mrs. Rodriguez came to be facing across the table, on the 26th floor of a Wilshire Boulevard building, Jackson Bridgeport III, with a lawyer fresh out of an unaccredited law school. Bridgeport did not even acknowledge his presence.

Mrs. Rodriguez was sworn as a witness by the court reporter. Then without even the preliminary formalities of introduction, and without looking up, Jackson Bridgeport began the pretrial deposition:

Q: Mrs. Rodriguez, you claim to have injured yourself at the a clothing store in the Los Angeles Valley Mall on May 8, 1975, is that right?

A: Yes.

Q: Mrs. Rodriguez, what part of your body do you claim to have hurt when, according to you, you injured yourself at the mall?

A: I fell on hangers laying there. I fell on my bottom and hurt my back.

Q: Mrs. Rodriguez, this isn't the first time you have claimed to have fallen and injured yourself, is it?

A: I don't know what you're talking about.

Q: Mrs. Rodriguez, didn't you injure yourself when your husband pushed you and caused you to fall?

A: No.

Q: Mrs. Rodriguez, your back was injured when your husband beat you, wasn't it?

A: No, that's not true. I fell on hangers at the mall.

Q: Mrs. Rodriguez, let me show you a request for a restraining order signed by you wherein you told the court your husband had beat you, injured you, caused you to fall, and you feared for your safety and that of your unborn child. Did you tell that to the court?

A: Yes, but...

Q: Were you lying, Ms. Rodriguez?

A: No. No. That's different. I hurt my back when I fell on the hangers at the mall.

The second hour began, without a break.

Q: Mrs. Rodriguez, you're an alcoholic, aren't you? Have you told the social worker assigned by the court, in the custody proceedings to assess your fitness, that you have been drinking since your alleged back injury?

By 11:15, when Bridgeport asked that a driving under the influence record of the Department of Motor Vehicles be marked as the next exhibit in order, Mrs. Rodriguez had had enough. She asked for a break, went to the restroom, took the elevator to the ground floor, walked out of the building, and never came back. Her case was dismissed for failure to comply with the court order to complete her deposition. Costs were awarded to Bridgeport's client. He had the statement of costs served personally on Mrs. Rodriguez with a demand that she pay his client for the unfinished deposition.

The *Los Angeles Daily Journal* chronicled the Sypnicki case, featuring Bridgeport and his firm under the heading: "Hard Ball Litigation."

In the article, Jackson described his philosophy of litigation: "In war, there is the Geneva Convention relating to the treatment of combatants and noncombatants. In litigation, there is no such agreement. I take no prisoners."

His father cringed upon reading the quote. Not that he did not welcome the reputation for his West Coast litigation department. It was, he found, good for business in Los Angeles. What disturbed him was that the person uttering the crude description of what had once, he believed, been an honorable profession and family legacy, was his son.

The *Los Angeles Times* ran a softer version of the story with a family profile. Bridgeport permitted them to come into his home and even photograph him and Sarah, with their two children, Jackson IV and Amy, in the splendor of their huge estate.

"Mr. and Mrs. Jackson Bridgeport III," graced the Sunday section. Jackson gave full credit to his "very artistic wife" for totally renovating and decorating "our home," and creating three acres of gardens in "the classical Italian style." As to his fame as a litigator, Jackson could not resist describing it as "Darwinesque." It was, he said, "survival of the fittest." And, he suggested, he was not about to be eaten anytime soon. He even went so far with the analogy as to suggest that Jackson IV, with his genes, would likely be his father's successor in litigation.

Sarah did not welcome the publicity. For a week, she noticed more cars driving by, looking at the house and grounds. Neighbors now seemed to make a point of waving or attempting to engage her in conversation.

Her "art" had become the house and gardens. Jackson had readily acceded to her renovations. He told her to bill everything to the office directly. Nevertheless, she was scrupulously careful of costs, feeling she had no right to spend his money without a full accounting. Yet, he seemed oblivious to, and without concern for, cost. He knew enough to appreciate Sarah's knowledge of and skill in creating a unique home and gardens in the midst of what he considered crass, schlock, though expensive, estates.

It never occurred to Sarah that the *Los Angeles Times* article never once referred to her by name. She was "Mrs. Jackson Bridgeport III" throughout the article—and in life. She did not know Sarah Graves anymore, or even if she still existed. Her consolation: two children for whom she would willingly give her life.

By 8:15 A.M. the Sunday the *Los Angeles Times* article appeared, Jackson was on the phone to the office manager: "Get tear sheets of the *Times* article. And the *L.A. Daily Journal*. Send them to our major national clients. Show them how Bridgeport, Bridgeport, Hall and Pendergast practices law out here."

He reread both articles. Laughing, he thought of Sypnicki.

"Sarah, you know what that thief Sypnicki said to me about his client, Mrs. Rodriguez?"

Sarah did not answer.

"He was groveling for crumbs and whined, 'But she's really hurt!'"

He laughed again, even harder. So hard he began coughing. Sarah did not see the point. Then again, he was not expecting her to.

"Casualty of war," he muttered, pleased with himself.

Chapter 37

Brian

BRIAN WAS RIGHT about the Willie Swanigan case. He had held all the cards: a sure thing. That is how the Los Angeles Superior Court jury saw it, too, awarding $1.4 million against the City of Los Angeles and its police officers for the vicious beating that had left Willie with limited sight in one eye and a damaged knee causing a permanent limp. Brian had argued passionately over the violation of Willie Swanigan's civil rights, but he had argued just as forcefully about Swanigan's personal physical injuries using orthopedic and ophthalmological expert witnesses. What it meant for the firm was a 40 percent contingent fee of $560,000. What it meant for Brian and Shelly, finally, after 14 years of marriage, was the purchase of their first home.

In the three years since her ovarian cancer and the loss of the baby, Brian and Shelly had reached an equilibrium in their marriage. Brian turned down cases out of the area and paid attention to fee-generating work at the office. Whatever cases he tried had to be close enough that he could return home at night. Even if he was up most of the night for trial preparation, he was at home. He showed an interest, a genuine interest, in her work. For her part, Shelly was willing to discuss her students, share funny things that happened at school, and talk about the future—as if they had one—but not about the past. It was there, they both knew, but if they did not talk about it, maybe it would just go away in time.

Ironically, it was Charles Garry, the Black Panther attorney, who taught him the lesson: "The thing about a legal reputation is you're known for one thing, and that's usually what you did last. If your last case was a free case, people will call asking you to handle more free cases. You get inundated with free cases. If your last case was a paying case, it generates more paying cases."

214

Brian had seen it himself. Even his friends and people he had defended for free took their paying business elsewhere. "We didn't know you did that kind of work," they would often say with some embarrassment. "What kind is that? The kind that pays the rent?" he asked, although he could not really blame them. It was how he preferred to see himself—a warrior for justice, not a lawyer for money.

Garry himself had financed his civil rights and criminal defense work in large measure by handling personal injury cases. If a Panther's mother got in a car accident, Garry damn well better get the case.

Brian had started at the top of The Movement in the company of men like Garry and Kunstler. He had learned well to identify with the ideology of his clients and move it forward, through the law and in the media. He did not, however, have a history of practicing law and making a lot of money.

Now, with *Swanigan v. City of Los Angeles*, he saw how one case, one good case, could give Shelly and him a home. It felt good. They deserved it, he reasoned. Willie Swanigan did not begrudge him the fee. If it wasn't for me, Willie would have just pled guilty to keep his chauffeur's license, Brian told himself. He alternatively justified the $560,000 fee earned on the broken body of Willie Swanigan as back pay for all the free work he had given to The Cause—a cause that had benefitted Willie Swanigan, too, even if Willie was unaware of Brian's work on his behalf.

It was also unsaid between Brian and Shelly that the new house, a home, represented a new start for them. Together, they talked about the type of home they wanted, secluded among trees, away from the noise of the city. The furnishings, contemporary but comfortable, with bright art on the walls and sculptures in the garden. "There's got to be a garden with water sounds," insisted Shelly, "a deck and a hot tub for us to relax in at night under the stars. Just us, alone."

The home they found in Laurel Canyon met all of their requirements, and more. Perched on the side of the canyon, with massive metal beams vertically set in cement abutments, it hung out over what appeared to be a jungle 40 feet below. A sundeck greeted them as they stepped through sliding doors. The deck railings were horizontal cylinders of copper, with stainless steel cables forming a fence between. A hot tub was perched precariously on its own deck, three steps down, and off of the front of the sundeck, as if floating in air, giving a hidden, but unobstructed, view of the horizon in three directions. From Willow Drive, above the house, to enter the home, they had to pass through an inner courtyard, over a steel bridge, with see-through grate looking into the water below that flowed from an area at the front wall and seemed to disappear over rocks on the side of the house as if falling off the edge of the world. The gardens were lushly planted with tropical plants, many fed by overhead sprinklers. The entry to the home was stone, which dropped immediately into a sunken living area. The master bedroom was above the first floor, back from the canyon so as to allow for its own deck on the roof. The canyon view was a rounded wall with glass covering 180 degrees—everything except the wall facing the front road side of the home. That wall was reserved for the master bed, from which the spectacular view and the night glow of lights over the next hill toward West Hollywood, in the distance, could be viewed.

It did not go unnoticed to Brian and Shelly, who were trying to hold their marriage together, that they were the beneficiaries of a divorce. The sellers of the home were in a bitter divorce and this, their dream home, was being sold quickly, and for a price that would never allow another to build the house with the precision and quality that they had lovingly brought to what neither could now permit the other to have.

The City of Los Angeles filed, on the last possible day, an appeal in the *Swanigan* case. There was no way the city would win the appeal. There was no way an appellate court could reverse the judgment, even though—Brian believed—it would if it could. Appellate judges were eager to find any excuse to reverse a big verdict against the cops. But the appellate process could take three years before he and Shelly—and Swanigan—would ever see any money. Sure, interest and court costs would be added on at the end of that time. But the house that he and Shelly had found would have been long sold.

Brian hated to do it—to give in to the bastards, to give them any satisfaction, to take even a dime less than the jury had awarded his client. In the end, he did not. Instead, he had his partner, Paul Zarick, make the final concession call. But before he did, his frustration and the importance he attached to the money became evident and undermined their negotiating position.

Brian had called the Los Angeles city attorney and argued, "You know there is no way in hell you can win this appeal. We are going to get interest at 7 percent on the verdict, court costs, and we are going to ask for sanctions for a frivolous appeal."

Brian stopped yelling. He waited. He did not slam down the phone. At that point, on the other end, the city attorney knew that Brian had called to negotiate.

In a week, the agreement was reached.

Paul's statement to the city attorney was overly formal: "I am authorized by my client to reduce the award by $400,000 and settle for $1 million payable immediately, in return for the city's dismissal of the appeal."

The "authorization" by the client Willie Swanigan never happened, just as Brian never told Swanigan that the District Attorney was willing to dismiss the original criminal complaint. Brian had always exercised a free hand to do whatever he wanted in the case, partly because he never told Willie everything and partly because Willie trusted him completely.

Instead of $560,000, the fee on the reduced $1 million settlement was $400,000, still enough to buy Shelly's dream house and possibly salvage a marriage.

It was Paul who reminded Brian that Jackson Bridgeport III had referred the case to the office in the first place.

"You need to call Bridgeport and work out a referral fee," Paul said.

"Why? He didn't do any work on the case."

Brian had already seen $160,000 be lost through the frivolous appeal of the city. Now his partner was suggesting, after years of work on the case, that the firm should split the fee again, with a lawyer who had done nothing to earn a fee and was, besides, one for whom he had no respect whatsoever.

"Fuck Bridgeport," he added.

"Brian, you can't fuck referral sources. It's standard practice. Someone refers a personal injury case, they get a referral fee."

It was apparent that Brian had not anticipated a referral fee in buying his new house.

"There is no guarantee Bridgeport will ever refer us another case. Besides, he referred the criminal case, not the personal injury case. We spotted the civil rights claim ourselves. Bridgeport wouldn't even know a civil rights claim if it kicked him in the ass."

"Brian, you are going to hurt the firm if it gets out that we fuck referral sources. It's not just Bridgeport; it's the legal community. We practice in the same town, and he's got a big mouth. Call him. Work the best deal, but don't ignore him. Brian, I am managing partner. If you don't call, I will. I think it would be better if you called him since you went to Boalt together. You know him."

Brian was boxed in, again. He had to get the matter resolved immediately. Escrow on the house was set to close.

"Yeah, I know him. That's why I don't want to call the pompous son-of-a-bitch."

But, finally, he called.

"Jackson, how have you been?"

"Fine. I hope you are not calling to tell me that one of those groups you represent is going to be doing a sit-in at one of my clients' centers."

"No, nothing like that. Actually, I just called to give you an update on Willie Swanigan's case."

"Who?"

"Willie Swanigan. You referred him to me when he was arrested."

"Never heard of him."

"Well," Brian began, seeing the beginning of a memo to the file, "maybe I was mistaken…"

"Are you talking about my housekeeper's husband? Black guy? I told her to have her husband call you when he was arrested for drunk driving. Frankly, I don't like to get involved with employees' personal lives, but it was disruptive. Our maid was saying that if he lost his license then she might have to quit. Okay, I remember. I just didn't know his name. So, what are you calling about?"

Brian had hoped he just would not remember at all.

"Well, I got him off on the drunk driving. Also kept his license."

"Good. She's still with us."

Brian went on tentatively.

"Well, we also filed a suit against the city for his injuries."

"Why in the hell would you do that?"

"Violation of his civil rights."

"Only you would believe that, Brian. He was driving drunk. He could have killed someone. Well, I understand that's what you do, and you're good at it. Frankly, I wouldn't allow anyone at my firm to file a suit like that."

Brian hesitated.

"We got him a good resolution. Since you referred the client originally, I thought I would talk to you about a possible referral fee."

Jackson Bridgeport III did not hesitate with his response.

"Our firm doesn't take referral fees for work we haven't done. I realize there are members of the Bar who do, and I think it's repulsive. Nor do I seek to benefit off of my domestic workers and their families. He wasn't a client I referred, he was the drunk-driving husband of my maid. So I suppose I should thank you, Brian, for being ethical in your ways and calling about your settlement, but we decline your request."

Brian could not believe it. Paul told him the customary referral fee was $33^{1}/_{3}$ percent—$133,333 of the $400,000 fee to the firm—and Bridgeport was calling him unethical for offering it.

"How much was the settlement?" Bridgeport asked.

Christ, thought Brian, he is going to take the money.

"We negotiated a reduction of the jury verdict to avoid appeal."

Brian was stalling. But he would have to get there sooner or later, unless interrupted. No interruptions came. "The final settlement was for $1 million," he finally said.

Bridgeport did not ask about the fee—nor did he suggest that his firm receive part of it. Instead, irritated, he yelled at Brian before hanging up: "Shit! Now she'll probably quit her job!"

Chapter 38

Rose

SHE COULD NEVER have done it had her father been alive. He would not have understood. Leaving her job, just as she was set to become a partner in a top San Francisco firm, to return to the Valley.

"We don't want to lose you, Rose." Anthony Hawk was pleading with her. "We'll open a Fresno office. You can run it. We have enough business in the Valley. With a presence, we could pick up even more. You would still be a partner with the firm."

Rose was appreciative, but his pleas made it harder. Leaving was not an easy decision. It had started with Gonzales and her brother's case. She had recognized the excitement. The pride. Her legal education felt like it had meaning. Reynoso—"Ernie"—had contributed to it. His commitment, mixed with criticism of her life, and the respect he engendered in ordinary people—people like her parents—whom he had helped. But her father would not have understood.

Since being confronted by Ernie, she had looked at her life. Hard. She had become more aware of comments made in her presence, especially by clients who had every reason to believe she was one of them—not a Mexican.

"Would Canadians be treated in the fields of California as Mexicans are?" Ernie had asked. She knew the answer.

As good as she was, she also did not feel judges and many of her opposing colleagues took her seriously. Some clients were clearly uncomfortable with a "girl" attorney.

Her father's illness brought her back to the Valley often, but she did not visit as often as she felt she should have. It was her brother Pablo, now a drama student at UCLA, who called. The note was on the conference room door, as she came out of a long afternoon deposition. She opened it:

"Urgent…call Mom." It bore the time of the call: "1:30 P.M." She had not been interrupted. It was an important deposition.

She was stunned by the news: "*Papá ha muerto.*" She fell back upon her training, to marshal the facts; to take charge. Arrangements had to be made. The funeral. A rental for mom—she could stay at the ranch house "until she found a place," they told her—since Dad would not be working for the company anymore.

"What did the doctors say?"

"*No sé.*"

"What made him die?"

"*No sé.*"

"We should get a copy of his medical records from the doctor," she told her mother.

Her mother answered, "*¿Porqué? Esta con Dios.*" Why? He is with God.

The funeral surprised her. The small Catholic church was packed. She walked behind the casket with her mother, her brother ahead of them. Families nodded to her in sorrow. She entered the front pew, next to her mother. Her brother, genuflecting, entered last.

The mass was in Latin, but the mariachis, hats in hand, sang in Spanish. Parishioners' lips moved in unison with the songs.

She heard him enter through the side door, the metal hitting it to hold it open as he adjusted the handles. She turned her head to see him struggling toward the pew. All eyes were on him. Their eyes met, he nodded and fell into place.

It was Pablo, not Rose, who was asked to come forward, sprinkle holy water on the casket, and address the congregation about his father's passing. He did so in Spanish. Of all the people present, only two were not Mexican: the priest and the company superintendent, and the priest spoke Spanish. Yet, even though only one of the 200 mourners was a non–Spanish-speaking Anglo, there was a conspiratorial feeling in the use of the common language.

Pablo, without notes, looked over the congregation:

> From the time I was little,
> my father told me to "be somebody."
> Yet he was just a farm worker.
>
> He sent me off to UCLA to pursue

a dream he didn't understand;
he worked so my sister could succeed
in a law career he could only imagine.
For he was just a farm worker.

He was born in poverty, in Mexico.
He came to this country and sent money
home to help his parents and siblings;
He married, raised two children,
who were never without
because he always provided.
Yet, he was just a farm worker.

He was sickened, and grew weary
from years of chemicals and stooping labor,
for he was just a farm worker.

Now he is with God.
Looking down upon us.
No longer a farm worker.

"Look, Señor Contreras," God says,
"see all of the people gathered in your honor.
You, Señor Contreras,
you were somebody."

At the reception that followed, the music was loud, almost festive. It was more like a family reunion. Introductions. Reintroductions. The theme was the same: "Your father was so proud of you…he always talked about you…you're doing so well."

They all knew her, through him.

Except Reynoso: "Rose, you never returned my call."

"When did you call?"

"Three years ago."

"Yeah," she answered with some resignation, "I've been busy. I guess I've been bad at returning calls for a while."

"Can I help?" he asked.

"This may not be the time, especially with my father looking down, and the congregation exuding his pride in my accomplishments, but I've been thinking of quitting my job. I'm not even sure I want to stay in law."

"Maybe this isn't the time to be making decisions," he remarked.

"I'm afraid if I don't make one soon, I'll be locked in forever. I'm feeling a sense of panic. Like my life is over unless I do something fast."

"Rosa, you're 30! Trust me. You're life's hardly begun."

He paused and then asked, "How long will you be staying in town?"

"All week. Got to help Mom find a place. Then I think I'll take a few days to sort things out before heading back to San Francisco."

"Okay. Let me cook you dinner while you're sorting. You never took me up on my Indian cuisine the last time you rushed through my life."

Rose smiled. "I'll call you."

"Sure?"

"Yes."

"Let me give you my number," he said, reaching for his wallet.

"I still have it. I've often thought of calling you, Ernie."

Chapter 39

Rose

"WHAT ARE THOSE?"

Rose did call Ernesto and the smells of his house, as she entered, told her he had been serious when he had talked of cooking Indian food. But since she had never tasted Indian food, a heavy aroma of marsala and curry, or even a little hint of cardamom, could fool her. Like real estate salespeople putting a touch of vanilla on a light bulb to make a house smell like freshly cooked bread.

"Well, in the Punjab, they may be called chapati. Or roti, or just nan."

"Looks like a tortilla," Rose observed.

"Same concept. Every society, it seems, has some form of flat bread. These roties are little different than those made thousands of years ago throughout Central Asia. The variations throughout societies seem to depend on the available grain and heat sources. Fortunately, we have it all, so we can bring together in an evening what might have taken a Bedouin, a Kurd, a Rajasthani or even a Mexican the better part of a day to collect and cook."

He picked up another ball of dough, rolled it flat, and pushed down in each direction. Then, with hands covered in flour, he picked it up and began moving it back and forth in a clapping motion. The circle expanded as he rotated it slowly on the upward clap. He laid it on a griddle and started on the next dough ball.

"You can paint the ghee on," he said, pointing to a basting brush in a cup containing a yellow substance. "That's real ghee—'usli ghee'—clarified butter. In the Punjab it's also used for religious and medicinal purposes."

He lifted the dough off the hot griddle and laid it across a burner with an open gas flame. The flattened dough began to rise, inflate rather, into something approaching a puff fish. He moved it about with his bare hands, flipped it, and then removed it quickly to a plate covered with a cloth.

"Ghee time."

"What do I do?" Rose asked.

"First lesson in Indian cooking. Brush the chapati with lots of ghee. Place it ghee-side up. Same with the next one. That way both sides are battered. Each time, cover them with the cloth to keep them warm. You don't want cold chapati with curry."

"You really can cook," Rose said with unconcealed surprise.

"Didn't you believe me?" He held his hands out, floured palms up.

"I dunno, I suppose I thought it was just part of the act. 'Zapata the revolutionary.' Iconoclast. Man of mystery. Fits in somehow with the smells of foreign spices," she answered him.

He did not respond. He kept on making chapati. She felt she had hurt him.

"Look, I didn't mean…"

"No," he said, "I understand."

They worked silently in the small kitchen.

"Rosa, have you ever heard about the three names of a cat?"

"A cat?" she said, relieved that the conversation was resuming and apparently steering away from revolutionary cuisine to sedate felines.

"Yes. A cat. A cat has three names. The first is the one everyone knows it by. The second is its real name. The third is its secret name that only it knows."

Rose smiled at the idea that a cat would have a "real" name, let alone a secret one.

"I think we're similar," Reynoso continued. "To be happy, it is important that others see us, in part, as we see ourselves, in our secret lives. We can affect how others see us by projecting parts of a persona. But first, we need to know who we are and ask whether we are who we want to be. Until that day, Rosa, we aren't going to be happy or, for that matter, as effective a person as we could be."

She knew her whole life had been summed up and found wanting, but he had delivered the verdict so softly that she knew it was meant to help.

"There is a part of me that wants to be a revolutionary," he continued. "Rob banks, blow up trains, break into grain silos and feed the peasants. But I do it with writs and briefs. Still seeking justice. Well, not justice, just what I can get for those who don't have much. So this is how I see myself.

"The 'act,' as you call it, is how I project myself upon the Anglo justice system. They, too, see me as a revolutionary; unpredictable, to be feared. I play on that. I wear this beard and moustache and keep them purposely shaggy. That way I look even wilder.

"When, instead of their women and children, I ask only for a modest nonrevolutionary increase in a child's medical benefits, or a mother's food stamps, they are relieved to give it. But, like in your brother Pablo's case, when I beat them with their own rules, it's a victory for the revolution.

"So, it's effective; it's who I wish I could be; and, it's fun. The Indian food, on the other hand, is pure indulgence. I love it."

He pointed to the pots simmering on the stove. "It's done."

"What can I do to help?" asked Rose.

"Nothing. It needs to simmer. Actually, if we turned it off and came back tomorrow, it would be better. Indian food is always better the second warming. But then, it took three years to get you here this evening, didn't it? No telling when I might see you again."

She did not have a ready answer.

"Well, let me show you to our table." She followed him to a large room off the kitchen.

A table was sitting in the center of an orchid-infested, glassed-in atrium at the back of the house. It had obviously been moved from the empty spot in the kitchen. An old pot-belly stove, its door open, provided visual and physical warmth. Large speakers stood in two corners, with smaller ones mounted high behind them.

"Do you like opera?" he asked, as she looked for the source of the music.

"Revolutionary opera?" she asked, smiling.

"Well, actually, it is Rimsky-Korsakov. Correction; it's Mussorgsky's *Boris Godunov* as revised by Rimsky-Korsakov. Uniquely Russian but pre-Revolution."

"First, fine cuisine; now, classical music. Seems I have a lot to learn."

"I don't mind teaching you," he answered too quickly. They were both embarrassed. She looked at the table. "My, you have been busy." Sitting on the table was wine, in a chilling ceramic pot, and chutneys in brass bowls, on a flat plate with a hard, thin bread. In the center of the brightly colored tablecloth was a brass statue of Shiva, with incense burning in a bowl underneath.

"I thought we'd start with my chutneys," he said as he pulled her chair out. "I make them myself every summer. One summer, when I was in the Marysville office, I canned so much peach chutney that all my friends got them as Christmas presents. Now, they expect it. Keeps me busy. This year, I also did a tomato chutney and a mango chutney with green chilies, red pepper pods, and black mustard seeds."

She sat. "Tell me what to do."

"Well, the bread is pappadam. I confess I bought it at the Indian market, but I did cook it in hot oil earlier. It is quite spicy. You can try each of the chutneys with it. Like chips and dip." He demonstrated.

Rose started with the tomato, assuming it would be the most familiar. She was surprised at the taste.

"What's in this?" she asked.

"Not exactly catsup, heh? Guess."

"It's sweet...with a little bite on the tongue."

"Good." He was genuinely pleased. "The 'bite' is ginger. There are also raisins and sweet onions and a stick of cinnamon. Like it?"

"Love it," she replied, as she spooned more on her pappadam. "I thought all Indian food was hot," she added.

"Another myth to dispel. It's like Mexican foods. The heat usually comes from adding red or green peppers. Americans think 'curry' means hot. Curry powder and most spices used in Indian cooking give character, not heat. Actually, my traveling companion, Madhur Jaffrey, taught me that even the order of ingredients put into an Indian dish can change its taste. For example, if a hot dried red pepper is browned in oil before being added to lentils, the dish will have an entirely different taste and heat than if the pepper is browned and cooked with the lentils."

He reached for the wine. "I'm sorry. I didn't offer you wine. It's a Gewurztraminer. I find that it stands up well to Indian food."

Rose sipped her wine. "Your traveling companion is Indian?"

"Madhur? Oh, God yes. I took her everywhere in India last fall. Constant companion. I wouldn't think of going to India without her."

Rose ate quietly.

"Could you help me plate up?" he asked. "I'm afraid I can't carry the plates in here. I usually eat at the counter in the kitchen alone."

"Sure." She followed him back to the kitchen.

"I'm afraid I got carried away when you said you would try my food. I wanted you to taste it all. You're going to have to make a number of trips.

Several of the dishes need to be kept separate. They complement each other and need to maintain their individual integrity."

He directed her to the refrigerator where a bowl of light green yogurt awaited. "Made it this morning. Wanted it to chill. It's the raita." He handed her two small bowls. She ladled the yogurt into the bowls and took them to the atrium table. When she returned, he had two more bowls. "Dal," he replied to her look. "A woman friend, Julie Sahni, gave me this recipe. It has tamarind."

"Another traveling companion?" asked Rose.

"Julie? Oh, no, I couldn't do that to Madhur. What kind of a man do you take me for?" He was enjoying himself.

He was leaning on one crutch and filling a plate when she again returned. "You're going to love this. This is a traditional Punjabi chicken curry, a chicken murgh masala. No matter what chicken curries I have, I always come back to this one."

He put rice next to the chicken. "This is basmati rice. The dish is called Patiala Pullao after a city in the Punjab. Don't eat the bay leaves or cloves."

When he lifted the cover of the final pot, the strong but sweetened smell of cauliflower followed the steam.

"What it that?" Rose asked.

"Gobhi Sobzi. Glazed cauliflower with ginger. I'm really on a Punjabi kick tonight. Actually, throughout India, vegetarian dishes are a staple, and not just with Hindus or Jainists."

He handed her the dish, grabbed his other crutch, and said, "Let's eat." As she walked ahead of him, he grabbed a worn paperback book off a shelf in the kitchen.

They sat, and he surveyed his table. He refilled their wine glasses. "Here's to your father and his children, Rosa." He lifted his glass.

"Thank you for coming to the funeral, Ernie. It really helped." They clicked glasses.

"Well, you wouldn't return my call…"

"You seemed to have done fine in my absence. What was her name? Your companion in India. And your woman friend, Julie?"

"Ah, yes, Madhur Jaffrey."

He handed her the cookbook. "As you can see, she is a little worn for wear, I carried her all over India, looking for her dishes. She was a wonderful companion."

Rose looked down: Madhur Jaffrey, *An Invitation to Indian Cooking*.

"Julie is young, beautiful, warm, charming. What can I say? The week I spent in New York at the Julie Sahni Indian Cooking School, that was different. Julie is real. Not that I fantasized in class, but given a choice, I think I'd take Julie Sahni to India or anywhere else she wanted to go."

Rose threw the book at him. He was laughing.

"You brat. You're a big tease."

"Like I said, what was I to do? You never returned my calls."

Rose smiled, "Well, I'm here now." She started to eat her food.

"Try the raita. It's chilled. The grated cucumber and fresh mint have a way of cooling the mouth as you eat the chicken."

"Ernie, you are amazing. Thank you."

"Wait till dessert. Gulab Jamun, which is a classic milk fudge with…" He stopped, mid-sentence.

"Don't do that!" he shouted.

Rose jumped. "What?"

"Use a fork to eat my Indian food. That's what the chapati is for. Here, watch."

He demonstrated, tearing off a strip of the warm chapati dripping with ghee. He expertly wrapped it around a piece of chicken, scooped some of the juices into it, and rubbed it against the chutney before lifting it into his mouth. After taking a bite, he told Rose: "Now, you try."

She tore off a piece of chapati and folded it as he had done. Then she reached in search of a piece of chicken.

"No! No! Wrong hand!"

Again startled, she asked, "What now?"

"Right hand, not left."

"Why?"

"Because Indians use the left for sanitary purposes. It's also suspicious. So don't do it again."

"But I'm not an Indian," Rose protested.

He had a look of satisfaction on his face. "That's what I've been trying to tell you all along, Rosa. You're a Mexican. Now we can work on who you want to be."

She just shook her head. "You don't give up, do you?"

"Not on you, Rosa. There is too much there."

Another uncomfortable silence. He broke it. "Why did you go to law school?"

"I suppose because people said I would be good at it, which I am," she added with emphasis.

"Why else?" he prodded.

"It's a career, something that takes advanced education. It has status attached to it. It pays well. It's more than anyone in my family has ever done. It can open doors to so many other opportunities."

"So far all the reasons sound like those that your parents might want for you."

She laughed. "My mother would rather I live close by and have babies."

"I'm surprised your father didn't want that for you, too, actually. Mexican fathers usually encourage the boys, not the girls, into careers."

"Maybe it was because I was the older. Pablo is nine years younger. Maybe he didn't expect any more children so he worked on me early. 'Be somebody.' It was me he told that to first. Over and over. I did what he told me, and when he died, it was my little brother, the male who is heir to the name, who was asked to deliver the eulogy." Her voice had been rising as she spoke. "It was me he told that to first!"

Reynoso tried to deflect the unease he felt at this surprising outburst: "Well, at least Pablo did a good job."

"You still don't get it, do you?" she shot back. "It was *my* job!" She was sobbing over her curry.

He got up from his chair and, with his crutches, moved behind her. He rested his hands on her shoulders and massaged her neck with his thumbs.

"Like I said, Indian food is always better reheated."

She laughed, rubbing her eyes with her napkin. "Only if you invite me back."

"You have an open invitation, Rosa," Reynoso said, his thumbs causing her head to sway back and forth, the tension receding with the ebb and flow of his hands.

Chapter 40

Michael

"MICHAEL, THE GOVERNOR could appoint you to the Municipal Court in Oakland, but I think you would be better off waiting." It was the end of Reagan's eight years as governor and last-minute appointments were being made as rewards to friends. After five years of practice, Michael could qualify—just barely—for a Municipal Court judgeship but was not eligible for the Superior Court, which had a 10-year requirement. But that was not what Ed Meese meant about waiting, and Michael knew it. No one doubted that Ronald Reagan was looking at the White House two years down the road, in 1976. The implicit offer was, if Reagan won, Meese would go to Washington and so would Michael.

"Whatever happens, you would probably be better off back in the District Attorney's Office. Get more experience as a prosecutor. Position yourself. Keep your options open."

Michael was thinking of his options too, particularly his options with his son, Robbie. The last three years in Sacramento had been hard. Robbie was eight and in school all week. Michael saw him only on weekends, and even then not every weekend. He missed laughing with him, rolling on the floor, putting him to bed, driving him and his little friends to McDonald's. He never forgot to call at night, every night. Often, he would excuse himself and call during a late evening dinner at Frank Fat's, Posie's, or one of the other Sacramento political meeting places. Most often, however, it was from the small, sparsely furnished two-bedroom—one for Robbie—apartment four blocks from the Capitol building. When it got really bad, Michael would walk into the empty bedroom, look at Robbie's picture, and rearrange toys. He wanted to go home. And home was where his son was.

Mai brought up the matter of divorce in early 1975. Michael's move back to Oakland, to rejoin the Alameda County District Attorney's Office, forced the issue. They had been "separated" in mind, body, and geography. Now geography was eliminated, and reality was difficult to avoid. So was Jeremy Mandel, an instructor in the Department of Social Work at San Francisco State College, Mai's companion. It was understood, though never discussed, that "separate" meant Michael and Mai had their own lives. Moving back to Oakland, and picking up Robbie two nights a week, after school, inevitably led to a greater awareness of her home life. And home life involved Jeremy Mandel most evenings and many of the mornings. Michael knew he would never be part of that home again.

Mai now had a picture of George McGovern in her study. It showed the former presidential candidate holding a newspaper. The headline read "Nixon Resigns." Written across the picture was the note: "Mai—we were right." It was signed, "George."

Michael Cassidy did not blame George McGovern anymore. He blamed himself.

Michael's father's only comment was, "I told you not to marry her." His mother was glad to have him back in the Bay Area. She fully expected to see more of him, which also meant seeing more of Robbie. She was right. Michael retreated to the only family left, his parents, and attempted to incorporate Robbie into their lives. He spent weekends in the city. He returned to the San Francisco Yacht Club and sailing on the Bay. Robbie became a familiar figure on weekends and, in time, an accomplished sailor. Also, with the passage of time, members stopped asking Michael, "Who's the Chinese kid?"

At work, he was technically just another Deputy District Attorney, but everyone knew he was being groomed. His future was not limited to the District Attorney's Office. Like others over the years at the Alameda County District Attorney's Office, he was an attorney-in-waiting.

Michael's assignments reflected his status. High-profile cases—those where a "law and order" position could be taken; a stand against permissiveness; a blow for decency; work against revolutionaries—were assigned to him. He was selected to testify before legislative committees on the threat posed by revolutionary groups such as the Symbionese Liberation Army (SLA), which had recently abducted Patty Hearst, a daughter of the Hearst newspaper publishers and granddaughter of the legendary William Randolph Hearst, from her apartment in Berkeley.

Michael advocated, in the case of the SLA, greater law enforcement surveillance of organizations that posed a threat to the rule of law. He acknowledged the right to protest—although he questioned its effectiveness—but opposed civil disobedience, violations of law, and, of course, criminal acts directed at other citizens in society. He had in mind not just the SLA—all the available evidence suggested that its members numbered less than a dozen—but the Black Panthers, war protesters who used illegal acts, and, of course, rioters, looters, and those whose slogan appeared to be "burn, baby, burn."

While he never revealed them to Brian Jacobs, Michael had reservations about the death penalty. He found it hard to integrate with his Catholicism. He acknowledged, in his own thoughts, the disparity of its application to blacks. But a society had a right to defend itself, he believed, just like in war. And what was going on in the streets of America was often a war, with a need for National Guard troops to restore order. There was no excuse, in America, he thought, for violation of laws. He could understand civil disobedience in the context, for example, that Mahatma Gandhi found himself in, but America was not an occupied country. It was a democracy. Here, things were changed through ballots and in the courts; not through bullets or in the streets.

Although Brian Jacobs and, for that matter, no one outside the governor's office would ever know it, Michael actually had advocated Jacobs' position to Meese in the matter of executive clemency for Stonewall Jackson. "Perhaps, in this climate of race relations in America, the governor might consider clemency as an act of reconciliation."

But he had no answer to the counter-argument: "If Stonewall Jackson was rightly convicted and sentenced, should it be a defense that other murderers were not rightly punished?"

He did not expect that Meese would be interested in poetry but the words of a poem about race riots, included in a law review article by one of his Boalt classmates, lingered:

I can't talk to you, you've never been there,
In the hate-haunted canyons of human despair.

He did not give the poem to Meese or to the governor. He was, after all, a lawyer called upon to make a legal analysis. Poetry was not the language of the law and hardly a tool of persuasion with the legal affairs secretary to the governor considering clemency for a murderer. But, while he rejected all lawlessness and was committed to the rule of law by reason and training, Michael was bothered because he knew what he did not know. He did not know why blacks would burn down their own neighborhoods; disproportionately commit crimes, especially against each other; or do so badly in school and employment settings compared to other poor people. He did not understand those his own age who were ready to condemn America and its democratic institutions while praising, uncritically, foreign countries and revolutionary movements.

"How can we have a society if everyone is free to violate the law?" he asked Mai.

"You and your fucking law!" she screamed and stormed out. On that occasion, the argument was over her support of the war protesters blocking ammunition trains leaving Port Chicago for the Oakland docks.

Michael was secretly relieved that Ronald Reagan lost the Republican nomination to Gerald Ford in 1976. Michael was not ready to go to Washington. More correctly, he was unwilling to leave Robbie and move East. He knew that if the call came, he would have to go. His position in the District Attorney's Office, with District Attorney Lowell Jensen, was because of Reagan, through Meese. If he broke that connection, he was just another Deputy District Attorney, another county-employed lawyer. He worried about his life without Robbie. He entertained the idea—briefly, very briefly—of seeking custody of Robbie if he had to go to Washington. He knew, in his position as a Deputy District Attorney, in a courthouse that knew his connections, that he stood an excellent chance of custody, especially if he was seeking custody as he went to Washington to serve the president of the United States. Mai's multiple arrests at a variety of protests and her cohabitation with a man not her husband would count against her. But he would not do it. He knew she was a wonderful mother. She gave Robbie the playfulness, the whimsy that he did not have. When he looked at Robbie, he saw her. Not just the Asian looks, but the ever-so-slight twinkle at the edge of his eyes when he knew he had you. He had even picked up her mime imitations. The first time he demonstrated his acquired skill was when he had tied himself to the main mast, with a full spinnaker ballooning in front of the yacht. Michael nearly ran aground on the west side of Angel Island, and other yachts lost their sail watching what appeared to be a Chinese mannequin, tied to the mast, rotating his head from side to side, up and down, with arms in short chopping strokes, as if running ahead of the mast. He was his mother's boy. Michael loved him so much, even though it hurt to look at him and see Mai.

Michael decided, before Gerald Ford won the Republican nomination, that he needed Robbie more than the president of the United States might need him. He would not be so lucky in 1980. Ronald Reagan beat incumbent President Jimmy Carter and became the 40th president of the United States.

Chapter 41

Leon

"WHY DO YOU get paid more than her?"

"Because I earn the fees."

"Doesn't she work on the same cases?"

"Yes, but I told you she is just the paralegal."

"She's got two kids and a house payment. She works on the same cases. You've got an apartment, no family, but you get paid three times as much as her? Is this how we raised you, Leon?"

It was Marx and Engels for dinner, the *Communist Manifesto*, which meant Leon was home for the weekend, in Seattle, with his parents.

"I am the one who funds the whole operation and the cases. Shouldn't I get a return on my investment?"

He knew this would send his dad up the wall. He did it for Angela's benefit: to show her the beliefs of his family; the stock from which he came.

But it was Angela who responded: "Mr. Goldman, I'm afraid Leon hasn't learned the lessons of *Das Kapital*. He still has a capitalist mentality: Using capital to accumulate more capital. Of course, certain classes of people in American society are shut out from access to capital. Hence, we have Leon, the capitalist, making three times what Cindy, the working mother in his office, makes."

Leon's father was nodding in agreement.

"If Cindy were black, a single mother, and got food stamps to supplement what your son pays her, we would have a starker picture of capitalist American society."

"Wait a minute. No one in my office is on food stamps!" exclaimed Leon. His father was also defensive.

"Black or white, it doesn't matter. It's a matter of exploitation of labor. Capital needs to be commonly owned, available to all."

"But Mr. Goldman," Angela answered, "black and white does matter in America. Labor unions have traditionally discriminated against blacks, which means blacks are a cheap labor pool outside of organized labor. Unions just play into the hands of the capitalists. Divide and conquer. Keep black and white labor separate, with blacks excluded from the more powerful white unions, and the capitalists have a reservoir of nonunion labor with which to break unions. Simple."

Now Leon and his father were talking over each other:

"...and my employees have the best benefits of any law office in the Bay Area..."

"...never turned down a Negro for membership in my union. They just don't do that kind of work."

It was Leon's mother who ended the debate by serving dinner.

The explanation given for their presence together in Seattle was a conference on housing discrimination and redlining by realtors—the practice of designating areas by race for sale and lease—but his parents knew he was "seeing somebody."

It had evolved slowly, given the teasing and sexual tension that had always accompanied their work together. At first, both were able to justify their time together because of their passion for The Cause while denying their passion for each other. Leon's passion was expressed intellectually while she intellectually used the expression of passion. Each respected and admired the other.

Then there was the matter of race, black and white.

"I gave up slavery once; I ain't about to be subservient to no man."

"Who's talking subservience?"

"Well, maybe that's how I see marriage."

"Who's talking marriage?"

"Oh? You just think I sleep round wid' anyone 'cause I'm black?"

"No, you sleep around because you're a dirty-mouthed bitch with a fabulous body that needs serving."

"Oh, now you is a servicin' me?"

"I've been trying."

"And I thought I was just trying to cure you of that thing you got for us black people."

"What thing?"

"That thing, like the missionaries. You know. White man's burden. You got to take care of us durin' the day. And fuck the women after dark."

"Angela, that's uncalled for. I have no problem with you being black. Besides, I couldn't hide you if I wanted to. You demand attention."

"Oh yeah? Then when do I meet your parents?"

He knew she had won. Again. He had told them of his girlfriend over the last two years, but had never mentioned her name—well, Angela—but not her last name—or, for that matter, that she was black.

"I don't suppose I can tell them you're Jewish?"

"Sorry. I think my tribe headed south out of Judea before Moses took your people to Egypt."

Now she was in his parents' home.

"Dad, Angela and I have been working on not just housing discrimination lawsuits but on building low-income housing. We're really excited about it."

"What do you know about building, Leon?"

"Well, nothing, but I am learning fast. My new partner was with HUD—the federal Housing and Urban Development agency—for the last five years. He's walking us through our first project. We've set up a corporation with a board of pretty prominent people in Oakland to apply for a loan to buy land in a redevelopment area and build 100 units designed for low-income families."

"So now my son's going to be a landlord?"

"Dad, isn't it better I do it than someone who's just using a government program to rip off people? We'll have a tenants' association to run the place. Much like a cooperative."

The idea had formed during an investigation of just such a rip-off. It had started when a black security guard working at a towing yard was turned away from a federally financed low-income apartment complex supposedly because he made more than the qualifying amount for the housing.

The 700-unit apartment complex was predominantly, but not exclusively, white, and was made up of steel workers from the nearby naval shipyard. The complex was owned by the Brotherhood of Steel Workers Pension Fund and had been built with a redevelopment loan from HUD. Rent was subsidized, with the U.S. Treasury paying up to 40 percent per month for families earning under guideline amounts. The employer, General Maritime & Defense Construction, which held the contract for construction of the latest nuclear-powered aircraft carrier for the Navy, certified employees' net pay to HUD, and HUD, in turn, paid the supplement to the landlord/union. To encourage development in redevelopment areas, the HUD loan was for 120 percent of the actual building costs, with low interest and favorable tax treatment, in addition to guaranteed minimum rent supplements.

Angela had complained to HUD. It was all perfectly legal, she was told. "This ain't public housing," she had fumed, "it's company housing for white union workers."

Out of the inquiry came Jonathan Bishop, a HUD attorney to whom Angela had been directed. For four years, at night school, Bishop had worked as a commercial real estate loan specialist at Bank of America's main real estate office in San Francisco. Upon graduation, he had taken a job with HUD. He was meticulous, with a bookkeeper's need for order, and an expert on real estate and government regulations. In his spare time, for relaxation, he liked to read the Code of Federal Regulations, the encyclopedic listing of every rule governing every action of every federal agency or program ever passed by Congress or issued in furtherance thereof. Worse yet, he remembered everything he read.

Angela brought Jonathan Bishop to meet Leon. "You ain't gonna believe this white boy. He says we can build our own housin'."

"Well, subject to certain restrictions," Bishop cautioned. "Also, I know you've handled cases against HUD-funded apartment complexes. You should be aware that federal housing discrimination regulations in the right case might allow you to evict the developers and have the ownership revert to the tenants."

Angela's eyes widened. "Didn't I tell you he's one smart white boy? How come you never thought of that, Leon?"

Jonathan Bishop had other ideas, too. He wanted to join the firm.

"Why here? We're pretty small-time," asked Leon.

"Well, I could go to a big firm, but that would mean doing defense work. I don't want to defend landlords. Besides, there can be some big payoffs in discrimination litigation."

Leon laughed. "You see any big payoffs around here?" he said, waving his arms at the adequate, but hardly richly adorned, offices.

"No, but I have some ideas about that, too."

"Well," responded Leon, "I have to be honest. We've had a pretty decent year, but I am in no position to hire a new attorney."

"I wouldn't consider you hiring me," Bishop answered matter-of-factly. "I want to be your partner."

Catching Leon by surprise, he asked, "How much do you pay a month for rent?" He asked it as if any amount would be too much.

"Fifteen hundred a month, plus parking, electricity, some miscellaneous costs."

"So, how about if we move to a nice place of our own, with a view of the Oakland estuary, have twice the space, and, with a build-out of the rest of the property, have our tenants pay off the mortgage for us? And with double-declining depreciation and money in the bank after close of escrow."

"What's the catch?"

"None. Just maximizing return for effort."

Jonathan Bishop explained the incentives for redevelopment, the same ones the union had used, available through HUD. But a further tax section provided accelerated depreciation for the renovation of historic buildings listed on the National Register. Through his work at HUD, Bishop was intimately familiar with all of the regulations and procedures. He also knew which areas were designated as qualified redevelopment areas and the buildings within each area that would qualify as historic.

Leon had never thought to spend his time in the tax codes. His gaze had always been directed to helping those who, for the most part, did not pay taxes. Again, he found, as in law school, that perhaps his ideology got in the way.

Goldman and Bishop moved to Oakland's "historic" Jack London Square in the spring of 1978.

*　*　*　*　*

Leon's mother turned the conversation to Angela. "Would you like some dessert, Angela?"

"Sure. You got any sweet potato pie, Mom?"

Chapter 42

Brian

IT WAS NOT just Shelly who kept Brian home. Nor his law partner, Paul Zarick, with his emphasis on billable cases. *Swanigan v. City of Los Angeles* had transformed Brian, overnight, into the "expert" on police brutality litigation Now, referrals came to him to handle personal injury civil lawsuits for money damages without regard to any cause, except money.

"I handle one jury trial and I'm an expert?"

"Think of it this way," a veteran personal injury co-counsel told him, "you've tried one civil jury personal injury case so you've got a $1.4 million average. Besides, in this business, you ride on your successes, and you can ride this one for years."

With the new referrals of personal injury cases, Zarick supplemented the library to accommodate *TRAUMA*, the set of books on medical evidence; Eisler on *Uninsured Motorist Law*, Cotchett on *Product Liability*, Van Alstyne on *Government Tort Liability*. He also signed the firm up for membership in the California Trial Lawyers Association. Other than the National Lawyers Guild, a membership he had maintained since law school, and a compulsory membership in the California State Bar, which he resented, the California Trial Lawyers Association was the first legal organization that Brian had joined in eight years of practice. He was immediately put on the calendar for the CTLA statewide conference to speak on "Handling Injury Claims Against the Police—A to Z." The Los Angeles Trial Lawyers Association asked him to join a panel, along with the Los Angeles city attorney, an insurance claims specialist whose company insured municipalities, and a young black lawyer named Johnnie Cochran.

The handout materials, at the Los Angeles Trial Lawyers Association meeting, prepared by a new young associate attorney at Brian's firm, included press clippings not just of the *Swanigan* case but also of Brian's successes on behalf of the Black Panthers, war protesters, and others. He was upset when the trial lawyers group did not reproduce the materials he supplied for conference participants.

"Mr. Jacobs, our trial lawyer association emphasizes civil litigation. The criminal law bar has its own organizations."

It was a subtle difference. When Brian had sued the Chicago Police Department for the wrongful death of Black Panther Emanuel Jackson, there had been nothing to lose. It had been a stunt. For The Movement. For the 5 o'clock news. For, one could argue, jurisprudential history: to show that the Klu Klux Klan Act was as valid in 1970s "Amerika" as in the 1860s. But Willie Swanigan was different. Sure, Brian invoked the Fourth Amendment's prohibition against "unreasonable force" and sought to bring the police to account. But, really, it was about money. Money for Willie, money for the firm. The firm "advanced" money to pay the costs of litigation, gambling on a big fee contingent on winning. Sure, there was publicity: "This will send a message to police departments throughout the country that the Negro cannot be treated like a second class citizen." But it was about money. The other message being sent by the publicity was: "Lawyers and clients, send cases to Jacobs and Zarick." Not the free Movement cases that generated more free cases, but the winning personal injury cases that generated big fees.

It was a subtle shift that did not elude Brian.

The predominantly white trial lawyers who had assembled wildly applauded the fiery oratory of Johnnie Cochran as he blasted the white legal system. But it was to Brian that they asked the questions: "Do you put your evidence in the claim or save it for trial?" "How do you decide how much to ask for in damages?" "Does your firm also handle product liability cases?"

A few weeks later, Brian was sorting through his weekend mail. He almost threw the announcement away with the junk mail, but his eye caught the name of Leon Goldman, a "progressive" member of his Boalt Hall class. He read the announcement of Goldman and Bishop's relocation to "Historic Jack London Square" in Oakland. "The firm continues its emphasis on housing and employment discrimination through class action litigation," said the announcement.

Brian smiled and put the card in his Rolodex. Nice to see someone else still dedicated to The Cause, he thought.

Chapter 43

Leon

THE DOCTRINE WAS called nuisance, public and private. The concepts were not new. Actually, they had a long history in the English Common Law. Leon pulled out his first-year Property book. It was all there: "Quiet possession and comfortable enjoyment of property."

What was new was Leon's use of the ancient remedy to attack a modern problem that was eroding black neighborhoods—drugs. Crack houses. Places where people congregated to shoot up. Places that ruined the investment of those who owned their own homes, posed a danger to persons using streets and sidewalks, and beckoned children to a way to make fast money. Places that were allowed to fall into disrepair because the economics of land ownership saw no profit in repairs.

It was not enough that drugs ruined the lives of children. The law, he knew, protected *property* rights. He remembered the arguments in class about "tenancies for a period of time"—what renters got—as constituting property rights. Even an easement over public lands, like the right to walk on a sidewalk, could be considered a property right, the interference with which would justify a nuisance suit.

The term "nuisance" actually came from the French, denoting a harm. In England, nuisance was originally punishable as a crime because it involved interference or encroachment on the property of the King. By the 1300s, nuisance included interference or invasion of public rights, like interfering with a public market, and, later, polluting water near private settlements. Yet, it was a crime then, not a matter of private lawsuit.

When the English law was implemented in the United States, which had no king, the idea of nuisance was exclusively to protect broad public rights, such as public health, safety, peace, comfort, convenience—and morals. In each instance, enforcement was tied to the effect on or use of property. If a brothel was closed, it was because of the use of property. If loud music was abated, it was because of its interference with another's enjoyment of his property rights. To bring a nuisance claim, a "property right," just as in feudal times, had to be involved.

In a parallel, but independent, development, as early as 1536, some enterprising English lawyer argued that if his property owner suffered peculiar injury different than the public at large, he should be able to sue for his unique damage. A brothel may be a public nuisance in a community, but should not the person next door, whose property is used for urination, whose tenants endure the nightly ritual of moaning and haggling, and whose property value plummets, be entitled to seek independent relief? Thus developed the twin concepts of public nuisance and private nuisance.

Leon sued not only the absent landowners, but the real estate management companies handling the properties. With about 100 neighbors suing for each crack house, Leon argued that each day of "continuing nuisance" was a new offense, another day of disruption of the neighbors' quiet enjoyment of property incident to ownership. The economics of private ownership dictated that the owners renovate or raze the offending structures. In each suit, the remedy included funds for neighborhood clean-up, financial assistance to neighborhood watch organizations, and, of course, attorneys' fees.

Leon was cleaning up Oakland, he felt, one block at a time. Better than one lawsuit to remedy one person at a time. Still, it was too slow.

He wanted to take on discrimination in a major way. As his father said, society would not be changed by an occasional victory by a black here, or a brown there. Attitudes had to change. The economics of racism had to be changed.

It was Leon's use of nuisance to go after the vertical chain of land renters, realtors, property managers, owners, and sellers that had first impressed Jonathan Bishop. The next logical step—with the potential of a big payoff—was a class action discrimination lawsuit. Leon had extended the English Common Law as far as it could go. It was time to expand American jurisprudence.

"Class actions are the only way to address the issues. But if we get bogged down in a major case, it'll bankrupt us. We have to have an exit strategy." Jonathan Bishop was more cautious than Leon. As a Legal Aid lawyer, Leon never had to worry about the personal financial consequences of losing.

But Leon knew the problem. "There really is no exit once a court accepts our argument that the case should proceed as a class action. The only way out is to win. If we lose, we'll be sued by the defendants for hundreds of thousands of dollars of their costs, and if we try to get out, our own clients will sue us for malpractice for abandoning them. Most likely, we will get sued by both, the defendants and our clients."

"We better be damn careful before we ever file," said Bishop. "It's got to be not just a sure winner, but one we can win before it exhausts our ability to continue. Maybe we should bring in some other firms to share the expense and work."

Leon shook his head. "That feels like selling off a piece of the case. I don't like it. Either we believe in what we're doing or we don't."

The planning was meticulous. Bishop's knowledge of the real estate industry, patterns of development in the Bay Area, and escrow documents, together with Leon's work on the pavement with Angela, converged into the strategy. For six months, multiple visits were made to major real estate brokers by black and white couples, separately but with identical financial qualifications, seeking housing in Alameda County and the contiguous counties of Contra Costa, San Mateo, and Marin. Some sought apartments. Others sought to purchase homes.

Leon had called his Property professor at Boalt Hall who, in turn, had posted a need for students to do "field research" in property law. Angela had provided professional black couples to help. Bishop even enlisted his parents to act as potential buyers.

After 26 weekends, with each of 10 couples making between two and ten contacts a weekend, the pattern was clear and consistent with the neighborhood housing pattern of the four counties. Leon was ready to file. Bishop was concerned if for no other reason than the fact that he was about to cross the imaginary bridge that separated him from all those in the real estate industry with whom he had been previously associated. He could never be trusted by "them" again. How would they respond to the suit? By crushing Goldman and Bishop?

"Why don't we test the market?" suggested Leon.

"Test market?"

"Yeah. I'm nervous, too. Let's approach one of the realty companies on behalf of a single client. Tell them our client wasn't shown available housing reserved for whites and see how they respond. Don't mention anything about lawsuits or a class action. Just treat it like a complaint rather than a lawsuit. Send a paralegal as a 'friend' to be a witness. No lawyers, even."

They did. The agent was apologetic: "I didn't want to embarrass you or waste your time. Those subdivisions out in Contra Costa County aren't going to sell to you. You get your hopes up, but they just won't even open escrow. The lenders. The developers. So we're not even supposed to show you the houses. I am sorry."

The strategy evolved from this interview: Sue all of the different levels in the purchase and ownership process, from landowners and developers to sellers, title companies, real estate brokers, and savings and loan lenders. In each category was included not only the largest company, but also some of the smaller firms who were only "following industry practices" and for whom a major lawsuit would be economically impossible.

"That's it," concluded Leon. "We have an 'exit strategy' but it's for those defendants who cooperate. Those who want out will testify against others, give us the evidence we need, and finance the litigation against the rest."

It was a pattern Leon would perfect on his way to becoming, as later described in a *Wall Street Journal* article, the "King of Class Actions." But in 1979, in order to pay to publish the notices required by federal rules for a class action, Leon Goldman put up his office building, the firm's assets and receivables, as well as his recently acquired two-bedroom modest Oakland home, as collateral for the loan necessary to finance the suit. Everything was on the line.

After the instant splash of publicity, upon the filing of the multimillion-dollar class action suit, came the motions by over 40 defendants to dismiss the suit and for sanctions. Each day the mail brought notices to take depositions, requests for production of documents, and every conceivable—and some inconceivable—excuse for 40 defense law firms to bill time. While the real estate agent to whom the paralegal had been sent acknowledged the "confession," his broker denied that any such company policy existed and fired the agent for discrimination. Bishop's parents were noticed for deposition, and a cross-complaint was filed against them personally for allegedly filing false documents to secure a loan as part of their application for housing. When Bishop appeared in court, on their behalf, the banking defendants sought to have him disqualified as the attorney for his parents, based upon the alleged conflict in his representation of the class and of his parents at the same time. The federal judge allowed him to continue but warned that he—and possibly his firm—could be disqualified from representing the class should a conflict develop before trial. The implicit threat was clear: The firm could be denied fees after years of work should it be removed prior to trial.

To avoid the potential conflict, Bishop was able to find a classmate from law school to front for him as attorney of record for his parents. The lawyer was paid hourly as a "contract attorney" to help on motions and document production, thereby freeing both Leon and Bishop from the tedium of sitting for hours with a room full of defense attorneys doing their best to wear them into dust. Not that they did not still put in 18-hour days. The time was just more effectively used on small fee-generating cases to keep the lights on and meet payroll.

Fortunately, the labor union group legal service contract with which Leon had begun his practice still accounted for a good portion of the firm's income, from personal injury cases, workers' compensation claims, miscellaneous DUIs, and the occasional will or divorce.

For the next 18 months, everything that came into the firm, after expenses, went into the class action. Leon fell behind on his house payments. The firm stopped ordering copies of witnesses' official deposition transcripts and instead relied upon meticulous handwritten notes, in order to save money. Everything had to be directed to the line of credit extended by the bank to finance the class action. Ironically, the line of credit was secured in part by Leon's house, upon which the mortgage company was threatening to foreclose!

"You gonna get us EE-VIC-TED, Leon? Shit, I bet that would be a first for yo white ass. Well, don't think you gonna move into my neighborhood. You'd haf be in by dark or the brothers gonna mess wid you. Beside, you can't pay yo haf of da rent."

They had not discussed her moving in because, after all, she had her own place. She just spent a lot of time at his house, they told anyone who asked, although few did. The extra bedroom was her "study," the place where she did her writing. It was filled mostly with journals and newspapers, with folders filled with clippings. In the midst of it all was the manual typewriter, perched on an unfinished door, which rested on bricks 14 inches off the ground. Just high enough for Angela to sit on a rug with pillows and cross her legs in front of the typewriter.

He ignored her taunts. She could slip into her street talk in the blink of an eye, but now it was done in humor between them.

"What are you working on?"

She hit the carriage and threw it back across the page. "Working on a piece to submit to the editorial page of the *San Francisco Bay Guardian*. A friend of mine from the journalism department at Columbia works there. We got to talking, and he suggested I submit a piece."

"What makes you think they would run it?"

"Well, it's an argument why local government should take a stand against racism at the international level, and since I'm the Executive Director of the Fair Housing Commission, I have some local credentials to argue the point. And, as you know, I am black."

"You never tire of reminding me."

"Your people never let me forget it," she smiled as she blew the sweet-smelling smoke of a joint toward him and lay back against the pillows.

He knew this signaled time out from her work and he responded. Standing at the raised platform on which she had her sitting area, he seductively loosened his shirt, took it off, and dropped it to the floor. She took another hit. He undid his belt and pushed his pants to his ankles. The phone rang in the other room. His business line. He turned and stumbled, his shoes caught in his pants. He shuffled, as she laughed, to get to the phone.

"They want to meet," announced Bishop.

"Who does?"

"All of them. Crosby called on behalf of the defense coordinating committee. He's the spokesperson."

"When?"

"He wants us to come over this week, suggests Friday. His office."

"Call him back. Not tonight. Wait till Thursday, mid-morning. Tell them that we can't do it on Friday but how about Monday morning."

"Why, Leon?"

"Because we need to meet with the lenders alone before we walk into Crosby's office. I'm going to call Jack Merchant. I have a feeling his people want out, and we can use your federal regulation angle on them. They have the least to lose by a settlement."

On Monday morning, Leon and Bishop did what appeared to be poor strategy in negotiations. They went to the turf of their opponent to talk settlement—into the luxurious 28th floor conference room of the largest defense law firm in Northern California. There, overlooking the San Francisco Bay, they met with the firm's senior litigation partner, Martin Crosby, Jr., flanked by his committee of defense attorneys representing the various levels of defendants. A number of corporate senior vice presidents were also in evidence, each being given careful deference by his respective representative attorney. Jack Merchant was absent.

Leon had never met Crosby before, since the senior litigator had been sending lower level attorneys to all previous court and deposition appearances. From Crosby's reputation, however, Leon knew he was not going to like him. Which was all right. It helped sometimes. Harder to really fuck an adversary if you liked him.

"Mr. Goldman, perhaps I should thank you," Crosby began. "Your class action has provided a lot of work for our firms." He smiled at his colleagues. Smug, thought Leon. "But I really don't like to bill my clients, contrary to what you might believe, for something that has no merit," Crosby continued. "Sure, when this is all over, we could get a judgment against your clients, possibly even your firm, but we all know that it would just end up unpaid—possibly even in bankruptcy court."

Okay, thought Leon, he's playing to the senior vice presidents. Good. That means they, not he, are making the decisions.

He remained silent, looking at the massive tabletop separating him from Crosby and his colleagues.

"We are all realists here," Crosby went on. "All professionals. Litigation is costly for everyone, even when we win. I'll be candid with you. I think class actions are legal blackmail and should be resisted forcefully. But my clients, our clients," he corrected himself, gesturing with his hands to the assembled group, "are willing to resolve the matter now to save the costs of litigation. Of course, if the matter proceeds, this offer will be withdrawn, and I can give you my personal assurance, Mr. Goldman, that we are prepared to spend whatever it takes to win."

Crosby paused. Leon said nothing. There was nothing in front of him on the very large conference room table. He had not carried in a briefcase. He did not even have a legal pad. He sat there, like a little boy called to the principal's office. Bishop sat back, behind him, his arms crossed, looking at the ceiling. Neither looked intimidated; just out of place.

"We are prepared to pay your class of clients $1 million"—Crosby said $1 million very slowly to let it sink in—"for any real or imagined slight they have endured and," he looked at Leon closely, "$1 million in fees and costs to your firm for its efforts in this matter." Leon sat looking into his lap as everyone watched him for any reaction. Bishop counted silently to himself: "One, two, three, four, five...nine...fifteen."

Leon leaned forward, his hands folded together on the table. The visible cuffs of the new white shirt showed the suit jacket did not fit very well.

"Marty"—he knew no one called Martin Crosby, Jr., anything but Mr. Crosby—"you invite me over here, threaten me, and then insult me and my clients, and conclude with offering me what amounts to a bribe to sell out my clients. I think I should report you to the State Bar."

"Listen, Goldman. I was on the board of governors of the State Bar. Don't lecture me on ethics. Get off your high horse. This case is about money, and we all know it."

"No. It's about discrimination, Marty, and stopping it. You could have called 18 months ago, before you guys ran up millions in fees, if it was just about costs. This case is about racial prejudice and keeping blacks out of white neighborhoods."

"Goldman. Where have you been? There are laws on the books against discrimination. It doesn't take a lawyer with a class action to end discrimination. You're just cashing in. The only question is how much, and I am telling you $2 million. You'd better take it or it's off the table. We'll run you into the ground, and you'll be back at Legal Aid with your girlfriend."

Leon smiled. So they had checked him out, thoroughly. He hid well his shock at the mention of Angela. He stood up, leaned on the table with both hands, and spent a few seconds on each corporate vice president, after passing his eyes over their attorneys.

"Here's how it's going to be, gentlemen. We will settle with each group separately. The first group will pay the least; the next a bit more; and so on. The last to settle will pay the most."

"Don't think for a moment that we are going to separately..." started Crosby.

Leon ignored him and continued. "In addition, each will agree on a statement of nondiscrimination and monitoring by a master appointed by the federal court. Goals will be established. Recruitment and hiring of black salespersons, agents, closers, loan officers, title officers, and other personnel who interface with the public will be part of the settlement. Penalties will be in place for noncompliance."

This time he looked at Crosby.

"You should know that I met with Jack Merchant on Saturday and Sunday, and we have arrived at a settlement, signed last night, that includes all of the provisions I just outlined. The lenders group of defendants have agreed to pay $40 million in settlement with our guarantee that each remaining group will pay more."

He shifted his eyes around the room again. He sensed the shock bordering on panic.

"So, gentlemen, I suggest each of you call me when you are ready."

He turned and walked to the door.

In a pause, a finger to the lip, and a turn he had learned from TV's Peter Falk as Lt. Columbo, he threw down the gauntlet softly.

"And Marty, I hope you're the last to call, because I really want your clients to know how they got fucked because of you."

It was a good month. The firm had settled with the one group of the class action defendants for what would become the first in many multimillion-dollar payoffs in this and other cases. The bank extended payment on his credit line based upon the $40 million initial settlement, pending its receipt, but the electric company would not cancel its interruption of service for 90-day nonpayment. Leon had to borrow $800 from his dad in an emergency loan to keep the lights on at the office. It had been that close.

Angela's article for the *San Francisco Bay Guardian* was picked up throughout the country by major newspapers and, overnight, she became a national spokesperson and a respected writer. Her article read, in part:

SECTION B, CELL 5

There sits, in Section B, Cell 5, on Robben Island in the South Atlantic, a prophet. A man who argues to his nation, and reminds ours, in the words of Abraham Lincoln, that we cannot have a nation part slave and part free. His struggle is our struggle, for he can show us the way, in a black-majority country, how equality and reconciliation can be achieved in the white-majority society of America.

It is not time for black Americans to return to Africa, as Marcus Garvey argued, but for all Americans, black and white, to learn from Africa, and bring home to America the unfulfilled promise of this country.

It was eloquent and reasoned in its appeal to white Americans. But Angela could not resist showing her credentials in the alternative warning with which she ended the piece:

"Change will come, inevitably, sooner or later, peacefully or through calamity, 'cause, as we say in the black community, 'God don't like ugly.'"

Congressman Ron Dellums called the morning of the publication. He was taking up in Congress what she was advocating locally: Boycott by every level of American government of South Africa and its apartheid government. He asked that she fly to Washington to help mobilize support for such a campaign.

In a few weeks, word came to Angela that the prisoner in Section B, Cell 5, would very much like to meet her. She considered *Ebony* and some other black magazines and papers through which she might obtain credentials to visit the prisoner in South Africa. Instead, she accepted the invitation of the *Los Angeles Times* for the assignment. She knew that the chances of getting the interview, getting through the racist regulations of the terrorist state of South Africa, were better with credentials from a mainstream, major newspaper like the *Times*. She also knew that she was writing to convince a white audience, not a black audience, of the immorality of apartheid.

The *Times* flew Angela and Leon to South Africa, with Leon acting as a photographer. On the strength of their *Los Angeles Times* credentials, and after months of prearrangements by the newspaper to authorize the visit, they were permitted—not without a strip search—to meet with the prisoner for a 30-minute interview. Afterward, at his suggestion, they went on to Lusaka, Zambia, where they were greeted by members of the executive committee of the African National Congress at the Mulungushi Conference Center. Over the next two days, Angela was given an in-depth education into the history of apartheid in South Africa, the black opposition, and the reasons why the opposition needed the West, and particularly the United States, to be outspoken in its condemnation of apartheid and forceful of its sanctions to bring down the white-majority government.

Her article appeared in the *Los Angeles Times* and was, once again, picked up throughout the country. In it, she stressed—some said parroted—the position of the ANC. "Quiet diplomacy and constructive engagement, which appeared to be the policy of the Reagan Administration, are futile. No one would argue for constructive engagement with Hitler. Quiet diplomacy with the devil is immoral. International pariahs must be isolated and brought down."

To the argument made, especially by the conservative *National Review* and its editor William F. Buckley, Jr., that boycotts would only hurt the blacks of South Africa, she posed the question, "Why do conservative white people in America feel that black people in South Africa, who themselves are demanding this boycott upon their own country, don't know what is good for them?"

Her article was also the first, at least in a major white newspaper, to bring to the American people the words of the African National Congress Freedom Charter. She quoted it, in part, and compared it to the American Constitution. First published in 1955, it proclaimed:

> No government can justly claim authority unless it is based on the will of all of the people...our people have been robbed of their birthright to the land, liberty and peace by a form of government founded on injustice and inequality. Our country will never be free until all of our people live in brotherhood, enjoying equal rights and opportunities...without distinction of color, race, sex or belief.

"Is this radical?" she asked in her *Times* article.

> Is this any different than "government of the people, by the people, and for the people," of which Abraham Lincoln spoke in the Gettysburg Address? And isn't our country also one that was founded on injustice and inequality when our own Constitution specifically provided for the counting of the Negro as three-fifths of a human being, for purposes of representation by the states, even though this three-fifths of a person it never contemplated would vote?

Leon and Angela were both on their way, in their respective careers, to prominence, effectiveness, and a lifelong commitment that, while never including the institution of marriage, was enhanced by the birth of their daughter. They named her after the "prophet" in Section B, Cell 5, who would become their dear friend. Conceived in South Africa, Mandela Goldman was born on April 3, 1981.

Chapter 44

Rose

IT IS EASY to know what is being harvested in the Central Valley at any given time: Whatever litters Highway 99 that runs down through its middle with fields on either side, hundreds of miles beginning above Sacramento and extending through Stockton and Modesto, on to Fresno, Visalia, Bakersfield, and to the foot of the Tehachapis. Governor Edmund G. "Pat" Brown—the father of Jerry Brown—would always say that he would decide whether to run for office "when the snow falls in the Tehachapis." Highway 99. A sharp curve littered with tomatoes; an adjacent train track where a set of doubles burped up sugar beets; oozing grapes that had fallen off a field trailer; the smell of garlic smashed by tires; decapitated heads of lettuce; rejected peaches dumped in a field along the road. In California, it is not "littering" to cover a highway with feathers. It is an inevitable consequence of hauling chickens and turkeys, and is specifically exempted by the California Vehicle Code.

In winter, fog regularly makes the highway visible no more than two or three center line dashes ahead. Not that anyone slows down. The predictable situation is of a tractor crossing the road to the field on the other side and a fiery pile-up of cars and trucks, with the death toll exacerbated due to the number of Mexicans crammed into a van or sitting on wood benches in the back of a pickup.

Towns associated with a particular agricultural product: Lodi, where every child by the fourth grade could recite that "97½ percent of the world's Tokay grapes are grown within a six-mile radius of downtown Lodi" (as if there was a "downtown" Lodi); Atwater with its almonds; Yuba City and cling peaches; Delano with table grapes; Livingston for chickens; Turlock for turkeys; oranges in Visalia. Small towns. One looking like the other (except for feathers and farm products on the highway outside of town). A hundred and ten degrees in the summer.

Sure, there was Fresno (with its raisin festival), Stockton ("come to the asparagus festival"), even Sacramento (sometimes called Sac-a-tomato). But, in reality, they were just Valley towns, too. Boring. People just lived there. Dreamt of leaving if they had any motivation. As for legal services, even the city and county governments looked to San Francisco or Los Angeles for law firms to handle important work. What was left for local lawyers was the scraps, or, for those like Zapata, small revolutions, skirmishes really.

Rose did not see herself leading a revolution. She was not intellectually comfortable with the rhetoric. "What does *La Raza* mean?" she asked Reynoso, confrontationally. "The race? What race? The descendants of Aztecs? Mayans? Omecs? Toltecs? Zapatecs? The Spanish colonialists? Descendants of the 450 years since Hernan Cortes? Is glorifying race effective? Are we in favor of illegal immigrants' 'rights' because they are Mexican immigrants?" She knew it could not, anthropologically, be about race. *La Raza*. It was a political term. Like "us" and "them."

Not only was she not sure she knew how to lead, she was not sure anyone would follow. Yes, Dolores Huerta was given credit as the co-founder of the United Farm Workers of America, but it was Cesar Chavez they followed; Cesar who fasted; Cesar at the front of the parade.

But Rose had come back to the Valley for a reason. To find herself; to get off the track that someone—her father?—had put her on. Ernie suggested that she would find it in recognizing that she was, first and foremost, a Mexican. He was wrong. She would find it in recognizing that she was, first and foremost, a woman.

Her mother refused to leave Gonzales, if for no other reason than that was where Rose's father was buried. She did not drive and wanted to be able to walk every morning, after mass, to her husband's grave. On Saturdays, she took new flowers. On Sundays, Rose accompanied her. On *Dia de los Muertos*—the Day of the Dead—she sat all night at the grave, decorated with marigolds, as millions were doing all over Mexico with their deceased loved ones. Rose sat with her.

It was obvious to Rose there was not enough legal work in Gonzales to support a law office there. Nor could she expect to start up a law firm located in the Valley doing what she had been doing in San Francisco. Bond work for cities, irrigation districts, and special districts required the name of a prestigious, established firm, and the signature "Rose Contreras, Attorney at Law" at the bottom of an opinion letter would not sell bonds on Wall Street.

"You have to be a general practitioner in the Valley," Reynoso told her. "Whatever walks in the door. You also need a good car because you're going to be up and down the Valley constantly. The courtrooms and towns will blur together, and you will feel like you're on autopilot."

"How would you know about private practice?" quipped Rose.

"Tried it; hated it."

"When?" Rose asked.

"When I got out of law school in 1956, I…"

"1956?"

"Yes, '56. What's wrong?"

"That makes you about 45! Jesus!"

"I am 43, Rose, since you asked. And you're 30. Now that we have established that, how old did you think I was? Your age?"

"Of course not, Ernie. I mean, I just have felt so comfortable with you. You've become my mentor in many ways. I knew you were older. It's just that I've never had a close relationship with an older man. You know what I mean. Friends."

"Older man. God…you make me feel so old, cuddly and impotent, all at the same time."

"I didn't mean it that way."

"For the record, it's just my legs that are crippled from childhood polio. Nothing else."

Rose looked down, embarrassed.

"For the record," she looked up, "you are probably the person singularly responsible for me questioning who I am and who I want to be. As difficult as that is, I cherish the fact that you have done this and hope it is because you care for me as much as I respect and care for you."

He smiled at her.

"I also appreciate the potency information because I have wondered," Rose added, "especially since you haven't made any moves in that arena."

"Prepare to be moved," he announced as he struggled with his crutches to get out of his chair.

"Wait a minute. Hold it. I am a good Mexican Catholic girl. If you want a date with me, you will need to come by the house, sit and talk with my mother, and take me on a proper romantic evening."

He fell back into his chair.

Rose changed the subject. "Now, back to my practice of law. Where would you suggest I open an office?"

Rose opened her office, as Reynoso suggested, in Salinas. Not just because his CRLA office was there, although he assured her referral of all fee-generating cases, since CRLA was not supposed to take cases for which private attorneys could make money. Nor because it was central; nothing in the Valley is very close to anywhere one needs to be. She expected that the contract work she would do for her old firm would require her attendance at board meetings and conferences. In any given week, it might be at the Merced Irrigation District, the Fresno Board of Supervisors, or, God forbid, the Kern County Wool Growers Cooperative—a five-hour trip each way by car. More important than clients, Salinas was 25 minutes up Highway 101 from her mother.

The office furniture was used, the Selectric typewriter on a 90-day loan from the salesman, with no payments until the new one was shipped. Rose's biggest investment was a Xerox machine.

The best advice she received as a new attorney was from a judge on the second morning of her move to Salinas: "Hire an old, experienced legal secretary and learn from her." Rose's testosterone levels presented no impediment to learning from the experience of a woman. She did as she was told, left the details and court forms to her secretary, and concentrated on learning the practical aspects of the law: that which was not taught at Boalt Hall.

Tony Hawk called as soon as he got the notice of her office opening. As promised, he had work assignments for her, on a contract basis, with clients of her old firm in the Valley.

"Actually, we would like to retain you one day a week. It appears that the Fresno County supervisors don't want to lose you either. They will provide you with an office at the county counsel's office for your personal use. You are not restricted to use it for their work. They just feel they, too, have too much invested in you. Any work you do for them will be billed through us."

"Tony," Rose protested, "you don't need to do this."

"It's not all gratuitous. We don't want to lose the client. Besides, we are going to bill the county a hell of a lot more than we pay you!"

They both laughed.

"Rose, I don't expect you'll stay forever, but, for now, this works for both of us. Use the day in Fresno to build up your practice. You know the county people; you went to college there. Get your name around. A practice is built on the ripple effect of each client served.

"Oh, by the way, Rose, why is your name different in Spanish?" Hawk added.

The announcement mirrored her entry door and the two sets of business cards on the reception desk. Actually, it was one card with two holders showing opposite sides. On one side, in English:

Rose Contreras
Attorney at Law

On the other, in Spanish:

Rosa Contreras y Baca
Abogada

She explained to Tony Hawk that the Spanish name was, in the Mexican tradition, the addition of her mother's maiden name—"and Baca"—to her father's surname of Contreras. It was, for her, she said, a way to acknowledge and honor her mother and the sacrifices that she, too, had made for her children.

"That's marvelous," responded Hawk, genuinely moved by the recognition of both parents.

Reynoso's response was predictable as he flipped the card back and forth. "Still can't decide who you are?"

Reynoso also knew his history. A Mexican moving to the United States might put the mother's name as a middle name to avoid confusion as to the "true" last name: "Rosa Baca Contreras." Especially since Immigration and Social Security hated hyphenating a name: "Contreras-Baca." In Mexico, she would have been Rose Contreras Baca. In taking Contreras "y Baca," Rose was going back further in time, to a tradition more Spanish than Mexican. Honoring her mother, yes, but clearly not politically correct for *La Raza* or as a *Chicana*.

It was, in essence, a feminist statement, not a Mexican fist in the air.

Chapter 45

Rose

ROSE HAD TO admit she knew nothing about it.

She was in Fresno usually one day a week and otherwise for court appearances when necessary. She tried to bunch all of it, and the work for the county, on the same day, even if it meant driving back and forth from Salinas to Fresno in one day: Driving through Hollister, "the earthquake capital of the world;" checking the level of the San Luis Reservoir, coming over 152 into the Valley, onto 99 south, down the center of the Valley to Fresno. She had it all on Memorex, fast forward, reverse: Was it real or taped?

"The item came up for report on the board's agenda last week, right after flood relief."

"Jim, I was probably rehearsing my presentation in my head. I just didn't hear it; what's it about?" Rose asked the county counsel.

Jim Hanes was county counsel for the County of Fresno, the county's "attorney." His grandfather had been one of the first Superior Court judges in the county. Jim had been a star fullback at Fresno State and might have been drafted by the pros if he had gone to a bigger, more recognized college. The only time he had been away from Fresno was during law school at Hastings College of the Law in San Francisco—the "other" law school affiliated with the University of California. He had returned and joined the largest firm in town. (For Fresno, that meant eight attorneys). He was gregarious, knew everyone, and was elected to the city council at age 32. After two years, he had announced that he would take the position of county counsel and had abruptly resigned from the city council and his firm. The reason seemed to be a closely held secret among Fresno's elite.

"Well, they were a pretty ragtag looking group of females, but they managed to get some community support for the idea of a battered womens' center. Dr. Simmons' wife is big on them, which means Judge Puchini's wife, Ann, will be involved, too. Those two do everything together, from St. Dominic's Women's Auxiliary to golf every Thursday. They even vacation together with their kids."

"Why are you telling me this?" Rose asked.

"The county is willing to give them space, phones for their emergency crisis line, even some money. But we want it supervised. They're a bit wild; radical feminist types. If they want to help beaten-up women, fine. But we don't want them running some kind of anti-male thing or getting in the way of the police doing their job. We also want to keep an eye on our money. Make sure it doesn't go out the back door into someone's pocket."

"So, audit them," Rose said.

"Well, Rose, the Board of Supervisors trusts you. We were thinking you could be on the board of this women's center. We would all feel a lot more comfortable backing this thing if you were there to keep an eye on them."

"You want me to spy on them?"

"No, no," Hanes said, holding his hands up as if to ward off a charging animal. "Help them. Make sure it's done properly. Just do your fiduciary duty as a member of a nonprofit board. That's all. Ann Puchini and Gloria Simmons will also be on the board."

"I take it nonprofit means I don't get paid," Rose muttered. Jim smiled.

"It will be good for business. Good contacts," he responded.

"Business from women who get beat up?"

"No, the board members. Prominent people. It will be helping them feel good with this charity thing for battered women."

"Can't you find someone else?"

"Where am I going to find a woman lawyer with your credentials in Fresno?" Hanes said.

"Tell me again, Jim, it was my credentials that tipped the scale, not the fact that I'm a woman, right?"

"Jesus Christ, Rose, it is a women's center, after all," Jim replied, which did nothing to assure Rose. He paused.

"Can I tell the supervisors you'll do it? Because if you aren't on the board, I don't think they're gonna give these women the money."

"So, I stand between Fresno getting a women's center, is that what you're telling me?" Rose asked, now annoyed.

"That's about it," Jim replied without apology.

Rose gave up. "You tell them they owe me big-time."

She meant the Fresno Board of Supervisors. Jim Hanes thought she meant the "wild radical feminist types."

"I'll tell them." He smiled.

In the four weeks that followed, Rose was copied on all letters between the county counsel and the Fresno Women's Center, as it was called, even though it was only a concept with a post office box.

"This will confirm that the county board of supervisors has approved funding of the Fresno Women's Center on a three-year grant, subject to certain requirements…"

"This will confirm that the Fresno Women's Center shall be incorporated as a California nonprofit corporation and shall meet all the requirements of IRS Code §501(c)(3)…"

"This will confirm that Rose Contreras, Attorney at Law, is preparing the incorporation papers and applying for §501(c)(3) status…"

"This will confirm that the board of directors shall consist of five voting members, including Rose Contreras, Gloria Simmons, Ann Puchini, and two others selected by the board. The executive director, Alejandra Delgado, shall be an ex-officio member reporting directly to the board…"

As a group, they were awkward with each other. In the conference room of the county counsel's office, Alejandra Delgado and two Hispanic women sat side by side. A large woman, apparently breast-feeding a baby, covered by a blanket, sat at one end of the table, on their side. Opposite them, in heels and impeccably dressed, sat Mrs. Simmons and Mrs. Puchini, chatting with each other. Jim Hanes sat at his desk across the room. When Rose entered, Puchini and Simmons appeared relieved. Delgado and the others acknowledged her more out of curiosity. On which side would she sit?

"Hi, I'm Rose Contreras. I am an attorney and I have been asked by the Board of Supervisors to help out. Alejandra?" she asked, turning to Delgado, "nice to meet you finally after talking on the phone for weeks." Rose had called often to get necessary information to prepare the incorporation and the other documents.

Rose sat at the head of the table, with each group flanking her from its own side.

"Perhaps we should start with introductions," Rose said, putting her briefcase beside her and a three-ring binder on the table.

"I am Mrs. Jerrold Simmons. My husband is Dr. Simmons. We have been supporters of Alejandra's work at Concilio Neighborhood Center. Dr. Simmons volunteers his medical services doing well-baby exams. My role has been fundraising with friends in the community."

Eyes turn to Mrs. Puchini.

"I am Ann Puchini. Gloria asked me to help. I really know very little about all of this. I'm not sure what I can contribute."

"Her husband is Michael Puchini, Presiding Judge of the Superior Court," interjected Gloria Simmons, "and they know everyone who is anyone in Fresno."

Since Ann Puchini did not know those on the other side of the table, this comment suggested that they were not anyone in Fresno.

Unaware of this slight, Mrs. Simmons added, "I am sure we can count on Judge Puchini and the courts to be supportive of the women's center's efforts."

"Not really." The voice came from the other side. It was Alejandra. "We can't get the judges of this county to issue kick-out orders to husbands even after they have beaten women in the presence of their kids. The judges say they don't want to 'break up the family.' If the woman leaves, the judges give the husband custody of the kids because they claim the mother has abandoned the children or because the father, after all, has the 'stability of the family home.' If she turns to the priest, he says, 'Honor your husband; submit to him. Divorce is a sin.' If she goes to her family, they say, 'Don't break up your family; don't ruin the lives of our grandchildren.' If she pleads with her husband, he threatens that if she tells, he will ruin her in the eyes of family and friends, and that she will never see the children again; she will be destitute and alone. Women have nowhere to turn and, especially, in this county, not to the courts."

Mrs. Simmons had a soothing answer.

"I'm sure there are many good men, like my husband, out there, sensitive to women's needs."

"Not really," replied Alejandra. "Men are the problem."

"I think that's very anti-male. Women have to take some responsibility..." Mrs. Simmons' voice was rising. She was not used to being challenged, especially by those less fortunate whom she attempted to help.

"Hold on, hold on," Rose interrupted. "I think we are here to put together the organizational aspects of the women's center, not decide whether men are responsible for all of the problems of women in society."

Ann Puchini excused herself, visibly upset at the exchange, and left the meeting.

"Ann...Ann..." called Mrs. Simmons. She turned on Alejandra.

"Why did you have to spout all of that radical ideology? I thought we were here to help other women, not tear down men. You do that in the community, and they will think you are a bunch of lesbians. You'll frighten people off, just like you did Ann."

Rose was also uncomfortable. "I can tell you if the Board of Supervisors were sitting here right now, we wouldn't get a single vote for the women's center grant with that speech."

It looked as if the idea of a women's center was likely to be stillborn. It was the mother with child at her breast, at the end of the table, who saved the day.

"I am Emma Fields." She shifted the baby on her nipple as she leaned forward at the conference table. "My husband is a black man. Most of you others here have Mexican men in your lives. Mrs. Simmons, you have that very nice Dr. Simmons, a good white, Jewish man. But they are all men, and all of our societies burden them with certain roles, call it patriarchal, authoritarian, head of the household, cock of the walk, breadwinner, or just men. Whatever you call it, it makes them act in certain ways toward women. Our job, as I see it, is to free men of this burden and, in the meantime, protect women and children from the results. We just want to liberate everyone to be free, and caring, and respectful of everyone else."

Everyone was nodding.

Rose brought the conversation around to the Articles of Incorporation.

"Okay, can we agree, then, in Section I, Statement of Purpose, that the primary purpose of the women's center shall be to aid victims of domestic violence?"

Rose added, legalistically: "That's gender-neutral."

Too legalistically.

"No." It was Alejandra.

"It's a women's center, not a men's center. We're here to help women. It should say to 'help women who are the victims of domestic violence.'"

"What about the children?" asked Mrs. Simmons. "Aren't they victims, too?"

Jim Hanes had sat quietly, off to the side, not at the table. For the first time, he spoke up.

"Don't men get abused by women, too?"

Alejandra was on him.

"According to FBI statistics, over 90 percent of violence between men and women is directed at women by men. Nine out of ten women murdered in the United States are murdered by men. Most attacks on women are by husbands, lovers, or acquaintances. The most dangerous place for a woman is in the home. The most likely reason a woman goes to an emergency room is because she has been beaten by a man." She paused, before adding, "so don't start this crap that men are abused by their wives or that women egg men on to beat them."

Rose did not want to lose the group again.

"The Board of Supervisors has approved the concept of a women's center so I think for whatever reason it has bought off on the idea of helping women. So this can be our 'primary purpose.' No one will dispute that domestic violence affects children. We can list assistance to children as a 'specific service' in furtherance of our 'primary purpose.'"

She added "care and assistance to children" to the list of services in the draft Articles of Incorporation.

"Alejandra, do you have any problem with listing 'counseling of batterers' to the list of services?"

"I don't see that it will do much good. I think our services are for victims, not batterers," Alejandra replied.

"Well, if we could stop batterers, we would help victims, right?" Rose asked rhetorically.

Alejandra just looked at her.

"How about 'explore ways to alter battering behavior?' Can you live with that?" asked Rose.

Alejandra shrugged. "If I have to."

Rose smiled. "Politically, you have to."

Jim Hanes smiled too. He knew he had picked the right woman for the job.

Ann Puchini was there, sitting next to Dr. Simmons' wife, at the next meeting of the women's center board. She had not wanted to return. Her husband, the presiding judge, had made it clear to her that he wanted her to serve on the board, along with Gloria Simmons. Ann Puchini did what her husband told her to do.

Chapter 46

Rose

THEY WERE JUST busy, they told each other. And they were.

Rose's practice in Salinas had grown quickly in the two years since she had come. In Salinas, most of her clients were Mexican residents and seasonal farm workers. Most of their problems were immigration-related or minor criminal matters—traffic mostly—and an occasional injury. She saw more clients in Salinas but made more money in Fresno. The county work brought her into contact with landowners and developers—the more affluent members of the community.

The county counsel, Jim Hanes, had been right about the women's center. It got her name around town. Through Gloria Simmons and Ann Puchini, Rose was invited to social events thrown for what passed as the high society of Fresno. Most of her Fresno work involved commercial leases, real estate transactions, and local work for corporate clients of her old San Francisco firm.

Ernie's work had taken a dramatic turn. After years of leading the charge, in state and federal courts, against the Reagan Administration in California, and the Nixon and Ford administrations in Washington, he woke up in 1977 to find that a Democratic president, Jimmy Carter, was in the White House, and Jerry Brown was the governor of California. An expert on state and federal welfare laws, he had almost single-handedly tied up Governor Reagan's "welfare reform" in the courts for eight years, to Reagan's great frustration—"That son-of-a-bitch is just what he claims to be, a Communist revolutionary." Now, he was called upon to draft welfare legislation. He was in Washington often for weeks at a time. When he was in California, the new governor's staff wanted his help in Sacramento.

When Rose and Reynoso were in Salinas, they were together at his home where he had first cooked for her. He still did the cooking. The glass-enclosed porch, with its freestanding wood-burning stove and the full sound system, became their bedroom. "Like living in the middle of a forest" was Rose's description. His small bedroom they now shared as a home office with three two-inch by twelve-inch, side-by-side boards resting on two half-sized file drawers, forming a work surface across one wall, her side meticulous, his piled with books and papers.

His side had a poster of the Mexican revolutionary Emiliano Zapata. She hung the announcement of the opening of the Fresno Women's Center on the wall facing her chair. His new status was hard for him to accept. It was like going off to the battlefield only to find that the other side had called in sick. For her, the women's center represented the birth of something for which she had provided legal conception.

At 34, Rose occasionally wondered if she would participate in conception beyond the women's center. Her mother ignored the fact that Rose and Reynoso were living together "in sin." Her approach was simply to ask, "Rose, when are you going to get married?" meaning, "When are you going to have a family?"

The truth was that Rose and Reynoso were both satisfied, comfortable with the situation as it was. They had their very separate careers but enjoyed each other's company, long talks, good food, classical music, eclectic books. Looking back, Rose would see the experience as a tutorial, he the professor, she the student. But it was a warm, protective, highly intellectual, and comforting experience. It was what she needed.

The sex was instructive also, since most of her experiences in high school and college had consisted of a lot of groping, hands under sweaters or in her pants. She had had only one long-term boyfriend. "Long-term" meant a week short of a year, in San Francisco right after law school, and his attempts at sex were less than memorable, at best.

With Ernie, it took time. Not because his legs were useless, but because he was experienced enough to make good use of what he could. Sex was not a few moments of physical contractions. He planned it out. The after-dinner sweet wine to sip. Undressing at the edge of the bed. Covering her only with a sheet and taking parts of her body to rub with oil. Using his hands to rub and warm the oil on the skin. Caressing her face, using his thumbs, with only the candle flickering light across her face. The Indian incense burning in the statue of Shiva.

His upper-body strength, from years of carrying his body on crutches, allowed him to lift himself on her or, just as likely, to lift her fully on him.

He was caring of her, and she loved him. He was, as Mrs. Simmons said of her husband, "a good man."

*   *   *   *   *

Ernesto had not sought the job, but once he decided he wanted it, he put all of his energies into getting it—U.S. District Judge for the Eastern District, Fresno branch. The inquiry had come from an old friend, Art Salazar of the United Farm Workers. Salazar had been appointed to the new Agricultural Labor Relations Board by Governor Jerry Brown on the recommendation of Cesar Chavez.

"Cesar wants to know if you want to be a federal judge, Ernesto."

Reynoso had responded, "Cesar doesn't pick federal judges, Art. The president of the United States does. Cesar's just the president of the United Farm Workers, not of the whole damn United States. At least not yet." They had laughed.

"Well, the president of the United States talks to Cesar. And he asked him for his recommendation for the Fresno federal court. He is looking to appoint a Chicano. Cesar will put your name in if you want it," Salazar said.

"Why in the hell would I want to be a federal judge?" Reynoso asked.

"Because Cesar is asking you," Salazar replied, "and because the president of the United States is asking you. Because, as a federal judge, you could shut down an entire prison system, welfare program, school district, or discriminatory housing tract, with the stroke of a pen. A single federal judge can have more power than the entire fuckin' Congress. You know why you want to be a federal judge."

Reynoso knew, as he hung up, that he could not pass up the honor of being the first public interest Chicano attorney to be appointed to the federal bench in California. The revolution was not over; it was moving to the next level. Consolidating. At some point, even he had to admit, he had won. It was time to take the reigns of power. Be on the inside for a change.

He really was a loner. Writing legislation, consulting with others had been frustrating; writing the definitive statute only to have it committeed, reconstructed, compromised to a skeleton of its former self by people of lesser ability, behind closed doors. It wasn't for him.

There was, he knew, no one more powerful in the law than a federal district court judge. Appointed for life, not subject to election, a single judge could, as Art Salazar said, bring justice "with the stroke of a pen."

Zapata a federal judge, he mused to himself. The legend goes on.

He called Cesar Chavez directly and told him he would be honored if Chavez would put his name forward with the president of the United States.

"The president will nominate you right away, before the election, and submit your name to Congress," Chavez assured him.

Next, Reynoso called Rose. She was in Fresno and would be home late.

He did not tell her the news. He simply told her that he would make Indian food and that he had a surprise for her.

"What?" she asked.

He would not tell her, but she could tell it was big.

"Oh, come on, come on, Ernie. Now you've got me excited."

"Matter of national security. I'm prohibited from discussing it on an unsecured line. See you at 9:00." He hung up.

He heard her car pull in the gravel driveway 15 minutes early. She opened the door and, standing in the doorway still holding the doorknob, asked immediately: "What's the surprise?"

He was leaning against the back of a couch for support, his hands holding a champagne glass.

"Champagne?" he offered.

"What are we celebrating?"

She smiled and took the proffered glass. She could smell the curry. She looked toward the table set for two, a bottle of Gewurztraminer chilling in a bucket of ice. Just like the first time. It had to be big.

"Now you've got me scared, Ernie. What's going on?"

He sipped his champagne. He was smiling.

"Have you ever considered the possibility of marrying a federal judge?" he asked.

Her mouth dropped.

"You are going to be a federal judge?" Her face expressed shock and disbelief.

"Yes. The president will nominate me next week. We need to be in Washington on Monday to go through some preliminary screening, FBI, etc. But it's a done deal."

He raised his glass of champagne. She was still processing what he had said.

"Don't you have to go through local committees, screening, all that before your name is submitted to the president? How could this all happen without us knowing about it?"

"This one came from the top down. It's important to get it in before the election. Demonstrate that the president is an equal opportunity employer. The election is six months away. The president contacted Cesar. Cesar gave him my name. That was good enough for the president."

It still seemed strange. But she went back to his original statement.

"So it's possible I might marry a federal judge? Someday?" she asked.

"Well, I thought it would look a whole lot better if we were to go back to Washington as husband and wife. You know how some of those Republicans look dimly upon conjugal visits for federal judges without the benefit of the sacrament of marriage. We wouldn't want to embarrass the president."

"No," Rose said.

"No what?"

"No, I won't marry you to save embarrassment to the president of the United States."

"Rose, I was joking. I have always thought we'd marry. Why not now?"

"Because you haven't asked my mother; you haven't spoken to my brother about it; and four days is not enough time to plan a wedding in the church where my father was laid to rest." She was upset.

"Maybe you should go to Washington alone so that I don't embarrass you," she added. She turned and walked out the door.

It was close to midnight when she called him. She was at her mother's home in Gonzales. "My mother and I are having a glass of wine. If you have anything to say to her, you can come over." She hung up the phone softly. Reynoso went to his closet and pulled out his suit. He only owned one. He changed, picking the better of his two ties, and headed for the door. He stopped and took the roses from the vase on the set table. Then he drove to Gonzales in his pickup.

Mrs. Contreras answered the door, acting as if it was normal for her to do so at 12:45 A.M. on a weeknight. He followed her to the parlor where Rose sat. Her eyes were bloodshot but dry.

He handed Rose the flowers and turned to her mother.

"Mrs. Contreras, I would like to marry your daughter."

Rose's mother had been well coached.

"When?" she asked in Spanish.

"When the proper arrangements can be made at St. Dominic's for a formal mass of the marriage sacrament with Father Quinn. Until then we will be engaged."

"Do you have an engagement ring?" Rose's mother asked.

Rose smiled. Mom was holding out.

Reynoso reached into his pocket and pulled out a small box.

"Yes. May I put it on her finger?" he asked, turning to the shocked Rose.

*   *   *   *   *

It was the second time in her life that she had left California. Both times for Washington, D.C. She toured the Smithsonian while Reynoso met first with an assistant to the president for Legal Affairs, then a deputy attorney general, and, finally, two FBI agents. The assistant to the president congratulated him on having Chavez's confidence, praised Chavez at length, and assured him that the president would back him 100 percent. Was there anything in his past, the assistant asked, that might embarrass the president with this nomination?

"No, nothing."

The deputy attorney general reviewed the exhaustive list of cases handled by Reynoso that he had been asked to bring. "Have you published anything?" he asked. "They always quote out of context in an attempt to embarrass the president."

After an hour of questions, the deputy shook Reynoso's hand and told him: "You'll be introduced as Ernest Reynoso. No need to use the Spanish spelling. Not *Ernesto*; and no Z. No point drawing attention to your middle name. Just inflame people unnecessarily."

The FBI men got ugly. "Have you been affiliated with any radical groups? You've never been married? Have you lived with anyone? Can we have the names of any long-term girlfriends you've had during your adult life? Have you fathered any children in or outside of marriage? Have you ever sought counseling or psychotherapy?"

It felt like a strip search, in public. Finally, the FBI ended the inquiry session with the assurance that it was "better we ask than some bimbo stands up at a televised hearing and says she had your baby, understand?"

270

He was exhausted. He and Rose stayed in and ordered dinner from room service.

At 10:00 P.M., the phone rang. "Just a moment please, Mr. Reynoso. Lance Jordan, assistant to the president, calling."

A voice came on after a beep.

"Mr. Reynoso, your stool samples have come back clean. We'll go ahead with the announcement day after tomorrow. You'll need to check in at the West Gate of the White House by 9:00 A.M. They will have everything there for you. Congratulations."

Reynoso was sitting up now.

"Oh, and Judge, it would be better if Ms. Contreras had her own room at the hotel. Washington can be a little prudish."

Rose was now awake. "Who..." He put his index finger to his lips, for her to listen but to be quiet.

"Tell the president we'll be there," Reynoso said.

"Uh, the announcement will involve just you, the president, Senator Cranston of California, representatives of the major national Mexican-American organizations, and, of course, Cesar. Since you are not married, we thought..."

"Mr. Jordan, if my fiancée isn't included, I'm out too."

Rose looked at him horrified.

"It's okay," she mouthed.

He held up his hand, firmly. There was silence in the room and on the phone.

"Please understand, Mr. Reynoso. We mean no disrespect. It just raises questions if she's there. None of us want that."

There was silence, again, at each end.

Jordan cleared his throat before speaking.

"Please bring your fiancée, Mr. Reynoso. The president will greet you both, and you and he will proceed to the rostrum. Ms. Contreras will be seated with the distinguished guests. The West Gate will have passes for both of you."

They exchanged "good nights."

Reynoso turned to Rose.

"The president of the United States would like to meet the future Mrs. Reynoso."

Rose hugged him, and they laughed playfully, in the king-size bed, in the middle of Washington, D.C. Just to confirm that they had not sold out to convention and Washingtonian politics, and to spite the Republicans, they made love. They were going to the White House. Together.

At the White House, Jordan knew as he hung up the phone that whether Rose accompanied Reynoso would not make much difference in the long run. Either Jimmy Carter would be reelected or he would not. No nomination of a federal judge, especially a controversial one, would move to the floor of the Senate until the election was settled. If Jimmy Carter was reelected, with the help of Mexican-Americans and other minority voters, Reynoso would be approved. If Carter lost, Ronald Reagan was not likely to reward an old adversary from his days as governor. Twice Rose had come to Washington. Twice she did not know the rules.

President Carter had a way, even across the room, of affixing his attention upon you, as if you were the only person who mattered. Up close, with a handshake, it was exhilarating to feel that the president of the United States was genuinely interested in you.

"Ms. Contreras, I read you're a lawyer also. Boalt Hall. Perhaps I'll be appointing you next," the president said as he held her hand.

They laughed. Ernesto had introduced her after shaking hands with the president.

Carter turned serious. "Reagan has no regard for the poor. He will scrap all that we've done with programs like CRLA. I don't have to tell you, Ernesto. You fought him for years. We can't let this happen."

There was a hint of panic in his words before he refitted his grin to walk on stage as they heard the announcement: "Ladies and gentlemen, the president of the United States."

*　　*　　*　　*　　*

The wedding was everything she had wanted as a young girl, except her father was not there to give her away. Pablo, now much taller than she, walked her down the aisle.

Two months later, Ronald Reagan crushed Jimmy Carter for the presidency. Rose knew she would not be married to a federal judge. Reynoso's nomination was still in committee. It would never come out.

On the transition team, Ed Meese was asked to gather for the new administration a list of all pending presidential appointments. In the meantime, Governor Paul Laxalt, a former senator from Nevada, asked, on behalf of the Reagan transition team, that Congress delay action until the new president had an opportunity to review the list.

Meese directed Michael Cassidy, his new deputy, to meet with Lance Jordan, the Carter liaison to the transition team, to obtain a list of all pending presidential appointments, and to prepare a report on each judicial nominee in particular. Reagan understood, from his California days, that the enduring legacy of a chief executive was the selection of judges. This was even more so in the case of federal judges who serve for life. He had every intention of changing the face of the federal judiciary. Ed Meese had already been given the assignment.

Michael Cassidy submitted his report to Meese in a week. There were 67 pending federal judgeships. Next to the name, Ernest Reynoso, Cassidy wrote one word: "Zapata."

Ed Meese made it official, with pleasure:

> President-elect Reagan will withdraw all pending judicial appointments from consideration. After a thorough review, he will personally submit the names of only those candidates who meet his high standards. This blanket action, as to all nominees, is taken because, for example, even a preliminary review has disclosed a nominee like Ernesto Z. Reynoso. This is a man who hung a poster of the Cuban Communist Che Guevara in his federally funded Legal Aid office, urged high school students to revolution, and used his government-paid legal services position to thwart and obstruct welfare reform in California.
>
> We can only assume that this "Zapata," as he calls himself, is representative of the other nominees of the departing administration. Therefore, we ask that all be withdrawn.

Rose watched the television with Reynoso at their home in Salinas. The phone rang.

"Mr. Reynoso? This is Mike Simmons, UPI. Do you have a response to Ed Meese, who, on behalf of President-Elect Reagan, has withdrawn your name from consideration for a federal judgeship?"

Reynoso knew that months of walking on eggshells, avoiding controversy, were over.

"Sure. Tell President Reagan that Che Guevara wasn't Cuban."

"How do you feel being responsible for all 67 federal nominees being withdrawn—because of you?" the reporter asked.

"Guilt by association. Ed Meese is Joe McCarthy's younger brother."

He hung up the phone.

"I know that guy." Rose was pointing at the television screen.

"Who?" Reynoso asked.

"The guy behind Meese. That's Michael Cassidy. We were at Boalt Hall together. He didn't read *Palsgraf* because his wife had a baby first year."

They watched as Meese left the podium and Michael Cassidy followed him off the stage.

Chapter 47

Michael

"I, RONALD REAGAN, do solemnly swear…"

Michael was sitting in the January cold in 1981, with his son Robbie, now 14, at the inauguration of the president of the United States. He could see his boss, Ed Meese, four rows ahead with cabinet members and other high-level officials of the administration. Michael's own title, "Assistant Counselor to the President," gave him full access to the White House. Thirty-six years old and in the White House. Very heady stuff.

If Ed Meese was disappointed with his title of "Counselor to the President," after handling so much of the transition between the humiliating Carter exit and the triumphant Reagan entrance, he did not voice it. Everyone, especially Meese, had assumed he would be Reagan's chief of staff. Or attorney general. Not a glorified lawyer in residence. Meese, or "Ed," as he insisted everyone call him, with his soft, friendly, easygoing manner, worked 16-hour days, six days a week, and took home full briefcases and armloads of paper every night. Ed Meese was totally loyal and dedicated to Ronald Reagan. Dedicated was not right. He idolized him. He lived and breathed for Reagan. He devoted his life to the man. Or, as they said in the movies, would take a bullet for him.

Michael felt it himself. As he had told Mai long ago, the man—Ronald Reagan—was bigger than life; just filled a room. It was hard not to like him. No; admire him, be in awe of him, when in his presence. If anything, on those occasions when Michael had accompanied Meese into the Oval Office, the man sitting there had been even more impressive. Yet, even as president, Ronald Reagan would always recognize Cassidy and say the same thing: "Ed, I see you've still got that student from Berkeley with you. Have we turned you around yet?"

They would all laugh, every time.

They were not laughing, however, on March 30, 1981, just two months later, when an unusually frantic Meese called from George Washington Hospital.

"Michael, the president's been shot. He's going to undergo surgery. The vice president is in the air from Texas. Research the 25th Amendment. If the president is under anesthesia, in a life-threatening situation, do we invoke the 25th Amendment and make Bush acting president? I need an answer fast. Call me through the White House switchboard."

Up to this point, Michael had felt like a glorified law clerk. Now he was asked to decide who was the president of the United States. He heard someone say, "I'm in charge here." He looked at his television monitor and saw Secretary of State Alexander Haig at a podium.

"Christ."

It was the only time Mai called him at the White House.

"I was worried. You weren't there, were you?" she asked.

"No, but the president's in bad shape, and everyone is really shook up. I can't believe this is happening again."

"Just be careful, Michael. Rob and I were worried."

With Michael in Washington, D.C., visits with Robbie—or Rob, as he now preferred to be called—were more difficult. Actually, since Rob had started high school, he preferred time with his friends anyway. But visiting D.C. and the White House was special. He clearly enjoyed it, even though his mother might be visceral when it came to the inhabitant of 1600 Pennsylvania Avenue. She was ecstatic, however, when Rob was named a congressional page for the summer of 1981, in the House of Representatives, on the nomination of Alameda County's congressman, Ron Dellums.

Dellums had extended the courtesy to fellow Alameda County resident Ed Meese, at the latter's request. Dellums, a black man, was the most outspoken liberal in Congress. To the dismay of many conservatives, he was a member of the Armed Services Committee and the Intelligence Oversight Committee. As such, he had access to some of the country's most guarded secrets. To mix and paraphrase metaphors, some of them felt it was like putting a "Communist in the woodshed."

Michael made it a point of calling Congressman Dellums' office and leaving a message of thanks. The congressman called him back personally.

"Michael, this is Ron Dellums."

"Yes, congressman. I just wanted to thank you for sponsoring my son as a congressional page."

"It's Ron. Please call me Ron. Your son is a nice young man. Maybe we can contribute to his political education." The congressman was laughing.

"I think his mother has already done that," replied Michael.

"Well, maybe his father's then. Michael, keep in touch."

Michael was learning that Washington was a town of back channels. Nothing of substance happened out front, in public view. Matters were decided by private meetings, late night phone calls. Deals were struck; information given or "leaked." Things were not always what they seemed. "Keep in touch" meant "call, if we can ever do business." It was an invitation; a back door. Rob's appointment was a gesture of goodwill; good politics between adversaries.

Michael would not use the door until 1985. When he did, it was not for politics; it was for conscience. Since Michael was a counselor to the president, an attorney to a client, Dellums would never know what Michael did with the information he provided. He could guess. But he would never know for sure. Michael would tell no one. Not even those present at the meeting in the Oval Office in September 1985 knew the source of the information Michael would impart to the president of the United States.

Meanwhile, a summer in Washington, especially with access to the White House and Congressman Dellums' office, ignited an interest in Rob for politics. From then on, when he returned home, phone calls between Rob and his father were full of questions about national and international issues. To the inevitable "mom says," Michael grew patient and would ask Rob, "What do you think?"

But in the five-and-a-half years Michael was in Washington, Mai never missed a beat:

"Star Wars is MAD—Mutually Assured Destruction—in space."

"He's trying to make homelessness a choice freely arrived at."

"Trickle-down economics means the rich are going to piss on the poor."

"He's not a president. He's a rich man running a country club."

"He's a puppet."

"He's a nut."

Of course, there was always the generic, all-purpose, "He's a fascist."

Mai was unremitting in her disdain for Reagan's ignorance of basic facts.

"Michael, you can't let this guy out alone. He'll get lost. They've got him on a string. He's scripted, playing a role, with others directing him."

"You're wrong, Mai. He may not have command of details like a Jimmy Carter, but he is a hell of a lot better president. He inspires. He leads. He has a vision of America."

"He's reading off of 4x6 cards, for Christ's sake, Michael. What does that tell you?" Mai responded.

"But Mai, I've seen them. They're in pencil!" Michael answered.

"So?" asked Mai.

"So, he wrote them himself. If someone had written them for him, they would be typed out."

"I'd believe that if they were written in crayon," responded Mai.

"There is just a lot more there, Mai, but you liberals are just too damn closed-minded and arrogant to see," he said in frustration.

"And I think there is just less there than meets the eye," added Mai, knowing that they had come to the usual end of their conversation—deadlock.

At the beginning of Reagan's second term, after Ed Meese had finally been appointed attorney general of the United States, Michael told Mai that he would be in California during the State of the Union address.

"Isn't that a big deal?" she asked. "Why wouldn't you be there for it?"

"The attorney general is going to be in San Diego. It's a rule that one cabinet member isn't at the Joint Session of Congress in case something should happen."

"I'm glad you told me, Michael," Mai replied. "I'll call off the Weathermen attack. I shutter to think, 'President Edwin Meese III.'"

"Don't even joke about something like that," he told her, worrying that her words might be picked up by satellite monitoring and set off an alarm somewhere at the National Security Agency.

The evening of the State of the Union address, Michael was with Attorney General Edwin Meese in San Diego, at a seafood restaurant near the harbor. In the background he could see a television over the bar. He knew there was no basis, in fact, but all evening he shot glances at the television screen, waiting for the report that the Capitol had been destroyed. When he went to bed that night, the Capitol intact, he just shook his head: "Oh, Mai," he whispered.

Chapter 48

Leon

LEON'S PARTNER, JONATHAN Bishop, could smell it. He took the records to Leon.

"Leon, remember a Victor Hall? One of the iron workers who helped us on the housing discrimination case."

"Sure. What about him?"

"Well, to make sure he qualified as a prospective buyer of a house in Orinda Heights, we got a letter from his employer, General Maritime Construction. Here's the letter saying he's paid $28 an hour." The letter, on company stationery, was from the headquarters in Maryland.

"What's the problem? That sounds as if it would make him a qualified buyer," replied Leon.

"Yeah, but it wouldn't qualify him to live at the low-rent complex owned by the Brotherhood of Steel Workers Pension Fund," Bishop answered.

"What are you getting at?" asked Leon.

"This. Here are the records subpoenaed from the local union by the Crosby firm. They show our guy making $8.50 an hour, as certified by his supervisor in compliance with HUD regulations."

Leon looked at the records.

"Good thing they didn't catch it before they settled. We'd have egg on our faces if our prospective black buyer wasn't financially qualified," said Leon.

Bishop lifted a box onto the desk.

"Well, he wasn't the only one. I went back and checked. We used a bunch of the iron workers because, you remember, it was Angela's efforts to get people into that complex that got us going down this path in the first place. Every one of these iron workers shows the same pattern."

"Have you asked Mr. Hall what he really was making?" Leon was now curious.

"Yeah. Neither figure! There is something going on, Leon, and from my HUD background, I'd say it's a fraud on the government."

Bishop explained what he thought the records meant. Leon listened, growing more interested as Bishop described the facts he had uncovered.

"*Qui tam pro domino rege quam pro se ipso in hac parte sequinter*," Leon said out loud, to the ceiling, as he leaned back in his chair.

Leon dropped his feet, stood, and walked around to the front of his desk.

"God, I love the English Common Law. The symmetry of it all. *Qui tam*. The ancient action on behalf of the King."

Bishop had not really had time for "pleasure reading" into the history of the Common Law while in law school. Working days, going to school nights, he was limited to learning what needed to be learned in order to pass the Bar exam. Leon, on the other hand, had always had an abiding interest in history. It was in history that Karl Marx and Friedrich Engels rooted their philosophy. Leon had handed out pamphlets with his parents on the historical analysis of class struggle, before he could even read. In law school, when confronted during his first year by his Contracts professor, he had taken up reading Holmes' *The Common Law*. This only whetted his appetite, leading to the definitive work, Blackstone's *Commentaries on the Law of England*.

It was clear Bishop was not familiar with the term.

"*Qui tam* lets an individual sue for fraud on the government," Leon explained.

"But how is our guy hurt? He's in housing provided by the union, with his rent supplemented by the United States Treasury. He is making a good wage. Where's the harm? Nobody's defrauding him."

Bishop pointed at the documents before him. "Am I missing something here? I think I know what the employer is doing with the Union Pension Fund, giving it numbers so employees can qualify for the HUD loan and rent supplement, but why would corporate headquarters give us hourly figures so much higher than what employees are actually making?"

Leon was excited. Not so much about Bishop's discovery but what he saw as a historical thread emerging from the ages.

"It's pretty obvious. General Maritime Construction is charging the United States Navy $28 an hour for a worker, who is paid $14 an hour but is certified to HUD as getting $8.50 an hour so that the Brotherhood of Iron Workers can have its building underwritten and supported by the Treasury."

Having given the explanation of a complex fraud he was able to dissect instantly, he resumed his fascination with history and *qui tam*.

"*Qui tam* comes from a Latin phrase meaning 'he who brings an action as much for the King as for himself.' It always involves recovery for the sovereign. In the 13th century, the only way a suit could get into the royal courts was by joining an interest of the King with a private interest. At the same time, some enterprising individuals took up suing just for the King's interest in hopes of getting a reward of sorts for recovering on behalf of the Crown. They were variously referred to as 'informants,' 'bounty hunters,' 'lewd,' and 'the worst kind of people.'"

Leon laughed.

"Isn't that pretty much what old Marty Crosby called us for bringing the discrimination class action?"

Leon turned back to history with enthusiasm.

"You know the major use of *qui tam* in the United States? Against contractors, just like these sons-of-bitches, who are screwing the taxpayers while building a nuclear aircraft carrier." Leon returned to his desk and leaned back in his chair.

"During the Civil War, when thousands of Union soldiers were dying with faulty military supplies, Abraham Lincoln pushed for the passage of the False Claims Act. It provided penalties for defense contractors who defrauded the government. Here's the kicker. The person bringing the suit to expose the fraud got 50 percent of the recovery."

Bishop's mouth dropped open. "Fifty percent!"

"Old Abe was a trial lawyer," Leon explained. "He knew what motivated lawyers: A contingent fee! Congress has reduced the percentage, but we're still talking potentially huge incentives. We're talking a percentage of the cost of a goddamn nuclear submarine."

"All for doing the King's work," added Bishop, laughing.

"Let's get all of those workers in here. But quietly. Don't even tell them what it's about until we're ready to file. We need to figure out a way to check the defense contracts and verify the numbers General Maritime is using, but without raising any suspicion."

Bishop looked worried.

"What's the matter?" Leon asked.

"What about the Union? They're in here up to their eyeballs. Once we disclose the overcharging on the defense contractor's end, it's going to come out about the understating of income on the Union housing."

Leon had already thought of that. If he sued a union, he was going to lose the union support that had been the backbone of his law firm. He was also going to have a serious problem with his father. He did not hesitate.

"We have no choice. It's all one suit. We sue them both."

Bishop did not like it, but he knew Leon was right. Initially, they would get the information from their Union clients without letting on that they would be suing the Union. Their real "client" would be the U.S. Government. Bishop had put his finger on the obvious. The Union members themselves had experienced no harm, but had benefitted from the conspiracy of employer and Union to defraud the government.

Leon knew where he could get the defense contractor information, the documents submitted to the government on a cost-plus contract for the building of the Navy's new nuclear aircraft carrier. But he did not even tell his partner. He did not want to take a chance anyone would find out.

When he was alone, he called Angela.

"I need your help."

"You got that right, baby," she answered.

"I need you to arrange a meeting for me with Congressman Dellums."

Angela had been in daily contact with Dellums' office for the last 18 months. She had known Dellums for years and had gone from walking precincts for him to now acting as the national coordinator of the Free South Africa Movement, which had its headquarters in the congressman's Washington office.

Most of her work was on the phone, out of her home or at the congressman's district office in Oakland. She had quit her job at the Fair Housing Commission with the birth of the baby, Mandela Goldman. Now she fully devoted her time to writing and organizing. Leon's income spared her from worrying about money. Together they moved into a new large home with more room for the baby and a study for her to do her writing.

Leon had insisted on a nanny to live in and help because of their busy schedules. Angela had resisted initially, preferring to take the baby to her mother's home. She relented finally because she would rather have the baby in the home while she worked. Without help, she could do very little at home. Her mother did not drive.

"But she's going to be black. I'm not having my daughter raised by no white woman."

Speaking for the congressman, as she knew she could, she suggested that Leon accompany her to Washington the following week.

"We're gonna hold a major demonstration at the South African Embassy, to coincide with the congressman introducing comprehensive economic sanctions against those racist bastards. It's been a while since you've been on a picket line, Leon."

Then she asked, "What's it about?"

"Actually, Angela, I've never been on a picket line. That was my dad. Just tell the congressman it's a matter of national security."

* * * * *

The crowd was waving signs: "Freedom Now," "Boycott South Africa." Congressman Ron Dellums, his booming voice aimed from across the road at the South African Embassy, was rocking back on his heels:

Immorality cannot be condoned with "the quiet diplomacy" of George Schultz. There can be no "constructive engagement" with evil, as suggested by Ronald Reagan.

There can be no rest until apartheid is destroyed. There is no place in the world for a terrorist and racist regime like the white government of South Africa.

The crowd roared its approval. If there were people in the Embassy, they were not getting any work done.

Leon had met Dellums at the congressman's fundraisers in California but had not really spent any time talking to him directly. Dellums knew Leon and Angela were together and knew that the ever-increasing substantial contributions to his campaign, by Leon, were because of Angela. He agreed to stop by for "room service breakfast" at the suite Angela and Leon had at the Four Seasons Hotel in Georgetown.

The morning after the demonstrations at the South African Embassy, Angela, wrapped in a robe of the hotel, its moniker falling away from her breast, greeted Ron Dellums at the door.

"Ron!" They hugged. "Leon, the congressman is here."

Leon was in the next room of the suite where he had breakfast waiting. As he had requested, Angela took her cue.

283

"You guys go ahead. I'm going to be getting dressed. See you back in California, Ron."

Leon got right to the point. He explained the discrepancies he and his partner had recently found with a number of black clients they had represented in a class action housing discrimination case. The congressman knew of the case since it occurred in his district and was widely reported. The employer was telling the Navy one thing for cost reimbursements while actually paying employees half of that amount claimed, Leon told the congressman. He left out any reference to the Union and its pension fund housing.

"It looks like the government is getting ripped off. If our numbers are right, it could run close to $100 million on this one carrier," Leon concluded.

Dellums sipped from the glass of orange juice he had requested.

"How can I help you?" he asked.

"All we need is to verify that the documents actually submitted to the Navy for payment have the false costs. If some class action lawyer like me starts snooping around, word would get back to General Maritime and there would be evidence-shredding parties, witness intimidation, everything. But if a congressman with an interest in military matters asks for the cost documents of a project in his district, no alarms should go off. I want those documents in hand before I sue one of the biggest shipbuilding companies in the world and charge them with defrauding the United States Government," Leon said, his eyes focused on Dellums.

Dellums was thinking.

"Of course," added Leon, "nothing I ask of you is illegal. Fraud by a military contractor is within the purview of the committees upon which you sit and, I'm sure, a major concern to you as a congressman."

"But tactically, to help your case, it would be better for you if I obtained them?" asked Dellums, suggesting it would be a personal favor to Leon.

"The primary beneficiary will be the United States Government when fraudulently obtained taxpayer money is returned," said Leon in reply.

Dellums laughed.

"Minus a percentage, right, Mr. Goldman?"

"Well, lawyers have to live, too," replied Leon.

Dellums looked around the large expensive suite at the Four Seasons and back at Leon who was wearing a handmade monogrammed shirt.

"Yes, they do. Yes, they do."

He stood, shook hands, and turned to leave.

"Let me see what we can do together for the taxpayers, Mr. Goldman."

As he reached for the door, he asked, "When will you be back in California?"

"Angela and I are taking a week in London and then Paris. We'll be back on the 23rd," said Leon.

"Paris. You'll enjoy Paris. Very different attitude about interracial couples. And the black people there…" He paused. "They speak French."

He opened the door and walked through, laughing and slapping his thigh over his joke.

Chapter 49

Brian

IT WAS LIKE they could not forgive each other. He was not there for her when she needed him. She had betrayed him. As much as they tried, neither could forget.

The success of the firm, with significant personal injury settlements, made their lives easy. Easier than confronting the problems that persisted, unspoken. Trips to Hawaii with the Los Angeles Trial Lawyers. Drinking. Madrid with the American Board of Trial Advocates. Drinking. Entertaining in their beautiful home with its to-die-for view over the canyon. Drinking. It all helped. They were either surrounded by people or, in those moments alone, could count on the buzz of a few martinis and the warmth of the hot tub to make them forget.

It was a marriage.

He still thought of himself as a radical, a Movement lawyer, but the press of product liability cases left him little time for The Cause. He kept his membership in the National Lawyers Guild, but its bulletins went from the receptionist directly to the library, unread.

The election of Ronald Reagan made him doubt that an armed revolution could be avoided in America. The rich were getting richer, with Reagan's help. The poor, especially blacks, were getting the finger.

Brian brought the same fervor to fighting big corporations as he had to fighting oppression by the government. Now, Ford and General Motors' deception in producing unsafe cars with exploding gas tanks or transmissions that shifted unexpectedly from park to reverse replaced illegal government surveillance of radical groups for his attention. Those deprived of civil liberties took a backseat to children burned so badly that their chins melted into their chests, their bodies covered with biological pigskin dressing from, the nurses told the kids, pigs kept in the basement of the hospital.

Crusading on behalf of the injured—"because big corporations cut corners on safety to add pennies to the bottom line"—gave his life meaning. Another cause.

If the coming police state, presided over by Ronald Reagan, was not enough, Brian shared the fear of nuclear war that appeared heightened by Reagan's rhetoric and his Strategic Defense Initiative—SDI—known derisively as "Star Wars."

"The son-of-a-bitch wants to dictate, from space, to the rest of the world! If he launches this, the Soviets will have no choice but to make a preemptive strike. Nuclear war. He's nuts."

Brian read extensively about nuclear arms issues, reports from the Institute for Strategic Studies in London, the Stockholm International Peace Institute, and the Doctors for Social Responsibility and the Freeze Movement. He helped form Attorneys for Nuclear Sanity, and he kept the office fax machine busy sending "urgent action" memos that prompted attorneys to contact their congressmen on MX missile votes, "Star Wars" funding, and military appropriation bills. For credibility and access, of course, the firm contributed substantial amounts to those leading the fight against Reagan—California Senator Alan Cranston and congressmen like Phil Burton of Los Angeles, and, of course, Ron Dellums of Oakland.

But there was no one to sue to stop "Star Wars." He wanted to use the legal system, his weapon, to advance The Cause. Ironically, it was Jackson Bridgeport III who gave him his opportunity.

Brian received a call on a Saturday morning as he was catching up on his office mail. It came on the back line.

"Hi," he answered, expecting Shelly.

"Mr. Jacobs?" the young voice asked.

"Yes, who is this?"

"Abby Greenfield. I am the coordinator of Freeze volunteers. We were given your number to call if we ever had problems soliciting for signatures on our petitions."

"What's the problem?" he asked, pleased that the Nuclear Freeze volunteers carried his name and number as their champion.

"Well, we're at the L.A. Valley Mall. We started collecting signatures on the petition to Congress to declare a freeze on all nuclear weapons, and the mall security tells us that we have to leave," she responded.

"Where are you petitioning?" he asked.

"On the sidewalk, outside the stores. I know the drill," she added. "No disruption; no blocking; no going in stores."

"Let me talk to the security officer," he requested.

He heard words exchanged that he could not make out. Someone came to the phone.

"Who's this?" Brian asked.

"Who's this?" the voice asked back.

"Attorney Brian Jacobs. I represent the Nuclear Freeze volunteers who are trying to exercise their First Amendment rights."

"This is private property," the voice answered.

"Right. So is most of America. But the First Amendment covers the whole damn country. Who is this?" Brian demanded.

"I have been told to ask them to leave. If they don't, we're calling the police and having them arrested."

"You're an idiot," Brian snapped. "Let me talk to a representative of the mall management."

"You just did," said the voice and hung up on him.

He waited. Abby did not call back. He was furious at a rent-a-cop hanging up on him. But he also realized he had let the conversation get out of control by calling the cop an idiot.

Brian got in his car and drove for 20 minutes, expecting that if the police were called, a citation on a citizen's arrest, with a promise to appear, would be the usual procedure to handle trespassing. The volunteers would probably be sitting in their cars, in the parking lot, waiting for instructions.

What he found when he arrived at the Los Angeles Valley Mall was a large crowd and television cameras. One was broadcasting live, on Channel 4, from the scene.

The scene consisted of seven young people sitting on the sidewalk, their arms interlocked, with a young attractive red-haired woman in the center. She was holding a sign saying "No Star Wars—Freeze Now." They were ringed by mall security, apparently unsure what to do with them.

The cameras were rolling.

"Mr. Jacobs," a voice shouted. It was the young woman in the center of the demonstration. "I'm Abby."

He walked over to her and crouched behind her, speaking quietly, "Why didn't you call back before doing—?" He was interrupted by the siren of a

288

police car sounded to clear a path through the crowd. He assessed the situation quickly and walked to the television reporter who was reporting live. Without losing a beat, the dapper, tan reporter, in a sports coat and tie, added to his live report: "...and well-known Los Angeles attorney Brian Jacobs has just arrived, apparently to end this standoff."

Turning his body partly to make room for Brian to enter the picture, he remarked, "Well, Brian, this isn't exactly Attica Prison or Wounded Knee, but we have a problem here. What can you tell us?"

Equally comfortable in front of a camera, Brian picked up on the reporter's comment: "No, it's not Wounded Knee, but it's just as important to every American. The Los Angeles Valley Mall, in lockstep with the Reagan Administration, is trying to prevent Los Angeles residents from exercising their right of free speech and to petition government to stop the insanity of Star Wars deployment. If there is no free speech allowed where our people gather, in malls, then there is no freedom anywhere."

The reporter interrupted: "What do you plan to do to resolve the situation?"

Brian had an immediate answer, as he always did for the press: "Nothing. Our people were exercising their constitutional rights. If the Los Angeles Valley Mall wants to have them dragged to jail for that, let them. But if they do, hundreds will be back here tomorrow to shut this shopping center down as un-American."

Brian saw the chief of security being escorted to his office. He came back and handed Brian a portable phone. The voice on the other end said, "Brian, so good to see you again. I was watching television."

"Who is this?" Brian asked.

"Jackson Bridgeport. You're standing on my client's property."

"You're not going to threaten me, too, are you, Jackson?"

"No, no. Don't be silly. I thought I could save you and your protesters..."

"They're petitioners, not protesters, Jackson," Brian corrected him.

"Well, I am looking at a bunch of people blocking the sidewalk, doing a sit-in at my client's shopping center. I'd say that's a protest."

"Your private cops stopped them from petitioning..."

"They were just following orders."

"Just following orders. That has a ring to it," Brian instinctively retorted.

"Brian, I didn't call to argue with you. Give it a rest. We have procedures. Your people ignored them. They didn't even apply to petition. They just showed up. I'm not stupid, Brian. I know we can't keep them out, but we have reasonable time, place, and manner regulations. Trust me, our rules comply with the latest Supreme Court pronouncements."

Brian was on the defensive. He had not been given all the facts by Abby Greenfield.

"So are you telling me you're going to have them arrested in front of television cameras and bear the consequences?" Brian asked, a little less sure of his position.

"No, Brian. You've seen to that. Why don't you announce that the Los Angeles Valley Mall has declined to prosecute and welcomes your clients to petition for their cause because the Los Angeles Valley Mall believes in every American's right to free speech. We can all go home. Tomorrow, they come back with their petitions, and we give them a copy of our rules."

Brian looked at the waiting cameras. "And Brian," added Bridgeport, "this is two you owe me."

Brian made the announcement. While he praised the Los Angeles Valley Mall for its "foresight" in allowing the petitioners, his announcement sounded enough of a victory to the protesting volunteers to cause yelling, hooting, and—on their feet now—shouting to the assembled cameras of "Stop Star Wars Now—Freeze. Freeze. Freeze."

Brian and Jackson were both good lawyers. In the confrontation brought on by their clients' actions, it was the words of the country western singer, Kenny Rogers, not that of a Supreme Court opinion, that they had both heeded:

> You gotta know when to hold 'em;
> know when to fold 'em.
> Know when to walk away;
> know when to run.

"Ms. Greenfield, may I talk to you?" Brian asked her as the cameras left and the crowd began to disperse.

"Sure, Mr. Jacobs. Good job," she answered.

"Well, Ms. Greenfield, it wasn't made any easier by you."

"What do you mean?" she asked.

"You never told me when you called my office that you hadn't even applied to petition. Is that true? You didn't even tell the mall you were putting petitioners in here?"

"Yeah, but their regulations are bullshit. I think they're unconstitutional," she said with a wave of her head.

"Unconstitutional?" He looked at her. "So you're familiar with all the cases in constitutional law dealing with time, place, and manner regulations, are you?"

"Enough," she said with a cavalier attitude.

"Enough! And you thought you could just sit down on the sidewalk and obstruct mall customers because you decided you knew enough about the Constitution?"

She did not like being lectured. "After I called you, and they reacted as they did, I decided we would sit in. That wasn't planned."

Her attitude annoyed him. "Even if they were wrong to deny you the right to petition, for which you never applied, that did not mean you could just sit in. How did you plan on avoiding arrest for obstruction or trespass?"

"I knew they wouldn't arrest us on TV," she said with confidence. "That's why I called Channel 4 instead of calling you back."

He looked at her closely. She was young, beautiful, and smart. He smiled.

"What do you do?" he asked her.

"I'm a law student at UCLA, third year."

Abby Greenfield was tall, with green eyes. She was smiling back at him. She knew she had pulled off a coup and hoped he would admire her tactics.

"It was a pretty risky stunt, Ms. Greenfield, especially for a young person who wants to be admitted to the Bar."

His tone was now conciliatory, that of a mentor to one of his best students. He did not know how good a student she was.

"If you want to be a lawyer, confine yourself to the courtroom. If you want to be a Movement lawyer, take your case to the streets," she said as if reciting a mantra.

He recognized the words he had often used in speeches to law students. He laughed out loud. She looked around. Her friends had left.

"Could you give me a ride home?" she asked.

He held her gaze with a long pause. "Sure."

As they walked to his Mercedes, she asked, "So how am I doing so far?"

He put his arm around her shoulder while they continued to walk. "Well, I give you an 'A' for media manipulation, a 'B' for sizing up your opponent, and an 'F' for planning."

She put her arm around his waist. "Maybe you could teach me. I'd really hate to flunk out of 'Movement Law.'" He sensed that the subject of the conversation had subtly changed and had to again give her another "A" for manipulation.

They were still talking a half hour later when he pulled up to her apartment. She had graduated from Mt. Holyoke and followed her boyfriend out to California where he was in medical school at Stanford. After three years, the relationship was over, but she at least had a master's degree to show for the years in Palo Alto.

"What's the master's in?" he asked.

"Business Administration. Can you believe it? It was his idea. Thought I could run his clinic and handle investments." She laughed. "That's all he talked about. He studied the Tax Code as much as he did medical books."

"What happened?"

"Nothing. Exactly nothing. He was so boring. I woke up one day and realized every mother's dream that her daughter should marry a doctor was my nightmare."

He had turned the engine off as they sat in front of her apartment.

"Brian, can you come in for a few minutes? I at least owe you a drink for saving my ass from jail."

He watched the ass he had just saved rise out of the passenger seat and exit the car.

"Coming?"

"Sure," he said as he got out.

He sat on the couch. She took off her UCLA sweatshirt to reveal a thin white blouse and went to the kitchen. She returned and handed him a rum and Coke. It was the closest she could get to his request for a "real drink." He had turned down the jug Almaden white wine that she now brought, along with a glass for herself, and put on the floor, where she sat in front of him.

"So, how did you get from a would-be doctor's wife to UCLA Law School?" he asked.

She leaned forward to pour her wine. As she did, her blouse fell forward, fully revealing her breasts as he looked down upon her. She held the position, pouring slowly, her wine. He held his position, too, admiring. Finally she looked up and smiled at him, making no attempt to conceal what was so nicely presented to him.

She took a sip of wine.

"A girlfriend invited me down for the weekend. We hung out at the beach. Went to a few parties. I ended up staying. This place is alive."

"That explains L.A. Why law school?" he persisted.

"After six months of parties, I started to have that feeling again, wondering is this it? Smiling while some date tried to impress me about some deal he was putting together: a building construction, a film production, a stock transaction. Or a lawyer telling me about his courtroom prowess—which usually turned out to be the only thing he was good at.

"What came out of all that, I guess, were two things. First, I wasn't going to be dependent on some man for the quality of my life. Second, this society has its priorities totally fucked up. I figured I could do something about both with law school."

There was something challenging about her independence. She appeared to be in her late 20s, and he was 42. Those 12 to 15 years seemed to represent a lifetime.

"I have no doubt you will succeed in both," he said, raising his glass of ice. He had finished his rum and Coke.

She rose onto her knees, resting one arm on his knee, and reached for his glass.

"You're going to have to help me finish this bottle of wine. I don't have any more rum," she said.

He held on to the glass. Both of them were holding it. He leaned forward and kissed her. She put her other hand behind his head, holding his lips to hers, and rose and pressed her body against his, all the while they held on to the glass, now over his head.

"I thought you didn't want to be dependent on some man for the quality of your life," he said when she lifted her head back.

She leaned back and picked up the wine. She poured a full glass for each of them. Then she sat astride him.

"Oh, I don't think the quality of this afternoon is going to be dependent on just you."

She undid her blouse, fully exposing the breasts he had seen earlier just from above. "I'll have a lot to say about it," she added.

He got home late. Near 9:00 P.M. He and Shelly were hosting a dinner. The extra people saved an immediate confrontation and allowed a collective unquestioned explanation.

"Hi, folks. Sorry I'm late. I had to meet with an expert witness. Goddamn cardiologist at Cedars-Sinai. Whole case depends on him and he wants to talk over dinner and drinks. Like I have nothing else to do."

Everyone nodded at the unreasonableness of the cardiologist.

"Well, you're here now, Brian." It was Jerry Bacharach, a fellow lawyer, drinker, and golfer. "Can I get you a drink?"

"God, thanks, Jerry. Let me take it in and change out of this suit."

Brian took the drink, went to the bedroom, and locked the door. As he did, he heard someone yell, "Hey, Brian, saw you on TV." He quickly undressed and got in the shower, with the drink. Vodka on the rocks. He let the water run over his head as he tried to relax. Then he soaped down his body with one hand in case the smell of powder or perfume—or any other smells—lingered. Then he gargled with vodka but swallowed when he finished.

He dried off and looked in the mirror. To his horror, he had nail tracks on his chest. God! He remembered the moment. She certainly had shown she was not going to wait for him in anything. In her ecstasy she had dug her nails into his chest. But he had been in no state, at that point, to object to pain, or stop her. He dressed quickly and joined the people in his house. All of them greeted him warmly. Except Shelly. He caught her eye. When he did, she turned and walked away.

The confrontation never came. She went to bed. He followed, in the dark, leaving a t-shirt on in case she woke before him and saw the scratches on his chest.

He continued to see Abby for about six months. She even came into the office occasionally as a "law clerk" doing research for Brian at UCLA. When she suggested that she could join the firm in the fall, after graduation, Brian knew he had to do something. But he did not. Abby decided for him. She knew it had run its course. She was already seeing someone else.

Brian did not see Abby again for three years. When he did, he was with Shelly.

They were at a fundraising exhibit of photographs of the Chernobyl Nuclear Reactor disaster, circulating throughout the United States under the sponsorship of Physicians for Social Responsibility. Nuclear Reactor No. 4 at Chernobyl, in Ukraine, had been destroyed in the worst accident in nuclear history, sending radioactive isotopes around the world. One hundred and thirty-five thousand people had been evacuated from a 25-mile radius, much of which remained uninhabitable. The photo exhibit was part of the world-wide effort to show the dangers of nuclear power plants and to shut them down.

Brian saw Abby standing, applauding the speaker, the noted plastic and reconstructive surgeon Jeffrey Ward from UCLA School of Medicine. Dr. Ward had organized surgeons to go to the Soviet Union to help treat radiation burns. One of the pictures showed him in Ukraine, examining a reactor worker whose skin was hanging off his torso.

When Dr. Ward completed his comments, he stepped down and returned to a young woman, who gave him a kiss that conveyed deep passion. It was Abby.

In moments, they were walking toward Brian and Shelly. Dr. Ward and Abby. Abby was holding onto his arm and smiling as people greeted Dr. Ward. She glanced, just one couple away, and saw Brian looking at her. Her expression did not change except for slight recognition. She looked quickly at Shelly.

"Thank you for coming." It was Dr. Ward, in front of them, with Abby.

Brian shook his hand. "This is my wife, Shelly." He did not know what to do next.

Abby, again, decided for him.

"Hi, Brian. How are you? Jeffrey, I was a law clerk in Brian's office during my last year at UCLA Law School. Brian is a nationally known attorney and longtime supporter of the Nuclear Freeze Movement."

Shelly looked at her. "I'm Mrs. Jacobs," she said. She did not offer her hand.

Jeffrey Ward was in thought, retracing their relationship. "Oh, right. I remember you told me when we met that you were working at a law office."

Brian felt pain in his chest like he had been hit hard with a tire iron.

"How are you involved in this exhibit, Abby?" Brian asked, attempting to keep his voice modulated.

Dr. Ward answered for her. "We were in the Soviet Union together, on a trip for people interested in nuclear issues. Right after she finished law school and took the Bar exam. We were even in Ukraine, just nine months before the Chernobyl meltdown. Since then, she's been helping me raise funds for medical research and treatment for nuclear injuries and illnesses. This exhibit is a big part of that."

Dr. Ward pulled Abby closer and kissed her cheek. "She's not just beautiful. She has an MBA from Stanford," he said with pride.

Brian looked at her. "I remember."

"Nice meeting you," Dr. Ward commented as he and Abby moved on down the line.

Brian did not know if he hated her, hated himself, or hated Shelly. He watched Abby walk away. She was everything every man in his right mind could want, was the thought that pushed to the forefront.

He had never felt guilty about Abby. Just emptiness. And anger at Shelly. When he reflected on his six months with Abby, he reasoned that it had not been betrayal. Shelly had done that to him. It was just tit-for-tat. Getting even.

He had a few more drinks before getting in the car to go home. Shelly drove. They were silent, each with his or her own thoughts, for the first 30 minutes.

Shelly shot him a glance.

"So. She was the one," she said. A statement; not a question.

He did not answer her.

It was two years later that the marriage counselor explained it as a universal truth: "Wives *always* know."

Chapter 50

Michael

THE ATTORNEY GENERAL, Edwin Meese III, asked Michael to gather information to support the president's expected veto of the Dellums Bill working its way through Congress. All indications were that President Reagan would face the issue of vetoing an economic boycott of South Africa by Christmas 1985.

"Emphasize the legal implications," said Meese. "Enforcement problems. Requiring divestiture would probably compel breaches of contracts, huge losses with constitutional arguments for compensation, including losses by colleges, universities, and municipalities that have pension plans invested in companies doing business in South Africa."

He added: "Bill Buckley can give you the numbers."

Michael gave his report to Meese. He never expected that he would be asked to sit in and directly address the issue with the president of the United States.

In the summer, Ronald Reagan had argued against sanctions, saying, "Punitive action will only hurt South African blacks." In response, black Archbishop Desmond Tutu had said, from South Africa, that Reagan was wrong. And even if he was right, blacks were willing to make the sacrifice.

In August, at a press conference, Reagan said that South Africa had eliminated racial segregation. The world laughed at him. Worse, the college students of America, who had marched in the spring in demonstrations reminiscent of the '60s, were coming back to school for the fall semester, reveling in Reagan's misstatement about and apparent ignorance of South Africa.

Unbeknownst to Michael, Admiral John Poindexter was, as National Security Advisor, the source of much of Reagan's information, telling the president that the black African National Congress was an extremist, probably Communist, element that had little or no support in South Africa. Michael's report did not agree.

"Mr. President," Michael began nervously. He had sat in on meetings where the president had been in attendance. He had even exchanged a few sentences, mostly in jest, with the president. Never before had he been asked to present an issue fully, with other presidential advisors present. He had provided issue papers, talking points, legal analyses, mostly to Meese, who, in turn, would modify, incorporate, or abandon all or part as he wished. This time, Meese had introduced him and told the president that Michael had a "different take" on the situation.

As always, President Reagan acknowledged him in the same way. "Michael, our Berkeley student. Does this remind you of when you were in school? All these student demonstrations?"

"Yes, sir, Mr. President." He paused to see if the president was going to go down memory lane.

"Well, let's hear your slant," the president said with a little chuckle.

"Mr. President, the issue is not whether the United States is going to boycott South Africa. The only question is the role of this Administration in the boycott that is already underway."

Poindexter looked up and put down the pipe he was lighting. The president frowned. Meese shot each an imperceptible glance.

"Forty major universities have sold over $300 million in stock of companies doing business in South Africa," Michael continued. "The pension funds of 100 cities, counties, and states, representing millions of people, have been withdrawn from companies doing business in South Africa. Millions of dollars of deposits from banks doing business in South Africa have been withdrawn. And not just by towns on the fringe. We're talking about Los Angeles, San Francisco, and New York, to name a few.

"Pepsi and Coke sold their interest in South Africa this year. Apple Computer announced that it will not sell computers in South Africa. The list goes on and on, and is growing every day. The effect of all this action has driven the South African rand down from its 1980s' value of $1.29 to $0.35 this month.

"So there is already a boycott, and it is growing daily."

Poindexter interrupted. "Well, some have cut and run, under the pressure of student demonstrations here in the United States, but there are still over $2 billion in U.S. investments in South Africa and over 300 American-owned enterprises."

Reagan picked up the cue. "I am not going to abandon the South African government because a bunch of students and their professors say to. There is no one else in South Africa to lead the country. You can't just have equality overnight. Most of the blacks can't even read or write."

Poindexter added an amen. "That's right, Mr. President."

"Well," continued Michael, "you should know that there is someone else: The ANC—the African National Congress—has widespread support in the country. It is just a matter of time, Mr. President."

He saw Reagan look at Poindexter. Meese interrupted before Poindexter could defend his position. "Tell the president what you found, Michael."

"Mr. President, while you have been led to believe"—he did not say by whom—"that the situation is salvageable, the major white-owned South African companies have been carrying out secret meetings with the exiled leaders of the ANC in Zambia, just across the border.

"What this tells us, Mr. President, is that those in the best position to know and with the most to lose in South Africa—white South African businessmen themselves—see the handwriting on the wall."

The president looked stunned. Again, he had been embarrassed and hung out to dry on the matter of South Africa.

"Have you confirmed these meetings?" he asked, looking at Meese.

"Yes, Mr. President," replied Meese. "Michael obtained a list of the representatives attending the meetings, times, places, everything. We've confirmed the information independently."

Meese did not mention where Michael had obtained the information. No one asked. Michael did not volunteer his source. The name of the black congressman from Oakland never came up. It was sufficient for discussion that the facts were true and independently verified. It was sufficient for Meese's purpose that Poindexter had been undermined in the eyes of the president.

"I still think this needs to be done in an orderly way," said the president. "We can't be accused of just abandoning the South African government. How would that look?"

There appeared to be not just frustration but anger in his voice. Michael spoke up.

"That's what we meant earlier, Mr. President, when we indicated the issue is not 'boycott or no boycott.' The boycott is, and has been, under way. The only question is this Administration's role. We propose you take charge of the situation."

The president's mood visibly improved as it appeared that someone had a way out. He smiled.

"When I was president of the Screen Actors Guild, and things were going against us, we used to say, 'If they're running you out of town, get in front of the crowd and pretend it's a parade.' Is that what you're suggesting?"

The president of the United States was looking directly at Michael.

"I'm suggesting, Mr. President, that we are on the wrong side of history when it comes to South Africa. How you respond will have implications for American leadership in all of Africa and the Third World."

Meese noted, to himself, that Michael had gone beyond the words of the report and was addressing the president of the United States from the first person. He no longer said "we suggest," but rather, "I'm suggesting." It was noted. But for Meese's purpose, it was effective.

"Thank you, Michael," Meese said as the president sat, looking at Michael. Michael knew that was his cue to leave. He got up, picked up his papers, and walked to the door of the Oval Office. He expected at least a "thank you" or "good bye" from the president. There was nothing.

Poindexter started as soon as the door was closed.

"Mr. President, we have to support our allies, no matter what."

Meese interrupted him. "Admiral, I realize it is a tradition in the Navy for the captain to go down with the ship, but that is not a position we should advocate for the president of the United States, especially when South Africa isn't even our ship."

"Maybe he's right," muttered the president to no one in particular.

"I agree," said Meese. "I think we need to get out ahead of this thing before Congress just passes draconian sanctions over your veto, Mr. President."

"No. Not that part," said the president, waving his hand. "Maybe we are on the wrong side of history."

In September, two weeks later, the *New York Times* carried the story of the "dramatic reversal" in Administration policy toward South Africa. By executive order, the president had put in place sanctions against South Africa's government designed to pressure it into ending apartheid in that country. The analysis attributed the change to "mounting pressure in Congress" and "an attempt to head off legislation, most particularly the Dellums Bill."

At a press conference, on September 13th, the following exchange occurred:

> *Sam Donaldson:* Mr. President, why have you backed down in your support of South Africa's all-white apartheid government and your opposition to sanctions?
>
> *President Reagan:* Now, Sam, let's be clear. We have never supported the concept of an all-white government in South Africa. The United States has always sought full representation of all people, of whatever color, in a democratically elected government. We have tried to accomplish our aims by constructive engagement and quiet diplomacy. But it is clear from events that time is running out. So we have changed our tactics, not our goal of freedom for all in South Africa.

Another reporter jumped in to ask a question. The president did not hear him. He appeared to be thinking. The room went silent. He began talking again, looking through, not at, Sam Donaldson.

"History will be the judge. In Africa and elsewhere, we support an end to minority rule." Again he paused.

"Never let it be said that the United States was on the wrong side of history, whether in the competition against Communism, or in any other struggle for freedom, in Africa, or anywhere around the world."

"Jesus, who feeds him these lines?" asked the 18-year-old, Asian-looking, black-haired boy sitting next to Michael and watching the television. He sounded just like his mother.

Michael smiled at the president's last lines. He knew. But he could not tell anyone. Not even his son. He was too good a lawyer.

Chapter 51

Rose

SHE HAD AN idea for the Fresno Women's Center. She had discussed it with her old boss, Tony Hawk.

"It could work, Rose. It would be a first," he told her.

The first battered women's shelter and counseling center in the country built with government-sponsored bonds.

"I don't see why not. If the county can issue bonds for off-street parking structures and convention centers, why not a battered women's center?" she had reasoned.

"But you need the support of the Board of Supervisors. That might be a tough sell in a county more concerned with irrigation," he warned.

Rose knew he was right. Only a public agency could issue bonds. But she was confident, after two years of assisting victims of domestic violence, and obtaining the grudging cooperation of the courts and the police, that the board would be receptive to the idea. After all, the original idea of county support for a battered women's shelter had come from this very board. And she would have the help of Gloria Simmons and Ann Puchini. They could be expected to make the presentation to the board, all of whose members had, at one time or another, been guests at their homes. Usually at fundraisers. Generally during election time.

Alejandra, the executive director, was guarded.

"Does this mean we have to answer to them about how we run the women's center? We're going to be government social workers?"

"No," Rose answered patiently. "It's our program. We're using their 'credit card' to charge a center. We pay it off, at low interest, it's ours."

"Sounds too good to be true," intoned Alejandra. "I just don't want any interference in our program from those men on the board."

"It's a wonderful idea," came the exuberant voice of Mrs. Simmons. "Rose, I'm so glad we have you to think up these clever legal initiatives."

"Well, it's still an idea. We have to sell it to the board."

"We'll take care of that," said Mrs. Simmons, including with a glance Mrs. Puchini in her assurances.

Ann had not said anything this evening. She generally said little, just sitting with Gloria Simmons, nodding in agreement when Gloria turned to her. She seemed pleasant enough. At social functions, she was always courteous to Rose, although the two had never had a one-on-one conversation. Ann was always with Gloria or, at social occasions, at her husband's side.

So it was out of the ordinary for Ann to approach Rose.

"Could I see you?" she asked, her voice dropping to a whisper.

"Sure. I'll be through in just a moment," Rose said as she loaded her briefcase.

"No. Not now. I mean in your office." Rose was taken aback.

"I understand you have a Salinas office. I would prefer to see you there. Not here in Fresno."

This made Rose nervous. The wife of the Presiding Judge of the Superior Court of Fresno wanted to see her. But out of town. It could only mean one thing: She did not want her husband, the judge, to know she was speaking to an attorney.

"Of course. I will be back in Salinas tomorrow. Do you want to come by after lunch, say 2 o'clock?"

"Thank you, Rose," Mrs. Puchini said, as if Rose had lifted a huge rock off of her body. Mrs. Simmons came back from the bathroom. "There you are. Let's go, Ann. See you later, Rose. Great meeting."

Rose stood watching them leave together.

The night was cold. As she drove over Highway 152, past the San Luis Reservoir illuminated by a full moon, she had the terrible feeling that all she had accomplished in Fresno over the last few years was about to be jeopardized by Mrs. Ann Puchini. She did not look forward to the meeting. Perhaps she could politely hear her out, sympathize with her, but make it clear that she could not get involved. She did not sleep well.

Mrs. Puchini was on time. "I got here early. Wasn't sure I could find your office, so I waited in the car."

Rose pulled out a legal pad and set it on the desk in front of her. At least, she felt, she should appear to be taking notes.

"Did you know I was a legal secretary once?" Mrs. Puchini began, without smiling. "After we got married, he told me he didn't want me working. Even though it was his office I worked in."

Rose did not know where this was going and sat with her pen quiet on her legal pad.

"I never worked after that. He would call me at lunchtime to see what I was doing. Then he would call in the afternoon, different times.

"When the babies came, he'd get angry if anyone came to the house during the day to see me. Both times he said he didn't think the babies were his.

"I can't go shopping by myself. If I need groceries, I tell him, and he takes me. He drops me off and comes back for me. Sometimes he just waits, watching, in the parking lot. If I take too long, he comes in looking for me. He'll be so angry. He doesn't say anything in public. Not 'til we get home."

Rose had not been taking any notes. She was growing very uncomfortable. Ann Puchini seemed to be telling a story by rote, something she had observed, without emotion.

"I never have any money to spend, except what he gives me. Then I have to give him the receipts. He pays all the bills. Checks each one, including the long distance calls. Even checks the mileage on my car.

"Rose," she said, looking up from the spot on the desk which she had been addressing, "our kids are grown. Our daughter Sarah is at Oregon State. Michael is a law student at Santa Clara. I have to get away."

This was Rose's chance. She took it.

"Well, Ann, there are a lot of good lawyers who specialize in divorce. I could help you find one. It shouldn't be too hard to find a good one."

"Rose, it will be hard. No one locally will take on a judge. He's very powerful. Besides, he'd kill me if he knew I saw an attorney."

Rose smiled nervously. "Now, I don't think..."

"That's why I can't go home," Mrs. Puchini added.

"What do you mean?" Rose asked, even more concerned that she was being placed in an untenable position.

"He's told me if I ever left, he'd find me. If I ever told anyone, he'd kill me," she answered.

"Pretty soon he'll figure out I'm not home, and he'll set out to find me. If I went home, he'd check the mileage on my car. I can't go home, and I can't let him find me."

Rose did not want to ask. She knew it was a trap. Like asking an expert witness "why" when you did not already know the answer.

"Told anyone what, Ann?" she finally asked.

"His sexual humiliation, physical abuse, that kind of thing," she said, clearly not wanting to elaborate. She looked at Rose with a wry smile.

"Pretty weird, eh? Makes me be on the women's center board, with Gloria Simmons, yet I'm not even allowed to drive there alone. Gloria is the only friend I have who he doesn't suspect of being a lesbian or at least bisexual."

She was now, finally, showing her emotions. Embarrassment. Guilt. Fear. Tears were welling up in her eyes.

"Now I've left. What did Alejandra say, at the women's center? 'The most dangerous time is when the woman leaves. That's when most are killed.'"

Rose tried to assure her. "He's a judge. He isn't going to do anything crazy."

"Rose, it's because he's a judge, he thinks he can do anything. He's probably looking for me already. He'll report the car stolen, just to get the police out looking for me. He's done it before. They all laugh. Pat each other on the back. 'False alarm. Sorry, judge.'"

"Where will you go?" Rose asked her.

"I don't know," she said. "I saved up $300 out of grocery and household money, mostly by returning items. I have a gas card, but I know he'll cancel it when he notices it's missing. I couldn't pack anything ahead of time, like they advise you to do. I just threw in the car what I could after he called at lunchtime. I had a 2:30 dentist appointment today. He's probably called there and found out that I didn't show up."

"I guess you haven't been listening at the women's center meetings. We tell women to have a plan before they leave," said Rose.

"I did. I have been watching you for two years," she said. "You're my plan, Rose."

There was no way out.

"I wish you had come earlier in the week. There is no way on a Friday afternoon we can get the papers together and over to Fresno for a restraining order," said Rose.

Mrs. Puchini looked alarmed. "No, you can't do that! You can't get a restraining order against him!"

Rose was surprised.

"You told me he's threatened to kill you. I can't protect you if you won't let me go to court," said Rose.

"He said he'd kill me if I told anyone," Mrs. Puchini answered with even more alarm in her voice.

"Well, you've told me," Rose pointed out.

"But I can't make it public. It would ruin him," Mrs. Puchini responded.

"I'm not trying to ruin him. Just protect you. We could keep it vague."

"No. A restraining order means I'm afraid of him. Like he's going to do something. You know how it would look."

"Ann, you *are* afraid of him," said Rose with growing exasperation.

"But I can't say that. It would embarrass the children. It would turn them against me."

"You think they really don't know?" Rose asked.

Now Mrs. Puchini was crying hard. Rose waited and then asked softly: "What do you want me to do, Ann?"

"Just talk to him," she said. "Just talk to him. Get the divorce quietly and make him leave me alone."

"Couldn't you do that, Ann?" Rose asked.

"No. He'll make me come back. Please, you talk to him."

"Okay, okay," Rose said, knowing that to press her any more would do no good now.

"Why don't you go next door and get a cup of coffee. Let me think about this."

Rose got up and led Mrs. Puchini to the reception area. Thinking better of the idea, she asked her secretary to accompany Mrs. Puchini to the café next door.

Judge Puchini had a reputation as a tough judge who liked to run an efficient courtroom with little regard for the litigants or matters that came before him. Stand when addressing the court. Sit until recognized. State the grounds for an objection; don't argue. Don't approach a witness without asking the court's permission. Never, never argue after the court has ruled on an objection or motion. He was precise. Autocratic.

Rose did not want to make the call but knew that if she did not, anything could happen. She had to let the judge know where his wife was and that she was all right. Then she needed to arrange an orderly and calm way to handle the matter with counsel for the judge. Get another professional in the loop.

It was already 3 o'clock. She looked up his courtroom number and dialed.

The bailiff answered, "Department 15. Deputy McMichaels." That meant the judge was off the bench, in chambers; otherwise, his clerk would have answered and the bailiff would have been in the courtroom with the judge.

"This is attorney Rose Contreras. May I speak to Judge Puchini, please?"

"What matter are you calling on, counsel?" She could hear him rustling through the docket sheets, looking for her name on the afternoon calendar.

"It's not on a case. Please tell the judge it's a personal matter," Rose replied.

"Just a moment."

She was on hold. She braced herself.

"Yes, Rose, how are you?" a voice came on the phone.

She was shocked at his friendly tone. Perhaps he did not know yet.

"Judge, sorry to bother you. Your wife asked me to call. Do you have a minute?"

"Ann asked you to call? What on earth for? Another fundraiser?" he laughed.

"No, judge. She has contacted me professionally. About a divorce. She was afraid you might be worried concerning her whereabouts."

"God. I had no idea. I can't believe this," said the judge sounding genuinely shocked.

"Let me come down and talk to her. Your offices are in the county counsel's building, aren't they?" he asked.

Rose hesitated. "She's not here right now, judge," she answered honestly, if not evasively.

"I know if I could just talk to her, we could work this all out," he said. "Maybe we could meet somewhere."

"Right now she just wants a little time alone. Perhaps you could obtain a representative, judge, so that we could work this out amicably and professionally."

He had been nothing like she had expected, but still she was uncomfortable dealing directly with him.

"Rose, I appreciate the professional courtesy of your call. Some people would just have filed and served. Restraining orders, all that kind of silly thing. Garbage. Just because I'm a judge."

"Do you have an attorney in mind, judge? Someone I might contact and discuss these matters with," she asked.

"No, Rose. I just don't think that will be necessary. If I could just talk to Ann…"

Rose was getting more uncomfortable. "Judge, I'd really like to deal with counsel—"

He interrupted her. He was not used to an attorney cutting him off.

"Counsel, you'll be dealing with me personally. Get used to it. If my wife doesn't call by 5:00 P.M., I'll hold you personally responsible." He slammed the phone in her ear.

Mrs. Puchini and Rose's secretary had not come back from coffee when Rose received a call from the county counsel's office. Jim Hanes was on the line.

"What's going on?" he asked.

"About what?"

"Judge Puchini. He just came in here looking for you. He was really upset. Asked for the number of Janrette, Hawk, Ross and Stephens in San Francisco."

"What did you tell him?" Rose asked.

"Well, I gave him the number. He insisted on looking in your office. Guess he didn't believe me. I told him you usually worked out of your Salinas office. I gave him the number. He wanted the address, too. He is not a happy camper, Rose. And he is not a guy to piss off in this county. What did you do?"

"Extended him a professional courtesy," Rose said. "Thanks for calling." She hung up as Mrs. Puchini came walking back. Now Rose was scared, too. She suspected Judge Puchini was on his way to her Salinas office.

"Ann, I talked to your husband. He was very insistent on talking directly to you. He has already been to my Fresno office since I got off the phone, and I think he is on his way here."

Rose did not expect what next occurred. Mrs. Puchini fell to the floor, holding herself across her stomach, crying. She had wet herself. "Oh, God; oh, God," she repeated. "He's going to kill us." She started shrieking. The secretary rushed in and was trying to sit her up.

In the noise, Rose saw the red light blinking. Her phone was ringing, but she could not hear it over the shrieking. She ran out of her office, into the reception area, and answered it.

"Rose, this is Tony…what's that noise?" he asked.

"I'm in the middle of something. Can I call you back?" she asked, starting to lean her head toward the receiver.

"Rose. Rose. Don't hang up. Is that Mrs. Puchini? Rose!" came the voice from the phone. She caught the name.

"How did you know?" she asked him.

"That's why I called," he said. "The judge just called here. He said you had threatened him with a restraining order and declarations with untrue and embarrassing allegations. Also, he said you were hiding his wife from him. Said if she doesn't call by 5:00 P.M., he will call the State Bar about your unprofessional conduct and the police to report a kidnapping, and will otherwise make your life miserable."

"I'm sorry I got you into this, Tony," she sighed with genuine frustration mixed with fear.

"That's okay, I told him that it didn't sound like our Rose."

"What did he say?" Rose asked.

"You don't want to know," he told her.

"You know, I'm getting really tired of this son-of-a-bitch already. I don't like being scared like this. I figure he's somewhere between Madera and Chowchilla by now on his way over here. I've got to get Mrs. Puchini off of my floor and out of here. Then if he wants to shoot me, he can do it in public. I'm not going to be driven into hiding by him. He's not going to intimidate me."

"Can I help?" Tony asked.

"Yeah, actually. Mrs. Puchini is a mess. Do you know of any therapists up your way who would take a crisis call tonight and a weekend patient? I'm afraid if I don't get her some help, she might do something to herself," said Rose.

"A couple. I'm thinking of one we've used here in the city. She's associated with Stanford, and I think she sees patients down there also. Let me give you a call back."

"Okay, but I don't want to stay here much longer."

It was a long ten minutes before Anthony Hawk called back. Rose had explained the situation again to Mrs. Puchini, who was anxious to leave Salinas.

Rose hoped it was Hawk, and not the judge, as she reached for the ringing phone.

"Rose, we're set. Call and confirm, but she says she will see Mrs. Puchini tonight at 6:30. We were in luck. This is the day she teaches at Stanford and takes afternoon patients at her Palo Alto office. She says it would be best if you get her up there right away. You were right. She says this is a very dangerous time, physically and emotionally. Can you get her up there by 6:30?" he asked.

Rose looked at her watch. "I think so. If she leaves right now."

He gave her directions.

"Do you know her?" Rose asked, referring to the therapist.

From the tone of Hawk's voice, she could sense a grin on his face. "Let's just say Sally Conrad and I have spent a lot of quality time together." Rose let the comment pass.

By the time they got to the parking lot it was apparent that Mrs. Puchini would never be able to drive to Palo Alto alone. She appeared exhausted. Beaten.

Rose asked her secretary to drive Mrs. Puchini's car, and Rose took Mrs. Puchini in her own vehicle. She just wanted to get on 101 and past Gilroy. By then, she figured, there was no chance that she would pass Judge Puchini coming in over 152.

Even after Gilroy, Ann Puchini did not relax. She was quite convinced that her husband had the power to call out the California Highway Patrol and the sheriff's departments of Monterey, Santa Cruz, Santa Clara, Alameda, San Mateo, or any other county he suspected they might pass through. She never believed they would make it to Palo Alto.

By San Jose, Mrs. Puchini had calmed down just enough to agree that Rose would find a hotel for her while she was meeting with the therapist…if they made it.

They did. Rose took out the directions she had scribbled on a pad of paper and turned the interior light on in the car as she reached Palo Alto. "Embarcadero Road—Stanford University exit, to Middlefield Road. If you reach the University, gone too far. Left. 1741," said the note.

They got out of the car together and walked up to the single story building. Sally Conrad was waiting for them on the porch.

"Thanks for waiting," Rose said.

"No problem. Gave me a chance to catch up on my paperwork." The therapist reached out her hand and said, "Hi, I'm Sally" to Mrs. Puchini, putting her at ease with her smile and calm, soft voice.

At 7:30, Rose and her secretary returned. They waited another 15 minutes until the door opened and Mrs. Puchini came out. She was smiling. Rose heard Sally, from inside the doorway, add, "And remember, it's not your fault." Mrs. Puchini laughed softly and brushed away a tear.

Sally saw Rose and her secretary waiting, and came down the steps.

"Rose, Ann is going to call my exchange three times a day, on a schedule, all weekend. If there is any problem, I'll call you. Monday morning, she'll call your office to proceed. Right, Ann?"

"Right," Mrs. Puchini replied.

"Rose, can I have a number where I can reach you over the weekend, also?" Sally asked.

Rose gave Sally her home number.

They left with Mrs. Puchini following in her own car to the hotel Rose had found for her.

"Are you sure you're okay?" Rose asked once they were there.

"Fine. Sally gave me some things to read. Affirmations, I think she called them. I have to check in regularly with Sally—just like with the judge," she said, but with a smile that showed the irony of her comment.

"Well, call me if you need to, also," Rose offered.

By the time Rose got home, she was exhausted as much by the anxiety and fear of the judge's ultimatums as by the day and drive. She told Ernie what had happened.

"What an asshole. I could never stand that arrogant son-of-a-bitch, but I didn't know he was a wife-beater, too," was Ernie's comment. "If he comes around here threatening you, I'll break him in two."

"Well," Rose said, rising from the couch, "he's going to have to come into the barrio and deal with our people to get to me. I want a good Mexican dinner and a lot of tequila tonight. I feel like getting drunk. Let's go to Gonzales."

"Oh," smiled Ernie, "now that some gringo judge is after you, you're a Mexican? *Our* people? What about me? I'm just a shield for you? You're going to get drunk and hide behind a big cripple? I'm the designated bull's-eye, eh?"

"Ernie, that's what a husband is supposed to do. Come on, macho man, protect your wife."

Rose was sure Judge Puchini had driven to Salinas, although she never saw him. She did not think he would come to her home—not with Ernie there. But she looked out the windows periodically.

On Saturday morning, Sally Conrad called. "Rose, I thought I should fill you in a bit."

"Is Ann doing okay?" Rose asked, fearing for her.

"Yes. I spoke to her this morning. She is relaxing. But I think you're in more danger than Ann is right now."

"What do you mean?" Rose asked, a chill going through her chest.

"You're on the women's center board, I understand. You know the dynamics of domestic violence. He exercises control over every part of Ann's life: who she sees, where she goes, what she wears, every dime she has, her body in whatever way he wants. Everything. He knows he can control her. Physically, verbally, mentally. But there is one thing in his way at the moment: You. He's got to get around you, over you, or through you, to get back his control over her.

"Now," she paused, "this is only a guess, but I don't think he'll do you any physical harm. He's used to getting his way. But he needs to preserve that at the same time he gets control back over his wife. Part of preserving his position is making sure he controls her. The last thing he wants is her talking too much. It would threaten everything."

"It wouldn't look good for a judge to have hit his wife," Rose agreed.

"Rose, hitting her is the least of it. This guy is really sick. He's got a huge pornography collection and has been acting out, forcing her to participate. Apparently, it's been getting rougher over the years to the point of forcible rape with restraints involved. I think what finally caused her to get out is that he's been talking about bringing others into the scene. He's not just kinky, he's brutal, really angry."

Oh, shit, Rose thought. This is getting totally out of hand.

In the afternoon, Hawk called again.

"Your judge has been busy."

"He's not my judge, Tony. What did he do now?" she asked.

"Two members of the Board of Supervisors called. Apparently, he called them and told them you had threatened him."

"That's crazy!" she exclaimed.

"I know it; you know it," responded Hawk.

"Why would he possibly call the Board of Supervisors? What does he want them to do?" Rose asked.

"Fire you," Hawk answered.

"Jesus, I'm sorry, Tony. I…"

She never got a chance to finish her sentence. "And I told them," Hawk went on, "that we would continue assigning work to you, as we have in the past, and if they didn't like it, they could take their files and shove them up their collective asses."

"Tony, this guy is really bad. I had no idea—"

Again, he interrupted. "Rose, you don't owe me an explanation. I know whatever you're doing is in your client's best interest. He's pulling out all the stops, though. Stay focused; stay firm," he advised.

There was a message on her office phone. "Rose, this is Gloria Simmons. Could you have Ann call me? Judge Puchini asked that I call. We're all very worried about her."

On Monday morning, the county counsel, Jim Hanes, called. "Rose, I'm sorry but the chairman of the Board of Supervisors called over the weekend. He says he has a legal opinion that we can't be letting you use county offices to conduct your private practice. I'm sorry. Not my call. Way above me. I think we both know where this is coming from."

The next call was from Judge Puchini. Rose's secretary announced from the reception area that he was on the phone. Rose thought for a moment, and then, loud enough so the judge would hear, said, "Tell him I'm not in and hang up." The receptionist did what she was told.

Rose counted. Eight seconds. About as long as it would take to punch up the phone number again. The phone rang.

"Let it ring," she instructed her receptionist.

The machine picked up. "Hello, you've reached the Law Office of Rose Contreras. We are presently unavailable. This message will repeat in Spanish and you may leave a message. *Hola, esta es abogada…*" Hang up.

Rose called Sally Conrad.

"Thanks for taking my call. I've been thinking about what you said about the judge's need to control and how best to approach this case for Ann. You were right. He's already brought an immense amount of pressure to bear. Now he's calling me directly. I have refused to accept his calls, and I have a feeling that will infuriate him. I'm not sure if that's good or bad."

Sally listened. "Your instincts are right. The worst thing for him now is if he loses contact with you, too. Then he does not even have indirect contact with his wife. It will make him panic."

"What will he do?" Rose asked.

"Find another way to make contact. Sometimes doing nothing is the best strategy," Sally answered.

"I think I'll take an early lunch," Rose said, picking up Sally's cue and also wanting to get out of her office which she could see, in her mind, going up in flames.

Rose drove down to see her mother.

The judge called seven more times during the day. Rose returned none of the calls. She left early for home, calling Mrs. Puchini and assuring her that time was on their side. She did not mention the calls. Mrs. Puchini was anxious enough. Her room charges were now nearing the $300 with which she had left home.

On Tuesday, mid-morning, the receptionist put the call through. "Mr. Jeffrey Arneson, attorney in San Francisco, calling on the Puchini matter."

Rose recognized the name. Jeffrey Arneson was a highly respected family law specialist who often spoke on the subject at State Bar conventions. He had served on the legislative commission that had drafted California's then-new No-Fault Divorce Law in 1969.

Rose picked up the phone.

"This is Rose Contreras."

"Good morning, Rose, Jeffrey Arneson. Judge Puchini has asked me to represent him in this matter. Have you filed anything yet?"

"Uh, Mr. Arneson, thank you for calling. It's been a little awkward dealing directly with the opposing party, especially a judge. But no, we haven't filed yet."

"Good. The judge really would like to explore reconciliation. Maybe the lawyers could get out of the way and let these two people see if they can work out their problems. I realize that Mrs. Puchini might be anxious, and I'm sure we could arrange for a trained professional counselor to meet with them. Sometimes, I think lawyers in the adversarial system just aggravate the situation, don't you?"

Rose closed her eyes. She knew Ann would have no chance in a room with her husband. Even with a therapist present. Joint therapy did not work when one of the parties was a batterer. Battered women who leave almost always go back—some five to ten times before they finally leave, if they ever leave. Rose was not going to facilitate re-incarceration for Ann. She would never get out again. The judge would see to that.

"Why don't we start by putting them on an even playing field, so each can make a free choice," Rose suggested.

"Of course we're talking about a free choice. My goodness, they've been married for 24 years. I'm sure no one can be forced to stay together for that long," said Arneson.

"Could we start then with your client sending his wife, say $5,000 for the month, so she doesn't have to worry about a roof over her head or how she's going to eat?" Rose asked.

"Well, is that really necessary? I mean, if they talk it out, then there really wouldn't be any need, would there?" he replied.

"We'd like the money in hand, and a draft separation agreement before we talk further. Let's just call it a show of good faith on his part. Could we do that?" asked Rose.

"I don't think he's thinking along those lines," said Arneson.

Rose felt it was time to end the charade. "Well, we're prepared to go in tomorrow for an *ex parte* order for temporary support and attorney's fees. Obviously, we'll also request that the Judicial Council appoint an out-of-county judge, since I doubt the other Fresno judges are going to want to hear this." She added: "Will your client stipulate to a restraining order?"

"No. I know he won't. He said you threatened him with that," Arneson replied sharply. "That you made false allegations about his conduct."

"What false allegations?" she asked.

"He didn't say."

"Maybe you need to have a long chat with your client, Mr. Arneson. I have never threatened him. I have never made any accusations of any kind. But if he attempts to contact my client, or me, I will file for a restraining order detailing all necessary facts to establish the legal basis for its issuance."

"There is no basis," Arneson objected.

"Talk to your client," Rose responded.

"You're just trying to use the threat as a bargaining chip. It won't work, Ms. Contreras."

"Talk to your client," Rose repeated.

"Let me call him and get back to you," he finally said. He was not about to call her bluff.

Rose was shaking when she got off the phone. She had to go out for a walk.

What if they don't agree? she thought. Would she have to file for a restraining order? Would Ann let her?

Arneson called back in an hour. "What do you have in mind by a separation agreement?" he asked.

"A document that confirms the separation of the parties, provides for temporary spousal support and an advance on attorney's fees, identifies the items of community property, and contains an enforceable agreement limiting contact between the parties."

"What if they want to go to counseling?" he asked.

"Fine," said Rose. "If both agree, through counsel. He just can't call her up, or have someone else do it, and browbeat her into it."

"And this agreement would be confidential, right?" he asked.

"Sure, unless breached. Then either party could file it with the court for enforcement as a stipulated judgment."

"Okay. He'll sign in that form. We'll come to your office for a four-way meeting. I'll fax you a list of the community property. Have your client look it over. Nothing is being withheld; it's extensive. I hope this is the good faith gesture that your client wants because he is sincere about wanting to reconcile."

"Mr. Arneson, I'll tell you right now. She'll be here to sign, but she is not going to meet with him separately, out of my presence, or talk to him. So tell him not to try, okay?"

"Okay. I'll tell him, but if after this is all signed and they want to talk, let's give them that courtesy, Rose. They are married adults, after all," he said.

When Rose told her client, Mrs. Puchini was relieved. Rose could hear the dread recede.

"Thank you, Rose. I couldn't have gone another day like this. God, it's over. Thank you."

"Well, it's not over yet, Ann," Rose cautioned. "But this gives you independence so you can think straight. We'll still have to go through the community property evaluation, appraisal, and division. That's going to take some time. There is a lot there. In the meantime, we'll get you an advance on the property settlement.

"You need to start thinking about what you want to do with your life, Ann," Rose added.

"I can't wait to talk to Sally," Ann said, sounding like a young girl about to go off to college.

The next afternoon, Jeffrey Arneson formally introduced his client to Rose and was polite with Mrs. Puchini, even solicitous. The judge smiled at Rose. "Thank you for your help," he said. She had no idea what that was supposed to mean. He stared at his wife who kept her eyes on the edge of the table in front of her.

Rose went through the formalities, aware that the judge was staring past her at his wife, as if trying to communicate telepathically. Rose could almost hear the message: "Do you think I'm going to let you get away with embarrassing me like this?"

The judge broke his stare long enough to smile at the notary. "Oh, I bet you need my driver's license. Can't trust a judge to sign his real name."

Rose gave a set of the duplicate signed originals to Arneson.

"Thank you, Mr. Arneson. Perhaps you could get me those tax returns also, and we can discuss this further later in the week."

"Fine. Thank you, Rose. Judge Puchini has asked if he could meet privately with his wife for just a moment. Perhaps, Rose, we could step out." He stood and walked toward the door with his briefcase.

Rose was caught off guard. Ann looked horrified.

"Mr. Arneson," Rose said, addressing him and not his client, "Mrs. Puchini has already expressed her desire not to communicate, at this time, except through counsel. Please respect that."

She was angry. When they had left, she apologized to Mrs. Puchini. "I'm sorry, Ann. They just don't let up."

"I just want him to leave me alone," she said, visibly upset again. "I'm going directly to Sally's. I knew I would be a wreck just being in the same room with him, so I made an appointment."

Rose tried to reassure her. "You did great. It's signed."

Rose was relieved. She had held her ground. Mrs. Puchini would have her own checking account and her own money for the first time in her married life. After the community property division, she would have income property, stocks, and a substantial cash settlement. Under California law, with a 24-year marriage, she would have lifelong spousal support.

The call came at 6:00 P.M. Rose normally would have already left, but she was going through the mail and other phone messages of the last few days that had been ignored since all efforts had been devoted to the Puchini case.

"Rose, this is Sally Conrad. Ann is here, but she's been beaten badly. He followed her here from your meeting. You need to come up right away."

"Oh, Jesus. I didn't think he'd do this," Rose said.

"Nor did I," Sally confessed. "But he still knows her better than we do."

"What do you mean?" Rose asked.

"She won't let me call the police. Not even medical care," Sally said. "You need to talk to her."

Rose called Ernie. She told him what had happened and that she had to get up to Palo Alto.

"Rose, you can't get involved with your client like this. Call the police," he advised.

"My client's just been beaten by the Presiding Judge of the Fresno Superior Court. I shouldn't get involved?" she asked incredulously.

"As a lawyer, Rose. As a lawyer. File for a goddamn restraining order. File assault charges. Splash it all over the papers. Take the son-of-a-bitch out. But don't play Florence Nightingale for Christ's sake."

"I gotta go, Ernie. I'll call you when I'm heading back."

"Okay, but at least take a camera. Evidence, counsel," he added. He was right. She grabbed the Polaroid.

Nothing Rose could say would convince Mrs. Puchini to call the police. "No," she kept saying. Rose convinced her to at least allow pictures, so she could talk to his attorney. Mrs. Puchini reluctantly agreed. "But don't file them with the court," she instructed. "I would be humiliated."

Rose took two of the pictures of Mrs. Puchini's bruised, cut, and swollen face, and put them in an envelope from Sally Conrad's office, addressed "personal and confidential" to Mr. Jeffrey Arneson. The brief handwritten note stated: "This is what your client did after our conference."

Rose signed it. Sally added, "Witness, Sally Conrad, LCSW."

Rose filed the petition for divorce in Fresno the next day, "but no restraining order," as directed by her client. While the petition contained no description of events, the mere fact of its filing by the wife of the presiding judge swept the legal community. By noon, everyone in the courthouse knew that Rose Contreras was either (a) "crazy enough" or (b) "had the *cojones*" to take on the presiding judge. The judge left the building soon after the filing.

Mrs. Puchini was again anxious about doing anything. "He's going to be really angry, Rose," she kept saying.

"He's always angry, Ann. I can't get you divorced without filing for a divorce. And I can't protect you if you won't let me."

"You saw what good a restraining order did. He signed it and then beat me up."

"No, Ann. We had a confidential agreement, not an order. He still believes you will not go public and, so far, he's been absolutely right," Rose replied. "He has more control over your case than your attorney," she added with some frustration showing.

"I just can't," Mrs. Puchini said, as if begging Rose to understand.

"What if we could keep it secret, but report him at the same time?" Rose asked.

"I don't understand."

"I've talked to Sally. The only way to stop him is to break the silence. As long as it's a secret, he's in control. We need to end his control."

"But I'm not going to humiliate myself and my children by making all this public."

"We don't have to. Let me explain," Rose said.

Jeffrey Arneson called before noon of the second day following the events. He had just received the Polaroids. "Rose, I had no idea. I'm truly sorry. We'll stipulate to mutual restraining orders. No need to put this in the media. Does no one any good."

"No, Mr. Arneson, he's never going to leave my client alone until he's stopped. I think you understand now that this isn't, and never was, a bargaining chip."

"But we're agreeing to a restraining order," he interrupted her.

"Mutual? When has my client ever harmed him?"

"Well, it would look better..."

"We're past that, Mr. Arneson."

Rose reached across her desk for the signed declaration of Ann Puchini.

"Yesterday, I contacted the Commission on Judicial Performance. I don't know if you've had any dealings with them. They are responsible for removing unfit judges. They confirmed that complaints filed with them are confidential. However, after they investigate, if they find a sufficient basis to warrant disciplinary action against a sitting judge, they then institute public proceedings."

Rose let it sink in.

"I emphasize 'a sitting judge.'"

Arneson was listening.

Rose continued. "Today, we filed a detailed declaration about your client, his sexual predilections, his years of abuse of his wife, and his recent beating of her, evidenced by the Polaroids I sent you. I'll send you a copy. I suggest you review it with your client. Should he decide that his talents are better spent somewhere other than on the bench, he would be free to resign. If he resigns, he would no longer be 'a sitting judge' and the Commission would have no interest or jurisdiction to proceed publicly against him. The declaration and photos would not become a part of the public record." She paused. "Unless, of course, he violates the stipulated restraining order you have agreed to."

The reason for Judge Puchini's decision to step down as a judge of the Superior Court was never clear to anyone in the Fresno legal community. Coming as it did so shortly after his wife filed for divorce, it was assumed that the two were related. But that was only speculation. No public record. He joined one of the largest firms in Fresno, and his income increased. His influence in the community seemed unaffected.

Rose thought that the county officials would allow her to resume working on county cases once the Puchini matter was over. They did not. When Anthony Hawk refused to assign her files to another attorney at the firm, the county terminated its relationship with his firm and switched to new bond counsel in Los Angeles.

New bond counsel was asked to review the proposal to build a battered women's shelter and counseling center backed by county bonds, as proposed by Rose through the women's center board. Its opinion was that such a use, while "innovative," would be "imprudent."

Shortly after, Mrs. Gloria Simmons quit the women's center board. Her friend Ann Puchini never returned to Fresno, and neither made any attempt to contact the other.

Sally Conrad wrote Rose a note a few months later.

Dear Rose,

I admire the way you handled Ann's case. You put the client first.

Most lawyers would be either too scared or relish too much the notoriety of publicly taking on a presiding judge. You did it quietly and with finesse.

I hope our paths cross again someday.

Warmest regards,

Sally

Surprisingly, once Ann Puchini moved to Sarasota, Florida, where she had a sister, Judge Puchini attempted no further contact. Rose had seen to it that spousal support checks went to a local bank account where, if not timely received, a clerk would call the judge. After the first call, the judge never missed a payment. Ann transferred money from this account to Florida as necessary. He knew she was in Florida. Their children visited her. He chose the next best thing to control, for him; he acted as if she did not exist.

But the children knew. Children are rarely fooled. They were supportive, critical only that she had not left sooner, but pleased to have a relationship with their mother free of their father's tyranny and the fear it had engendered throughout their lives. As Ann said in a Christmas card to Rose: "Thank you for giving me my life and children back."

As a consequence of handling the matter of *In Re Marriage of Puchini*, Rose had lost her office in Fresno, managed to lose the county account for her old firm, lost the chance of building a women's center with county bonds, and alienated a large portion of the power structure, including the judiciary, of the Valley.

Ernie was philosophical about it all: "That's the price you pay when you take on entrenched power," he said.

"So far, it looks more like the price I pay when I take on entrenched male power," she responded.

"What other kind is there?" he asked with a smile.

A couple of weeks later, when the receptionist forwarded the call, Rose did not recognize the name.

"Hi, Rose. I've thought of you so often, all these years. I finally found your number."

"Well, good," replied Rose, still not recognizing the voice or placing the name. "What can I do for you?"

"It's very complicated. Do you handle divorce matters?" she asked.

"Well, I've had some experience recently," Rose answered. "I'm sorry. I'm trying to place your name," Rose confessed. "Could you help me?"

"It's me. Mouse. We met at law school. My husband was in your class. Jackson Bridgeport III."

Chapter 52

Michael

NBC'S ANDREA MITCHELL asked the question of the president: "Did the United States condone an Israeli shipment of arms to Iran as part of the deal to release hostage Benjamin Weir?"

Michael's ears perked up. He had been following the press conference on the small television set on his desk in the Justice Department.

The president denied that Israel was involved or that arms were traded for hostages.

The attorney general had requested that Michael finish a report by the weekend. The question posed was whether secret arms sales to Iran by the United States would violate the Arms Export Control Act. No one had ever mentioned Israel or hostages.

Michael went directly to the attorney general's office.

"Is the General in?" he asked Meese's secretary.

"Yes, he's alone, Mr. Cassidy."

Michael walked by her and into the office, closing the door behind him. "Ed,"—Meese insisted on informality in private—"the president is being asked about Israel and hostages on the arms shipments. Is there something I should know?"

Meese was pensive.

"I heard it, too. That damn Poindexter isn't leveling with us. I want you to set out the facts as they were given to us. Make it clear we have never given anyone, in the name of the president, a blank check to violate the law."

Michael was uncomfortable. "Poindexter already doesn't like me because of the South African report I did. I don't want him using me or my legal opinions as a cover if he's doing something I don't know about."

"He won't. I'll see to that." Meese picked up the phone. Michael turned to leave.

"Michael," Meese said, covering the phone as it rang at the other end, and gestured for Michael to have a seat. "Admiral Poindexter please," Meese quietly spoke into the phone to the secretary.

"John, could we get together this afternoon at Director Casey's office? Perhaps you could bring Colonel North. Don Regan has asked to sit in, also. He's flying up to Camp David this weekend to meet with the president on this matter."

Meese waited, listening. "Fine." He hung up and turned to Michael. "We'll get to the bottom of this," he said, shaking his head. "Can I get you anything?" he asked as he led Michael to the seating area in his office.

"What are your plans," Meese asked, "when the president leaves office?" Michael had been expecting a question on arms export control.

"Well," he answered, "return to California. I had hoped my son would go to college here in the East, but he's opted for U.C. Santa Barbara, to major in surfing. Can't say I blame him. But I don't want to be on the opposite coast any longer than I have to."

"The president," Meese began—there was still respect bordering on reverence for the man he had served so long, Michael observed with admiration—"is two years into his second term. People are starting to leave. That's the way it is in Washington."

There was resignation and distaste in the last sentence.

Meese looked down at some folders on the coffee table. Michael noticed his name on one of them.

"When you ended your service in Sacramento, I told you that you weren't ready for a judgeship. I think you are now."

He handed Michael a letter from the folder. It was on the stationery of the governor of the state of California. It began "Dear Ed" and ended "Best regards, George."

George Deukmejian had enjoyed a long tenure as a state senator from Long Beach, serving much of the time on the Senate Judiciary Committee. He had been Minority Leader and then Majority Leader when the Republicans took control. He was known as a tough "law and order" legislator his entire career. Which is how he had become close friends with Ed Meese, the representative of the District Attorneys Association to the California Legislature.

"The governor," Meese said, summarizing the letter, "would be honored to appoint you to the Alameda County Superior Court."

In words that Michael did not fully understand but would appreciate later, the attorney general of the United States told him: "Michael, I think this would be a good time for you to get the hell out of Washington and go home."

He thanked Meese, shook hands, and went back to his office. He sat, looking out of the window at the White House. He thought he should be happy. Instead, he felt very depressed. He picked up the phone to call the two people in the photo on his desk: the smiling young boy draped by his mother hugging him from behind.

"Robbie, I'm coming home."

"Cool, dude," his son said with real enthusiasm.

Michael laughed. "Maybe you could teach me to surf."

"Sure, Dad. It's easy."

He felt better. He called Mai.

"Well, you always wanted to be a judge," she said matter-of-factly.

He was puzzled. "I don't think we ever talked about me being a judge," he said.

"Oh, my mistake. It must have been because you were always so judgmental, I thought you wanted to be a judge," she said with that wry smile he knew she was wearing.

He knew she had got him. Again.

Now she was rolling. "Well, Mikey, think of it this way. If you've been fired by Ronald Reagan and Ed Meese, maybe there's hope for you after all."

From almost 3,000 miles away, he could see her beautiful Asian face and deadpan delivery.

Chapter 53

Rose

"WHAT OTHER KIND of power is there?" Ernie had said. It was not a statement of his belief of how things should be; just how they were. Again, in Fresno, Rose had come face-to-face with the reality that power was wielded by men. She had represented a woman against a sick and perverted judge. She had won for her client but had lost a woman's center and employment in the process.

"They wanted me on the women's center board," she said of the board of supervisors and the county counsel, "but I stand up for a woman and they turn against me."

"Now you understand why you can't be on the inside, dependent on them. They wanted a woman they could control. A house nigger. Not who you turned out to be." He said this without any condescension. He was not patronizing her. Rather, it was a statement of fact for him. He took no pleasure in its revelation for Rose.

"Maybe I should have thought of the women's center first, not the client," Rose said.

"You know you couldn't do that. You had to help your client. She had no one else. Besides, I have learned you can never know the consequences of what you do. It's the proverbial stone thrown into the water. Effects hit distant shores you can't even see."

"What do you mean 'what I turned out to be'?"

"Well, you've become very passionate about these issues, women's issues."

"You're passionate about what you do."

"Yes, but, well, your issues seem to occupy you 24 hours a day."

"Maybe it's because I'm a woman 24 hours a day," came her agitated retort.

"I'm a Mexican 24 hours a day, but I take time out to cook Indian food, watch the Lakers, grow my plants," he said in a reasoned voice.

"Maybe it's because we have to put in twice the time and effort to get 70¢ for every dollar of compensation men get. We don't have time to waste," she snapped.

"Hey, take it easy," he shouted, "I'm not the enemy!"

"No, but you're the only man around to yell at right now," Rose said in exasperation.

She walked over to the La-Z-Boy where he was sitting and leaned over and hugged him.

"Tell you what," she said. "Let's compromise. I'll go sit in front of the television and see if the Lakers are playing. You heat up some Indian food."

He pulled himself forward, then up, and reached for his crutches. She patted him on the butt. "That's a good little husband. Maybe later I'll tie you up and humiliate you, just as you like it."

He turned to see if she was agitated again. She changed her expression in response to his and smiled. "Sorry, Ernie. I do love you, just not your gender at the moment."

Rose's meeting with Sarah "Mouse" Bridgeport did not give her any more confidence that the origin of the species and evolution could explain how men and women could be so fundamentally incompatible, yet able to mate.

"How did you find me, Sarah?" Rose asked. She insisted on calling her Sarah, not the diminutive "Mouse."

Sarah was impeccably dressed in a mustard-colored Ferre blouse with a dark blue jacket and matching skirt. The shoes were Ferragamo. She seemed too well dressed for Salinas, let alone to be called "Mouse."

"I called the State Bar and got your address," Sarah told her.

"Why?"

"Well, for one thing, no firm in Los Angeles will touch the case. For another, you're the only lawyer I've ever felt I could talk to who would listen to me." She gave a little smile of remembrance. "Well, you were a law student then, but I hoped you haven't changed."

Rose was impressed that someone had traveled all the way from Los Angeles to Salinas to see her. "Well, maybe we should talk, then, but I'm not sure I could get involved in a case in Los Angeles. Salinas is not the easiest place to get anywhere from," Rose said, knowing she had to at least listen to Sarah, who had come so far to see her. Of course, she could have declined the case on the phone and saved Sarah the trip, but there was something voyeuristic about delving into the intimate life of a classmate, especially one who lived a life of privilege at the pinnacle of the legal establishment.

Sarah had a folder thick with papers sitting on her lap. She handed them to Rose and began explaining.

"I've been pretty unhappy for years. I didn't want to do anything because of my boys. I talked to Jackson about going to marriage counseling. He said he didn't need it. It was my problem. If I felt I had emotional problems, I ought to go see someone by myself." She perked up as if proud of herself. "So I did. It took four years, but I finally was able to stand up to him and tell him the marriage was over."

Rose was listening and looking at the papers. The first was a Petition for Dissolution of Marriage filed in Los Angeles by attorneys on behalf of Jackson Bridgeport III, Petitioner. She shuffled the papers to find Respondent's Answer on behalf of Sarah. There was not one.

Sarah was still talking.

"He told me I was stupid. That I was in the United States because of the marriage and that if I left him he would take the children. I'd have nothing and have to go back to England." Sarah showed signs of panic as her voice broke.

"Then I got a call from one of the partners at the office to come in and discuss some matters relating to our house."

Rose looked up from the papers. The idea that Jackson would have his law firm somehow involved in his private affairs seemed unusual. "I went in and Jim Sammis, one of the partners in the Los Angeles office, handed me those papers from the firm headquarters in Bridgeport, Connecticut." She was pointing to a batch of papers clipped together on one side of the file. "He said I had 30 days to move out of my house unless Jackson and I reconciled our differences; that I owned nothing from our marriage. Oh," she added, "then when he walked me out of the office, he said he was sorry."

Rose saw the endorsement stamp of the Los Angeles Superior Court on the petition. It had been filed. They were not bluffing.

"What happened? These papers have been filed," Rose said.

"I went home after my talk with Sammis and told Jackson he couldn't do this to me and the children. The kids and I needed to stay together until school was out and if anyone moved out it should be him. He got furious and called up Sammis in front of me and told him to file the divorce papers."

"Did he move out?" Rose asked.

"No. He comes and goes. It's a big house. He's avoided me since then, but he hasn't moved out." Suddenly her composure appeared shattered. Her hands were shaking.

"Yesterday, he was waiting for me when I came home to greet the boys after school. He said they had been sent to visit their grandparents in Connecticut. I asked who took them, and he said a secretary from the office."

Rose's first thought was kidnapping. Taking children out of the jurisdiction. This was not just about money. Unless Jackson was using the children to negotiate. This guy is worse than I remember him, she added, inside her head.

Rose was trying to read the papers while listening to Sarah. The petition listed no community property despite 15 years of marriage. "None" was typed in the place for the listing of all marital assets.

"How can he do this?" Sarah asked.

"He can't," Rose answered, trying to assure her. "Sarah, men always threaten mothers with taking the children. I know it's upsetting, but the court won't tolerate those kinds of threats."

Rose had just turned to the document entitled "Residential Lease" on the stationery of Bridgeport's law firm. It appeared to be for the family residence.

"Who owns your house, Sarah?" Rose asked.

"We do. We've had this one for about nine years. Why?"

Rose did not answer.

"And your husband is a partner in the law firm?" Rose asked.

"Of course. It's been in the family for at least three generations. His dad runs it. Jackson's been there since he graduated from Boalt. About what, eleven years? He takes out whatever he needs. Money has never been a concern of ours." Sarah looked worried by the questions.

"He can't just take everything and the children, can he?" she asked again.

"No, of course not. But I do need to read these papers to figure out what's going on. There is something strange about how this is being handled.

Using his own law firm. And the firm sending you a notice to vacate your own home. If there were a legal basis to evict you, it would come in the form of a Los Angeles family court order, not a 'Notice of Termination of Occupancy' from the Bridgeport main office," Rose said, reading the title on the document.

Rose stood up from her desk and took the file of documents to a conference table in her office. "Let's get back together this afternoon. That will give me time to read all of these documents, do a little research, and better advise you, okay?" She knew she could not send Sarah back to Los Angeles without some answers and a little hope.

The papers formed a coherent endeavor—"scheme" Rose thought was a better word—by the law firm of Bridgeport, Bridgeport, Hall and Pendergast to protect the partners from their spouses. In fact, the firm was actually a trust established by Jackson's grandfather about the time his son—Jackson's father—had become a lawyer with the firm. All assets of the firm belonged to the trust administered by an executive committee of three senior attorneys, one of whom had to be a Bridgeport. There were no partnership interests—no "partners" as owners of an interest in the firm. Rather, all attorneys were "at will" employees of the trust for a fixed annual salary, below market, Rose could see. Jackson's salary was $90,000 a year at a time when comparable lawyers in Los Angeles were getting three times that amount. All "bonuses" were "discretionary" with the executive committee. There was no vested interest in the firm's pension plan. Vesting was discretionary, at the time of retirement or severance.

An attorney who, at the discretion of the executive committee, was provided with a residence, executed a "residential lease" for the property which, while selected and occupied by the attorney and his spouse, was owned by the trust. Rose noted, under a section entitled "Termination of Occupancy," that the lease could be terminated upon 30 days' notice for reasons including, but not limited to, the filing of a petition for divorce or legal separation, in which case the non-attorney spouse could be separately evicted.

By the time Sarah returned, Rose was visibly angry.

"What is it?" Sarah asked. "What's wrong?"

Rose explained.

Sarah listened quietly. For the first time, she realized that she actually had something in common with the other wives at Bridgeport, Bridgeport, Hall and Pendergast. Even Jackson's mother, it would seem, since the trust was established by her father-in-law in response to, or at least at the time of, her wedding to Jackson's father.

Then she remembered. "This happened to another wife of a partner at the Denver office," she exclaimed. "I heard she was thrown out of her house. No one understood. I talked to her. She said it was all confidential. She wasn't allowed to talk about it, but I know she was looking for a job after the divorce."

"If they have been doing it for a long time, then they are going to fight hard, Sarah. I don't want to kid you. This is serious," said Rose.

"My children are all I have, Rose. If we can get them back, I don't care about the money."

"I assume he took them to pressure you to settle without a fight on the community property," Rose said.

"No, Rose. You don't understand Jackson. He truly wants the children. It's not a trade. He wants it all. No one takes anything away from him, especially a woman."

Rose felt backed into a corner again, into a fight she did not want. Suing a classmate. It would look like a personal vendetta. Bridgeport would also enjoy the advantage of the home turf in Los Angeles. Christ, she thought, I don't even know where the courthouse is in Los Angeles.

"Let me think about this," Rose finally said, wanting to calmly reflect upon the situation without a desperate woman sitting in front of her, awaiting a favorable answer. Always easier to decline a case on the phone rather than in person. Just getting the client out of the office, after saying "no," could be another 45 minutes of pleading and emotions.

"In the meantime, call and check on the children. I'm sure they're fine. You might also see if you can locate that woman in Denver and find out how her case was resolved. You might get the name of her lawyer. I'll call you tomorrow. Promise. Okay?"

Sarah was not happy to leave. On the way out, she picked up two of Rose's cards at the registration desk.

More than anything, Rose wanted to discuss the case with Ernie. Her last divorce case, with Judge Puchini's wife, had tied her stomach in knots and had been enormously stressful. She did not like the feelings, especially the anger, she took home. Also, Ernie was spending so much time in Sacramento, writing bills for Governor Jerry Brown's Administration and lobbying the Legislature for their passage, that she hesitated about taking a case in Los Angeles. It would just add distance between them. Physical distance. Emotional distance.

The only reason she even considered taking a case in Los Angeles was because of an unexpected passion she had found: flying. It started with the practical thought that if she was going to have to traverse the entire Central Valley, visiting irrigation districts and other public clients of her San Francisco firm, flying a small private plane would save time. Driving the Valley was either exhausting when traveling its length, or virtually impossible going east and west. The Valley was made for north-south movement, just like the water in the viaducts built by the other Governor Brown. Flying, she could be home every night, she thought.

"Madera International Airport," she joked to herself, as she traveled north from Fresno on Highway 99, on the way to the 152 cutoff to the 156, on to Hollister, to catch 101 to Salinas. But even Mariposa, Columbia, Chowchilla, San Andreas, and most any place with a post office had a landing strip. Granted, not all of them were well-paved, and planes were often seen coming in over the heads of cows, almost sideways, to minimize the length needed to land in a "big" town like Gustine. Even a little Piper Cub might need to do a sideways slip to lose altitude approaching one of these short strips, since it had no flaps with which to increase its rate of descent.

On the other hand, some small towns had huge civil aviation airports disproportionate to their size, with a tower and instrument approach capacity but no commercial aviation to complicate the air space. Like the little town of Atwater, they were the beneficiaries of the windfall of an inherited, closed military base formerly used to land B-52s as part of the Strategic Air Command. The whole town could be collected and deposited on the long runways with room to spare.

Rose inquired and found that the Salinas Municipal Airport offered flying instruction. Her instructor, Chuck McFarland, had flown C-147s in Vietnam, landing them, he bragged, on the equivalent of a football field–sized clearing in a jungle. While she was comfortable with his experience, she was shocked during her first lesson when he handed over the controls to her and said, "Here, you fly." He knew there was nothing she could do at 4,000 feet that he could not undo, but for Rose the experience of holding the yoke and putting her feet on the rudder pedals was both terrifying and exhilarating.

She threw herself into studying the books to qualify for her pilot's license. Not because she had a deadline, but because flying fascinated her. She was studying for the sake of learning—something she had not done since her early years, reading as her parents worked in the fields nearby. Now it was a distraction from what she did for a living. Aerodynamics. Weather patterns. Radio communication frequencies. Instruments. The pitch of a propeller moving through air. Air speed versus ground speed. The effects of thin air at high altitudes on engine power and performance.

Every chance she could get, she was out at the airport, practicing with her instructor. Basic maneuvers, landing patterns, controlling air speed on turns, recovering from a stall. If he could not find her at the office, Ernie knew to leave a message at the pilots' lounge at Salinas Field.

Her instructor told her that she was a natural in the way she took to flying. In just weeks, she mastered the basic turning maneuvers with a smoothness that gave her confidence and no sense of fighting the plane. In response to disorienting exercises, where she was required to close her eyes or put her head down toward her lap while the instructor changed the configuration of the plane, she was able to quickly recover her orientation and right the plane, trusting her instruments over competing inner ear messages.

Her first "cross-country" trip was to Fresno, on a triangle pattern of stops at Merced and Madera, finally touching down in Fresno, only to take off again immediately—a "touch and go"—and return to Salinas.

Her next cross-country was in sight of the Sierras—of course, everything in the Valley is in sight of the Sierras—on a trip to Mariposa. On a clear day, she acquired a new respect for the Sierra Nevadas and the wind currents that carried the small plane high, then slammed it down without warning. The heat that rose off of the foothills had buffeted the little plane and shaken her confidence. She had turned over the controls to the instructor who handed her a headset to calm her nerves. He smiled at her as he put in the tape and she heard the words of the song: "I feel the earth shake under my feet. I feel the earth move…"

By the time they reached Mariposa, she had calmed herself sufficiently to retake the controls. She landed the plane on the undulating runway of the airport on the outskirts of the small Gold Rush town that, at 2,250 feet, had paved over some hills and called it an airport.

It was during the trip to Mariposa that Rose first saw the Yosemite Valley from the sky. She and her instructor went during the day, knowing full well that the air was rougher and more unpredictable than at night. However, if a problem developed in darkness over the Sierras or even the foothills, there would be no place to put the plane down. At least the Valley was flat, with many roads and, even at nightfall, some chance of illumination. Leaving Mariposa in the late afternoon, they were quickly in sight of Merced and the Valley floor. McFarland had her turn north and circle over Bear Valley and take in the mountains and the entrance to Yosemite. The view was spectacular. As she banked the plane to turn to-ward Salinas, she saw, as a pilot, her first sunset, then dusk and the emergence of stars in the deepening dark blue horizon. By the time Rose powered back on the landing in Salinas, she was a confirmed flyer for life.

Rose returned to the Sierras often. With respect. Not the respect for a worthy adversary, but of a lover to learn everything there was to know. Watching the smile of a sunrise; the laugh of an updraft; the anger of a storm; the siren song of danger; and the beauty of nature. She learned to fly with the moods of the Sierra Nevadas.

On a sunny afternoon she sought out sail planes, gliders, to catch the same drafts they used so she could lift her Cessna 150 when she found its fixed pitch propeller no match for the downdrafts coming over the Sierras and sucking her down as she tried to climb out of Minden, Nevada. On another afternoon, she waited for evening, for the mountains' calmer air, watching reports of a storm brewing over the southern Sierras toward Yosemite, before taking off from Reno to home. She had rented a Piper Comanche for the extra power to make the trip, aware of uncertain weather but determined to experience, even looking forward to, rough weather conditions. She knew, as every pilot was told, of the stories of World War II Mescherschmidt pilots bailing out in cumulus clouds and ending up as dead human popsicles. A small plane would be treated like a sock in a washing machine if caught in the power of one of those clouds.

She had no intention of experiencing the power of such a cloud. She simply wanted to witness the staggering beauty of the towering cumulus, as moist air was lifted tens of thousands of feet into the sky. The Sierras were their home.

As she crossed the peak from Reno and flew over the Tahoe Basin, she could see the lights of the casinos around the north shore and, to the south, as far away as State Line. On the west shore, she could see snow-covered hillsides illuminated. Night skiers. She adjusted her 230 compass heading (that would have taken her straight into Salinas) by 30 degrees left, taking her over Kirkwood and a little closer to the Yosemite Valley.

There they were, illuminated by the moon, like ruffled icebergs, towering cumuli rising, she estimated, 30,000 feet into the air. The air was calm. The stars were drowned out by the light of the moon made brighter by the reflection of the snow and the massive clouds ahead of her. They looked so benign, inviting, like a soft pillow to set a plane upon and get out and walk around. She knew better. She had no intention of getting any closer. In the back of her mind was the contingency of a sharp bank to the west into a glide path to San Andreas.

But it was her respect for the mountains that made her a meticulous flyer. On every trip, even those she had taken with regularity, she studied her sectional maps, confirmed weather all along the route, maintained radio communication in a professional and crisp manner without unnecessary chatter, and had a ready contingency plan for every emergency she could imagine and many she could not imagine but that Chuck McFarland had experienced and for which he had trained her. She had never been reckless in anything she did in life, and she applied the same discipline to flying.

Reynoso was reluctant about her taking a case in Los Angeles, but for tactical reasons. "They can run you back and forth from Salinas to Los Angeles daily with motions. They can back-door you with the judges they know. They can claim he shouldn't have to pay for his wife hiring a Salinas attorney, when there are so many in Los Angeles, and they will challenge your fees for travel time. It's not an even fight," were his thoughts.

"I don't want this to look like a personal thing between me and Bridgeport, either," Rose added.

"Why not? You said he was an asshole at Boalt. Why should you care?" he asked.

"Because I don't think you use the law to get even."

"Sure you do," said Reynoso with a smile. "It's part of the fun."

"Not for me. I just don't think I should get involved."

"If you did, you would need to end it fast. Hit them with everything. Go to the newspapers. Plaster their names all over the press. They aren't going to like that."

"Forget it," Rose said. "It won't work. This guy prides himself on being an asshole. Giving him more bad publicity just feeds his reputation." Inadvertently, she was now talking tactics, too.

"Rose, he wants a reputation for bludgeoning his opponents, not his wife and kids."

"Well, I'm not interested in being bludgeoned," Rose said, deciding that she would tell Sarah she could not take the case.

Sarah had gone home upset. She had hoped Rose would take on her husband. She knew all too well—had heard it for three years of law school—how "some woman" named Rose had bested him and all of the other men at Boalt.

Anger was a good thing, her therapist had told her, when used constructively. A person with no self-esteem was incapable of anger; just fear, self-pity, or self-loathing. After four years of therapy, Sarah no longer felt sorry for herself. She felt angry.

When she got home, close to 11:00 P.M., he was there.

"Where have you been?" he asked, seeming bored already before her response, yet apparently aware that she had been gone all day.

"Meeting with my lawyer!"

"You're wasting your time. You'd better work out a settlement with Sammis or you're going to be out on the street with nothing," he said with a smile that did not part his lips.

"You wait. She says you can't do any of this. You're going to be charged with kidnapping. You will probably be disbarred. Get out of my house," she screamed at him.

She reached into her purse and pulled out the card she had picked up at Rose's office. She threw it at him.

"Talk to my lawyer. Never talk to me again!"

He picked up the card. Someone named "Baca," he noted, as he put it in his suit pocket and left the room.

Rose had not called Sarah yet when she was interrupted by the intercom the next day. She had just arrived in the office, gotten her morning coffee, and sat down to plan her day.

"He says to tell you it's Mister"—her Spanish-speaking receptionist pronounced it meester—"Bridgeport calling."

"Oh, Jesus," thought Rose.

"Tell him I'm not in," she said.

In a moment, the receptionist came back on. "He said to tell you that he wants to speak to you *now*."

Rose thought perhaps there had been an accident. Did Sarah get home all right? She had left late for the long drive home. She had wanted to tell Sarah first, but if necessary, would just tell Jackson Bridgeport that she had declined representation. That would end the conversation.

She picked up the phone.

"Hello, this is…" She never finished her sentence.

"I know who this is, Ms. Baca. I also knew you were there. What kind of a fool do you take me for?"

"I really don't know what you're talking about," Rose answered.

"Don't play cute, Ms. Baca. You don't know who you're up against. I don't know why my wife went to Salinas for a lawyer, Ms. Baca, but you ought to check around before you decide to play ball in the big league. You're in way over your head, Ms. Baca."

Every time he said "Ms. Baca," it sounded like an insult.

"Jackson," she shouted to make sure she would not be interrupted again, "do you know who this is?"

He was holding her card in his hand. "Abogada," it said. He turned it over to the English side. He read, "Rose Contreras, Attorney at Law."

There was a long silence. Jackson Bridgeport III slowly, softly hung up the phone. Now he knew why Sarah had gone to Salinas to hire an attorney.

"That son-of-a-bitch!" Rose shouted. She was furious. She called Reynoso.

"Why are men so predictable?" she said as soon as he came on the line.

"What did I do?" Reynoso asked.

"Not you. Bridgeport. He just called here threatening me for representing his wife."

"Did you tell him you aren't representing her?" he asked.

"I am now, damn it. I can't just walk away after that. Not after how he treated me."

"How did he treat you?" asked Reynoso.

"Like I was a dumb Mexican girl who went to night law school through affirmative action."

"Was it more the Mexican or more the girl treatment?" he mused.

"Ernie, damn it. This guy is an equal-opportunity bigot. I'm a 'two-fer,' Mexican and girl."

"What are you going to do, Rose?" he asked.

"Jump on him with both feet. Not because I'm pissed, but because you were right, tactically. He needs to be slammed, hard."

She called Sarah and informed her that she would represent her. She explained the strategy, what she would do.

"By the way, how did your husband know you had talked to me?" Rose asked.

Sarah hesitated. "He must have seen your business card," she answered.

The strategy was complex but necessary. Even when Rose had thought she was not going to handle the case, she had lain awake contemplating how she would handle a case against a law firm that had conspired to deprive women of their community property rights without their knowledge, abetted in the kidnapping of children, held in its name property belonging to the community for the benefit of the male surviving the divorce, and represented one spouse against another despite an obvious conflict of interest.

It is what lawyers do: Think through the entire case from beginning to end, every attack, counterattack, ploy, and response, so that the execution is pulling off the shelf a plan laid there in the hours that invade sleep.

Now Rose began what had been the night before only hypothetical.

First, she listed all of the marriage property as community property, even though held in the law firm's name: the house, the cars, the pension plan, personal jewelry and effects, and an "undetermined amount of cash" owed by the firm to the community.

Second, she listed "the community property interest" in the law firm itself, despite the claim that it was not a partnership.

Third, she listed "the value of a law degree from Boalt Hall School of Law" as an asset of the community. She smiled. Must have a value of at least $200,000 a year for the next 20 years of Jackson's practice. She typed in "Estimated value: $4,000,000."

When she was researching the Puchini case, Rose had read an article in the *Los Angeles Daily Journal* entitled, "Doctor Ordered to Share Value of M.D. Degree With Ex-Wife." Why not a law degree as community property?

"Go for it, girl," she told herself.

Fourth, she named the law firm of Bridgeport, Bridgeport, Hall and Pendergast as a party to the dissolution of marriage. Since it was claiming an interest in the property, it was, she reasoned, a "necessary party" to the action and must be "joined" for a determination of ownership of all of the property at issue.

"Due process," she said to no one. "You are going to be processed as is your long overdue." She was getting into the mood for a fight.

Finally, she prepared a Petition for Temporary Custody, again naming the law firm and alleging that the children of the marriage had been "kidnapped" and removed from the jurisdiction of the court with the aid of the law firm. It asked that they be immediately returned to the jurisdiction and to the custody of their mother.

Sarah called back in the afternoon. "I contacted Veronica in Denver," she said.

"Who?" asked Rose.

"Veronica Benton. She was the one who lost her house to the firm. She said her lawyer found out there were others over the years."

She gave Rose the name and number of the attorney. Rose called. He was very sympathetic.

"These are evil people you're dealing with," he told Rose. "They have unlimited resources. It's hard for one distraught woman to take on her husband's huge law firm. They'll offer you a settlement. Your client will probably take it."

He hesitated. "I've got to be careful. I had to sign a confidentiality agreement about the case and the settlement. So I can't tell you how many other women, if any, I found out about at the Los Angeles office, the Denver office, the Houston office, the Baltimore office, the Chicago office, or even the main office, in Bridgeport, Connecticut, even if I knew one way or the other about one or more women getting screwed out of their marital rights at each and every, or some, or none of those offices I have mentioned, or others for that matter."

Having uttered the sentence without taking a breath, he stopped. He then added: "I do hope you understand, Ms. Contreras, no?"

"Yes, I understand. Thank you, Mr. Porter. I appreciate all the help you were unable to give me."

"You're welcome, Ms. Contreras. Good luck."

She had her secretary call the Los Angeles Superior Court and set an *ex parte* hearing for temporary custody. The secretary got the time and day confirmed and gave the obligatory 48 hours' notice to the Bridgeport attorneys, overnighting the papers Rose had prepared. On Rose's direction, she also phoned and got the name of the managing attorney at the Los

Angeles office of Bridgeport, Bridgeport, Hall and Pendergast, and arranged for him to be personally served with a Notice to Appear. Finally, she express mailed a copy to the firm's head office and the attention of its executive committee chairman, Jackson Bridgeport's father.

Rose then prepared what would be the second of the two feet that were going to come down on Jackson Bridgeport III: the federal action. She would be personally carrying it to Los Angeles, not sending it by mail for filing.

The response to her initial foray was not long in coming. More threats. This time in a long, hand-delivered letter, under the signature of James E. Sammis, but with a tone that sounded strangely Bridgeport: "You have obviously been misinformed...no property interest in the residence...no vested rights...the law firm is not properly joined in a divorce case... sanctions...attorneys' fees...frivolous claims...sanctions...dismiss the firm or bear the consequences...defamatory claim of kidnapping...sanctions ...State Bar..."

Predictable, Rose thought, although not without her stomach beginning to turn, the knots tightening, the apprehension growing.

"Almost time to send them scrambling," she said as she placed their letter in the file. "Tomorrow," she told her secretary, "have this delivered."

It was a Notice of Motion to Disqualify the law firm of Bridgeport, Bridgeport, Hall and Pendergast from representing Jackson Bridgeport III in the divorce action. Since at issue was the question of whether the firm owned the residence and other property, or whether they were community property, there was an obvious conflict of interest.

"Unless the firm relinquishes any claim," the motion concluded, "it has a conflict of interest as a party in interest to the dispute."

Rose flew to Los Angeles International Airport commercially. She had too much on her mind this trip—for this first court appearance—to fly herself. With only an occasional look at the Sierras out of the left side of the PSA airliner, she reviewed the federal action in her lap.

I hope I'm right, she thought. She knew she was out on a limb but had not the Denver lawyer told her there were others? Or had she misunderstood what he was trying to tell her? If she was forced to reveal him as the source of her information, could she honestly say he had told her anything? Or had he refused to not tell her anything? Or implied..."shit"...She was getting panicky.

Even when the taxi driver at LAX asked, "Where to, lady?" she was not sure whether to say "Federal Courthouse" or "Superior Court, Family Law Division."

It came out "Federal Courthouse."

When they reached the federal court, she asked the cab driver to wait. She had no idea how long it would take to find another cab. When she returned to the cab, she asked him to take her to 111 North Hill Street: Los Angeles Superior Court. Her secretary had written the address and the number of the department "on the eighth floor," with the helpful information that to get to the eighth floor Rose needed to take the second set of elevators from the entrance, not the first set.

"Call the first case, please," the judge directed. The court clerk read: "*In Re the Marriage of Friedman.*"

Rose watched as the judge consulted his notes. The issues were routine, and the judge was polite, but firm.

"Counsel, I've read everything you filed. Late last night. You don't need to repeat it. Unless you have anything else?"

"No, your honor, we just feel—"

"I know how you feel," the judge interrupted. Then, turning to opposing counsel, who had not yet spoken, the judge asked: "Submitted counsel? I don't need to hear from you."

The attorney was apparently experienced with the judge. He took the cue: He need not say anything to win.

"Submitted, your honor," he snapped like a military salute.

The judge ruled in his favor.

"Next," said the judge before the attorneys could pick up their papers.

"*In Re Marriage of Bridgeport,*" announced the clerk.

Rose stood to walk through the gate to the counsel table. As she did, two attorneys with large briefcases walked in front of her. One stood at the gate, blocking entry.

"Your honor, James E. Sammis. Could we pass this matter to the end of the calendar?"

The judge looked up, the file in his hand.

"Why, Mr. Sammis? Most attorneys would be pleased to be at the head of the docket."

"Well, your honor, this is a sensitive matter involving unfounded allegations against a member of this Bar. We would prefer that it be taken up, in private, at the end of the Court's calendar."

"Is counsel for Mrs. Bridgeport here?" the judge asked.

"We haven't had a chance to meet with her yet, your honor," responded the attorney blocking the entry.

Rose pushed forward. "Excuse me. Rose Contreras, your honor. We would like to proceed."

"I see no reason to treat this matter any differently than any other case, Mr. Sammis. Let's proceed. Please, counsel, identify yourselves for the record and state who you represent."

Rose introduced herself again, handed the bailiff a card for the court reporter, and introduced her client, Sarah Bridgeport.

"James Sammis and Leonard Marks representing Jackson Bridgeport," came the response from the opposing side.

"Is your client present?" the judge asked.

"No, your honor, but he's available by phone."

"Well, I suggest that you call him, counsel, and get him over here. We have a little problem," said the judge, looking at Sammis.

"Your honor, we represent him, so I don't think he's required..."

The judge's voice changed slightly from accommodating to directory. "See, that's the problem, Mr. Sammis. I don't think you can represent him before this Court, unless, as Ms. Contreras has argued, the law firm is prepared to waive its claim to assets she says belong to the community. Are you prepared to do that, Mr. Sammis?"

"No, your honor. I'm not here representing the law firm. We think the firm is improperly named."

"But, Mr. Sammis, you are the one who delivered the Notice of Termination of Lease to Mrs. Bridgeport on behalf of the firm. How can you say you don't represent the firm?"

"We believe it is improperly named," Sammis repeated.

"Was the firm served to be here today?" asked the judge.

"Yes, your honor," interjected Rose.

"So, where is it, Mr. Sammis?"

"It was improperly named," Sammis repeated, again.

"If no one is here representing the firm," said the judge, "then perhaps I should either enter its default or issue an order re contempt."

Mr. Marks returned. He had called Bridgeport as directed by the judge.

"Your honor, Mr. Bridgeport will be here in 10 minutes."

"Good of him," said the judge. "Why don't you all have a seat and we'll proceed with the next case until he arrives."

Sammis and Marks started for the door to warn Jackson Bridgeport.

"No, no. Gentlemen," said the judge. "I want you to stay right here where I can keep an eye on you."

There was a smattering of smirks and chuckles from the audience of attorneys whose interest was obviously piqued by the unfolding drama.

Jackson Bridgeport arrived just as the judge was dividing a single, inadequate salary to feed two households-to-be. He finished and reached once again for the Bridgeport file.

"Mr. Bridgeport, come forward, please," the judge said, obviously recognizing Jackson Bridgeport on sight.

"Now, counsel, if we might revisit this matter."

All of the attorneys returned to the counsel table and remained standing.

The judge turned to Rose.

"Ms. Contreras, you contend that property standing in the name of the law firm actually belongs to the community?"

"Yes, your honor."

"And you allege that the firm actually entered into a conspiracy with Mr. Bridgeport and others to deprive women of their community property interest and benefits acquired during marriage?"

"Yes, your honor."

"On the temporary custody motion, you allege that the law firm aided and abetted the removal of the children from the state?"

"Yes, your honor."

"Serious charges, Ms. Contreras."

"Yes, your honor. Very serious." She was not giving an inch. Not now.

The judge turned to Mr. Sammis. "I am prepared to disqualify your law firm from representing Mr. Bridgeport. You're going to be busy representing your law firm, Mr. Sammis."

The judge turned to Jackson Bridgeport. "Since you are an attorney, Mr. Bridgeport, you may proceed *in pro per* to represent yourself today. Do you have anything you would like to add to the papers already filed?"

Sarah was loving it. Finally. Jackson Bridgeport III at a loss for words.

Rose spoke up. "Your honor, I wish to advise the Court that earlier today we filed in the United States District Court for the Central District a lawsuit naming Mr. Bridgeport, members of his firm, and its executive committee as defendants and alleging violations of the Racketeer Influenced and Corrupt Organizations Act related to the conspiracy to systematically violate the marital property rights of women, including my client, through extortion, wire fraud, and kidnapping. Since Mr. Bridgeport is now appearing on his own behalf here, I would like to lodge a copy of the suit with this Court and ask the bailiff to serve Mr. Bridgeport."

A loud murmur spread among the audience. The bailiff stood and cast a stern look in order to regain quiet.

"It might also be appropriate, your honor," Rose continued, "to advise Mr. Bridgeport and his law firm of their Fifth Amendment right against self-incrimination."

"Mr. Bridgeport," began the judge, "I'm ordering that Mrs. Bridgeport have exclusive use of the family home pending determination of these issues. I'm also ordering temporary support of $10,000 a month, child support of $4,000 a month, and advanced attorney's fees of $25,000, as prayed."

He looked up from his notes and directly at Bridgeport. "You, Mr. Bridgeport, and you, Mr. Sammis, are ordered to have those children back in this jurisdiction and in Mrs. Bridgeport's custody by Monday, or show cause on Tuesday why you should each not be held in contempt. Are there any questions?"

There were none.

"Good."

The judge shut the file and looked at the lawyers: "And, Mr. Sammis, someone better make an appearance for the law firm at the next hearing. I find that it is properly joined and a necessary party. Especially in light of the federal lawsuit now on file."

He turned to Rose.

"Ms. Contreras," he said, giving a very slight nod to her. "You're also arguing that Mr. Bridgeport's law degree should be considered community property?"

"Yes, your honor."

"How did you get the value of $4,000,000? I'm curious."

"Well, your honor, it's from the top law school in the state. Boalt Hall." A number of the lawyers in the audience laughed.

"Ms. Contreras, you're not from these parts, I can tell. Most practitioners before this Court know I went to Stanford Law School—of which I am very proud."

A thought flashed through her mind: Go Indians? Or was it Cardinals?

"Number two is not bad, your honor," she replied.

Again laughter.

"Well, Ms. Contreras, we'll see. We'll see." He smiled briefly at her as if he had sized her up and found her more than adequate for the task at hand.

"Mr. Bridgeport, I suggest you get yourself a good lawyer." He looked at his clerk. "Call the next case."

As Rose reached the courtroom door, she was aware of someone following her out. He held the door. She glanced at him. He was impeccably dressed in an expensive Italian suit, silk tie, and bright blue shirt, and was grinning, not smiling. His hair was jet black and his complexion slightly brown. With his tan he could probably pass for Mexican in the summer.

"Well, well, well…" he said in a heavy Indian accent.

Rose turned, the lyric of his voice strangely familiar.

"Professor Van Dyke would be so proud of his student. Yes, indeedy. Yes, indeedy."

She laughed as she faced him.

He stuck out his hand and dropped the accent.

"J. J. Rai, Boalt Hall, class of '69. That was one hell of a performance, Rose."

"J. J.," she said, remembering the playful accent in class. "How are you?"

"Fine. Just here on some airplane litigation. Practice out of Sacramento. Here, let me give you my card. If you ever get up that way, please call and use my office, meetings, depos, anything."

"Thanks, I will," replied Rose and reciprocated with her card.

Her opposition was coming out of the courtroom and she wanted to get her client, Sarah, away. She abruptly left J. J. holding her card.

Jackson Bridgeport and his lawyers reached the courtroom doors and J. J. rushed to hold a door open for them.

As Jackson passed within a foot of him, J. J. whispered to him, again in his Indian accent: "In my country we have a saying. 'Man who beats his wife is an egg beater.'"

Jackson's head spun to look at him. J. J. was already moving.

"Pardon me, pardon me. Coming through," J. J. said loudly, without a hint of accent, and entered the courtroom as the bailiff called his case.

"Present, your honor. Jawaharlal Jallianwalla Singh Rai for the plaintiffs."

Bridgeport had no idea who he was.

The *Los Angeles Times* carried a long story on the case in Monday's edition. Rose had been surprised when the reporter had called. She declined comment. The story focused on her argument in court—calling it "cutting edge" (with not-so-subtle implications)—that a spouse could claim her husband's law degree as a community asset. Of course, the article quoted James Sammis as denying that the law firm consisted of racketeers and kidnappers. Rose's prior representation of the wife of a Fresno judge was featured in a box with her picture under the title "MAN-SLAYER: Salinas Attorney Takes on High-Powered Men." It was not a role she had sought or one with which she felt comfortable. Reynoso had said, "Some men are born to power; some seek it; some have it thrust upon them." She thought that could apply to women, too.

Rose was disturbed to read, in the box feature about her, the statement:

> And if Ms. Contreras prevails against Bridgeport, it will not be the first time. Contreras graduated number one in her class at Boalt Hall in 1969, taking on all comers. Bridgeport was a member of the same class.

If Rose was upset about the *Los Angeles Times* story, Sarah was elated. She had chosen right. She was well-satisfied with her representation. It had turned out exactly as she had hoped. Exactly as she had planned. She had known what Jackson's reaction would be to the selection of Rose as her attorney. After the hearing, she had immediately called the *L.A. Times* herself, told the news desk of the filings, in state and federal court, and given the reporter the case numbers. She had even given him a copy of the *Fresno Bee* story on the Puchini case that she had herself researched before calling Rose. She was, of course, the source of the information about law school.

Sarah's satisfaction was not just in the fact that she had won or that it was a woman who had beaten her husband. It was that Rose Contreras had beaten him. She had sought her out, found her, and put her on Jackson. She knew that it was the worst thing that she could have done to Jackson Bridgeport III.

It was the joining of the law firm in the action and the federal RICO filing that brought Jackson's father into the case. Mr. Porter of Denver proved to be right. There was an offer. It was taken. But the offer was from Rose: Two million dollars to Sarah and the scrapping of the company's policy that allowed attorneys to hide assets in the firm on divorce. It was, of course, confidential.

In 1984, the California Legislature passed Family Code Section 2641 to limit the claim of a spouse to a law, medical, or other professional degree earned through special training or education during the marriage. The official legislative history referred to the legislation as a response to a case called *In Re the Marriage of Sullivan*. There, according to California Supreme Court Justice Rose Bird's opinion,

> Janet Sullivan sought to introduce evidence of the value of Mark Sullivan's medical education, obtained during the marriage.

In Los Angeles, however, those in the know called it the Bridgeport Amendment. Those who went to Boalt Hall had no problem believing that their degree was worth $4,000,000, as Rose Contreras had claimed. They just did not want their spouses to know it. The legislative change came too late to help Jackson Bridgeport.

Most satisfying to Rose, however, was the letter from the dean of Boalt Hall: "We are all very proud of you, Rose."

It was signed Herma Hill Kay, the first woman dean of a major law school in the United States—and Rose's Family Law professor in 1968.

Chapter 54

Rose

SHE WAS 37 when she finished the Bridgeport case; Ernesto was 50, closer to her mother's age of 54. She was reflecting on where life would take her. He was the elder statesman of La Raza. If he was comfortable and confident in his role as a Mexican revolutionary, she was still wrestling with what it meant to be an articulate and strong woman lawyer. Not just a lawyer. A *woman* lawyer.

Reynoso could expect, even revel in, pejoratives. If a Republican state senator referred to him as "that fuckin' Mexican," it probably meant Reynoso had killed his bill in committee. It might even be spoken in grudging admiration. When a Valley lawyer called her that "Mexican bitch," it was a double hit unrelated to her abilities. It was never a compliment.

She, too, had gained some degree of prominence—thanks to her representation of women against powerful men. The first had resulted in the loss of most of her Fresno clients, the second in a one-day splash in the *Los Angeles Times*. Good for the ego and for recognition among lawyers, but not likely to lead to more big city clients. After all, she was in Salinas, not Los Angeles. Mrs. Bridgeport was a "special case"—not likely to cause other women of means to beat a path up the Valley from Los Angeles to the "Mexican woman lawyer" in Salinas.

If all politics is local, so is fame. People locally like to say, "She was in the *Wall Street Journal*" or "He was on *60 Minutes*." The people who remember forever are at home. Just like obituaries appear in local papers.

So it was with Rose. She was known among those who were likely to be her clients by what was written about her. Divorce cases. Or, as the practice is euphemistically called, "family law." Or from what was known about her, more generically, it was said of her: "She helps women."

Family law practice in Salinas, among the Mexican farm and cannery workers, was not lucrative. Many of them had immigration reasons, or fears, not to voluntarily bring themselves before a court. Few had enough resources to divide and support a second household. Then there was the church. For religious reasons, families stayed together. When they did seek an attorney, the women came to Rose.

Her "fame" brought her a fair share of the wives of professional men— doctors, dentists, and even lawyers—who became her main source of income. With them, there seemed to be a wives' network that broadcast regularly: "She's the one who sued the Los Angeles lawyer to make his law degree community property." Of course they also knew of Judge Puchini, but a *Los Angeles Times* story carried more weight than a local *Fresno Bee* story. Each of the women she represented seemed to broadcast on her own bandwidth to a new audience: wives of osteopaths, veterinarians, professors at U.C. Santa Cruz, surgeons at Manteca Hospital, administrators at San Jose State. Periodically, she would even get a resident of 17 Mile Drive in Monterey.

While Rose's career had fallen into family law, her mother's concern was for Rose's family, or rather, the absence of children.

It was true, as Rose argued, Ernesto was home very little, spending most of the week in Sacramento. Also, she had been busy building her own career over the five years they had been married. When she came home late at night during the week, it was usually to an empty house.

It was not Ernesto's age or his physical condition.

"Yes," he was "all right." That was the closest her mother would get to asking if Ernesto could perform.

The truth, which Rose did not fully understand, or at least allow herself to consider, was that she had little interest in sex with her husband. He was her best friend, her confidant, her mentor, her teacher, and her supporter. She loved him. She enjoyed him. More than anything, she respected him. Like a father.

Rose had never been very experienced sexually. Most of her friends in the law were men, since most attorneys she dealt with were men. She related well to secretaries, as a woman. However, she avoided conversations about sex or what was "normal" or "average" for sex within marriage. She did not read *Vogue* or other "women's magazines," or magazines at the checkout with articles like "How to Turn Your Man On" or "Ten Steps to Revitalize Your Sex Life." Most of her clients complained that their husbands wanted too much sex or wanted it in ways that repulsed them. She did not really know but had the sense there was something wrong with her.

It took her a long time before she could bring herself to talk to Ernesto about her feelings. If Republican George Deukmejian had not been elected governor, forcing Ernesto to return to do "battle in the trenches" of the Valley with CRLA once again, she might have delayed the conversation for four more years. It was not something she wanted to face. She did not want to hurt him.

She broached it as he was cooking. "I've been thinking. I think it would be a good idea if we got a little help," she said almost casually, despite the days and nights she had spent formulating those two sentences.

"What type of help?"

"Well, you know, with our marriage."

He turned with the sauce pan in his hand. "What's wrong with our marriage?"

"Well, you know, sex."

He put down the pan and turned off the gas. He shuffled to the faucet and rinsed his hands. While wet, he ran them through the sides of his hair. Looking at the floor, he began to speak.

"I realize it's difficult for you, with my paralysis—"

She cut him off. "No, it's me. I have problems with myself. I know I'm not a very sexual—"

It was his turn to interrupt. "I think you are very sexy, but you don't seem interested in sex with me."

"It's not you. I'm not interested in sex with anyone," she blurted. "That's why I want to see someone."

He reflected. "Okay. Why don't you?"

"What?" she asked.

"See someone."

"I don't know," she said. Then she added, "I've been waiting to talk to you."

"About what?"

"Going. Together."

"If you think it's your problem, why do you need me to go, too?" he asked.

"Because it's our marriage."

"Okay," he said, as he reignited the burner.

"Okay, what?" she asked.

"Okay, I'll go," he said, without enthusiasm.

They ate without exchanging the normal stories of their day: a court hearing, a new client, a legislative challenge. After dinner, she picked up the dishes and cleared the table. She returned and wrapped her arms around his neck from behind, kissed him on the head as he sat at the table, and said, "Thanks."

"For what?" he asked.

"For being a good, patient man," she answered.

"I'm Zapata. I can be patient only so long!"

She laughed. He grabbed her, pulled her around to his lap, and kissed her softly.

"Well, maybe for you a little longer," he whispered in her ear and she hugged his head.

She called Sally Conrad the next morning and left a message. At 9:50 A.M., she got a return call promptly, as she always had when representing Ann Puchini.

"Hi, Rose. I'm between appointments. How have you been?"

"Fine. I wonder if we could make an appointment," Rose ventured, a little nervously.

"Sure. Is this an emergency matter again or can your client wait a few weeks?" Sally asked.

"Well, it's not exactly an emergency, and it's not for a client."

"Who is it for?" Sally asked.

"Me. And my husband," Rose told her.

Sally was silent. Then an "oh."

Finally, Sally asked, "Can I call you back after 5:00 tonight? I think we need to talk a little."

"Sure," Rose responded, assuming Sally's next client had arrived. He had not. Sally just wanted time to reflect and decide whether she could be a therapist to Rose Contreras.

By 5:00 P.M., she had decided. "Rose, this is Sally. I don't think I can see you and your husband."

Rose was a bit taken aback. She managed to recover. "Well, could you just see us to give us some direction? Like whether we even need marriage counseling. I don't want to waste some other counselor's time. I mean, I don't want to waste your time either, but we trust you. I mean, I trust you. Ernie trusts my judgment, and I've told him about you."

There was a hint of desperation that Sally heard in "I trust *you*," as well as a connection Sally could not let go of, although she knew better.

"If I were to see you and your husband, it would only be to determine an appropriate person to send you to, not for therapy." Then she added, attempting to soften the rejection: "I really don't see many couples. Mostly individuals."

"Well, if it turns out that I am the only one who needs help, then could you see me as an individual?" Rose asked. "I think it's me who has the problem, anyway."

"I don't think I could be your therapist, Rose."

There was silence.

"Oh," Rose finally said. She did not know where this left her. She was not going to consult the Yellow Pages, and she would not subject herself and Ernie to the scrutiny of marriage and family counselors who found their way into most courtrooms to testify for hire.

Sally wanted to help but knew she was the wrong person to counsel Rose.

"Let's all get together and explore some options," Sally finally offered. Relieved, Rose made an appointment for herself and Ernesto.

At the session, Ernesto was clearly uncomfortable in the presence of the two women. For the better part of the hour, Rose spoke of Ernesto in glowing terms: how considerate he was, how attentive, intelligent, supportive. Ernesto interrupted to point out that Rose made more money than he, so far as being "supportive" was concerned.

Sally let them talk for the first 40 minutes before she finally interrupted. "So what's the problem? You both sound wonderful. I should be so lucky to be married to you two."

They laughed, and Rose looked nervously at Ernesto. "It's not Ernie. I just don't enjoy sex. I have no interest. He doesn't say anything. He holds me. But it's not fair to him."

"Let's get a man's point of view," Sally said, "before you decide what's fair for Ernesto." She turned to him. "Ernesto, on a scale of 1 to 10, with 10 being highly frequent, your wife sounds like a zero in bed. Do you agree?"

"I didn't say never," Rose objected.

Ernie came to her defense. "No. We hold each other. Caress."

"Just no sex?" Sally asked.

Neither said anything.

"How does that make you feel, Ernesto?" Sally persisted.

"Less than a man. Less than even a crippled man."

Rose's eyes welled up.

"Okay," Sally said, after letting it all sink in, "we have a problem here." She reached for a pen and a piece of paper. "I'm going to give you some names. I suggest you each start seeing a therapist separately. You need to be honest with yourselves before you can be honest with each other. That's going to take some time."

Sally was right. It was over a year before she heard from Rose again.

"You knew, didn't you?"

"Let's just say I had a feeling."

"How long have you had 'a feeling'?"

"From the time you came to my office with Ann Puchini."

"That was four years ago."

"Yes."

"You didn't say anything."

"That wouldn't have been professional."

"And Sally is always professional?"

"Yes."

"Is that why you wouldn't see me in therapy?"

"Yes."

Rose took it all in, wondering whether to be angry or flattered. She could see Sally at the other end of the phone: sitting with her feet curled under her, her short blond hair riding above her collar, her pale blue eyes as they generally looked over the coffee cup she held with two hands while listening intently to what you had to say.

"How is Ernesto?" she heard Sally ask.

"We're separated. He moved up to Berkeley and is full-time at Boalt now, teaching."

"Have you told him?"

"No. I have to, don't I?"

"Yes. So he won't blame or doubt himself."

"Is that the therapist talking?"

"No. Just a friend, Rose."

Chapter 55

Brian

AS HE SAT at the reunion listening to the conversation about law swirling around him, he could feel the sweat on his body, the pounding in his chest, and the throbbing in his head. He wanted to scream, "Don't you know who I used to be?"

In the din of wine glasses clinking and soup spoons being properly laid to rest, he raised his glass and sipped his Diet Pepsi, on ice. Brian Jacobs was a drunk. Every Thursday for the last nine years he had stood up in front of his group and introduced himself: "My name is Brian and I am an alcoholic."

He had not believed it when he had walked into the Chinese Palace restaurant in Los Angeles for what he thought was a birthday party for his wife, Shelly. He did a double take when he saw William Kunstler of New York City, Charles Garry of Oakland, and Mike Tigar of Houston, with his parents from Florida, and each of his partners sitting in the reserved room.

"What's going on?" he asked, truly not knowing but fearing some calamity had occurred to bring three of his best friends and the leading criminal defense attorneys in the country to Los Angeles, unannounced, let alone his parents, and the rest. He did not like the silence.

William Kunstler stepped forward, his glasses resting on his head, in his typical fashion. As he did, Shelly stood behind him. She feared Brian's outburst. She feared the consequences. Mostly, she feared it would do no good.

"Brian, we love you. We can't stand by and watch you destroy yourself."

Confused, Brian responded, "What the fuck are you talking about?"

Michael Tigar, the Boalt Hall legend after whom Brian had patterned much of his own career, stood up. "Brian, your drinking is destroying you, and it is killing us."

He was stunned. He looked around the room. He had been ambushed. He was being humiliated, wrongly, by those he loved and most admired in the world, and why? Who put them up to this? Shelly!

"I don't know what you have been told," he started slowly, "but I am recognized as one of the top criminal defense attorneys in the fucking country! I have tried more death penalty cases than any of you. And, not to get personal, but since my partners are apparently part of this conspiracy of duplicity, it is my fucking name on Jacobs, Zarick, Stein and Moore that brings in the money. And I remind you, it's a lot of money. We don't have to hang around waiting for court appointments for clients anymore. And the reason is *me*. So the idea that I have a problem with drinking is fucking absurd!" He was screaming as he ended, and his face had been sucked dry of color, which had been replaced by white fury.

Charles Garry stood slowly. The order was choreographed ahead of time as they were advised, professionally, they should do. Garry was like a father to him. Brian had worked that second summer of law school for Garry. It was Garry from whom he had learned the first principle of criminal defense. An eager summer intern, Brian did legal research for Garry, the attorney for the Black Panther Party, on the theory of self-defense. Huey Newton, chairman of the Black Panther Party, had been stopped by an Oakland policeman. What ensued was unknown except that, when the dust on the East Oakland street cleared, Huey was wounded and Officer Frey had been killed, with his own gun.

Garry had obtained a reversal of the first trial conviction. That summer, he was preparing for the second defense of Huey. Trying to better focus his legal research of self-defense, Brian, the eager law student, had asked, "Mr. Garry, what does Huey say happened that night?"

Charles Garry sat gazing at Brian for what seemed a very long time. He looked down at his desk while thinking through his answer. Finally, he looked up, studied Brian carefully, and simply answered, "I don't know. I have never asked him."

Brian now saw the same intensity in Garry's eyes.

"Brian," Charles Garry said quietly, "you're an alcoholic."

Chapter 56

Brian

HE WAS RIGHT. Even as a drunk, he was one of L.A.'s best lawyers. He could coast on his reputation. But he was in the office less, would not show up at court hearings, and missed deadlines for filing papers. He had enough residual respect with judges and chits with fellow lawyers that they would excuse him, extend time, or accept his vague explanations. The firm also covered for him.

Brian had not stopped drinking despite the intervention attempt of his friends and family at the Chinese restaurant in 1987. Instead, he had sulked. Drunk more. Closed himself off from people who he thought were against him. Especially Shelly.

Shelly was adjusting. For the day he would no longer be there. Brian could see it. Her life was going on. Her students at the school occupied all of her time and thoughts, it seemed to him. Every night she would be in her study, cutting out letters, pasting maps on boards, making miniature historic monuments out of papier-mâché. She had installed a workbench in the garage where she had taught herself soldering. She had a three-foot Eiffel Tower partly constructed using HO gauge toy railroad tracks as girders. She did not show it to him. He saw it sitting there when he pulled into the garage late one evening and hit the workbench with his car.

They had stopped using the jacuzzi, at least together. Shelly did not say it, but she did not want him to fall on the steps of the deck or fall asleep in the hot water, in his usual condition. Besides, their sex life had come to a halt. What was the point of a jacuzzi without sex?

Shelly was not planning on leaving. She was waiting for him to come back. The Brian Jacobs she had met, loved, admired, respected, and married. The one she had hurt, she knew. But it was never discussed. He drank. She soldered.

Shelly had the idea for a long time. Perhaps as the way out. The way on. For both of them. But he was still drinking. Her 45th birthday seemed to impose a deadline upon her, at least in her mind. Certainly no one at the adoption agency had said this was the outer age limit when she had spoken to them, off and on, over the years.

"Thursday's my birthday," she mentioned to him. "Could we have dinner at home, just the two of us?"

"Wouldn't you rather have a party downtown with friends?" Brian asked.

"No. I'd like just the two of us. To talk," she replied.

"I didn't know just the two of us did anything together," he answered, sounding more agitated than hurt, as if the only way to get it out in the open was to start a fight.

"Let's try, okay?" Shelly asked, not taking the bait.

"Fine. It's your birthday," he said, pushing his glass into the ice maker in the refrigerator door for more ice cubes.

He refreshed his drink and went into the library, shut the door, and pulled a file from his briefcase. Another black man shot by the LAPD.

"When I think thus of the law…" he bellowed, reciting from his Boalt Hall days, but adding, "I see white slave masters with guns."

Shelly heard him in the library. It was not unusual for him to recite whole speeches: "I've been to the mountain…I've seen the promised land." Or the words of famous documents: "We hold these truths to be self-evident; that all men are created equal…"

She just wished he would talk to her.

Brian had consumed a few drinks, but he was sober when he arrived home for her birthday dinner. He brought her red roses, boxed.

"I couldn't figure out how to hold them in the car in a vase with water," he explained.

She clipped the ends to arrange them for the table while he poured himself a drink. A bracer for what he feared was coming: another discussion about his drinking.

He was surprised to see her pour one also and bring it to the table.

"Cheers," she saluted him, as she raised her glass to meet his.

"Happy birthday," he said.

"I want to adopt a baby," she said, looking down at her food, without so much as any introductory small talk.

"I know I've let you down, Brian. I'm sorry. But I can only be sorry for so long. I can't change the past. I would like this for both of us, but I can't decide your future. Our future."

He had prepared for ultimatums, accusations, not this. He did not know what to say.

"Shelly, I feel like such a failure. This isn't how it was supposed to be. Us. Everything. I've been so busy trying to change the world, I've lost you in the process. It all got blurry somewhere along the way. What good have I done? Here we are in a luxury house, on the edge of a beautiful canyon, with a ravine between us."

Obviously, he had been privately looking at his own life. Her lack of accusations allowed him to be open and honest.

He shook the ice in his glass and looked into it.

"You have me, Brian," Shelly said, after a moment.

"Well, it hasn't exactly been the Love Boat around here, has it?"

"No, it hasn't," she answered quietly.

"I don't see why you think having a baby will change everything," he said, waiting perhaps to be told things would be different.

"I don't expect it will. I just want a child. If things don't change, you can always go. I wouldn't expect you to stay. I will keep her," Shelly said. Not as a threat but as a way of relieving him of any responsibility to change if he did not want to or could not.

For the first time he offered a faint smile to her.

"You'd kick me out? The father of our little girl?" he asked.

"No. We would want you to stay with us, always," she said with tears in her eyes.

Chapter 57

Brian

IN THE 14 months after Shelly had said she wanted to adopt, Brian quit drinking—a number of times. He and Shelly started counseling together. Not for his drinking. She never asked him to quit. She knew it would not do any good. He would do that on his own terms, if and when it happened. Their counseling was for their marriage.

It was not easy, because they both knew that they had to discuss the past if they were going to have a future. As long as he kept showing up, Shelly thought, there was hope. As long as she did not leave, Brian thought, there was a chance.

"We just seem to have separate lives," he told the therapist.

"He just always seems annoyed at me," Shelly remarked.

"She doesn't seem interested in sex," he said.

"He won't stay in the same room with me, avoids any contact—even if I brush by him—let alone intentional touching or hand-holding."

It started as a ballet of complaints descriptive of behavior. They tried to improve their behavior. But the anger remained.

It was months before anything substantive came of the counseling. When it did, it was an explosion. Brian arrived late. He had obviously been drinking. Shelly was annoyed and embarrassed in the presence of their therapist.

"I thought you cared enough to at least come here sober," she said to Brian.

"Maybe I can only be with you when I'm drunk," he snapped. "Did you ever consider that? You should try it, Shelly. Maybe we could have a sex life."

"Maybe if you were ever sober at night, you'd be awake long enough for sex," Shelly shot back.

"Were you sober when you fucked him?" he demanded.

It took a moment. But Shelly knew what he meant. "That was 14 years ago, Brian. I'm sorry. I'm sorry. How long are you going to punish me for that one mistake?"

"I was in trial for months. I doubt it was just one mistake!" he yelled, his face contorted with anger. Then he hurt her as badly as anyone could. "That's why we can't have a baby of our own! That IUD."

She was sobbing and yelling back. "I had cancer, you bastard! I could have died. Where were you? Where were you?"

The therapist did not intervene. She knew this had to come out. Whether the marriage survived the outpouring of buried emotions was another matter. For another session.

Shelly and Brian left separately. Brian left first. He had a plane to catch. To Las Vegas for a speech he was to give to the Los Angeles Trial Lawyers Association: "The State of Civil Liberties in America After Reagan." Shelly stayed behind to dry her eyes and compose herself before returning to school for parents' night.

"Now we can begin talking about the real issues," the therapist told her as she left. It was not reassuring to Shelly at the moment. It was too painful; perhaps not worth it.

The call came after she was in bed.

"Shelly, this is Paul. I'm here in Las Vegas." Shelly brushed her hair back and looked at the clock. It was 2:30 A.M. Why was Brian's partner calling her at this time of night? She was confused and still disoriented.

"Didn't he get there?" she asked, half asleep.

"Yes, he's here. We flew over together, Shelly. He was really drunk when he got on the plane. They wouldn't serve him, but he had his own bottle. When we landed, he got belligerent with people trying to get past him and wouldn't get off the plane. The airline called security. It took everything we could do to not have him arrested."

Now she was sitting up.

"Where are you now?"

"At an emergency room. He's okay. The hospital wants to release him, but the cops say that if he's released, they're going to arrest him."

"What do you want me to do?" Shelly asked.

"We think he needs a detox center. He won't go voluntarily. If you agree, we'll check him in and the cops will walk."

Shelly quickly agreed. "Do you want me to fly over there, Paul?" she asked.

360

"No, Shelly. This has been coming for a long time. We all know it. He needs to sort this out for himself. I'll call you back when we get him checked in, and I'll give you the information."

Brian stayed the full 30 days. He exercised, went to meetings daily, and kept a journal.

"Write down the things that are important to you in your life," the AA counselor told the group, a fair number of whom, Brian noticed, were lawyers.

"Then write down whether you can have each of those things as a drunk," the counselor added.

Brian listed "practicing law" and made a rather convincing argument that drinking was not only compatible with the practice of law but a necessity.

"National reputation," which he also thought might be enhanced by the ability to hold his liquor well.

"Making a difference" which, if he was successful, he felt, entitled him to drink. If unsuccessful, he needed to cover his failure.

The entries in his journal, at the beginning of the second week were: "Shelly. Shelly. Shelly. Shelly and Shelly."

On the question of having Shelly and being a drunk he wrote: "Not for much longer."

He added "our baby" to the list. Next to that he wrote: "Not as a drunk."

The adoption agency woman had felt the same way. She was impressed that he had completed 30 days of detox but noted, correctly, that "most drunks go back to drinking."

The interview was humiliating, especially in front of Shelly. For once, there was no argument he could make to convince the trier of fact otherwise. He was not even a lawyer representing himself. He was a drunk representing a drunk. All he could do was ask: "When can we come back?" The agency placement representative looked at Shelly, knowing it was not fair to her, but was uncompromising: "Six months." She smiled. "Six months and we'll see where we are."

Where we are, thought Brian as he and Shelly drove home. If I'm drunk is what she really meant. He did not have to say it out loud.

"This is it, isn't it, Shelly?" he said quietly to her after a while.

She looked out of the passenger side window. "Yes," she said softly.

Chapter 58

Michael

"ALL RISE!"

It was a good feeling. Wearing the robes of a judge. Being announced by the bailiff of his own courtroom, and having lawyers and litigants all stand in unison. He took the two steps quickly up to his high-back chair behind the bench.

Most of the cases of the Alameda County Superior Court involved criminal charges. This was the area with which he was familiar, having practiced as a prosecutor. But it had been a while since he had practiced law, real law. When he had started in the early '70s, it was often hard, in the Bay Area, to tell the attorney from the client. Either could have long hair, a shaggy beard, sandals, or a sweater. He was happy to see, as he took the bench, that decorum had been restored and attorneys were, once again, clean-shaven and suited.

His reputation, however, preceded him. He was "the former D.A.," "Meese's protege," the "White House lawyer." No reputable criminal defense attorney would take the chance of letting him decide anything substantive or allowing him to sentence a client. Defense attorneys routinely filed a "170.6 challenge"—a procedure to disqualify a judge for "prejudice" without the need to make any showing more than the attorney's signature on the motion papers. As a result, he received miscellaneous cases, one-day civil trials, small claims appeals, and the garbage of the courthouse.

Michael took it. He did not complain. He offered to help other judges who were overburdened and took on administrative matters for the court. Things other judges preferred to avoid. As a result, to the surprise of those outside the judiciary, Michael was named Presiding Judge of the Alameda County Superior Court by his fellow judges in his third year on the bench.

As such, he controlled the assignment of all cases each day and ruled on all procedural motions affecting the court's calendar. He was the "Judges' Judge."

Toward the end of his term, as promised by Ed Meese, Governor George Deukmejian submitted Michael's name for appointment to the First District Court of Appeal in San Francisco.

While his nomination was pending, Michael, as Presiding Judge, was called to rule upon a Writ of Prohibition that almost derailed his appointment. A group of Berkeley college students had burnt an American flag as part of a protest against the University. They were promptly arrested. The Writ, in which the students were joined by a number of distinguished professors of constitutional law at Boalt Hall, sought to stop their prosecution and declare their conduct to be protected speech under the First Amendment. Michael ruled in favor of the protesters.

The governor was furious. He felt he had either been misled by his good friend Ed Meese or unnecessarily embarrassed by Michael. He went so far as to contact Ronald Reagan, now living near Santa Barbara, directly. Reagan thought Deukmejian was right: "If they want to burn the American flag, they should leave the country, not be judges." This only fortified the governor in his feeling that he should withdraw the nomination.

It took everything Meese could do to keep the dispute in house and out of the public view. He talked to Michael. Then to the governor. He explained that it was "settled law," that Michael "had no choice." The Supreme Court had ruled. Finally, the governor settled on a public statement that blasted the demonstrators and not the judge:

> It is unfortunate that some citizens abuse the freedoms that only America gives its citizens and burn the symbol of freedom, the American flag, for which braver citizens have died.
>
> I urge Congress to adopt a Constitutional Amendment to protect this symbol of freedom so our judges' hands are not tied and those who desecrate our flag can be prosecuted.

Michael not only agreed with the statement, he helped write it.

When the appointment to the First District Court of Appeal went through, Michael decided it was time for him to move, with his job, to San Francisco. With his son Rob at college and the Court of Appeal in San Francisco, there was really no need to stay in Alameda County. He had not expected the move, just across the Bay, to cause such a feeling of loss—that his real home was no longer in Oakland; that Mai was a part of his past, not his future. It was not rational, he knew. She had not really been a part of his life for many years, except for the scheduling of holidays with Rob and the periodic caustic comments about his politics. He became seriously depressed.

There had never been anyone, other than Mai, he felt he could talk to. He did not know how to address his feelings. There was no one now to turn to. He had said goodbye to his colleagues on the Superior Court bench. The members of the Court of Appeal were all new to him. While they met in conference once a week, and on three-judge panels while sitting in court, each retreated to his private chambers. As one of his fellow justices, Justice Pacino, had told him after his swearing in, "It's like being in a medieval, Irish monastery, painstakingly working by yourself on manuscripts that no one will ever appreciate."

It was while working on one of these manuscripts that he read the sentence in a brief: "Sally Conrad, LCSW, of San Francisco, a recognized family therapist and a consultant to the California Commission on the Status of Women, testified…" He read her credentials: "Undergraduate, Vassar; master's degree, Stanford; visiting instructor in Psychology, Stanford; private practice." Her testimony in the particular case was "sensible," he thought. Not "wacko psycho-babble." A "real expert," not a "paid whore willing to say anything." The law firm that had retained her in the case, he noted, had an excellent reputation: Janrette, Hawk, Ross and Stephens of San Francisco.

He called her. From chambers. He was desperate. His heart was pounding in his ears when he received her answering machine.

"Hi, this is Sally. I check this machine periodically during the day and evenings. Leave a message."

He had not rehearsed what he would say.

"My name is Michael. Could you call me this evening at my home number in San Francisco? 555-1320."

Then he hung up. He immediately had second thoughts. Why had he called her? Perhaps a man would understand better. She sounded nice. What if she told anyone he was an appellate court justice? Maybe he should go out of town. What if someone saw him going into the office? Why her?

He worried about his call all afternoon, as he watched the clock. By 3:30, he decided to go home. He was not getting anything done anyway. He packed his briefcase with the trial transcripts for the opinion he was writing and left. He rode down to the garage with Justice Pacino, who was also carrying a large briefcase.

"Working late at home tonight?" Michael asked, making elevator talk.

Justice Pacino opened the briefcase. It was full of tennis balls.

"Practicing my serve." He smiled.

When Michael got home, he sat and looked out onto the deck of his second-floor apartment. He had a bougainvillea on the trellis facing south and a small table with two chairs for morning coffee and the *San Francisco Chronicle*. At $108,000, his salary did not go far in San Francisco. He may have counseled the president of the United States, but he had not made any serious money doing it. What was left over each month, he had paid for trips to see his son and for Rob's college. College had been the subject of many transcontinental discussions. At 24, Rob had earned, in five years, off and on at Santa Barbara, 68 units (or the equivalent of just over two years of college credit) with no end in sight. He just could not decide what he "wanted to be." Maybe a "graduate," suggested his dad. But Michael kept sending the rent and tuition, while he simultaneously urged his son to become "self-supporting."

It was still warm out when he decided to sit on the deck. He left the door open in case the phone rang. He thought he heard it a couple of times. Once he walked in, but it was not ringing.

At 6:10 P.M., she called. "Michael? This is Sally Conrad. You called?"

"Yes, thank you for calling back. I was recommended to you. I'm a lawyer. I wonder if I might see you? Professionally."

"Can you give me an idea of what this is about?" she asked. "I see a good number of lawyers in my practice, mostly men, individually, but sometimes with their spouses."

"I think the main problem is that I'm in love with my wife," Michael said, surprising himself both by his candor with a stranger and by his answer.

"That's generally commendable," Sally commented.

"Well, I thought so too, but we've been divorced for about 17 years," Michael replied. "It's gotten worse since I moved back to the Bay Area."

"Okay. We have a problem, then."

"You mentioned you treat lawyers. I would have a problem sitting in a waiting area. A matter of confidentiality."

"That's not a problem. I handle all my own calls and scheduling. The entrance and exit are separate. Of course, everything is confidential."

"Well, I'm not exactly a lawyer. Perhaps we could discuss this further when I see you."

She was a little puzzled. "All right. Friday morning work for you?" she asked.

"I would prefer the end of the day. A little difficult taking off work during certain parts of the day."

They made the appointment. She hung up and wrote it in her book. Just the first name. That is all she had. "Michael. 4:00 P.M. Friday. June 14."

The rest of the book had first names, or initials, in case she lost the book. Confidentiality was not just a professional responsibility; it was a creed for her. She told no one. Not even to acknowledge that she had seen a client referred by another client. It could be the referrer's brother or sister. The two clients could talk to each other about what they had said to Sally. But she would never even acknowledge to one that she was seeing the other.

She would, if she could, have confessed a bit of intrigue over the identity of a new client. Potential client. She knew some never showed up, even after finally making the call and setting up the appointment. Some called years later. Sometimes without telling her it was they who had called earlier.

Michael was not sure either that he would actually keep the appointment. What if an attorney who appeared before him saw him going in? Maybe a public defender. An hour later it would be all over the P.D.'s office that "Cassidy is seeing a shrink."

On Friday, Michael drove by the building early to see its layout. It was a large medical complex in the old California Pacific Hospital on Clay near California and Webster. "Room 211," she had said. He could take the stairs and avoid the elevator, he thought. Anyone seeing him in the common area might assume he was in for a medical check-up. No reason to believe he was seeing a therapist. He took the stairs. He walked past her door on the second floor. There was only a number; no identification that it was a therapist's office. He tried the handle. It was locked.

"Michael?" asked a voice behind him.

He jumped as if startled while burglarizing a home.

"I'm sorry," said the woman with short dark blond hair holding a paper coffee cup with a plastic lid.

"I just slipped out for coffee. I'm Sally Conrad."

He shook her outstretched hand. She had blue eyes, no makeup or jewelry that he could discern, and a certain playfulness in her smile. He guessed she was about 40.

She did not wait for him to speak. It was apparent he was not going to.

"Let me unlock the door. It's always locked. As I told you, one way in; another way out. This door doesn't open until I'm ready for you. You are early today, but there is no one ahead of you, so come on in."

He followed her through the door into a small hall with two doors. She unlocked the one on the left. As she did, she pointed to the other. "Sometimes, I have to separate the people." She added with a smile, "Or else they might kill each other." Then, with a frown: "Or me." She smiled again.

He did not smile back. He was obviously nervous and remained standing as she sat on an overstuffed chair, pulling her feet under her.

"Sit down, please, Michael," she said, motioning to a chair with an ottoman in front of it. He realized that he had not known what to expect. Perhaps a Freudian couch. Perhaps something out of a Woody Allen movie. Hardly a warm and friendly, slender woman, in long khaki pants, sitting on an overstuffed chair with her legs pulled up, sipping from a coffee cup with an Italian name stenciled on its side.

He sat, rather rigid, with his feet on the floor.

"Do you know who I am?" he asked her.

"Michael, isn't it?" Sally asked, sipping her coffee.

"I'm Michael Cassidy. I'm a judge."

"Sorry," said Sally, her face showing no hint of recognition. "Now, if you had said David Cassidy, I would have asked for your autograph."

He did not recognize the name.

"Michael," she said, putting her coffee down on a lamp table, "relax. Put your feet up. We are two people who are going to spend a nice Friday afternoon getting to know each other. Want some coffee?"

"Sure," he said, his first decisive act of the day.

"It'll be burnt and thick. That's why I went out. But it's hot."

Sally came back with coffee in a ceramic 49ers cup.

"Put your feet up," she said again, holding up the coffee as a prize for obedience. He did.

"Good," she said, handing him the cup.

He smiled a bit. "Thanks."

"So tell me about your wife. After 17 years, you should be through anger and at fondness, not stuck at love. She must be a doozie," Sally opened.

"She is. Was," he corrected himself.

For an hour he described Mai. They both laughed often, but Sally laughed more at Mai's antics since she was hearing the stories for the first time, whereas Michael had lived and relived each incident a thousand times in his mind.

There was no diagnosis at the end of the hour. No advice. No shared insights. Sally just asked him if he would like to come back and talk some more. He said he would.

When he left, through the rear door, she wrote "MK" in her appointment book, the variation of his initials she had decided upon for Michael Cassidy. She put them at the following Friday, 4 o'clock, his next appointment. Same time. Same place. Then she took out a new notebook, put "MK" at the top of the first page, along with the date and a few notes of their meeting. Notes no one would ever see. If a client's records were ever subpoenaed, she would provide only the list of visits on her billing records. There were no "records." This notebook did not exist. Yet, out of her normal caution, she kept even this nonexistent notebook cryptic:

MK. Reep. Rawhide. Uncomf. Self. In love with a mime. Stuck at the Buena Vista.

She knew who he was. He was a "Reep," a Republican, which partly explained his problem, she mused, when put in context with Mai, the "mime" he had first met and fallen in love with at the Buena Vista. She knew, from newspaper stories, that he had been in Washington as an assistant to Attorney General Edwin Meese and "Rawhide," the not-so-secret code name for President Ronald Reagan. It would all come out in time. No point in volunteering things that would scare him off. He seemed like a decent enough person, "for a Reep." Maybe she could "cure him." She smiled at the thought. He was clearly uncomfortable with who he was and yearned for a person who was all that he was not.

It was Friday. She thought briefly of getting a drink. Maybe at the Buena Vista?

"Go home, Sally," she told herself.

Then she added in his notebook: "A mime is a terrible thing to lose."

Chapter 59

Michael

IT WAS NO secret. Michael Cassidy was being groomed for the California Supreme Court. His appointment to the Superior Court, directly out of Reagan's Justice Department, and then to the Court of Appeal in San Francisco after just three years on the bench, made it clear that he was on a special track and had powerful supporters. By 1990, with the election of Republican Pete Wilson as governor, it was only a matter of time until a vacancy occurred on the Court. Pete was going for 16 years of Republican control of the governorship and completion of the destruction of the liberal California Supreme Court, which demise his Republican predecessor had championed in 1986 with a bitter recall vote and ouster of Rose Bird, Cruz Reynoso, and Joseph Grodin—"the bitch, the Mexican, and the liberal" left over from Jerry Brown's days.

Bitterness begets bitterness. There were those who vowed that Michael Cassidy would never sit on the California Supreme Court. Chief among them was Ernesto Zapata Reynoso.

It was not his political enemies that Michael feared in seeing a therapist. It was his own embarrassment that he needed someone to logically walk him through his feelings; that he could not work them out for himself. It would be an acknowledgment of weakness; of failure. That others would know was just the public acknowledgment of his failure. He did not want to appear pathetic. A person to feel sorry for. He wanted his loss to be private. Accomplishments, not feelings, were what mattered. Satisfaction came from a life of accomplishments. He hated liberal judges who anguished publicly. They wrung their hands. Complained that the system was not fair, that they so wished the law was different and they did not have to do what they did, but they did it anyway and told everyone how sorry they were. But they did it. And all the liberals said, "What a wonder-

369

ful, humane, and decent guy." Better yet, if a liberal found himself in a crowd of judges, one "decent, humane, and wonderful guy," he could write a dissenting opinion saying how terrible the rest of his colleagues were. Being a dissenter, Michael thought, meant never having to take responsibility. He told Sally all of this, and more.

Sally Conrad's style permitted a recitation of the facts of his life, his upbringing, his marriage, career, and divorce, and the resulting depression Michael felt and the continuing longing he called love, for a half dozen sessions. Enough to get comfortable with each other. Enough that he put his feet on the ottoman without prompting. Then she started her work.

"Michael, will you do something for me?" Sally asked.

"Sure. What?"

"Go fly a kite!"

He laughed, thinking she was commenting on his statements to her.

She was smiling but not laughing. "I mean it. I want you to go fly a kite. Go down to Chinatown. Get one of those great big box kites or a dragon kite or whatever you want. Then go out to the beach. Maybe up near the Maritime Museum. Always guaranteed wind there. And fly a kite. Just you. Alone. Think you could do that?"

"What's the point?" Michael asked, realizing that she was serious.

She leaned forward. "That's the point, Michael. There is no point. It's just play."

He did not seem persuaded.

"Would Mai go fly a kite because she felt like it?" Sally asked.

"Sure, but she would do just about anything crazy," he quickly responded.

"Right, and you love that about her. Spontaneity, 'crazy' things. Things you could never bring yourself to do, right, Michael?" She added, "Do you think you could act like a mime on a street corner?"

"Of course not. I'm a judge. What would people say?"

"They might say, 'That's one wonderful, humane, decent guy,'" Sally said as she threw the phrase back at him.

"What's the harm in harmless acts? It's inside us, isn't it? Something that won't let us do it. Makes us uncomfortable. But we admire it in others. Why do you think that is, Michael?"

"I wish I could do those things," he finally admitted.

"We all do, Michael," Sally said reassuringly. "That's what you miss so much in Mai. She gave you that part of yourself. She's gone, Michael. But you still have it in you to develop; that freedom in yourself."

He knew she was right.

"God, I miss her," he said, his voice choked.

"Of course you do. You still love her, but you're not in love with her, Michael. You love the memory. What it represents. You've clung to it because you're afraid to let yourself go. I bet you didn't even do pot or drugs in the '60s because you didn't want to lose control."

He wiped his eyes. "You're right, again."

"Let's stop fantasizing about Mai and work on you, Michael. Okay?" she said to signal the end of the hour.

He stood up and looked at Sally like an embarrassed, vulnerable little boy who had just wet his pants in front of his first grade teacher.

He got his first hug from Sally.

"See you next week. Let me know how the kite flying goes."

He hugged her back. He managed only one word.

"Thanks."

Chapter 60

Michael

ERNESTO Z. REYNOSO had joined the Boalt Hall clinical program teaching staff in 1985 with the establishment of the Center for Social Justice. At age 53, he had left a distinguished career at California Rural Legal Assistance recognized as probably the top public interest attorney in the country. His duties as Director of the Center included teaching public interest litigation, filing *amicus curiae* briefs in major public interest cases, and running a clinical program of practical experience for second- and third-year students. His career path, as an activist and public interest attorney, was not the traditional path to a Boalt professorship—which usually required attendance at a prestigious school, law review, clerkships, and a brief stint at a major corporate law firm—but it was more in keeping with the new look of Boalt. The same look that made room for the *La Raza Law Journal* in room 585 of Simon Hall at the law school. Ernesto was selected by the students to be its faculty advisor.

Reynoso was also an active participant in Moot Court, acting as one of three judges assigned to evaluate students' advocacy skills. The Moot Court is a law school tradition that pits two teams of law students against each other to argue a hypothetical case before judges acting as an appellate court. As is expected of lawyers in a real appellate court, the students need to be prepared on the law and the facts, and any possible cases that might bear upon the issue. It is not infrequent—in fact part of the exercise—that judges interrupt a student's presentation at any time with questions or comments that might deliver a crushing or glancing blow, depending on how the student handles the intrusion. Some students demonstrate mental facility; some are so rattled as to lose all ability to speak.

In the fall of 1989, the hypothetical question at Boalt Hall's Moot Court was stated as follows:

John Doe, a white male, was denied admission to the school of law at Berkeley, California, even though his grades and LSAT scores were higher than those of a number of black, Hispanic, and Asian males, and a number of females. He contends that his rejection was because of his race and gender, and the use of each in the selection process was in violation of his constitutional rights under the Fourteenth Amendment's guarantee of equal protection of the law.

The University argues that certain races and the female gender have been historically underrepresented in the field of law and that an affirmative program is needed to recruit such persons. It denies that it selected students based on race, but claims that it merely took into consideration economic status and diversity of life experiences, illustrated by essays written by persons who would not otherwise have made the list of slots available for entering students based on grades and LSAT scores alone. Applicants were urged to submit a photo of themselves with their application.

Michael Cassidy had accepted the law school's invitation to participate as a Moot Court judge. It was not unusual that he was asked to serve. Whenever possible, Boalt preferred to use its own graduates who had achieved high standing in the judiciary. Nor was it unusual that a member of the faculty would participate on the panel.

Cassidy found, on arriving at the Gordon Johnson Moot Court chambers, that he had been paired with Judge Melvin Huffsteider and Ernesto Zapata Reynoso.

Melvin Huffsteider was a federal judge and a Boalt graduate. A Carter appointee, he had come to the bench after a distinguished career defending major media clients in free press and speech cases. He had enjoyed the luxury of being a partner in a large Los Angeles law firm with Establishment credentials, while arguing constitutional law on behalf of companies with unlimited assets. It was a rare position for a constitutional scholar.

With Huffsteider and Reynoso, Cassidy knew he would be in the minority with his conservative views. Nevertheless, he meant to have a good time challenging the students and putting them through their paces. It was, after all, "moot" court, not the real world yet, for these students. The object was to get the students out of their prepared speeches, to force them to defend their positions against unexpected arguments.

A student seeking to strike down the University's affirmative action policy began the oral argument. He ran into Reynoso immediately.

"Counsel, do you really think 'equal protection of law' can happen by simply ignoring 300 years of American history? Most minorities, especially blacks, didn't start out equal. We have a history of repression, the effects of which are still with us. How can we wake up one morning and declare that everyone is now equal?"

"Well," began the student, "it's a…slippery slope when the law starts using race as one of the conditions for admission—"

He was immediately interrupted. "Well, isn't it a slippery slope we've put minorities on when they are systematically excluded by our requirements from higher education and therefore never to have a fair chance to participate meaningfully in our society?" asked Reynoso.

"Does the same argument apply to Asians?" Cassidy interjected.

The question hung in the air since it was not directed so much at the student as at Reynoso. The student looked at both of them.

"Asians," Cassidy continued. "I understand that few white students get into the hard sciences, like chemistry, at Berkeley, because Asians beat them out on grades and test scores. Apparently there are other departments, like engineering, where foreign students are filling the slots. On merit. So, to give white people a chance against Asians, or Arabs, or Pakistanis, is it all right to have a preference for white people?"

The student immediately picked up the argument. "Of course not. That's my point, Justice Cassidy. Once we start assigning seats by race, who is to say where it will end? It would be equally improper to assign seats to white people."

Reynoso was now looking directly at Cassidy but addressing the student advocate. "But counsel, there has never been a need to assign seats to white males by race. They have always had a disproportionate place at the table, have they not?"

But it was Cassidy who replied. "Until now, it appears. It seems whites can't compete with Asians in math and science, at least here at Berkeley."

Judge Huffsteider noted that the student's time to argue had expired and called on the proponent of the University's policy. In an appellate court, time waited for no attorney. The fact that the litigants had spent less of their time arguing to the Court than being used as foils by the judges to argue among themselves did not change the rules.

"If it pleases the Court," said the young woman who had stepped to the podium. Reynoso did not wait for the student to deliver her prepared statement. He knew Erin Polansky was a top student. In fact, one of his best.

"Ms. Polansky, how would you answer Justice Cassidy's argument for white preference or set-asides at the University?"

Cassidy smiled. Of course he had not argued for white preference. But it was Moot Court. Let the student handle the issue.

"I sympathize with Justice Cassidy," Ms. Polansky answered, causing Reynoso to look up quickly and arch his eyebrows.

She continued: "It must come as a shock for the white male, who has always enjoyed the full benefits of our society and the premier position of power, to find that he must now compete for that which was always his birthright. But the difference is that when a woman or a minority achieves a position usually reserved for a white male, it is by overcoming the odds, not by taking advantage of them. What we argue for is not the exception achieved at unfair odds, but a leveling of the playing field to take into consideration the historic realities and other indices of academic success and life experiences."

It was a good, in-your-face argument; bold, Cassidy thought. She would be a good advocate, although she acted a tad condescending and left the weak point in her argument at the end to jump upon.

"Thank you for your sympathy," Cassidy began. The audience laughed. "We white guys appreciate it," he added, gesturing to the bench.

Reynoso did not appreciate being included in the sweep of Cassidy's hand. He shot him a look.

"Other indices of academic success and life experiences," he repeated. "It's not really 'life experiences' the University is asking for, it's really an invitation to give information about race and ethnicity, isn't it, Ms. Polansky?"

"No, applicants can talk about whatever they feel would reflect upon their special suitability for study at Berkeley. That's what the application says. There is no reason to believe the University is using this as a subterfuge," she replied confidently.

"Why then does the University ask for a picture with the application except to ascertain whether an applicant is black or white, brown, Asian, or 'other'?" Cassidy asked.

"The picture is optional," the student pointed out.

"Yes, it says that, but any black kid who knows the University is trying to recruit more blacks would be stupid not to attach a picture, right?" asked Cassidy.

Judge Huffsteider spoke up. "Ms. Polansky, why can't we all put our cards on the table? If, as you say, there is a historical imperative that demands we use race and gender to achieve equal protection of the law, why can't we just say so and stop talking about 'life experiences'?"

Ms. Polansky looked pained. "I agree, your honor. There is no question, as Professor Reynoso says, that equal protection can only be achieved by using race and gender preferences. I believe that is supported—indeed, compelled—by the Fourteenth Amendment, especially when one looks at the historical origins of the Amendment rooted in the movement to give rights to the freed slaves. But..."

"Does that history include women?" interjected Cassidy.

She turned quickly, facing him with her whole body. "I think we could make a strong case that slavery has been practiced with regards to women, too."

She paused, holding her stare. She then turned back to Huffsteider. "But our job as attorneys appears to be to disguise the remedy sufficiently to make what is constitutionally required publicly acceptable. Given that, this Court need only uphold the University's action on the basis that it is not for the Court to assume an improper purpose on what appears to be a gender- and race-neutral selection process."

She sat down. Her team partner stood and approached the lectern.

"Do you agree with what your co-counsel just said?" Cassidy asked, as the young man reached the podium.

"You mean about women being slaves?" he asked.

Everyone roared with laughter. Even Ms. Polansky. Cassidy laughed too, then picked up the question again.

"Well, I was thinking of her point that we all know what's going on here, but as a Court we shouldn't go behind the words. I guess close our eyes to discrimination is her argument. Do you agree?"

Ms. Polansky startled everyone when she jumped up and shouted, "I never said close your eyes to discrimination, Justice Cassidy. I said open them!"

There was stunned silence.

Michael Cassidy folded his hands at his chin, resting on his elbows, and gazed at Ms. Polansky without saying anything. She sat, satisfied with herself, as her partner tentatively returned to his argument. Michael said nothing further during the presentations.

There was a large story, complete with a photograph of Justice Cassidy, in the *San Francisco Chronicle* two days later. A box carried the quote of Ms. Polansky's statement: "I never said close your eyes to discrimination, Justice Cassidy. I said open them!"

His probing questions about preferences now sounded like an argument for 'set-asides' for whites who could not compete with "Asians, Arabs, or Pakistanis." The quotes were there, evidence that a recorded transcript had been made and shared with the media.

Justice Pacino came by Michael's chambers mid-morning to offer condolences. He knew how the hypothetical Moot Court was supposed to work.

"Michael, you've been set up," he offered.

"And I know by whom," Cassidy added. "They've made me sound like a racist." His thoughts turned to his son. He picked up the phone and called Robert Fong Cassidy—"Robbie."

It hurt, he admitted to himself. And he admitted it to his therapist, Sally Conrad. To everyone else, he appeared defiant, arrogant, as he refused to comment on the controversy surrounding him.

If Reynoso thought the controversy and label "bigot" would derail Cassidy's career, he was wrong. Governor Pete Wilson's first nominee to the California Supreme Court, when the opportunity arose, was Michael Cassidy.

Chapter 61

Brian

THEY NAMED HER Randy—and she changed their lives.

Brian could even joke that it rhymed with brandy.

Brian and Shelly became expectant parents—but with only four weeks' notice. The adoption agency, once it agreed to accept them, with assurance from Brian's counselor, notified them that an available child was to be born in a month, on November 15, 1989. Shelly decided that she would take hormones to simulate a pregnancy and hopefully develop breast milk to breast-feed. Brian was worried, given her history of cancer, about her taking hormones. At his request, they met, together this time, with her gynecologist and decided that the importance to Shelly of bonding with the child outweighed the slight risk associated with hormones in a 46-year-old adopting mother.

"Besides," she added, "you always wanted me to have big breasts."

"That's not true. I love you the way you are."

"Yeah, but you'd love me more if I had big tits."

"Well, sure, but…"

She threw a pot holder at him as he ran from the kitchen, laughing.

With only four weeks, they prepared her room and purchased all of the furniture and clothing for a child. They knew the baby would be a girl. They both wanted a girl.

"A dad is very special in a girl's life," Shelly told him.

He worried whether he would be up to the responsibility, since he felt he had failed so miserably as a husband.

When the agency had asked if they were interested in adopting a minority, impaired, or foster child, Shelly had said "no" immediately. Brian had not given it any thought until that moment. But he had said nothing. When he thought about it later, he felt maybe they should consider, politically, the option and be open to the idea. But the more he thought about it, the more he felt, emotionally, that he wanted a child he would not have to explain. Not black. Not brown. Not a crack baby. A little girl about whom teachers could say, "She looks just like her mother, Mr. Jacobs."

Shelly knew him well enough to save the political anguish. She relieved him of the soul searching and guilt. "No," she had answered firmly.

Randy did look like her mother: a tall Ukranian girl of 23, with dark hair, long eyelashes, a thin nose between hazel eyes, and delicate, long fingers. The mother had been studying music at UCLA and had "gotten herself pregnant," is how it was put. She obviously knew who the father was, but would not say out of fear. She could not tell her fiancé in Kiev, to whom she was to return at the end of her two years of study. The nondisclosure of the father's identity worried Brian. Proper notice of adoption could not be given to him in order to cut off his rights to the child. What if he came forward later? On the other hand, it sounded unlikely that he was in a position or wanted (if he even knew) to assert parental rights. Shelly did not care. She wanted the child.

Randy was three days old when they took her from the hospital. On seeing her in Shelly's arms and the tears of joy rolling down Shelly's face, Brian knew he could never drink again.

Randy came home to a house better designated "baby central." Monitors were in place in the nursery, on the main floor, capable of picking up the slightest sound and transmitting it to one of the two portable, clip-on speakers provided. The baby was to spend the first three months in a bassinet in their bedroom. The stairway from the bedroom had a child gate in place, screwed into the wall as recommended (not just pressure mounted), even though the baby would not crawl for eight or nine more months. Brian had managed to install it himself, using extremely large wood screws, into the wall studs he was able to locate with his new stud finder, obtained with a comprehensive tool set he felt he now needed with a child in the home.

As planned, Shelly gave up her teaching job to be a teacher for one. Everything she had ever learned about children had been in anticipation of this job as a mother. They had talked at length about parenting. How he should have one day a week alone caring for the child; how they would alternate feeding the baby, putting her in her bed, playing with her; and how, as she grew, they should have meals together as a family. At first, Brian thought Shelly was giving him responsibilities because of his alcoholism—testing him, aiding his recovery. He was taken aback when his therapist suggested that it was not about him, but rather about Randy. Shelly's focus was on what the child needed, not what might help the father with his recovery.

"It's not always about you, Brian" was the phrase that resonated with him.

He took off from work most of the month to be with Shelly and Randy. There were two hearings he just could not change or get someone else to handle: an oral argument at the Court of Appeal on the constitutionality of a Los Angeles city ordinance used to regulate topless bars—he was still the lawyer for the porno shops that had paid the bills when the law office opened—and the arraignment, in a new case, of an aging Black Panther, who had shot it out with the LAPD when the police had attempted to serve an out-of-state warrant on Bobbie D. Cleveland, now Mohammad Asiz.

Driving to work, he had to admit that while he was restless for the courtroom, he felt good having something called a family to come home to. Especially, to come home to sober. To hold the baby, without fear that he might fall on her or drop her. He knew he still had a long way to go with Shelly. He understood, intellectually, that she was guarding against the day he would fall back into the pit. She was not going there with him. Not again. Not now, with Randy. Not ever.

Intellectually, he understood. Emotionally, he was hanging on. Hanging on to the hope that he and Shelly had a future. Everything they planned with Randy was the assurance of another day together. Ironically, he knew, Randy made it easier for Shelly to leave because, with Randy, she could have a future with no past to burden her. She could wrap herself in Randy and be happy. As she had told him, "If things don't change, you can always go. I will keep her." She had been honest. Shelly never saw the baby as a means of changing their relationship. She just wanted a baby. At this point in her life, he was optional, and he knew it.

The invitation was thrown out casually. But it had been a long time, and the import did not escape him.

"Why don't you put Randy to bed and I'll turn on the jacuzzi," Shelly said as the sun was setting over the canyon walls.

His automatic thought was to get the champagne they always drank in the jacuzzi. He could taste the cold bubbles with the smell of chlorine rising from the warm water.

Then he remembered. The jacuzzi had not been used for over a year. He had not taken a drink in 11 months.

"Shelly, we're going to have to drain and clean the jacuzzi before we can use it. Maybe I could call someone in and we could use it this weekend."

Shelly handed him the baby and walked toward the sliding door that opened to the deck. As she did, she was talking.

"I had it cleaned this afternoon while you were at work. It's at 101 degrees."

She reached the door and slid it open.

"Why don't you put Randy to bed and bring the monitor."

She undid her robe and let it fall to the floor. She was naked.

"Bring us some plastic glasses of water."

She looked over her shoulder and smiled: "And a tall glass of crushed ice cubes. See if I still remember what to do with them."

Brian started toward her, then realizing he was holding Randy, turned and bolted for the stairs. He heard Shelly laughing behind him. Laughing as he had not heard her laugh in years.

Chapter 62

Michael

"JUSTICE CASSIDY, WHILE you were on the bench this morning, an attorney called from Los Angeles. He said it was important for you to call him back."

Ruth Chin had been Michael Cassidy's secretary for only a few months, but she had been with the Court of Appeal for 18 years. It was rare for a lawyer to seemingly direct an appellate court justice to call him back; rather, the protocol was to ascertain when the judge might be available to take a call. If the call was on a matter before the Court, which would be a standard question Ruth would ask, Ruth would make it clear to the caller that any *ex parte* communication was prohibited.

He waited for an explanation.

"Frankly, he was very abrupt but said the call was personal and that you were together at Boalt Hall."

For months, the fact of Michael's legal education at one of the leading—read that, liberal—law schools in the country had been used against him by one of Boalt's leading leftist professors, Ernesto Zapata Reynoso. Since the governor had announced his intention to name Michael to the California Supreme Court, Michael had been called a "bigot" and his life of service summarized as the waste of a fine legal education. No one at Boalt had rushed to defend him. After all, he had aligned himself with Attorney General Meese and, therefore, Ronald Reagan. So it was with some concern that he reached for the phone message held out to him by Ruth Chin.

Jackson Bridgeport III. (213) 555-1000.

"Call by 5 P.M. today."

He remembered Jackson from school. Tall. Well-dressed. Arrogant.

His first instinct was to throw the phone message away.

Ruth pointed to the note: "He said he was going into a State Bar meeting at 5:30."

The governor's office had warned him not to make any statements about his nomination to anyone except through its channels. He was aware the State Bar was to pass on his qualifications, and while its determination was not binding, it could potentially derail his nomination, if unfavorable. Now a classmate was calling on the very eve of a State Bar meeting. Was this another Boalt ambush?

He walked back to his office and sat at his desk. What would Bridgeport ask? He jotted a list: death penalty; Rose Bird; mandatory State Bar dues; tort reform. He knew the standard evasive judicial responses and also how to suggest that he might yet do what the listener wanted. His judicial record was meager and thus hard to pin down. Which is why opposition had focused on the politics of his patrons.

Then, with annoyance, he crumpled up the list and threw it into the garbage. At the same time, he picked up the phone and dialed Bridgeport's number. He was surprised with the almost-immediate, and impatient, response: "Bridgeport!"

"Is this Jackson Bridgeport?"

"Yes. Who's this?"

"Justice Cassidy, returning your call." Apparently the number Jackson had left was his direct line.

"Oh, Michael." Jackson could not bring himself to the deference solicited by the title of "Justice" Cassidy. "Listen, this is a confidential and personal call. I've been appointed to head up the State Bar committee to evaluate you on your nomination to the Supreme Court. You probably didn't know that, did you?"

"Well, no. The governor's office has been handling all aspects of the nomination."

"They're idiots. I requested the appointment to head up the committee and had enough clout to get it."

"Why, may I ask?" Michael was not sure this communication was ethical, but he could not put a stop to it.

"Because if someone with balls doesn't stop it, you are going to get railroaded by the State Bar. They are dominated by left-wingers; not in numbers, but in action. That's why they are out there taking all kinds of social policy positions on the death penalty, abortion, immigrants, and every popular cause in the Legislature, instead of focusing on the profession. No one wants to stand up and say, 'enough.'"

"What's that got to do with me?" asked Michael.

"First, I want to know, are there any skeletons in your closet, illegitimate kids, kickbacks, anything that is going to embarrass me?" asked Jackson.

"No, of course not."

"Don't kid yourself, Judge. There are very few of us who could weather the scrutiny you will be under without something coming out. I just want to know whether to go out on a limb for you."

Michael reflected. He and Jackson had not been friends in school, just classmates. He had not seen him since law school and, as best he knew, Jackson's firm had never appeared before him in court or sought his help in the state or national political arena.

"Jackson, why would you want to go out on a limb for me, anyway?"

"Well, don't let it go to your head, Michael, but I think you are a pretty decent guy. That's how you impressed me in school. If I was governor, I wouldn't nominate you. But I think you're reasonably qualified. You're not a genius or a scholar, but you are bright enough and hardworking. Since you've spent your life in public service, I know you haven't made any money. I think the way you are being treated is just plain wrong, and I want to take the politics out and bring some integrity to the judicial selection process. Governors come and go; the institutions of the law are what's important. End of speech."

Michael did not know what to say.

"So," added Jackson, "be a damn good judge. Don't let me down. Oh, and don't tell anyone I called."

Michael was going to thank him, but Jackson hung up.

Chapter 63

Leon

IT WAS NOT the first time he had been to their Oakland home. The first time was in 1987. Though they had no reason to know, it was the same night Brian Jacobs was entering a Chinese restaurant in Los Angeles under the impression that he was going to a birthday party for his wife.

Their visitor had sought them out, that first time, as many did, to introduce himself "and share ideas." The occasion was a $1,000-a-plate dinner, in their spacious garden, for Senator Alan Cranston. The fact that he had invited himself, and stayed late with a small group in the library, was more a measure of their national reputation than his bad manners. They were impressed with his intellect and his ideas, although Leon was put off by his accent.

As his standing rose, so did their interest in him. The next time, in 1989, the small "gathering of friends" at the house was for him, at their invitation. He stayed the weekend, and they talked into the night about racism, poverty, economic justice, the Third World—issues that passionately moved him. When he left, they were convinced that he was genuine. He could make a difference.

By November, 1991, they had raised over $1,000,000 for him, $100,000 of which was their own money. Leon's money.

But this time was different. A "who's who" of California Democratic politics and their major contributors lined the steps outside Leon and Angela's residence for the exclusive invitation-only party. Guarded barricades ringed the surrounding streets, holding back crowds of photographers, supporters, demonstrators, and the just curious. Leon and Angela stood at the open door, at the top of the stairs, with their daughter in front of them, standing tall like her mother, long ebony arms hanging along her brightly colored dress. She was, her dad always said, just like her mother: "Tall, beautiful, intelligent, and with a mouth on her."

The noise level increased in anticipation as the limousines pulled up to the front steps of the manicured garden leading up the steep entry to the house. An athletic-looking young man quickly reached for the rear passenger door as another two cleared the area for exit, their eyes watching the guests, row by row.

He was, as always, relaxed. Comfortable with himself. Enjoying the spotlight. He looked up toward the crowds and waved. He stepped slowly, as athletes often do before a burst of energy. Taking it all in, biting his lower lip, conserving his reactions. He was shaking hands, on each side of the walkway, when his eyes met hers.

"Mandela!" he exclaimed. He brushed through the hands reaching for him and bounded the remaining steps to the half-circle stone bench on the right side of the top landing where she stood. As he did, he grabbed her hand and sat her on the bench next to him.

"My God, you've grown! Look at you. Y'all look just like your mama. And I hear you're just as smart, too."

Mandela smiled and, without showing any sign of intimidation, replied: "Smarter."

They all laughed, and he gave her a hug as the cameras clicked.

Leon and Angela both looked on with pride and satisfaction. Parents could not want for much more.

He seemed just like the person he had been on every other visit. But now it was different. William Jefferson Clinton was the president of the United States.

Chapter 64

Brian

WHILE RANDY WAS in Montessori preschool, Shelly loved spending mornings in her garden. Back to her Israeli roots, as Brian called it, making the desert of Los Angeles blossom as had her parents in the desert of her childhood in Israel. It was she, not he, who carried the rocks down the embankment under the house to make the steps. She built the forms and had the cement poured for the greenhouse foundation. She cleared the weeds and cut the wild canyon manzanita back, worked the soil with additives, and planted the garden. Looking over the balcony decks, over the back of the house, visitors would marvel at the maze of rocked pathways, covered with moss, with Virginia creepers and other small leaf, ivy-like plants crawling over the retaining walls. Under the cantilever house was deep tropical vegetation moistened by misters Shelly had personally hung from the floor joists: tree ferns, birds of paradise, daily flowering hibiscus, and even orchids in the hot summer (that would be returned to the hothouse in the winter).

She did not fault him for not participating in her gardening. It was her solitude. Her meditation. Her pleasure. She enjoyed sharing the results, walking with him in the garden and showing him her day's work. It was all hers. Satisfying. A visitor to the garden did not even have to look over the railing for the garden to evidence itself. As if seeing someone approaching, the banana bushes on the lower level, the trumpet vine trailing up into the tree, the large magnolia blossoms down the hill hanging over a small pond, and even the sweet-smelling gardenias among the small ferns gave away their presence. Especially at night.

An evening walk through the garden, with a tall glass of ice and Diet Pepsi—Brian's new dark drink of choice—was a requirement most spring and summer evenings, especially if Shelly had been planting. If it was dark when he arrived home, the least they would do would be a visit to the railing.

Randy, now 3½, even had her own garden area, bucket, shovel, and watering can. With little leather boots, tan shorts, t-shirt, and dark hair, with what could pass for Mediterranean coloring, she looked the part of a little Kibbutzer. Her garden turned out to be a rock garden. Her little toy shovel and bucket were really made for the beach. Shelly let her play in a pile of sand. All the rocks Shelly cleared from her own garden, Randy took and built miniature paths within hers. But Randy was adamant about the plants she wanted at the nursery—cactuses. She kept herself busy rearranging her paths, carefully, through the small cactuses, and little rock houses, and watering all of it repeatedly after preschool. She, too, wanted daddy to see what she had done in her garden each day.

Some days, if a court day was cut short by a lack of evidence, or a deposition finished early, Brian would call Shelly and pick up Randy from preschool. Not often, but enough that Shelly kept her cell phone in the garden. He treasured those times. Going to the school. Not just to save Shelly the trip, but to have the experience of Randy seeing him, running with delight, and grabbing him around the leg, shouting, "Daddy, Daddy, Daddy!" It was rarely planned because his movements could not be planned. If a client called, he would be on the phone. If a deposition ran late, he could not just walk out. He did not mean to forget; he did not love them less. But the practice of law, his way, was all-consuming. The client came first. No; the case came first. *Winning* the case came first.

Shelly long ago stopped competing with the law. Sometimes, it demanded his complete, undivided attention. Other times, she could distract him for periods. Blocks of time, between major events. But it was always there, the noise in his head, planning, tactics, devastating cross-examinations, summations of oratory for closing arguments. He had explained to her once the theory of his success: "I've seen the trial a thousand times played out in my mind. I've walked through every minefield. Avoided every blow-up. Found the way to victory. The trial is anti-climactic, but it is a gauntlet I have to go through."

They were exhausting work, these trials in his head. Especially since they went on 24 hours a day, regardless of where he was or with whom, and what else was going on around him.

So it was unusual that Randy's school called him at 5:30 in the afternoon to ask who was picking up Randy. He was in with a new client, regarding an "alleged"—as he would say—gang-related shooting by a 23-year-old unemployed black defendant, who somehow had the $25,000 retainer to hire one of the top criminal defense attorneys in Los Angeles. It was not Brian's job to ask where his client obtained the money. His focus was on the government's burden to prove, with constitutionally admissible evidence, that his client was guilty of the crime charged. Nothing else. It was not for him to say, "Where did you get $25,000 in cash?" Or to ask of the new client his relationship with the former client and "alleged" gang member who accompanied him to Brian's office.

An associate attorney had taken the call since the secretaries had left for the evening. He did not know enough not to interrupt a new case interview. Brian believed the first meeting between an attorney and a client was the most important; it was there a bond was established and trust developed with the client. Taking phone calls during the interview meant that the new client was not the most important thing in the lawyer's life, as he ought to be—at least for that hour.

Annoyed, Brian excused himself to call the preschool teacher back from an adjacent office. His personal life was not a proper subject to interject into the somber tones of a P.C. 145—attempted murder—interview. He left his associate with his client. "Never leave a client, or opposing counsel, alone in your office," he always said, "unless you want them to see something you set out for them."

"Hi, Ms. Morgan. This is Brian Jacobs. What's the problem?" He listened to Ms. Morgan. "No, her mom was supposed to pick her up. I have no idea. Why don't I call her right now? I'll call you right back." He listened again. "Yes, I appreciate you close at 6:30. I'll call you back immediately."

He hung up and punched in the cell phone number for Shelly. If she was in her car, stuck in traffic…but then she would have called…or she forgot and was still working in the yard…but she would never forget. Had he said he would pick Randy up? No, he never did that going into the office. He would never know in advance. He could not understand what could have happened.

The phone rang. Once. It was picked up, then went dead. He called back. No answer. He called repeatedly. No answer. Perhaps, he thought, Shelly was at the school and shut off the engine, killing the phone, to run in and get Randy.

He called the school. They had not seen or heard from anyone but wanted someone there right away to pick up Randy. It was almost 6:00 P.M. Brian needed to get back to his client. The client would be restless and starting to complain to the associate: "Well, if he's too busy to take my case..." It was not like Shelly. "Maybe she has been in an accident on the freeway," he thought.

He needed Randy picked up. Maybe he could ask the associate to go and get her while he finished the interview.

He stopped at the closed door to his office, his hand on the doorknob. "Where were you?" He shuddered on remembering her voice.

"I had cancer, you bastard. I could have died. Where were you? Where were you?"

He was not going to fail her again.

He opened the door but did not step through. "Parker, will you finish up getting the information and retainer? I have an emergency."

He did not wait for a response. He turned and ran out of the building to his car.

At 17:46, May 8, 1993, according to the official report of the Los Angeles County Sheriff's Department, Officer Brandon Cory was on routine patrol in the residential area of Laurel Canyon near Mulholland Drive when he stopped a BMA—black male adult—driving an older model Ford van in a "suspicious manner."

> Subject appeared apprehensive upon seeing the marked patrol vehicle. RO [reporting officer] followed subject for approximately one mile during which subject made a number of turns which appeared designed to evade RO. Finally, subject was pulled over to establish identity and confirm ownership of vehicle. Upon approaching vehicle, RO noted that subject appeared to lean forward as if to hide or reach for something. RO ordered subject out of the vehicle and onto the ground. Upon a search of the interior of the vehicle, a cellular phone was found under the driver's seat.

It was Shelly's cell phone.

Chapter 65

Brian

HE INSISTED ON seeing everything. The scene. Pictures. He forced himself to read every word. The police report. The statements. Even the preliminary autopsy report. Just as he would if he were defending the case of a person accused of murder.

He had read hundreds of coroners' reports. They were all so clinical. The format everywhere the same: Jackson, Mississippi; Chicago, Illinois; Los Angeles, California. Coroners all went to the same schools of pathology. Out of habit, he looked for discrepancies.

Name: ___Shelly Jacobs___ Case No.: ___93-00137___

Date of Autopsy: ___May 9, 1993___ Time: ___0950___

Age: ___49___ Ethnicity: ___Caucasian___

Sex: ___Female___ Length: ___66 (inches)___

Weight: ___135___

The body is that of a well developed Caucasian woman whose appearance is consistent with her listed age of 49....three plus rigor present...post mortem lividity is noted along the lateral aspects of the torso...the decedent is identified by a coroner's tag attached to the left great toe.

The report proceeded with the external description, in the usual manner, from head to toe, then over to the back. The second paragraph described the neck:

The neck is symmetrical and normally formed. A deep laceration is seen approximately 10 cm across the anterior neck exposing

a severed trachea with a laceration extending through the esophagus, dissecting the carotid artery, the jugular veins to the level of
the cervical spine at C4...

He kept on reading.

> There are multiple small punctures of the back with imbedded
> glass. No other abnormal trauma is noted externally.
> The external genitalia are those of an apparently normally de-
> veloped adult female without evidence of trauma. A well-healed
> vertical scar, presumably surgical, from the umbilicus to the pubis
> symphysis, measuring 15 cm, is present.

He never asked. No one had said anything. But he wanted to know.
He began the section on the internal examination.

> The standard Y-shaped thoracoabdominal incision reveals...

He passed over the cardiovascular, respiratory, gastrointestinal, and
hepatobiliary systems, to the genitourinary system:

> The internal genitalia show no signs of recent trauma. Exami-
> nation reveals presumed surgical absence of the uterus, cervix and
> fundus, fallopian tubes, and ovaries bilaterally. There are no cysts,
> lesions, or other abnormalities.

There was no evidence Shelly had been raped.

The laceration of the throat, the trauma and small punctures to the
back, the location of the blood—and her cellular phone—all fit. Brian
knew she would have been in her garden all afternoon, down below the
house. She always kept the phone with her in case he called. She would
have come up at about 4:00 or at least by 4:30 to clean up and drive down
to get Randy.

A splattering of blood was at the door leading from the house onto the
back deck. Footprints in it. Then a torrent of blood all the way to the
railing, and her body found below, having crashed through the glass roof
of her hothouse, onto the cement floor she had installed. He knew, from
her injuries, that she would have died as her body racked to inhale one last
time with a lacerated esophagus and a severed aorta pumping blood everywhere, before she was pushed over the railing.

She did not show any signs of putting up a fight or warding off blows. Nothing under her nails, no cuts or bruises, no defensive marks such as lacerations on her arms. She probably saw him as she entered the sliding glass door, turned to run, and was caught from behind. One slash of a knife and she was a few seconds from death.

He also knew that if David Rodney Hall had a competent lawyer, he would walk. Brian did not need a Deputy District Attorney to tell him about the Fourth Amendment. He was Brian Jacobs, nationally known criminal defense attorney and constitutional expert.

In the ten days after Shelly's murder, Brian barely slept. He had not spent a night in their house. When the police left at 1:00 in the morning, he picked up the sleeping Randy from her room—he had picked her up from preschool and rushed home. They spent the rest of the night at his partner Paul Zarick's home.

That first morning, lying on the bed, still fully dressed and without sleep, he got up early and realized that he had no clothes for Randy. He drove back to the house to get them, determined to take Randy to school and pick her up as if nothing had happened.

He drove to his home before dawn. The police tape had been taken down. But the house looked different. Shrubs had been stepped on near the front door. A ceramic pot lay broken, the foxtail fern and exposed root ball on the entry steps. A coroner's gurney track cut through the scotch moss at the shaded curve in the walkway. The sprinklers were running. The door was unlocked.

Brian entered, his mind expecting to see Shelly sleepy-eyed, in the long t-shirt she often pulled on, to stagger out to the kitchen, and make him coffee and toast before he left for work. He saw her, one last time, and realized that her faint smile was saying goodbye. He looked through her, to the glass door, at the deck, and saw the blood. His body jerked, and he ran back outside and heaved into the shrubbery.

As he was bending, holding onto his knees, the fragrance of daphne brought him back. The daphne she had planted in the morning sun along the front of the house so that the bouquet would drift up to the open bedroom window in the late spring and early summer, and surround their bed with every breeze.

"...and here, last night, the wife of noted criminal defense attorney, Brian Jacobs, was murdered..."

The television camera peered into the gate and caught him standing there, with vomit on his shoes, disheveled, in the clothes that he had worn for 24 hours.

He ran at them, screaming, as if they were committing a sacrilege.

"Get out! Get out!"

The camera kept rolling. He looked for something to throw. The fountain statue.

They kept rolling.

He could not hear what the reporter was saying during the live broadcast, the blood was pounding so loud in his head. The TV crew kept its ground. The statue would not budge. Brian retreated to the house, locked the door so that they would not defile her memory with "live" blood shots promoted all day in teasers, between the soaps. He ran to the garage. He started the car. Before opening the garage door, he thought a moment about keeping it shut with the motor running, but then hit the remote and backed out at high speed. As he swerved onto the street in front of the house, the cameraman was running to get into position, with the flawlessly coiffed, on-air talent running with her remote microphone in hand, her high heels sinking into the grass surrounding his wall and gate.

"Mr. Jacobs. Mr. Jacobs...how do you feel..."

He sped off. It was the only time in his career he had not readily consented to an interview.

*   *   *   *   *

"We have some problems with the case, Mr. Jacobs."

Nelson Marquart was the Chief Deputy to the District Attorney of Los Angeles County. He was personally handling the case, in large measure in deference to Brian's status in the legal community. The conference was not offered to every victim or family member of people killed in L.A. District Attorneys are too busy. Prosecuting. Juggling hundreds of cases. Making deals. Not holding hands. This was special treatment.

"The search," Brian offered.

Marquart was relieved. Brian understood. It would make things easier.

"Yeah. The officer went too far. He was obviously inexperienced. His guts told him there was something wrong about this guy out there, but he had no basis to search the car."

"You mean because the suspect was a black man in a white neighborhood?"

"Well, that's what you…what the defense attorney is going to argue. Racial profiling. Unconstitutional search; maybe even the stop," added Marquart.

"So the man who murdered my wife is going to walk?" he asked Marquart, calmly.

Marquart squirmed. "Well, we need to meet with his public defender. See if we can get a plea." He paused. "To something."

"Like jaywalking?" asked Brian. Again, he said it quietly, as if he were genuinely entertaining the possibility.

What was he going to do? Would he explode? Hurt himself? Hurt others? Marquart wished he had brought in another deputy D.A., just in case.

"I propose we offer them burglary. It's a lesser included. This guy had about everything of value in your house lined up next to the front door. If your wife hadn't—"

"No," Brian interrupted, "we won't offer burglary." He said it as if he was in charge. As if with the word "we" he was the prosecutor rather than the bereaved husband. "This guy knows the system. I've seen his rap sheet. You offer burglary on a murder, he knows we have no case. He'll push for a suppression motion and roll the dice."

Marquart interrupted. "The P.D. has the police report. He knows the problem we have. He knows the search of the car is no good, and without it, there is nothing to tie this guy to the crime."

Brian was out of his chair. "You get the P.D. and that little scumbag that killed my wife in a room. You hand him a new information charging him with capital murder. Tell him he killed the wrong fuckin' woman and the D.A., the mayor, and the governor all want to see him in the gas chamber and it's your job to put him there."

Marquart started to answer. Brian held up his hand. "You tell him you can convict him without the search. You got his vehicle, make, model, and license plate. What's he doing up there? With a van? He has no visible means of support? And he drives a van around an exclusive area in L.A.? Tell him the cop can I.D. him positively with or without the stop. That gets you enough for his shoe size at the scene. Tell him it was in the blood. Tell him his prior burglaries will come in for M.O."

It was shaky. They both knew it.

"Then you tell him the cop wasn't real good at writing everything in his report. He's new. But at the preliminary hearing, and at trial, with proper preparation, he's going to make it absolutely clear that he observed the defendant make a 'furtive movement' as if to hide or conceal something, that when he looked into the van, he saw 'in plain sight' the edge of a blood-soaked t-shirt that appeared to be partially concealed between the seats, with the cellular phone and no corresponding attachment in the van, and it was then that he feared for the life of a potential victim of a crime. Tell him it was in these 'exigent circumstances' that he was constitutionally permitted to look at the phone and confirm with dispatch that the number belonged to my wife. He rushed to her home, just blocks away, reasonably, but too late to save her life."

Marquart looked at him. "But the officer didn't see any of that."

Brian exploded. "For 25 years, cops have taken the stand against my clients and sworn to 'furtive movements' and 'plain sight' and their 'reasonable' fears. They do it because they believe the defendant is guilty. Well, this motherfucker is guilty! Of murder, not burglary. You tell the P.D. the cop is going to testify to all the things I said, and he'll believe you. You make him believe you."

Brian was quiet again. Reflecting. "In all those cases, the judges knew the cops were lying. The juries knew the cops were lying. But if they believed the guy did it, they didn't care. Nobody is going to cry any tears over this murderer being sent to prison for murder. No matter what the cop did or didn't do. No one."

He was right. He sat on the aisle, back row, when *People v. David Rodney Hall* was called.

"I understand the defendant is prepared to enter a plea this afternoon," said the judge.

"Yes, your honor. Peter Boyle, Deputy Public Defender, appearing with the defendant. Your honor, the defendant is prepared to enter a plea of guilty to second degree murder. The People will drop all other charges. Sentencing will be left to the Court without any promises as a condition for the plea."

"Is that correct, Mr. Marquart?" asked the judge.

"Yes, your honor."

"Very well. Mr. Hall, do you understand…and you're pleading guilty because you are in fact guilty and for no other reason…right to trial by jury…right to…right to…right to…and you're waiving…," etc.…etc.…

Brian had heard it a thousand times. Or, it had been said in his presence and he no longer heard it. It was a recording played over and over. Did anyone really hear it? Did it have any more meaning than reciting Humpty Dumpty? "Big fall…over the wall…you're going down."

The judge motioned Brian forward after the defendant had been taken from the courtroom.

"Brian, why don't you go through my chambers and down the back stairs. The press is waiting out in front of the courtroom, in the hall."

The bailiff led him through.

As he entered the back hallway, the public defender was returning from lockup. "Brian, I wish there was something I could say."

Brian waved him off. "Thanks for getting him to plead."

"I just laid out the options," Boyle responded, with a wry smile bordering on disgust.

"Well, if it's any consolation, Peter, if he had walked, I would have killed him myself. So maybe you saved his life."

Brian walked out of the Los Angeles County Courthouse, scene of some of his greatest triumphs, for the last time.

When Shelly's murderer came up for sentencing, Brian—under the new California Victims' Rights Act—had the right to address the Court and the defendant about his loss and on the issue of sentencing. He did not bother. He was through with the criminal justice system. He and Randy were in Montana. At exactly 9:00 A.M., California time, sitting in his car, he looked at his watch and knew the sentencing hearing had begun. He did not want to know the outcome. Not then. Not ever.

Instead, Brian watched Randy run out into the preschool yard and greet her friends and the large, slobbering labrador retriever that was their playmate. Brian had four hours before he had to pick her up. Enough time to build the rabbit cage he had promised her for Benny, her bunny. He smiled, as tears rolled down his face.

"Shelly, she's you," he said, as his voice broke.

He had walked into his partner's office three months before on his last day in Los Angeles, after the court hearing where the defendant had pled guilty, and said only, "Paul, I can't do it anymore."

Chapter 66

Rose

"UNFINISHED BRIDGES" BY Sarah Graves. Mendocino Gallery. Highway 1. Mendocino.

The 4x6 postcard was stark white with a thin black border. "Unfinished Bridges" appeared in black. "Sarah Graves" was bold, in red. In between, a 1-by-2-inch rectangle had been punched in the center of the card, through which the viewer looked upon a very small pastel watercolor depicting an incomplete painting of a bridge. More clouds than bridge. But for anyone who had ever lived in the Bay Area, it was recognizable, through the mist, by its towering suspension structures.

Rose threw it aside with the catalogs and junk mail. As she opened her electricity bill, she looked back at the flipped card and the writing, again in red, on the other side.

"Hope you can make the show." It was signed, "Mouse."

Sarah "Mouse" Bridgeport had gone back to her maiden name, at least as an artist.

The show was to open with a wine-and-cheese reception on Saturday, November 14—Rose's 40th birthday. She had nothing planned. She had not spoken to Ernesto in months. Her mother, of course, wanted her to come down to Gonzales for the weekend. Or she could just go down to the office and work. There was plenty of that. Her staff had urged her to "get out; see someone." But Salinas, she knew, would not be the place to meet someone.

She made herself a drink. A stiff one. Gin and tonic. Not the wine she normally drank with dinner when Ernesto used to cook for her. She sat in what had been their bedroom, with its look of a converted greenhouse. He had let her have the house because he decided to leave Salinas. She offered to buy him out, but he declined the money. Neither of them had filed for divorce or signed any separation agreement or consulted an attorney. They were dealing with personal issues, not legal ones.

Rose held the card and contemplated. It was a valid reason to call. An art opening. Chance to fly the plane. Birthday weekend. Out of town.

She had expected—well, really hoped for—the answering machine. She was shocked when the voice answered before the second ring.

"This is Sally."

"God, you scared me. I was expecting your machine. What are you doing at the office so late?" Rose asked.

"Rose?" Sally asked.

Rose had not, in her alarm, identified herself, and they had not talked in months, since Rose had told her that she and Ernesto had separated.

"Yes."

"How are you? I've been worried about you."

"I'm fine. I am sorry I haven't called. I've wanted to, but I've been having a difficult time."

"But you have called," Sally said, making Rose even more nervous.

"Well, to be honest, only after two stiff drinks."

Sally laughed.

"Oh, Rose, am I that intimidating?"

"No, I'm that scared."

They both laughed, understanding what remained unsaid. Then there was silence. Rose was the one who broke it. "It's my birthday."

"When?"

"This weekend." She rushed through the rest.

"One of my old clients is having an art opening in Mendocino on Saturday, and I was wondering whether you would like to go. It's in the afternoon, and I thought we could go up there for the day."

"I'd like that, Rose," Sally said warmly.

Rose could feel the excitement as her whole body responded to Sally's voice. She opened her mouth slightly, ran her tongue across the inside of her lower lip, closed her eyes, and visualized Sally.

"Shall I give you my home address?" asked Sally.

"I'd like to fly up in the Piper Comanche since we'll be going up the coast. It's a much smoother ride, and the coast is just spectacular," Rose said with enthusiasm. Can you drive over to Concord or down to San Carlos? I'll fly in and pick you up. I want to avoid the San Francisco Airport airspace."

"Oh, God, Rose. I'm terrified of flying. I'm sorry. I really want to go, but you'd have to drug and diaper me. If I woke up in an airplane, I'd crap my pants. Not a great visual for a first date."

"That's okay. I could drive up from Salinas and we could drive together to Mendocino and back. We'd just have to go a little earlier."

"Rose, it's your birthday. That's probably eight hours of driving for you. That's not fair."

"Just a minute," Rose said.

Rose put down the phone and went to get her thin briefcase—the one in which she carried her pilot log and sectional maps.

"Okay. I'm back. We are going to spend my birthday together come hell or high water," Rose said, unfolding her map of Northern California airports, restricted zones, radio frequencies, and landing strips.

"There is an airport at Sea Ranch," Sally volunteered. "I have a friend who owns a place there. I'm sure you could land and park at the airfield. If I met you there, we could drive up to Mendocino. It would be less than an hour."

Rose was unfamiliar with the north coast by land, although she had flown as far as Fort Bragg along the coast, then up to Idaho.

"Then you'd have to drive," Rose replied.

"It's an easy drive for me, out of San Francisco on 101. I know a cutoff that puts me at Stewarts Point, just a few miles from Sea Ranch. I can be there in a little over an hour."

Rose was looking at a map. Stewarts Point was on the coast at the end of a wavy line across the hills from 101. She could see the logic. Her sectional showed the Sea Ranch airstrip. It was private with no tower or weather service.

"You sure?"

"Yes," replied Sally. "Then we'll have my car to drive around the north coast and explore."

"What kind of car?" asked Rose.

"What? Maybe you won't take me if I don't have a good enough car?" Sally asked, laughing.

"No. No. I just wanted to know what to look for."

"Look for a woman sitting safely on the unmoving ground at the end of the runway, holding a flower, anxious to see you, Rose."

Again, that feeling.

They finalized the arrangements and said goodbye.

Rose got up and walked over to the stereo and put on a tape. Then she sat back and finished the remains of her drink.

"The first time ever I saw your face…" Roberta Flack sang.

Rose imagined Sally touching her face and shivered.

*   *   *   *   *

There she was, as she had said she would be. Almost. Not on the runway, but behind the fence, sitting on the roof of her Jeep Cherokee, her feet through the open sunroof, slowly waving a single red rose like a Navy quartermaster doing semaphore aboard a ship. Rose was much too busy preparing to land to look for her. Sally watched as Rose circled the field, checking the wind sock, and then lowering the retractable landing gear of the Comanche as she came in for a landing into the brisk wind. Rose did a forward slip with one wing dropped toward the gust coming off of the ocean and used the rudder on the opposite side to keep the nose straight to the runway. The gear touched down on one side and then, with a thump, on the other. Finally, Rose dropped the nose wheel. Seeing this and feeling the gusting wind off of the ocean, Sally felt very glad she had not flown.

Sally watched as Rose taxied to the transient tie-down area. She heard the propeller unwind and the engine sound change as the power was turned off. Then she saw Rose exit the plane. Rose waved, and she waved back. Rose reached back into the plane, standing on the Comanche's wing, to retrieve a small travel bag. Then she got off the plane, put the bag on the ground, and attached the tie-down chains to the underside of the wings and to the rear tail hook. She stopped and spoke briefly to the Chevron truck driver fueling another of the planes, turned, and ran to the fence.

The two of them reached for and grabbed each other's hands, resting on opposite sides of the chain link fence, like a visitor and prisoner might.

"So, are you the woman with the flower?" Rose asked.

"Maybe. Who wants to know?" Sally asked, her eyes darting dramatically as if to see if she had been followed. "Rose. One red rose. Must be for you," Sally said, as she reached to put it over the six-foot fence. Rose took the flower and smelled it, not taking her eyes off Sally.

In a few minutes they were driving north on Highway 1 along the ocean. As they crossed the bridge into Gualala, Sally pointed to an old wooden building with chipped paint and faded lettering, on the right side of the highway, facing the ocean, at the edge of town.

"That's the Gualala Hotel. Funky. Pool table. Jukebox. And a long bar right out of the Old West. Complete with the locals. Especially this time of year. We can eat there this evening before you fly out, unless you want something fancier."

"Sounds like fun," Rose said enthusiastically.

"A birthday dinner," added Sally, smiling back at Rose. "So tell me about this artist client of yours," she added, looking ahead as she began maneuvering the curves out of Gualala.

Rose told Sally of the Bridgeport case, the elaborate duplicity of the law firm to protect its attorneys from their spouses, the men from the women.

"Someone must have gotten really burnt a few generations back," Sally offered after hearing about the unraveling of the scheme. "Wasn't he a classmate of yours at law school?"

"Yes, how did you know?" Rose was surprised.

"'Rose Contreras: Slayer of powerful men. Defender of women.' I read the articles about you. I even kept the clippings."

"Really. Why?"

Sally smiled. "I don't know. Pride, I guess. Admiration."

Rose turned away and was quiet. After a few miles, Sally asked, "What's the matter, Rose?"

"I'm 40, and I don't feel very admirable. I never expected to end up practicing as a divorce attorney in Salinas, California, as the culmination of my life's work. I guess I thought I would have done better. Believe me, I never went looking for those cases; they came to me. I didn't make a conscious decision to do what I do."

Ruefully, she added, "There was a time I believed that I was going to clerk at the United States Supreme Court. Go on to an important career in the law. Perhaps become a judge. Maybe even a law professor. Not this."

Suddenly, Sally swerved across the road and jammed on the brakes in time to stop before hitting the barrier at the edge of a cliff. As the cloud of dust cleared, they could see the ocean beneath them softly washing seaweed-clad rocks on its way out. It was low tide.

"Goddamn it," Sally shouted, "don't make me put on my therapist hat! Look at that ocean. The empty beach. You're exactly where you're supposed to be. With me. Now get your whiney ass out of the car. We are going tide-pooling."

Sally jumped out and ran to the back of the Jeep. She opened the hatchback and produced two matching children's sand buckets. "Here, happy birthday," she said, handing one to Rose, and started down the trail to the low tide fields.

Rose caught up with her and put her arm on Sally's. "Okay, okay. But I'm a Valley girl. You'll have you tell me what I'm looking at."

Sally mocked her. "Oh, like for sure. Like, you know. Like, wow, a whale."

"Wrong valley," responded Rose.

"Well, if you're good, I'll find you a Gumbo Chiton, lots of starfish, some sea anemone, and maybe an octopus."

"You're kidding. About the octopus."

"No, really," Sally assured her as she jumped from rock to rock, heading for the furthest pools of the receding ocean. "They get caught in the deeper pools and have to wait for high tide to get out." As she spoke, she was sprayed with a sheet of salt water. Rose slipped off of her rock, laughing, and was knee high in seaweed.

They arrived at the Mendocino Art Gallery late in the afternoon, with pants still wet and smelling of seaweed, their shoes squeaking. They were relieved to see that most of the guests gathered on the veranda were in jeans and boots, or the loose long dresses of the Russian River and north coast reminiscent of the '60s flower children. Their own appearance, even wet, was not terribly out of place, although theirs was the only thing close to a new model vehicle in the parking lot.

The table on the veranda featured two cardboard boxes of wine, plastic glasses, cheese wedges, and an announcement of the show. Sally surveyed the table and asked, "Red or white?"

"Quarter of a glass of red. I'm flying, remember."

"Right," said Sally, as Rose wandered into the gallery.

Sally found Rose in the front room looking at a very small painting—actually, a very large canvas with a very small painting in the center. She looked around. The room was full of similar paintings. "What do you think it means?" asked Sally.

"I thought you were the therapist," said Rose.

Each work appeared unfinished in some respect. Some with a full sky of clouds or fog and then the beginnings of a structure. Others with an almost-complete bridge and the beginnings of a sky or sea. None was signed.

None was titled. At the entry to the room, a sign on a triangular easel bore the name of the show, "Unfinished Bridges by Sarah Graves."

"Why does art have to mean something?" asked Rose.

"I thought you were the art critic; I'm just a guest," responded Sally.

They were totally unprepared for the second, larger room. As they entered, their eyes were drawn upward, over the heads of a group gathered in the room, to the upper half of a brightly colored painting, at least 9 feet high and 12 feet long. As they turned their eyes around the room, reds, bright yellows, and lime greens sprung out from every wall as did the nude bodies of women. At the end of the large room, arched like a chapel window, with two hinged wings of comparable size, hung a painting structured in the style of a Russian icon.

Except for the triptych with its gold leaf highlights, the huge brightly colored paintings were reminiscent of the South Seas work of Paul Gauguin. In content, they made no apology for being nude. Not as Toulouse-Lautrec might feature them, gaily entertaining, or as Rubens might paint them. Nude, yes, but not as viewed by a man. Not coy. Not submissive. Erotic? Definitely.

Rose approached one of the paintings. In the bottom right corner, quite large, the artist had signed, in red, "Mouse." She shook her head. "I don't believe it."

"What?" asked Sally.

"This. All of these were painted by a person who calls herself 'Mouse.'"

"I used the gold leaf to give it a religious overtone. Like she's the Virgin Mary. But that look of satisfaction," she said, pointing to the head tilted back over the pillow, "implies she's no virgin."

The group laughed appreciatively at the artist's comments.

Sarah Graves saw Rose and excused herself. Her head was so closely cropped that it looked like it had been shaven. Large rim glasses—without lenses, Rose noticed as she got closer—filled the center of her face. Equally large yellow hand-painted, circular, wooden earrings hung from her ears. The yellow was matched by very small yellow panties visible through her white cotton see-through dress, as were her small breasts, around which she—or someone—had painted yellow circles.

She wore no shoes, which made her appear even shorter than her 5'1" stature.

Sally whispered, "Why didn't you tell me you were bringing me to erotic art of the north coast?" She gulped her drink as she kept her eyes on the approaching circles under the dress.

"Rose! You made it."

Rose was not used to being hugged by her clients. Even a former client. She stiffened.

"Sarah, this is Sally Conrad, a friend of mine." Sarah let go, turned, and hugged Sally enthusiastically. Sally hugged her back with equal enthusiasm. "Nice show. Are you the Mouse?" she asked.

"Yeah, that's me," Sarah answered, laughing. "I used to hate the name. Rose can tell you about the asshole and his family who called me that. But you know, therapy does wonders for you."

"Yes, I know," said Sally, smiling at Rose.

"Sally is a therapist," Rose interjected.

"Well, then, you understand," said Sarah, turning back to Sally. "What is it you therapists call it when you take something and just jam it up their ass?" Sarah gestured with an upward arc of her fist.

"We call that 'butt-fucking,' Sarah," Sally replied.

Rose choked on her wine and had to be patted on the back.

"Yeah, well, it's very satisfying, whatever it's called," said Sarah. "It was my therapist who suggested I start painting large paintings, bolder colors. Said it would mirror the growth of my self-esteem. It has," she said looking around. "It was also my therapist who suggested I do a show in L.A. and invite all of our old social set, at least the women. Since I didn't need the money," she added, smiling at Rose and acknowledging her work, "the gallery made it a benefit for battered women."

"Nice touch," said Sally with appreciation.

"Why did your therapist suggest that? Is your therapist involved in art, too?" asked Rose.

"No, it was that thing you said, Sally."

"Butt-fucking," responded Sally, confidently.

"Yeah, right. Felt great. So it kinda caught on. Huge pictures by a Mouse. The reviews have been so good, and now I have such a following in L.A., I couldn't change if I wanted to. Which I don't. I feel good about myself every time I sign a finished piece of work."

"So why do you show the unfinished bridges?" asked Rose.

"Reminder," Sarah said.

"Of your ex-husband?"

"No. Reminder of what happens when you lose yourself. After this show, I'll burn them. I don't think I need them anymore."

She smiled at Rose and hugged her again. This time, Rose hugged her back. Sarah let go and stood back, holding onto Rose's hand.

"Thanks for coming. It means a lot to me. I've always looked up to you, Rose."

Rose was embarrassed. She deflected the comment. "How are the kids, Sarah?"

"Great. We spent three months in Europe in the spring. I home-school them. We can get away with that up here in Mendocino County. Took them to see the galleries of Europe. Look around, you'll see the influence in these paintings. Gold leaf, orthodox forms from the Hermitage. The colors of the German Expressionist school from the Thyssen-Bornemisza collection. Pechstein. Karl Schmidt-Rottluff. Of course, Gauguin. The kids loved the Van Gogh Museum in Amsterdam. I told them it was too weird for me. Reminded me of their dad." She laughed again.

"Are they here?" asked Sally.

"No, they are in New York with jackass's parents. It's only fair they see that side. Besides, little Jack's long hair drives them all nuts, but he is so smart and sweet, and reads just about everything, they don't know what to do with him. Amy doesn't understand why her dad doesn't call her more. It's pathetic, really. He just can't connect, but his kids keep trying."

"Well, thank you for thinking of me. We better let you visit with your other patrons. We'll see the rest of the exhibit, but we'll need to run shortly if we're going to make it home tonight," Rose concluded.

Sally hesitated. "Rose, why don't you wait for me in the front room? I need to go to the bathroom."

As they were driving off, Rose asked, "Can you believe that? A therapist actually directing her career. Sounds bizarre."

"Sounds like a damn good therapist to me," said Sally. "Obviously a 'real bitch of a therapist'—and I mean that with all due respect and admiration."

"You're kidding, right?" Rose asked.

"No. Mouse was beaten down. She had to be raised up. Battered women have low self-esteem. Battered women aren't angry. They don't even think they are entitled to be angry. So getting her to anger, to enjoy and direct her anger, and get even, is wonderful therapy. She has taken the name 'Mouse' and her diminutive paintings and turned it all around. Like she says, every time she signs that name to one of those giant paintings, it is a reaffirmation of strength and power as a person."

"But the show in L.A.?" Rose said. "That was a bit much. Was that really necessary?"

"Necessary? I'd call it daring. But this therapist must have felt she was ready. She could have just left town with all that money you got for her, I guess. But my professional opinion is that it would have kept her in therapy for years. She needed to confront him; not leave quietly. A woman therapist would know that. A man therapist would have probably urged her to 'move on' with all the money."

"And the public thinks it's we lawyers who are ruthless," Rose observed.

Sally laughed. "Most of my clients are lawyers, and I can tell you they are no match for me. Or else why would they be coming to me to fix *their* lives?"

They both laughed.

"Got you a present," Sally said after a few miles.

"What is it?" Rose asked, looking around the car.

"Can't tell you now. You'll have to have dinner with me at the Gualala Hotel so I can present it to you properly."

Sally raised an eyebrow. "Okay, I think I have time," she said, looking out at the ocean to her right. The tide was coming in, and the tide pools were covered with the crushing waves, the sand bubbling with salt foam.

The sun was low when they arrived and pulled up to park at the hotel. Once on the veranda, Sally guided her to the door on the left, away from the restaurant entrance. "You've got to see this bar first," she said.

A fire was going in the giant hearth. A single bartender was standing at the end of the bar, near the window, talking to an old couple. Three or four people sat midway down, and a lone person sat at the far end of the bar, near the jukebox. Nobody looked up.

They took seats at the bar, with Rose catching her foot on the boot railing at the base of the bar. The bartender kept talking to the old couple. Rose and Sally heard the music begin as a person sat down next to them, singing to the music—something about looking for love but in all the wrong places. His drink and a bowl of chips had been sitting there. He had been selecting the song at the jukebox.

"Ladies," he greeted them loudly, his speech a bit slurred.

"Hi, there," said Sally, smiling. "What do we have to do to get a drink around here?" she inquired.

He looked each of them over, up and down, and answered, "Well, you'll have to choose which one of you wants me because I can't afford to buy both of you a drink."

"I meant how do we get the bartender's attention and get him to come over here?"

"Oh, him. He's deaf," he said. Immediately, he yelled at the top of his lungs: "Hey, Byron, they chose you over me! Get your ass over here! The ladies want a drink."

"I thought you said he was deaf," Rose said.

The man turned and looked directly at her nose. He took a drink, spilling some of it on himself, and answered her. "He reads lips."

The bartender came over, put some chips in front of them, and asked, "What'll you have?"

He looked over at the man sitting next to them. "Jesse, did you tell these ladies I was deaf?"

"You are fuckin' deaf. I can't never get no drink when I want one," the man replied.

"Jesse here," the bartender pointed to the man, "is drinking himself into his disability policy. If he doesn't stay drunk, he'll be declared sober and lose his only visible means of income."

"I got some invisible means," replied Jesse.

"I'll have a margarita," Sally said. "What would you like, Rose?"

"I'd better stick with 7-Up. Flying," she gestured with a hand to the bartender.

"I'm flying, too," interjected the man they now knew as Jesse, holding out his arms like wings and sputtering over the bar.

He turned to Rose. "So what are you? A flight attendant or something?"

"No, I'm a lawyer," Rose answered.

He gagged. "Jesus Christ. My ex-wife had a woman lawyer. A real hellcat. A barracuda. The way she went after me you'd think I was married to her."

He took another drink. "That's why I moved up here. Cash economy, if you know what I mean." He drew on his cigarette like it was a marijuana joint.

"No visible means of support," he said, laughing into his drink.

"So, what about you?" he asked Sally. "You a lawyer, too?"

"No. I'm a marriage counselor," said Sally—not exactly the truth, but designed to get a reaction.

Jesse did not disappoint.

"A marriage counselor? Maybe you can tell me: What's wrong with my ex-wife? Hiring a woman lawyer like that."

Sally looked at the ceiling, her hand across her face, as if divining an answer.

"Well, perhaps your ex-wife is a lesbian," she answered with a furrowed brow.

Jesse slammed his drink down. "Christ, I never thought of that!"

He pondered the diagnosis as he sipped, then downed his drink. "Right. You're absolutely right. What I need is a real woman."

Sally looked at Rose. "So do I, Jesse. So do I."

As the sun set across the street, Sally and Rose went into the dining room for dinner.

"Can I get you a drink?" asked the waitress.

"Sure, I'll have another margarita. Rose, what would you like?"

"7-Up."

They studied the menu. From the front, they could hear a pool player racking the balls. From the bar, they could hear Jesse yelling, "Byron, read my lips. Give me a fuckin' drink."

"Nice place," Rose said.

"Cozy," agreed Sally. "Out of the way," she added with a smile.

"Kinda like *Deliverance*," replied Rose.

"Well, in the winter, it's mostly locals, but the coast is actually clearer, the weather more interesting, and it's not crowded.

"Perfect place for a birthday party," added Sally.

"What now?" Rose asked. "You've got that look."

"Wait here," Sally said, and got up and went out to the car. She returned with something wrapped loosely in brown paper.

"I'm sorry, I didn't have time to get it wrapped. Close your eyes."

Rose closed her eyes. She heard the rustling of paper. Then she felt something being placed on her lap.

"Okay, open your eyes," said Sally, standing beside and slightly behind her, her hand resting on Rose's shoulder.

She recognized it instantly. Both the image and the rendering. It was one of Sarah Graves' unfinished bridge paintings, except she had signed this one: "To Rose...Mouse."

"Oh, my God, how did you do this?" Rose exclaimed.

"It was hard getting away from you, but Sarah and I worked it out. She had someone put it in the car when we were all talking together."

"It's wonderful!"

"Here's to unfinished bridges, Rose," Sally said, holding up her drink. "Happy birthday."

Rose pulled Sally down by the arm and kissed her. On the lips. Hard. Then she just looked at her.

"Well, right," said Sally. "We need to order dinner," she said, as she straightened up and went to her side of the table, across from Rose.

One of the pool players was watching over the swinging doors. He chalked his cue. "Rack 'em up," he said to his competitors, "I feel horny."

After they had eaten dinner, Sally quietly waved off dessert. "Wait here," she said again and departed for the car.

When she returned, it was with a small birthday cake, a glowing candle, the waitress, and a busboy. As Rose looked up, they began singing: "Happy birthday to you…" Within seconds, they were joined by Jesse and a large American Indian, clapping out of time with the song, adding their attempt at the birthday refrain. At the end of the song, Jesse shouted "drinks for everyone" and disappeared back into the bar.

"How could you hide all this from me?" Rose asked.

"You're not very observant," Sally answered. "Here, put on your Gualala Hotel t-shirt. I got us a matching set."

"You're crazy," Rose said.

"Crazy about you."

Rose took a deep breath and pretended it was to blow out the candle. As she did, she noticed the frown on Sally's face.

"What?" Rose asked.

"Well, when I went out to the car, I noticed it's dark."

"So?" asked Rose.

"Well, I guess this means you can't fly out tonight."

Rose blew out the candle.

"First, you try all day to get me drunk. Then you try to ground me by stalling until dark." Rose smiled. "Are you trying to get me to spend the night with you, Sally?" Rose asked.

"Did it work? That's all I want to know," Sally asked.

"No."

"Why not?"

"Because I'm instrument-rated and fully qualified to fly at night. Now, if I had flown into Oceanridge, Gualala's airstrip up the hill, 940 feet above town, with deer on the runway, a runway with a hump so large you can't see the other end, and which closes down at 10 P.M., your plan might have worked. But I'm at 26 feet above sea level on a bluff at Sea Ranch. I've been watching the weather, not the clock, and it's a beautiful, clear night without fog down here. Typical of this time of year."

"Damn!" exclaimed Sally.

"Actually, I've also spent over 60 hours in instruction with ILS in the Comanche," Rose added.

"What's ILS?" Sally asked.

"Instrument Landing Systems. It gives you not only distance, like VOR, but a glide slope for precision with an audio beeper panel in the cockpit. Of course, I'm also trained in VOR approach and the use of nondirectional beacons."

"Of course," said Sally throwing up one hand, realizing her plans were going astray.

"On the other hand," added Rose, looking at the birthday cake, "the Sea Ranch airport isn't equipped to handle ILS. It doesn't even have a beacon."

"What does all that mean?" asked Sally. "I don't understand a thing you've been saying."

"It means I'm trying to impress you. Actually, to get out of this airport on a clear night, I don't even need instrument rating. Night flying can actually be easier than day flying. I just want you to know that I'm a damn good and highly trained pilot. I also want you to know I can choose to do whatever I want with this evening, Sally."

Rose put a fork into the birthday cake, scooped off a petal of the red icing forming a single rose, made a display of slowly rubbing the cream-covered fork across her tongue and lower lip, and asked: "Why don't you just ask me, Sally?"

Sally watched the dissolving petal of icing and tried to formulate a response.

"You know," Rose continued, "for a therapist, you certainly aren't very direct."

Sally was speechless.

"Why don't you buy me a drink, Sally? And see if you can get us a room. I'll be in the bar," Rose added, as she stood, picked up her painting and placed it under one arm, and lifted the birthday cake.

Jesse greeted her as she entered the bar. "You've decided! My regrets to the runner-up. Byron," he yelled, loudly as was his custom, "I've got some action down here! Get the lady a drink."

Sally returned, excited. "We've got the suite. Second floor, with a balcony. Looks out to the ocean."

"I've got a camper," Jesse said, putting his hand on Rose's leg.

"Let's take that margarita up to the room," Sally said, putting an arm across Rose's shoulders.

"I think we should have a pitcher," said Rose.

"Bartender, the lady would like a pitcher of margaritas, to go!" Sally yelled, reminiscent of Jesse.

"Go where?" asked the bartender.

"To our suite," Sally said triumphantly.

"We don't have no pitchers, except for beer, and no room service. You can take the blender, but bring it back in the morning."

"Won't you need it tonight?"

"No one drinks blended drinks around here, except tourists. And you're it."

Rose downed her drink with excitement and a little apprehension. She poured another from the blender to drink as she went up the stairs. She gulped from it while still carrying the cake in her other hand and the painting under her arm. It was all very awkward.

The room was unlocked. "They said just lock it from the inside." As they entered, they could see the lace curtains blowing in the open windows that looked out onto the white sand and the dark ocean across the road with surf illuminated by a partial moon.

The balcony promised was the roof overhanging the veranda, accessible only through their windows.

"Come on. Let's sit in a window."

Rose put the painting down, and carried the cake and pitcher of margaritas out the window.

Sally climbed out the other window and walked across to sit next to Rose. She placed the pitcher back on the floor of the master bedroom and began the first of a number of toasts.

Sally was first. "Here's to us. Happy birthday."

Then Rose. "Here's to Jesse. First runner-up. Does that mean you're my birthday present?" she asked Sally. Her apprehension was eased with her third margarita.

They woke up in bed together to the bright morning light and the sounds of a Harley Davidson going up Highway 1 toward Mendocino. They were wrapped in each other's arms, wearing only their matching Gualala Hotel t-shirts.

"I hope I was a good birthday present for you, Rose."

Rose kissed Sally softly.

"I'd say I've been waiting 40 years for you, Sally."

Chapter 67

Leon

"YOU JUST SUE everybody. You get rich. What good is that? Doesn't change anything. Except now you're one of the big shots."

Leon had strayed a long time ago, according to his father. Had lost his conscience. It was not just suing a union, although that was unforgivable in his father's view; it was all the other cases, especially the class actions.

"The government should pass a law making these things you sue about illegal. Then put a few big corporate leaders in prison. That would send a message like you keep talking about. Leon, the only message you are sending is, 'Pay off the lawyers and it's business as usual.'"

It was an argument they had had many times before. Yet, Leon always took the bait.

"You don't think that if an insurance company pays $400 million for years of discrimination against women and minorities, it doesn't change anything? You don't think every other insurance company, and every other big corporation seeing that, doesn't change its practices?"

"No. They just pass it on to the people who buy insurance. Put the president of the company in jail. Take away his home. Put his family on the street. Now, that will change things."

Mr. Goldman saved his anger, however, for the class action Leon was then pursuing against German, Austrian, and Swiss manufacturers, seeking compensation for slave labor camps during World War II.

"You think Churchill would have accomplished anything with a stupid lawsuit? Who are you suing? Hitler is dead. Goebbels is dead. Eichman is dead. Mengele is dead. Hunt the murderers down. Kill them. Don't sue them with some lawyer getting 25 percent. It's an insult to the six million Jews who died in the Holocaust."

He looked at Leon as if he had failed him as a father.

"It was the Holocaust for God's sake! Not an opportunity to make money."

"But we can't just let them get away with it..."

"They didn't get away with it. The Nazis are dead. Israel is alive. We are alive."

"But the money they stole..."

"Everybody steals. America stole America from the Indians. England stole Australia from the Aborigines. Your mom and I taught you about colonialism. So what are you going to do? Have a lawsuit to right every wrong in history? How far back are you going? And for what? So someone alive today can get some money earned by a relative who died through injustice in the past? What right does such a person have to that wealth? Inheritance? That's what has perpetuated class wealth over work. That is what my son does?"

It always came back to Karl Marx.

As critical as Mr. Goldman was of Leon, he always mixed it with praise for Angela.

"Angela understands. Marches. Boycotts. Getting arrested. Revolution. She shuts down corporations. Takes back countries. She doesn't file lawsuits for money."

"That's not my style," Leon responded. "I can be effective through litigation."

"Right. Your style. You'd rather write a check from your multimillion-dollar house. Nelson Mandela freed a country from a jail cell, not a mansion."

And it always came back to defending, as he saw it, his success.

"I'm not going to apologize for having earned a lot of money. When I finally collected on my first discrimination class action case, it was after years of hard work, risking my money, everything. Sure I made millions, but I put tens of millions of dollars in my clients' pockets."

"You should have put it all in your clients' pockets. They were the victims. Not you," interrupted his father.

"And I should work for free?" asked Leon.

"No. You should work for wages, like other people. Like your clients. Like you did when you were really representing people. At Legal Aid."

"Well, I understand you have a problem with me earning a lot of money, but I give away millions—"

"You should give it all away…"

"—and I am not going to let German companies keep the benefit of years of slave labor by Jews."

"And when it's all over, what will your clients get? A coupon for a Volkswagen at half price? Or to buy a Krupps coffee grinder?"

His father was now pleading with him. "Don't reduce the Holocaust to a lawsuit to be settled. There is not enough money in the world. It can never be undone. It can never be settled."

Chapter 68

Rose

NOT EVEN WITH help from Ernesto, a member of the faculty, could Rose get her article accepted for publication in the *California Law Review*.

The 25ᵗʰ anniversary of California's passage of the landmark 1969 Family Law Act, with its "no fault" provisions, was to be marked by a retrospective on the law by the *California Law Review*. It was Professor, now Dean, Herma Hill Kay's article in the 1968 edition that had formed the basis for discussion and ultimate passage of the "reform." Rose had been the editor of the review that year and had worked closely with Professor Kay, a leading expert in the field of family law.

Ironically, Rose found herself both a practitioner of family law under the "reform" and an ardent critic of the law that she had so fervently advocated in 1968. The equality and freedom arguments made at the time by women's groups were, she realized, misplaced. "Equality" generally meant for most women and children a 40 percent drop in their economic lifestyle. Legal equality did nothing for the economic reality that men still had the ability to earn a dollar for every 60 or 70 cents a woman could earn, even if doing the same job.

But what really bothered her was the adversarial system with its dueling lawyers charging by the hour with no incentive to stop, each attempting to "win" or "crush" or "destroy" the subject of his or her client's emotional wrath. She might even concede them that right, a couple's desire to hurt each other, but not within the legal system. Not by the hour and not if children were involved.

In the years since Ernesto had left, Rose had spoken out at family law sections of Bar conferences on the need for counseling instead of contention; mediation instead of litigation. But she was often asked in her own practice: "How do you conciliate in an adversarial system? How do you negotiate from strength when the other side is throwing everything at you, seeking your client's capitulation?"

Her disenchantment with the adversarial system was not changed by her reputation as the "manslayer." Rather, she argued for a family law system where a Jackson Bridgeport could not threaten his wife; a system where her adversarial skills were unnecessary.

Rose's interest in counseling and mediation as an alternative to the adversarial system was fueled by her association with Sally. At first, she perused Sally's library of marriage, family, and clinical social work texts. Then she began looking into mediation for her family law cases, since a number of retired judges had formed a group to mediate complex civil cases. Their interest appeared to be the clogged calendars in the civil court system. They offered fast, expedited—and expensive—"rent-a-judge" alternatives for litigants willing to pay. To some, these "retired" judges appeared to be creating a two-tier system of justice—one for the rich who could afford to rent their own judge, and one for the rest in the adversarial system in clogged courthouses.

The idea was slow in implementation, but Rose decided she would prefer to be a mediator, solving problems for families, rather than a litigator, representing one side in a fight. She redirected her practice, training as a mediator, and returned to Fresno State to work on a master's degree in child and family counseling.

It was a little different returning to Fresno as a student. Now, she flew back and forth from Salinas in her Cessna 172. And she resumed her role as a board member of the Fresno Women's Center, which had managed to lease a building for a shelter in the years since she had been involved.

Rose's new business card was a little confusing to her clients:

Rose Contreras y Baca
Attorney, Mediator and Family Counselor

But she felt free of the constraints of litigation. She was not your normal lawyer. She did not follow the usual path of a top law student and successful litigator. But then, nothing had ever been normal for her in the law.

Ernesto genuinely tried to help. He took her idea for a law review article to the student editor of the Family Law Project. He pitched the idea of a practitioner, who was also a mediator and family counselor, doing a piece for the review. "A different point of view," Reynoso argued.

"They just feel the *California Law Review* is a national scholarly publication and reserved primarily for law professors and judges, with few exceptions," Reynoso told her when he called.

"And I don't meet their criteria for an exception," Rose said. She knew it, deep down, but had hoped she could parlay her position as the 1968-69 Editor-in-Chief of the law review that had published the landmark article as entree. Also, she thought that her notoriety as a "manslayer" in family law litigation might appeal to the review's woman editors, a number of whom were prominent on the law review's masthead.

"Let's face it. I'm just a lawyer in Salinas as far as they're concerned. Not even a major Valley town. Who are we kidding?" she said with resignation.

"A damn good lawyer," Ernesto responded.

"Oh, don't patronize me, Ernie. I'm fine with who I am. I appreciate your help."

"By the way," Ernesto asked, "did you see Pete Wilson nominated your classmate Michael Cassidy to the California Supreme Court? It's in the *Chronicle* this morning."

"No! Really? After what you did in Moot Court to expose his views?"

"Well, I'm going to testify at the hearing against him," said Ernesto.

"What good would that do?" Rose asked. "Is there any chance of derailing the appointment?"

"None. But you remember he's the same son-of-a-bitch who cost me my federal judgeship," said Ernesto.

"Ernie," she said, smiling into the phone, "I think 30 or 40 million voters who voted for Reagan cost you your judgeship."

"Well, I've got to make sure he knows we are watching him. He is evil."

"You watch him for me, Ernie. I've got to run. Thanks again. I love you, Zapata," she said, smiling at his revolutionary resilience.

"Hey, I love you too, Rose," he said, with a passion that caused both of them to pause.

"Have you told your mom, Rose?" he asked, breaking the silence.

She was annoyed with him. He had no right to ask. He knew the answer.

"No, Ernesto. It's the hardest thing I've never done."

After the rejection by the "scholarly" *California Law Review*, Rose submitted her article to the *California Lawyer*, the journal of State Bar practitioners, and it was accepted. She was asked, however, to change the title, and the magazine added an introduction and a "teaser" to the piece. Instead of the original title, "An Evaluation of the Family Law Act in the Adversarial System," the article appeared under the heading, "Getting Lawyers Out of the Family and the Family Out of Court." Rose's picture appeared in a box, with a description of her headline-winning exploits against Judge Puchini and "hardball L.A. litigator Jackson Bridgeport III" and a caption: "Man-slaying divorce litigator argues that lawyers need to be taken out of family matters and the family out of the court system."

When the magazine appeared, she took it to her mother's house to show her. She explained the article's content to her, even though her mother could read English. Her eyesight was poor and she read little. Rose told her how more than 150,000 lawyers throughout the state would be receiving the magazine from the State Bar.

Her mother looked at the article and the picture of Rose.

"I liked your hair longer," she finally said. She took her glasses off and put them in their case.

"Did Sally help you with this paper?" her mother asked, pointing at the magazine with her glass case.

"Yes, Mom. She read it. Many times. As a therapist, she has worked with lots of divorced families over the years."

Her mother pondered her next words. Mulled them over. "Good. Sally is very nice."

Her mother looked up at Rose. Rose's eyes welled up with tears, and she hugged her mom.

They left it at that.

Chapter 69

Jackson

JACKSON BRIDGEPORT III had not read Rose's article when it first appeared in the *California Lawyer*. But in early 1999, he came across the article while reviewing old issues in preparation for his position as the newly elected president of the California State Bar, the organization to which all California lawyers paid mandatory dues and which regulated attorneys' conduct.

He instantly recognized the name this time: "Rose Contreras y Baca. Salinas, California."

He clicked on the title and pulled up the article on his desktop computer. He pushed "print" and dropped the article into his briefcase for evening reading.

Jackson had been a member of the board of governors for eight years, moving into the chain of officers that led him to his selection as president. As the senior named partner of the California branch of a large national law firm, he had the time and resources to devote to the prestigious position. He did not need to do a single billable hour of work to reap the benefit for his firm. Holding the position of president of the State Bar was a time-honored tradition for rainmakers at major law firms. His picture and title were prominently featured on all firm brochures. National clients knew that when they retained Bridgeport, Bridgeport, Hall and Pendergast, they were getting the firm that included "the president of the California State Bar." His name, on a brief filed in a California court, was all they wanted; younger lawyers did the grunt work. Clients also knew that they were hiring a firm trained in the style of "hard-ball litigation" associated with the name Jackson Bridgeport III, even if Jackson's own image was tempered by his service to the Bar.

Jackson believed everyone had a right, maybe even a duty, to have a lawyer. In what some saw as contrary to his representation of big businesses, he had argued for greater funding of Legal Aid for the poor. He felt strongly that practicing attorneys should volunteer their time and money, and otherwise support legal services for the poor. It was part of his concept of law as a profession, not a job.

He did not feel government should fund Legal Aid or that legal services for the poor should be used to pursue class actions, or "social or political agendas of radical lawyers." His view, in summary, was that the profession should represent those less fortunate, on an individual basis, as needed. Like charity.

Jackson's law firm committed $100,000 a year for legal service centers, and through his presidency of the Bar, he established a "check-off" system where lawyers would send all the interest earned on their client trust accounts to support legal services for the poor. The results were impressive.

His position put him on a first-name basis with the Chief Justice and associate justices of the California Supreme Court, and the hierarchy of the profession throughout the state and nation.

Rose's article on mediation confirmed what he had always believed. Privately. Women did not have what it took, over the long haul, for combat. Sure, she had beaten him once, but now she was throwing in the towel and he was still a respected and feared litigator.

If there had been any doubt—which was unlikely, given his intractable arrogance—whether he would show up at the reunion at which his ex-wife's attorney would be present, Rose's article of surrender dispelled it.

He tossed the article onto the nightstand and smiled as he turned out the light. "See you at the reunion, Ms. Baca."

Chapter 70

Michael

ROBBIE HAD SURPRISED his dad when he told him he had decided to go to law school. It seemed out of character for the surfing dude who had taken time off to teach English in Thailand and had returned professing an affinity for language and writing. He had then spent two years at Columbia, bouncing between courses in literature and journalism, finally getting an M.A. in Asian literature.

Now he was in his second year at Boalt. Robert—his mom and dad still called him Robbie—phoned his dad frequently just to discuss the law. As so many other students, he was anxious to get past the Commerce Clause of the Constitution and into "real" constitutional law like free speech and press. His dad pointed out that the origins of civil rights protections had been conceived through the Commerce Clause: "The way Kennedy and Johnson justified so much of the civil rights legislation was the argument that discrimination affected commerce between the states," Michael told him.

"Don't just go to the index to the Constitution, be creative," he urged his son. "Look at the impact on commerce. Look at the taxing powers. Nowhere in the Constitution do you find the word 'privacy,' but since *Griswold v. Connecticut* there is absolutely no question that it is a fundamental constitutional right."

"You're one to talk. Your old boss Attorney General Meese was the architect of Reagan's 'original intent' doctrine: that judges are supposed to look at the actual words in the Constitution and discern what the Framers had in mind," replied Robbie.

"Don't quote me, but that's bullshit," said his dad. "Think about it. What was the Framers' intent when they guaranteed equal protection of the law? Since they provided for slavery, effectively, right in the Constitu-

423

tion—after all, the Negro was counted only as $^3/_5$ of a human—they didn't mean for blacks to enjoy equal protection. Or what did they intend for speech on the Internet when everybody in the world is now an instantaneous 'publisher' of material?"

The exchange of ideas, privately between them, was open as it had never been on any other subject or any other aspect of their lives.

"What is important, also, is some semblance of order, though," Michael added. "It can't just be what any given judge feels like. There has to be a discernable body of rules."

"Mom always said you were hung up with rules. Dad, sometimes good things can come out of the synergy of chaos."

"Chaos is not a basis for jurisprudence," Cassidy said, laughing, "even if it is your mother's guiding principle."

"It can be fun, Dad. You ought to try it."

"Well, maybe I will. Speaking of chaos, can I come by your apartment and take you to lunch Saturday? I've got my 30th law school reunion to go to."

"Sure, but I've got some work to do at the law review afterwards. Maybe you could come by there, too, if you want."

"You didn't tell me you were working on the *California Law Review*. I never made it myself when I was at Boalt."

"Well, it's the *Asian Law Review*. You just sign up and submit a paper which may be selected for publication."

"Do you have a topic?"

"Yeah. Reparations to Japanese-American internees."

"What does your mother think?" Cassidy asked.

"She thinks people should live in the now and move ahead."

"I'm surprised. I thought she'd be all for reparations."

"No, she told me to tell you it's like *Yick Wo*. The law shouldn't have taken the laundries away from the Chinamen—that was her term—in the first place. She said you'd understand."

"As unpredictable as ever," Cassidy said, again laughing, thinking of Mai. Robbie knew his dad had genuine fondness for his mother.

Justice Cassidy could not walk the halls of Boalt Hall without being recognized and receiving deference. Even students, at least those who knew Robert, knew "Dad" was Justice Cassidy of the California Supreme Court.

Robert was meeting with editors of the *Asian Law Review* to discuss his paper. Justice Cassidy was invited to sit in.

One student was openly hostile. "Rob, doesn't this whole reparations issue smack of affirmative action based on race?" he said looking at Justice Cassidy as if to illustrate an ideological rift between father and son.

"No, it's restitution, just as for any wrong in the law. The wrong was based on race; Japanese-Americans were rounded up and interned because of race. The restitution is to identifiable victims and their heirs," responded Rob.

"I don't know. What do you think, Justice Cassidy? Doesn't this smack of affirmative action?" asked the editor.

Justice Cassidy smiled. There was nothing like a law student with newly found terminology, assumptions, and a penchant for analogy.

"If I stole your truck, would I owe you restitution?" he asked the student.

The student did not hesitate. "Sure."

"If I stole your farm, would I owe you restitution?" Cassidy asked.

"Yes," replied the student.

"If I stole your life, would I owe you restitution?"

"Well, I suppose that would fit under wrongful death."

"So if the government did all this, would it owe restitution?"

"Certainly the government is no different. Yes. It would owe restitution."

"So is there any question that the government took the trucks, farms, and lives, and incarcerated people of Japanese descent without trial, for a period of years, without any legal basis?" asked Cassidy.

"So you're in favor of reparations for the Japanese-American internees, Justice Cassidy?" challenged the student.

"I'm just asking questions," Cassidy answered. "Let me ask you a couple of other things," he continued, looking around at all of the editors and Asian students listening. "If these internees were Jews, and were subject to slave labor, should they not be similarly compensated?"

No one said anything.

"And instead of being Japanese internees for 3 or 4 years, or Jews in concentration camps until most died, what if these people were subjected to 253 years of slavery, deprived of their language, culture, history, children, and lives, and thereafter subjected to legally enforced segregation and discrimination for another 100 years, would they, too, be entitled to 'reparations,' or would that be called 'special treatment' or 'affirmative action'?"

They were stunned.

"Are you saying…"

"I'm a judge. I don't render decisions on cases not before me. I'm just exploring the logic of an argument with a group of Boalt students."

He looked at his watch. "Well, I've got a reunion to go to tonight, so I better get back to the hotel and get ready."

He got up to leave and his son followed him out.

"You really had them going," Rob said.

"About what?" Cassidy asked.

"The argument for reparations to African-Americans for slavery."

"Is that what it was?" He smiled at his son as he got in his car and raised a fist in salute as he pulled away from the sidewalk at Boalt Hall.

Chapter 71

The Reunion

"SO, RANDY, ARE you giving some thought to being a lawyer?" Rose asked.

"Well, I was more thinking of being a judge. My dad said being a lawyer was too hard." Everyone laughed.

"Can I tell you a story about your dad?" Rose said.

"Sure," said Randy, as she began spooning the ice cream put in front of her.

"Well, your dad was a very famous lawyer in Los Angeles. I was at a conference one time, and I heard a young lawyer from your dad's law firm tell a story about him. And I want to tell it to you."

Brian looked at Rose in surprise. They had never encountered each other in the years since law school.

Rose kept looking at Randy.

"Well, this young lawyer was in the office with your dad working very late one night. And the lawyer had a little girl at home. And he told your dad how he had gotten to work very early in the morning while the little girl was still asleep. And when he would get home at night, his little daughter would be asleep, and he wouldn't get to see her at all that day. And he told your dad how working as a lawyer often meant that he didn't get to see his little girl. And you know what your dad told the lawyer?"

Randy just shrugged her shoulders.

"Your dad said, 'Young man, that's the price you pay for the privilege of being a lawyer.'"

Rose looked at Randy. "Do you know what privilege means, Randy?"

Randy twisted her face up a little and squinted her nose. "Is kind of like it's real special?"

427

"That's right. That's what your dad meant. Being a lawyer is very special. But it takes very hard work."

Randy thought about it for a while.

"Well, I think he should still have gone home and seen his little girl."

"So do I, Randy. So do I. But it just means that if you want to be a lawyer or a judge, you have to work very, very hard. And it's an honor. And you can be a judge if you want to."

Rose now looked at Brian and then back at Randy. "Randy, your dad was a very famous lawyer and worked very hard. But it looks like he has spent a lot of time with you, too."

"I'd like to recognize, at this time, some distinguished members of the class." It was the dean who had taken the podium.

"Of course, Justice Michael Cassidy of the California Supreme Court is with us, and Jackson Bridgeport III, president of the California State Bar." Each received light applause, as did various Superior Court judges and Appellate Court justices, District Attorneys, and a state legislator, but the most resounding applause was reserved for the class president, who insisted on being introduced as a "retired winemaker." He just raised his wine glass and declined to come to the podium.

Talk resumed at each of the tables as the podium was vacated while dessert was served.

Sally had, of course, seen Michael Cassidy when he first stared at her upon entering. His introduction as a Supreme Court justice brought polite applause from her and another look of recognition from him. She was surprised now to see him standing, directly across from her, at her table.

"Good evening," he said, addressing her.

"Justice Cassidy," came the surprised announcement of someone at the table.

"I just wanted to come over, Sally, and thank you." Looking at the others at the table, and at Rose, he continued, "This woman has been very special in my life. We spent a lot of Friday afternoons together, and she was most discreet, which, for a judge, is important. So, Sally, this is a first for us, meeting in public, so I thought I would publicly thank you."

"Justice Cassidy, is it?" asked Sally. "Well, nice meeting you, your honor."

Cassidy gave a slight bow of the head, smiled, and left.

"What the hell was that about?" asked Rose. "I didn't know you know Michael Cassidy."

"Who?" asked Sally, with her best professional face.

"Justice Cassidy of the California Supreme Court. Don't tell me he was also one of your clients?"

"Rose. I would never tell you that."

"Well, since it was in the *Chronicle*, I suppose you know he's getting married to his secretary. They are quite the couple in San Francisco society."

Sally could honestly say this time that she did not know. The article had appeared in the *Chronicle*'s society section on the weekend of the LPGA Tournament and she had missed it. Had she read it, she would have seen the lovely couple, Justice Cassidy and Ruth Chin, formerly his secretary at the Court of Appeal, and the announcement of their upcoming wedding set for the fall—"when the sailing on the Bay is best"—at the San Francisco Yacht Club.

Sally looked over, a bit surprised but clearly pleased, and saw Michael resting his hand upon the arm of an attractive Asian woman perhaps 10 or 15 years his junior. He made eye contact with Sally and smiled back.

Sally wagged her finger at him as if in disapproval. He held his fiancée's ringed left hand, arched his eyebrows, and smiled, as if to mime, "cured."

Rose also had her share of eye contact, but the one that was distressing and disappointing was with Professor Ernesto Zapata Reynoso—Ernie. She noticed him come in, caught his look, and saw his eyes immediately shift to Sally. Then they went down to the floor and never came back to her. He sat at the dean's table, purposely, Rose believed, with his back to her and Sally.

He acknowledged, intellectually, what she had told him after their separation, but he took it as somehow being about him, not her. He felt he had lost her to another—a woman. Now he had to acknowledge it emotionally, by being in their presence. He could not.

What did she expect? A wedding present? A champagne toast? He could not accept it. He had his machismo. He was Zapata. This, here at Boalt, must be embarrassing for him, Rose thought. But she was not going to turn her back on her relationship with Sally and walk the distance to his table, alone. Nor would she confront him with Sally. So, from time to time, she looked sadly at his back.

J. J. had returned to the podium.

"Thirty years! Thirty years! We come together and all the dean can talk about is whether we're going to include Boalt in our wills. It's nice to know that Boalt is following our careers, if only in the obituaries."

He paused, looking at his fellow classmates, and switched gears.

"How can we forget those days when we first came together? In 1966. The last graduating class of the '60s. At Boalt. In Berkeley. During those tumultuous times. 'The war' to us will always be Vietnam. The protests: 'Hey, hey, LBJ, how many kids did you kill today?' Black Power. With Huey and Stokely. We were on a first-name basis, right? And then there were Martin, John, and Bobby: 'Some people see things as they are, and ask why. I dreamed things that never were, and ask why not.'

"My kids ask me of those days and I wonder, as we reach 56, 30 years later: 'Are we who we were; and were we ever?'

"I have to confess to some nagging doubt, which I wish to confront tonight. Actually, I am confronted with it by my children, especially my daughter, Rebel, to whom cross-examination is instinctive."

Turning to Brian, he added, "I suspect it's the same with your daughter, Randy, here tonight.

"'Dad,' my daughter Rebel asked me, 'Were you at Woodstock?'

"'Well, no. But I was at Berkeley in the '60s,' I answer with pride, my eyes moistening as I look into the distance, or at least the blur left when I remove my glasses.

"'So you were in the Free Speech Movement?'

"I bask. 'Ah, the FSM.'

"'Well?' she asks, bringing me back.

"'Well, no. That was Mario Savio in 1964. I didn't get to Berkeley until 1966, so they went ahead without me. By 1966, I think Mario was a mailman.'

"'Mario? You knew him?'

"'Well, no. But everyone called him Mario. He came back during the People's Park Protest in 1969. Or, as we call it, the PPP.'

"'So, Dad, you were in those protests when Reagan called out the National Guard. Wow!'

"'Well, no. But Brian Jacobs went down and got beat up and arrested so we all wore "Free Brian" buttons as Reagan gassed the university.'

"'You were gassed by Reagan, Dad?'

"'Well, no. But Boalt Hall is upwind from the campus and it kind of blew up…we could smell it…so we protested finals.'

"'Really, you refused to take finals?'

"'Well, no. We delayed them. It actually gave us a little more time to study. We couldn't refuse to take them. After all, we needed the grades to get jobs in those big law firms. You can't go messing up your whole career for some cause.'

"'But you did oppose the war, right?'

"'Of course. We all did.'

"'And refuse to go to Vietnam? You stood up to Nixon and Kissinger?'

"'Well…actually, I took this draft class and got a 1-Y classification. See, the wife of a classmate got TB, and I exposed myself to her.'

"'Dad. Does Mom know you exposed yourself to a classmate's wife?'

"'That's not what I mean and you know it.'

"'Well, at least you went to a law school that recognized the equality of women.'

"'It was hardly equality. Rose Contreras was number one in the class, all three years. I'd call that female dominance.'

"'It's natural for us to lead, Dad. But, I thought Mom said you worked for the poor when you got out of Boalt.'

"'No, she said we *were* poor when I got out of Boalt. My first job paid $750 a month. Later, I did work for the ACLU—hey, did you ever see Peter Fonda in the movie *Easy Rider?*'

"'Who?'

"'He would pronounce it really slow, with a Southern accent: Aaa–Cee L–YOU—and I had an Afro for a while. I represented a gay lib group and even shut down a nuclear power plant, while making a little money, of course, in accident cases. How do you think we afforded all those big houses and travel, and the money I paid your Mom? The PSAs.'

"'What Public Service Announcements?'

"'No, Property Settlement Agreements. The divorces.'

"This is usually where it gets ugly.

"'Face it, Dad. You're an ambulance-chasing yuppie. Look at those $4,000 Armani suits, those $600 shoes.'

"I become defensive.

"'Damn it, I named you Rebel, didn't I? I worked hard to send you to an all-girls school. I even wrote the essay on your application: "Why I want to go to Mills College." So leave me alone.'

"'Dad,' she begins with the patience of a person saying the same thing for the hundredth time, 'it's a women's college, not a girls' school. And you wrote the essay because you are so controlling. Chill out.'

"'Listen, kid,' I say, my voice rising, 'I was politically correct before you were born. I rode with the Black Panthers in the streets of Oakland. I faced the Po-Lease. I can say any damn thing I want. I went to Berkeley in the '60s.'

"Last month, I was invited to a 35-year Woodstock reunion party. I don't know if any of the insurance defense and corporate attorneys present were at Woodstock. I know I wasn't. But that evening, they were all wearing polo shirts, shorts, and expensive sandals. Being a graduate of Boalt, at Berkeley, I decided it was time to dress appropriately.

"I wore an American flag as a cape, over a bare upper torso on which I had painted 'Fuck Nixon' in bright colors. I even personally made a peace symbol, as best I remembered, out of cardboard, painted it black, and put it on a leather string around my neck. I wore a black wig with hair hanging past my shoulders, and a red, white, and blue bandanna around my forehead. I went barefoot.

"To impress my children, I had my picture taken and sent it to them.

"At the party, I enjoyed being someone I had never really been.

"As I was leaving, I overheard an older woman say, 'Why is he still so angry with Nixon?'

"My daughter called me the next week, at my office. She had the photo I sent her in front of her.

"'Dad,' she asked, genuinely perplexed, 'if you're so politically correct, how come you didn't know you were wearing a Mercedes hood emblem around your neck?'

"Well, I still cling to an image of the law student at Boalt Hall, at Berkeley in the '60s, that perhaps never was. The one my children think I might have been. But there must be a reason the image is so important to me that I refuse to give it up. Maybe it's the lawyer that I wish I had been. I know that as a law student in the '60s I was never really comfortable with the concepts of personal wealth and country clubs. And here, 30 years later, we are at a country club, many of us wealthy, and it still doesn't feel right.

"The only explanation I can give you is summed up in a few words that I have uttered with pride over these years: 'I went to law school at Boalt Hall. Yeah, Berkeley.'"

J. J. looked up at his assembled classmates, raised a clinched fist, and said: "Power. Peace."

Chapter 72

Conclusion:
The Class of '69

EVERY LEGAL BRIEF, submitted in court, ends with a section entitled "Conclusion." It seems fitting here.

A third of a century has passed since they first came together in the late summer of 1966—the last graduating class of the '60s at Boalt Hall. Young, eager, bright, from diverse backgrounds, yet ready to take on the problems of society. It all seemed so clear—black and white. When did it turn gray?

Did they change society? The law? Anything? Or were *they* changed? Perhaps it was the legal education or the practice of law itself that determined their outcomes? You'll have to be the judge.

Leon Goldman and Angela Africa are so well known you could have just looked one or the other of them up on the World Wide Web under headings like "Class Action Litigation," "Holocaust Litigation," "Leading Black Americans," or "Democratic Party—Major Contributors." Saying "Leon and Angela" is like saying "Ted and Jane" or "Bill and Hillary"— couples recognized by their first names. They weren't at the reunion. He sent regrets, noting that he was in London at an Amnesty International board meeting. Angela has recently been asked to join the board of directors of Nike. They travel a lot, maintain a place in Paris, but still call Oakland home. Damn, are they rich! And he started out as a Legal Aid lawyer!

Leon chose class action litigation as his way to improve society. Maybe it's good his dad never lived to see the tobacco settlement. After billions in settlement, Philip Morris is doing better than ever. It's even spending $100 million to improve its image. Now the government can't afford for people to stop buying cigarettes; it needs the promised billions to be paid out of tobacco company profits as part of the settlement with the tobacco companies. And so do all the black kids promised scholarships and battered women's shelters promised money by the public relations department of Philip Morris. A partnership for a lawsuit-free smoking America has been formed. Leon's dad would have preferred the lying bastards be sent to prison.

But Mr. Goldman's argument is being heard in the Holocaust settlements. The lawyers are being shamed by Jewish groups into waiving their fees. Leon was first among those who have agreed to waive any compensation. His dad would have been proud of that, at least.

Brian Jacobs was consistent in his beliefs until he flamed out. Like so many dedicated zealots of the '60s and '70s, he paid a terrible price in his personal life. But, he was right. Public interest law must be public, sometimes more for The Cause than the client, grabbing headlines to reach the greatest audience. How much of it is the headlines, feeding an insatiable appetite for publicity, recognition, ego, and how much is for The Cause? Who knows? Did Brian? Did he ever admit it to himself? Is that really why he walked away from the law? While he still at least had Randy?

But, then, why did he come back? To the reunion with Randy? Perhaps he still believes that one man—or his young daughter—can make a difference. Or should at least try.

Michael Cassidy made it all the way to the California Supreme Court, proving once again, it's who you know, not what you know. Maybe that's unfair. He's actually a pretty decent guy. Just got mixed up with the wrong crowd. Reagan and them. If he could have just worked it out with Mai, life would have been different. Crazy maybe, but different. Maybe he couldn't do crazy. He's actually a damn good judge.

Jackson Bridgeport III, well, he's still an asshole. Maybe that is also unfair. At the reunion, he seemed more of a prick, which is an asshole who has power and position, and abuses both. Maybe that's being too hard on him, too. Maybe he's still just an asshole. A legal education doesn't always make you a better person. But yet, he maintained a strong (perhaps flawed) belief in the judicial system and what he saw as the responsibilities of practitioners. Perhaps, like his father, he yearned for the days when the law was a high calling practiced by gentlemen.

Finally, it comes back to Rose.

John F. Kennedy said something to the effect that "no one said life is fair." Did Rose know that as she studied for those first exams that pronounced her number one in the class? When did it come to her that the

THE CLASS OF '69

rule for women was exclusion, not inclusion? Even her. Number one in the class. At Boalt Hall.

The practice of law is viewed by practitioners as combat. It's an adversarial system. The jargon is that of war and sport. In America, the two are interchangeable. And in America, women have traditionally not been allowed in combat.

In the war metaphor, there have always been those who went out ahead. What were they called in those old westerns? Scouts? To reconnoiter. They weren't expected to fight alone. Just check out the situation. Get the lay of the land.

Maybe Rose was a scout. Now, Boalt is over 50 percent women. Does that give satisfaction to the life of a scout to know that others walked over her? That it was on her back that others climbed up?

Zapata would tell her it was nothing new for the squatting, bending, and lifting Mexicans of California. She would probably tell him it was nothing new for women, Mexican or otherwise, in California or anywhere else.

The new dean asked Rose after the reunion if she would be interested in participating in a conference at Boalt entitled "Women in the Law," or perhaps teach a class under that heading in the spring. Rose was moved to hear that Professor Reynoso had recommended her as a person who had "much to teach," but she declined.

At about the same time as the 30th reunion of the class of '69 was being held, a select group of young lawyers were making their way to the U.S. Supreme Court to take the most prestigious positions that can be offered to beginning attorneys, that of law clerks to justices of the Supreme Court of the United States. It was a little different than when Rose applied in 1969.

In the fall of 1999, the clerks included Rosemary, Debra, Sonja, Leslie, Shirley, Mary Beth, Rebecca, Kristen, Amanda, Deidre, Erin, and Ketanji.

At the reunion, Rose told Randy that famous story about her dad, Brian Jacobs, announcing to the young lawyer that absence from family was "the price you pay for the privilege of being a lawyer." Brian asked her later if she really felt it had been a "privilege" to be an attorney. "No," she said, "but I wasn't going to ruin your little girl's dream."

Perhaps that is what Rose did with the legacy entrusted to her: She allowed Randy to have her dream.

But it wasn't bitterness that Rose displayed at the 30th reunion. If anything, there was a certain playfulness and peace of mind, not in accepting defeat, but understanding the absurdity of the game and refusing to play by its rules. The relationship between Rose and Sally was obvious, though not flaunted. The matching Cal ties with the bear mascot were a nice touch. After dinner, Rose pointed out Jackson Bridgeport to Sally. They were both looking at him when he looked up and stared at Rose. It was his litigation stare of disdain for which he was famous.

Even from a distance, Bridgeport could make out what they were saying as Rose and Sally, arms around each other's shoulders, smiled broadly and saluted him with their wine glasses, each reaching around and lifting the other's Cal tie, and mouthing: "Go Bears."

*   *   *

Author Bio

JOHN M. POSWALL is the Senior Partner of Poswall, White, Kouyoumdjian & Cutler, a civil litigation law firm in Sacramento, California. He was born in Southampton, England, in 1943, and immigrated to the United States at age 10 with his English mother and East Indian father.

In 1966, he graduated with honors from Sacramento State College (now CSUS) as the Outstanding Graduate, Outstanding Student in Government, and Student Body President. Poswall graduated with honors from Boalt Hall Law School in 1969. He was an assistant editor of the *California Law Review* and upon graduation, was named to the national honorary society Order of the Coif. At Boalt, he published on topics including the First Amendment.

Author John M. Poswall

Poswall is recognized by his peers both in and out of the courtroom. He has been selected to the prestigious American Board of Trial Advocates and to the exclusive American College of Trial Lawyers. In 1995, he was named Sacramento County Bar Humanitarian of the Year for his work with battered women, and in 2001, Lawyer of the Year by the Doctor/Lawyer Organization of Sacramento.

Poswall has written and spoken extensively on the law. For two years he had his own talk

The author in 1969

radio show, on 650 KSTE, Sacramento, entitled "Poswall on the Law." His speeches have included titles ranging from "Good vs. Evil: Practicing Civil Law in the Public Interest and Making a Pretty Good Living" to "Would You Want Your Daughter to Be an Attorney?" and "The History of Marriage and the Role of Women."

His article "Fighting for My Life in the Medical System," published in the *Sacramento Bee*, chronicled his fight with leukemia and has been used to motivate others facing cancer. He also taught "Law and Mental Health" at the community-college level and lectured university doctors on "Traumatically Induced Pre-Frontal Lobe Injury" and the ABA on "Autologous Bone Marrow Breast Cancer Litigation."

"When David takes on Goliath," begins one media account, "he usually calls attorney John M. Poswall." The *Sacramento Bee* featured him under the heading: "Taking on the Giants." The *Sacramento News and Review* simply listed him under "Super Lawyers." In the legal profession, he consistently appears in the national publication *Best Lawyers in America.*

His causes have not always been popular. In his first year of practice, he sued his *alma mater,* Sacramento State College, and made headlines with the first court order in the nation requiring a state college to officially recognize a gay student group. During the Vietnam War he defended conscientious objectors and drew the ire of the *Wall Street Journal,* which editorialized against his successful federal suit to release a West Point graduate from his military obligation because of his conscientious objection to the war.

In 1995, he appeared on ABC's *20/20* defending the academic freedom of a lesbian college professor to deliver a graphic lecture on female masturbation. In between, he sued a black college president for gender discrimination in promotion.

Poswall has not limited his legal strategies to the courtroom. On television and in the media, he orchestrated the first referendum in the country to close a nuclear power plant. In litigation with an HMO, he took to the radio and put out an "All Points Bulletin" for the CEO of the health organization that was denying treatment to women with breast cancer.

After a successful jury verdict of $2.3 million for his client, he "seized" a Montgomery Wards store and went on television in front of the store urging the public to come down and shop since the money would help pay off the former Ward employee's judgment.

Poswall has successfully sued some of the biggest companies in America and obtained multimillion dollar jury awards. This includes the free speech "SLAPP-back" case of *Leonardini v. Shell Oil Co.,* which went all the way to the U.S. Supreme Court, with Shell ultimately paying $7.5 million in general and punitive damages. The issues in the case were spotlighted on *60 Minutes* and his success in this and other cases was featured in Ralph Nader's book *No Contest: Corporate Lawyers in the Perversion of Justice in America.*

Poswall is married to food writer and consultant Peg Tomlinson-Poswall. He has two children, Robert and Rebel, and she has one, Lisa. They have two grandchildren. John and Peg live outside Sacramento on 50 acres in the foothills.

This is his first novel.

Give the Gift of

THE LAWYERS:
Class of '69

to Your Friends and Colleagues

CHECK YOUR LEADING BOOKSTORE, ORDER HERE,
or go to www.thelawyersclassof69.com

❑ **YES**, I want _____ copies of *The Lawyers: Class of '69* at $14.99 each, plus $4.00 shipping per book (California residents please add $1.16 sales tax per book). Canadian orders must be accompanied by a postal money order in U.S. funds. Allow 15 days for delivery.

❑ **YES**, I am interested in having John M. Poswall speak to my company, association, school, or organization. Please send information.

My check or money order for $_____ is enclosed.

Please charge my: ❑ Visa   ❑ MasterCard
                    ❑ Discover ❑ American Express

Name _____

Organization _____

Address _____

City/State/Zip _____

Phone_____ E-mail _____

Card # _____

Exp. Date_____ Signature _____

Please make your check payable and return to:

JULLUNDUR PRESS
a Golden Temple Publishing company
1001 "G" Street, Suite 301 • Sacramento, CA 95814

You may call toll-free to: 866-449-1600
or Fax: 916-449-1320

or use our website: **www.thelawyersclassof69.com**